*The devil always gets his due...*

*Praise for*

## *Tangle of Lies*

"Fast-paced . . . a fantastic suspense thriller."

—*Midwest Book Review*

"A chilling, complex tale of revenge, betrayal, and long-kept secrets."

—*Library Journal*

"A tangled web of clues [with] a touch of spice thrown in for good measure."

—*A Romance Review*

"Great characters, a compelling story that's almost impossible to put down, lots of plot twists—*Tangle of Lies* has it all."

—*Romance Reviews Today*

"Exciting mystery with hot romance make this a winner."

—*Fresh Fiction*

## *Beloved Impostor*

"Ms. Potter has given us another thrilling drama. Every page proves the reason for her award-winning success . . . *Beloved Impostor* travels at a fast pace with outstanding characters and an expertly developed plot."

—*Rendezvous*

"A wonderful Scottish tale wrought with emotion, tender in its telling and heart-wrenching in its beauty. Ms. Potter captures our hearts and gifts us with another beautiful story."

—*The Best Reviews*

"[A] superb romance . . . It's Potter's unique gift for creating unforgettable characters and delving into the deepest parts of their hearts that endears her to readers. This is another masterpiece from a writer who always delivers what romance readers want: a love story to always remember."

—*Romantic Times*

"Ms. Potter is a very talented storyteller, taking a much-used theme, lovers from warring families, and manipulating it, adding plenty of new ideas and twists, until the end result is the original, highly satisfying *Beloved Impostor* . . . Ms. Potter very adeptly whetted this reader's appetite for more about these two Maclean brothers, but for now, there is *Beloved Impostor*, which I highly recommend."

—*Romance Reviews Today*

*continued . . .*

## *Dancing with a Rogue*

"Once again, Potter . . . proves that she's adept at penning both enthralling historicals and captivating contemporary novels."

—*Booklist* (starred review)

"Gabriel and Merry are a delightful pair . . . Patricia Potter has provided a character-driven story that her audience will enjoy."

—*Midwest Book Review*

"An entirely engrossing novel by this talented and versatile author."

—*Romance Reviews Today*

## *The Diamond King*

"From war-torn Scotland to the high seas to the jungles of Brazil, Potter takes the reader on a roller-coaster ride as a rake becomes a hero and a courageous, resourceful woman finds love against all odds."

—*Booklist*

## *The Heart Queen*

"This is a book that is difficult to put down for any reason. Simply enjoy."

—*Rendezvous*

"Potter is a very talented author . . . if you are craving excitement, danger, and a hero to die for, you won't want to miss this one."

—*All About Romance*

***More praise for Patricia Potter***
***and her bestselling novels***

"Patricia Potter has a special gift for giving an audience a first-class romantic story line."

—*Affaire de Coeur*

"When a historical romance [gets] the Potter treatment, the story line is pure action and excitement, and the characters are wonderful."

—*BookBrowser*

# Tempting the Devil

Patricia Potter

BERKLEY SENSATION, NEW YORK

**THE BERKLEY PUBLISHING GROUP**
**Published by the Penguin Group**
**Penguin Group (USA) Inc.**
**375 Hudson Street, New York, New York 10014, USA**
Penguin Group (Canada), 90 Eglinton Avenue East, Suite 700, Toronto, Ontario M4P 2Y3, Canada
(a division of Pearson Penguin Canada Inc.)
Penguin Books Ltd., 80 Strand, London WC2R 0RL, England
Penguin Group Ireland, 25 St. Stephen's Green, Dublin 2, Ireland (a division of Penguin Books Ltd.)
Penguin Group (Australia), 250 Camberwell Road, Camberwell, Victoria 3124, Australia
(a division of Pearson Australia Group Pty. Ltd.)
Penguin Books India Pvt. Ltd., 11 Community Centre, Panchsheel Park, New Delhi—110 017, India
Penguin Group (NZ), Cnr. Airborne and Rosedale Roads, Albany, Auckland 1310, New Zealand
(a division of Pearson New Zealand Ltd.)
Penguin Books (South Africa) (Pty.) Ltd., 24 Sturdee Avenue, Rosebank, Johannesburg 2196, South Africa

Penguin Books Ltd., Registered Offices: 80 Strand, London WC2R 0RL, England



TEMPTING THE DEVIL

A Berkley Sensation Book / published by arrangement with the author

PRINTING HISTORY
Berkley Sensation edition / September 2006


Cover design by Brad Springer.



ISBN: 0-425-21258-0

BERKLEY SENSATION®
Berkley Sensation Books are published by The Berkley Publishing Group,
a division of Penguin Group (USA) Inc.,
375 Hudson Street, New York, New York 10014.
BERKLEY SENSATION is a registered trademark of Penguin Group (USA) Inc.
The "B" design is a trademark belonging to Penguin Group (USA) Inc.

PRINTED IN THE UNITED STATES OF AMERICA

10 9 8 7 6 5 4 3 2 1

*With many, many thanks to my editor, Christine Zika,*
*for her invaluable input as well as infinite patience*

# author's note

Although the seed of *Tempting the Devil* was suggested by an actual event, the characters and events in the book are completely fictional, the result of the author's "what if?" mechanism.

# prologue

JUST OUTSIDE ATLANTA

Fear rushed through Jesse Carroll as he felt the barrel of a gun pressing into his back.

Why the hell had he agreed to Zack's invitation to sneak a few minutes off to smoke a cigarette and maybe take a swallow of that good 'shine Zack usually carried?

The rough, almost overgrown road was just off their beats, a piece of private property being held for future development. Even the entrance was difficult to see.

Zack had known the old man who'd owned it until his death two years ago. It was then purchased by a holding company. An old shack on the property still stood, but a heavy chain had been added across the entrance to block any traffic from entering.

The property was outside Zack's rounds, but he drove by every day on his way to the office, and tonight the chain was gone. He'd called Jesse on his cell and suggested he and his rookie meet him and take a look around. Jesse knew it was merely an excuse to meet. Zack always carried that 'shine Jesse liked, and he didn't like drinking alone. Like Zack, Jesse would have been alone if Kell, a rookie officer, hadn't been training with him.

Meeting like this wasn't in the training manual.

But it often got lonely and boring in this part of the county where little happened except for the occasional speeder. So on especially dull nights, Zack and Jesse sometimes met in a secluded place, shared stories, took a sip or two.

Why hadn't he said no? Instead, he'd sworn Kell to silence and driven down the road to the remnants of a cabin. He'd looked for Zack's headlights. Instead he saw the silhouette of a darkened blue-and-white squad car. Then another car behind it.

He stopped the car, took out his weapon and stepped out. Lights from the squad car flashed on, blinded him. At the same moment, something hard and small and round pressed into his back.

Jesse's heart pounded. A shadowy figure pushed Zack forward. His figure blocked the blinding light. One handcuff dangled from his wrist.

"What the hell . . . ?" He stopped, then started again. "This is one hell of a joke, Zack." He peered frantically into the darkness. "Who's out there? This ain't funny."

The figure seized his left wrist and hooked him to Zack. Still another man took his handcuffs from his belt and hooked his right one to Kell's left hand. It was done so quickly, so professionally, he knew it must be a cop. Had to be.

A joke. Had to be one. Probably aimed at Kell, the rookie.

He kept telling himself that. The only other explanation was too awful to consider.

So far he'd been the only one to speak. Kell remained silent, but Jesse felt the trainee's tension. Smelled the fear.

He blinked against the glare of the flashlight. He turned to avoid it and saw one man who stood alone. *Lou Belize.* He froze. God, he was a dead man.

A deer in headlights. That's exactly how he felt. And the truck was coming right at him! Did Kell realize they were up to their eyebrows in shit?

Fear exploded in him.

Hooked to the other two men, he couldn't run, though that was exactly what he wanted to do. Kell muttered something, but Jesse couldn't make out the words. Zack slumped, and now Jesse saw the blood on his face, the way his free hand clutched his stomach. Someone had worked him over.

Belize came up to him. "This pig said you just happened to come here."

Jesse nodded, afraid his voice might reflect the stark terror he now felt.

"No one told you about this place?"

Jesse tried to think. *Hold out and play for more time.* But Zack's expression revealed he'd already told everything. "We were just going to have a drink," he said, hating the tremor he heard in his voice.

"A cop? Isn't that illegal?" Belize sneered.

Jesse didn't answer.

Belize stepped back behind the light.

Jesse was only too aware of the revolver still pressed against his back. He closed his eyes and thought of Sarah, and little James. Jesse and James. It had been Sarah's little joke when she crawled over him on those nights they made love.

If he hadn't fought with her tonight, he never would have agreed to meet Zack for a quick bite of moonshine. Every bar would be closed on his way home, and a sip or two would relax him. Same old fight. She wanted him to quit and get a safe job. She couldn't understand why he loved being a cop, how he enjoyed the comaraderie he shared with others of the breed.

"Do it!" Lou Belize ordered.

He frantically looked around for help. Shadows. They were all shadows. Then he saw a figure he knew instantly. He couldn't see the man's face but he didn't have to.

*A mistake. It had to be a mistake.*

He started to call out, but the sound was interrupted by the blast of a gunshot. Kell's weight dragged him down.

"Sarah," he whispered.

He never heard the second shot, as the bullet tore into his skull.

# chapter one

*She'd never seen a dead* man before.

Much less three.

Robin Stuart turned away from the bodies of the three dead police officers. She had what she needed for her news story. Three men in uniform, their faces drained of life. A bullet in the back of each head. Little blood.

They'd seemed more like wax figures than men who had been alive just hours ago.

Yet she knew they had been, and her heart ached for them, and for their families.

Not professional. But it had happened before, this witnessing of tragedy and the resulting feelings she tried to mask. Today she knew she'd not mastered that particular skill. She'd often wondered how war correspondents learned to live with the death they observed daily.

At first she'd fervently wished she could. In her first months at the *Atlanta Observer*, a chartered plane carrying more than a hundred prominent Atlantans had crashed in Europe, and she had been called, along with other staffers, to write obituaries for an Extra. Several family members she'd contacted had not yet learned about the crash, and she'd had to break the news.

That had been her worst day as a reporter.

This was a close second. She couldn't stop thinking about the families waiting for the three to return home. Two were young—around her age—and the third was probably in his forties. She fought to keep tears at bay. She would never live that down among the other reporters.

Yet mixed with that was the adrenaline from knowing this was going to be a huge story.

The heat of an Atlanta summer bore down. She felt perspiration trickling down her blouse as clumps of law enforcement officers huddled together some space from the bodies, as if distancing themselves from the dead. A bright yellow ribbon isolated the bodies from the living.

But she couldn't avert her eyes. It wasn't like writing about a county budget, or a squabble on the county commission or even the occasional trial she covered.

She scribbled several observations in her notebook. Other reporters stood quietly rather than being their usual raucous and competitive selves. One was a police reporter for the opposition daily, and then there were several from local papers. The television media hadn't arrived yet, but they wouldn't be far behind.

Ordinarily, a crime story of this magnitude would have gone to the paper's police reporter or one of the veteran general assignment reporters, but she'd been covering this county and an adjoining one for six months and had been sitting in the sheriff's office when he received the call.

Trying to ignore the heavy brace on her left leg, she limped over to Meredith County Sheriff Will Sammons.

He was talking to another officer, but stopped when she approached. "Do you have the names of the victims?" she asked.

He frowned. "That's up to the county police to give out," he said. "I 'spect they'll wait till the families are notified."

"I won't print them until they are."

He sighed. "Can't do it, missy."

She hated the "missy," but he'd insisted on calling her that since she'd first met him. Since he'd turned out to be a good source on county politics and news, she'd never considered it important enough to object.

"What *can* you tell me?"

"That some sons of bitches executed three officers," he said.

"Do you know when?"

He shrugged. "Two called in at two a.m. and said they were taking a break. I don't know about the third. They must have chanced on some kind of illegal activity. Probably drugs."

"It doesn't look like there was a struggle."

His eyes turned hard. "Someone got the drop on them." His gaze left her face as he watched a photographer take photos and newly arrived officers from the police department expand the crime scene ribbon.

More people were filling the clearing now, including the first television van. She found her cell in her pocket and phoned Wade Carlton, city editor for the paper.

"I have enough for a bulletin for the first edition," she said.

He didn't waste words but handed her off to another reporter to take the story.

"Three Meredith County police officers were found slain this morning in a clearing near Wilson Lake in the northwest corner of Meredith County. They had been handcuffed together and each shot in the back of the head, execution-style.

"Meredith County Sheriff Will Sammons said all three officers were on duty last night. Two reported in to the police dispatcher at two a.m. They and the third officer did not report in at the end of their shift, and a search was instigated. Their bodies were found at eleven o'clock this morning, on a narrow dirt road leading to the private lake.

"The three officers—as yet unidentified pending notification to their families—are members of the Meredith County Police Department. The department operates independently of the county sheriff's office.

"Sheriff Sammons said there are no immediate suspects but that the officers may have stumbled on a drug sale or stolen car operation."

To Wade Carlton, when he came back on the line, she said, "I'll have more later."

"I'll send Bob Greene out there," he said.

Bob Greene was the principal police reporter for the paper. She didn't want the story taken away from her. "I know the people here. They trust me." She took a deep breath, then said, "They don't know Bob."

Wade Carlton hesitated, then, "Okay it's yours. For now."

She closed the cell phone, then went over to a deputy sheriff who stood alone. When she was first assigned the county, she'd had coffee with him several times at the café across from the courthouse and had talked him into letting her ride along in his squad car for several days. It wasn't quite against rules because there were no rules regarding reporters, but she knew he'd never reported it.

They had become friends, and he'd flirted with her more than once, though he often talked about his wife and son.

"Sandy?"

He turned to her, his usually pleasant expression harsh with anger. "Damn them," he said in a low voice. "Damn them to hell."

"Did you know the officers?"

"Yes," he said shortly. "Weren't close, though. Our department and the police department don't talk much."

She wanted to keep him talking. There was a rare anger about him that was explosive. She felt it, and an angry man often said things he might ordinarily be more cautious about.

She was aware of the tension between the two agencies. The county had a sheriff's office and a separate police department that covered the same area. She'd heard about some of the turf wars. The county police operated under the county commission; the sheriff's deputies under the elected sheriff.

"Two look really young," she prodded.

"They all have families," he said bitterly. "One was just married."

"What do *you* think happened?"

He cast a quick look at the sheriff, who was now talking to his second in command: Chief Deputy Paul Joyner. "What did the sheriff say?"

"They must have stumbled onto some illegal transaction and were ambushed."

He raised an eyebrow.

"You don't think so?" she probed.

"Three cops—two of them experienced?" he said in a low voice. Then he moved away and joined the sheriff watching the crime scene investigators at work.

She talked to several other deputies but did not try to approach members of the police department who were now flooding the scene. Instead she watched as they stood in numb grief.

The thump, thump, thump of news helicopters now thrummed from above. Reporters and local law enforcement thickened the crowd. The police chief arrived with an entourage and stalked over to Sheriff Sammons. The body language was angry, and she inched toward them, only to be told to stay back.

Still watching, she limped over to the editor of the local paper, an older man with whom she'd often shared cups of coffee and exchanged information. His paper was a weekly and thus they didn't have the competition that flared between daily papers.

"Sandy tell you anything?" Hank Conrad asked.

"Nope," she said. "Only that one was recently married. You have the names yet?"

"Yep."

"They wouldn't give them to me," she complained.

"You'll wait until the families are notified?"

"Of course."

He gave her the three names. "You'll have them before my paper comes out anyway. Rather you than those TV types."

"Do you know any of them?"

"I know all three. Good officers. Never heard anything bad about any of them."

"About 'them'?" She'd caught Hank's slight inflection on the word "them."

He shrugged. "There's always rumors flying around. Never been able to pin anything down."

"About who?"

"No one specifically." He turned around and approached the police photographer. She was left standing there alone. Again.

And, damn it, her leg was beginning to ache, the one she'd nearly destroyed when her car flew off the road and landed in a ravine. It was getting stronger day by day, but the brace she wore was heavy, and her muscles complained when they felt misused. She tried desperately not to show it. She'd worked too hard to get this far; she didn't want to go back to an inside desk job.

She used her cell phone again to call in the names of the slain officers. It was newspaper policy not to reveal names or contact relatives until they'd been officially notified. Sometimes there was a slipup, as she knew only too well, but she knew in this case they would hold back. Having the names, though, meant they could start on background. She was glad she wasn't part of the television media where the pressure to "get there first" often clashed with ethics.

She listened as other reporters tossed questions. She never liked to ask her own while others were listening. She would ask her questions later.

When they were through, the sheriff asked the news media to leave. The detectives and forensic people needed to do their work without a media circus.

Some protested as they were moved out. But she had more information than most since she'd been in the sheriff's office when he was notified and had been one of the first on the scene. She could describe the initial reactions of anger and disbelief of first responders. Meredith County was mostly a bucolic area with few crimes, and fewer murders. Most of the latter were domestic disputes.

She couldn't shake the image of the bodies. Who would risk killing three police officers? Every law enforcement official in the state would want their heads. Every investigative tool would be used to find them.

The pure cold-bloodedness of the crime was chilling.

What secret—or secrets—was behind it?

Her mind turned over what she'd heard during the past hour.

*"Damn them."*

*"There's always rumors . . ."*

She made a mental note to call Sandy and find out exactly what he knew. Or suspected.

She'd learned she had a talent for that, getting people to say more than they meant to say. She didn't have many others, but she knew how to listen. And listening was the key to getting answers to the questions she really wanted to ask.

It wasn't calculated. She had an immense curiosity. She always wanted to learn as much as she could about everyone she met, and people responded—usually—to that interest and often divulged things they'd never intended to tell.

Her mother used to scold her about it. "Curiosity killed the cat," she'd always warned.

"But a cat has nine lives," Robin always responded.

She wondered whether those police officers on the ground had felt the same way.

# chapter two

*Robin drove into Atlanta to* write the story. She always thought better on a keyboard than on a phone.

As soon as she arrived at her desk, she called the police chief's office and discovered the officers' names had been released along with their ages, the number of years they'd been with the department, addresses, and immediate family information.

She wrote the story she'd already partially composed in her head and signaled to the city editor, who read it on the computer. He then gestured for her to come to his desk.

"Damn good job," he said. "Bob Greene's calling the families and will do a sidebar on them. Your story will lead the front page."

A strange mixture of elation and guilt filled her. And relief. Relief that she wouldn't have to call the families. Elation at the praise for her story and its placement. Guilt that she felt any elation at all.

"You keep on the story," he said. "Work with Bob, though. He has contacts with all the law enforcement agencies."

"So do I," she reminded him.

She went back to the desk. The story was finished for the first edition, but there would be others, and she would be expected to add to it.

At eight, she left. Drained. Exhausted. Her leg aching like the devils in hell were pricking it with pitchforks.

*Poor Daisy.* The big bushy black and white cat she'd rescued a year ago would be stalking through the house in search of food. She'd found Daisy as a kitten next to her tire one day, the kitten's skin bare with mange and half her ear gone.

The drive to her rented house in an old part of Atlanta took less time than usual, or perhaps she drove faster. She was anxious to get home, feed Daisy, have a glass of wine, and think about where she could take the story tomorrow.

She parked in front of her home, a Victorian cottage. It was small and lacked a garage but was full of character. She loved every square foot of it.

Her father had been military, an enlisted man who climbed to sergeant major. They'd lived in military quarters all her early years, usually small plain quarters that looked like every other unit, no matter which base. She'd never felt at home in any of them, nor had she ever made best friends. She knew she would be gone the next year. Or the next.

But she'd decided when coming to Atlanta she would find her nest, no matter what else she sacrificed.

The cottage always welcomed her, even on the worst of days. One day she hoped to buy it.

The murder still very much on her mind, she locked the car and went inside. Daisy meowed and wormed her furry self against one leg, then another before jumping up onto the counter, meowing soulfully for her meal.

Robin rubbed Daisy's back for a moment, and the demand turned into a purr. It was amazing what an animal could do for you, particularly when loneliness wrapped around her like a shroud. It didn't usually do that, but something about today, about death, made her want to feel alive.

She thought about calling one of her two sisters, and dropped the idea. They had problems of their own. Lark was in the midst of a divorce, and Star—short for Starling—was near term with her first child. Their mother had loved birds, and Robin had always been grateful she hadn't been named Tufted Titmouse or House Wren.

She smiled at the joke she'd often shared with Lark and Star, then the loneliness closed in again. Their mother had died two years ago from a stroke. Home had always been where she was, and now there was no longer a place to go home to.

Daisy's purr turned into a demanding meow again, jerking

Robin back to the moment. She opened a can of tuna, spooned the contents into a dish and watched Daisy's greedy consumption. When the cat finished her meal, Robin poured herself a glass of wine and switched on a jazz CD. She took the glass outside and placed it on the table, then returned for her crutches.

Few things were more important now than removing the brace. For good. She could walk now without the brace as long as she used crutches and kept her weight off the left leg. She unzipped the leg of her specially tailored slacks and removed the brace. Just taking off the brace and the ugly heavy shoes it required was a huge relief. She ran her hands along the scarred skin, then balanced herself on the crutches and went outside and sat in her wicker rocking chair.

The sky was clear, the deep dark blue of dusk just lighting with stars. She took a sip of chilled wine, and wondered why she felt so lost. Usually a story of today's magnitude excited her, stirred the competitive juices. But now she remembered her mother's stroke, and her father's death in a desert far away, and she knew the despair that three families felt tonight. It was much too close to home.

She told herself to let it go. She was not often given to melancholy. She had always been an optimist, just like her chirping namesake. One of the older reporters—Jack Ross—called her his Holly Golightly, the fictional heroine from *Breakfast at Tiffany's*. She'd rented the movie after that and wasn't sure whether she was flattered or insulted.

But all too quickly, the images she tried to banish returned. How could someone get so close to armed officers? She kept trying to remember the look in Sandy's eyes. Anger. Raw anger. Or something else?

She finished her glass of wine and went inside to the room she'd made into an office. She went through her Rolodex and found Sandy's cell number. He had given it to her after learning that she often drove lonely roads at night; he'd told her to call him if she ever had car trouble.

Robin looked at her watch. Nine thirty p.m. She found herself punching in the numbers.

She was surprised when Sandy answered with a curt "Harris."

"This is Robin. I was hoping we could meet for breakfast somewhere tomorrow."

"I'll call you back," he said. "What's your number?"

She gave him her home number.

Ten minutes later he called.

"I can't tell you anything," he said.

"I just want to understand more about the way the police department works there. You know, the difference between you guys and them."

Silence.

"It would really help me," she pleaded.

A sigh. "I've been working since midnight and won't leave here until morning. We're all on double shifts. Interviewing everyone who lives within five miles of that road and stopping every car in hopes someone saw something last night."

"You'll need to eat."

He paused, then said, "There's a Waffle House in Gwinnett County." He told her how to find it.

"Gwinnett? Isn't that a long way for you?"

A silence on his side.

"I'll be there," she said. "What time?"

"Maybe around eight."

"I understand," she said and hung up the phone before he had second thoughts.

She looked at her watch and returned to the living room to turn on the news.

It was all about the murders. No new information, but they had photos of the three patrolmen when alive. Some film on the homes where they lived. An interview with both the sheriff and the police chief.

She thought about tomorrow. More phone calls to the sheriff and police chief, to plain citizens about how crime had hit their quiet community. Interviews with friends of the officers. Hopefully something from the medical examiner.

She wondered if breakfast with Sandy was worth the time. Yet she had an itch about him. He might well have scuttlebutt from the inside. And she'd always trusted those itches. They'd paid off for her in the past.

The newscast went off, and she gently pushed Daisy from her lap and started for the bedroom.

When she'd first moved in, she'd maneuvered clumsily around the house with the brace and crutches, but now she was stronger and more adept, and frequently didn't use the crutches at all. When she did use them, it was like having extra legs. She could swing along a street faster than most people could walk. But the brace, though she hated it, helped build the muscles in her leg. Another three weeks and she shouldn't need it. She would probably always have a limp, the doctor said, but it could have been far worse. She planned a brace-burning party.

She'd had the accident hurrying across two states to her mother's bedside after the stroke. She'd never made it, never had a chance to say good-bye. Instead she'd ended up in an emergency room with a crushed leg. It had taken several surgeries over two years to put the Humpty Dumpty leg back together again.

That was one reason this story was important to her. She'd been a rising star at the paper when she'd had the accident. After nearly a year's absence, she returned on crutches for six months between surgeries and was put on the city desk. When she'd returned after the last surgery, the city editor had wanted to put her back on the desk. She'd fought it bitterly and finally been sent to what she considered Siberia, a place where very little happened. Doing a good job—no, a great job—here would send her back to the action. She planned to prove she could do as good a job as anyone with two good legs.

She was determined to break through that protective cocoon the management had placed her in.

Robin put on a sleep shirt, then crawled into bed, placing the crutches next to it. Daisy jumped up and curled up at the end of the bed. Robin's leg still ached, but it was free from the heavy brace and, gratefully, she stretched out.

She thought about tomorrow. She needed sleep, though she knew it would come hard. She planned to be at that Waffle House no later than seven and that meant a five a.m. wake-up.

That itch was getting stronger all the time.

Ben Taylor turned on the news in his barely furnished apartment. He'd kept up with the story all day at his office, every fiber of his being wanting to go to the scene.

Unfortunately, as yet, there was no jurisdictional reason for the FBI to become involved. Not yet.

Not yet, but he sensed there would be. Hell no, not sensed. Knew it.

No one killed three policemen unless there was a damned good reason. And nearly every one of those reasons meant that sooner or later his office would become involved. Drugs. Corruption. Interstate transportation of cars, people, goods.

He had every lawman's repugnance of a cop killer. And now there were three dead cops. The way they died was particularly repellent. He would bet his last dollar that they knew their killer. Maybe even trusted their killer.

He'd asked his boss, the agent in charge of the Atlanta office, to go out there. But Ron Holland said no. Not until they were asked or there was undisputed jurisdiction. There was already too much friction between the office and local cops on the drug case they were currently working. Ron didn't want anything to unravel now.

Meredith County wasn't involved in the case. But the Georgia Bureau of Investigation was, and unquestionably they would be brought into this murder. They probably wouldn't appreciate the FBI stealing their thunder.

If there was one thing Ben hated about the job, it was pussyfooting around other law enforcement agencies. Shouldn't happen. They should all be after the same objective, but he knew some locals felt the FBI lorded over them, even when they were damn well trying not to.

He went to the kitchen, took out a frozen pizza, and put it in the microwave. He would much rather have stopped somewhere but he wanted to get home to see the news and whether there was anything new.

There wasn't.

He turned it off as he saw reporters crowding the yard in front of the home of one of the victims. Vultures. The whole bunch of them. Feasting off the tragedy of men and women trying to do a hard job.

Ben had come to despise the whole breed in his fifteen years as an agent. On rare occasion, they'd helped in the past. Lost and stolen children had been found because of them. But he'd yet to find one that he could trust, that cared about anything but the damned story, and to hell if they destroyed a case—or a person—by printing what should have been protected information.

One had destroyed his ex-wife in pursuit of a headline.

To him, freedom of the press was more of a freedom to yell fire in a crowded building than to protect the citizenry.

He took a beer from the fridge and strode up and down the room as the microwave nuked his pizza. Pasteboard with tomato sauce.

He remembered the meals he'd once shared with Dani. He could still see her dark hair falling over her shoulders as she carefully chopped ingredients. She'd loved to cook.

But she'd also loved the bureau. They'd gone through FBI training together and married two years later after being separated at different ends of the country. They had three good years together until she went undercover and became what she hated most.

He still wondered how he'd missed the signs until it had become too late. She'd divorced him when he tried to help her, and since then he'd spent nearly every cent he had to help her. Though the love was long gone, the caring was not.

Ben often wondered whether he hadn't been part of the problem himself. He'd grown up in foster homes and trust had never come easily. Nor had sharing a part of himself. She'd told him enough times that he couldn't relate to anything but a mystery.

Now she was in yet another rehabilitation program, and he came home to a frozen pizza.

He retrieved his pizza from the microwave and cut a slice. It tasted as bad as it looked. He ate it anyway, since he hadn't had anything for lunch. He'd sat in a meeting, one of many concerning the joint force drug case under way with the DEA. They'd netted some lower-rung fish, but they couldn't find the main source. They'd learned enough to know, though, that an organization had taken over much of the drug trade in and around Atlanta and sold everything from ecstasy to crack to black tar heroin. It seemed the dealers worked in cells, most of them unknown to the others, just like terrorists.

He was growing frustrated, and the murder in a rural

county forty miles from Atlanta nagged at him. Three policemen had stumbled onto something bad.

It was too much a stretch to believe they were connected.

Or was it?

# chapter three

*Robin walked into the designated* Waffle House at seven.

She didn't want to take a chance that Sandy might arrive early and leave. She might not get anything but color, the details that changed fact into a real human story. But she hoped for more.

"Coffee and wheat toast," she said when the waitress arrived at her table. She couldn't eat more. Her stomach churned this morning and she'd had precious little sleep. She unfolded the paper she'd picked up in a box at a gas station on the way. Her own had not yet been delivered by the time she'd left the house. Heck, the sun hadn't even come up.

The headline stretched across the width of the paper: THREE MEREDITH COUNTY OFFICERS MURDERED, EXECUTION-STYLE.

Her story was accompanied by several sidebars, one of which gave a brief biography of each of the officers and another of other police slayings in the state. A large photo of the three slain officers on the ground made her wince, and she closed the paper.

She flipped open her cell phone to call the sheriff's office. He was unavailable. She asked for the chief deputy. He, too, was unavailable. Then she asked for the deputy who acted as department spokesman on occasion.

"Sorry, Robin. Nothing new, but there's a press conference this morning."

"Why a press conference if there's no news?"

"Because we're being deluged by you people. The sheriff thought he would tell everyone at once that we have no news."

"Thanks for a preview," she replied wryly.

She then called the county police department, where she was told again that there would be a joint press conference at ten. She would go, of course, but she hated the mob mentality at press conferences. She would find a way to talk to the sheriff and police chief alone.

She drank several cups of coffee, grateful to the waitress, who seemed to recognize her caffeine addiction, and opened the paper again, this time skimming over other headlines. But she stopped every time a car drove into the parking lot and the door opened.

Her watch told her she'd been there an hour and a half, and the waitress was obviously tired of having one of the four booths occupied so long for coffee and toast. Robin ordered eggs and hash browns, then moved them around her plate.

She was ready to give up when the door opened and Sandy walked in. His eyes were bloodshot, and stubble shadowed his face. He glanced around the diner until he spotted her. He hesitated, then walked to the booth.

"I didn't think you would still be here."

She didn't reply, afraid he might run. Wariness was in every inch of his body.

He slid across from her, and the waitress was instantly there, a cup in one hand and a coffeepot in the other. "Coffee, hon?"

He nodded, and she poured coffee into the cup.

"What's your pleasure?"

Robin listened in amazement as he ordered a slice of ham, eggs, potatoes, and a waffle.

"Haven't eaten since noon yesterday," he said as the waitress left with the order.

His eyes went to the headline on the front of the paper as he took a quick swallow of coffee.

She waited as he nervously drummed the fingers of his left hand on the table. He radiated tension.

She took a sip of her own coffee.

He put the cup down. "Damn it, I don't know why I'm here."

"For breakfast," she said mildly.

"There's closer places."

"I wondered about that."

"Not a good thing now to be seen with a reporter. I used to come in here years ago when I went hunting. Don't know why I told you I would be here."

She did. Or thought she did. He needed someone to talk to. Somehow during those ride-alongs they had become friends. He'd told her he couldn't talk to his wife about some of the things he'd seen as a cop. He said other cops had much the same situation. They couldn't take their jobs home.

"You probably needed to talk," she said simply.

"If anyone knew I met with you . . ."

"They won't."

He stared at her for a long time.

She took a sip of coffee. "Is there *anything* you can tell me?" she finally asked.

"Orders are that everything come from the boss."

"The sheriff?"

He nodded.

"You told me before that you guys in the sheriff's department don't think much of the county police."

"They're still cops," he said roughly. "They have families." His hand shook slightly as he raised his own cup of coffee and took a long swallow.

"Training as good as yours?"

He turned as the waitress approached with a plate full of eggs, ham, potatoes along with a waffle.

She waited, afraid that more questions might spook him. He'd agreed to meet her for a reason whether he realized it or not.

"You gonna stay on the story?" he finally asked.

"For a while, anyway," she said. "Any ideas where to look?"

"Stay with the press conferences."

"I don't understand."

He took a bite of waffle, chewed it much longer than it deserved. Then he looked at her again. "I like you, Robin. Probably too much. If I weren't married . . ."

He let the words die, then shrugged. "Not that you had any interest."

She didn't say anything. She liked him, but he was right. She had no romantic interest. She was surprised that he said what he had. She was no beauty, and now she was hampered by the brace on her leg. Not exactly seductive.

He gave her a sideways look. "I think that's why. No bull-shit. No cute denial. You're the only woman I've ever talked to about my job."

She gave him a minute, then asked, "Why should I stay with press conferences?"

"Because someone killed three cops to keep a secret," he replied bitterly. "I don't think they would stop at a nosy re-porter. And you are the nosiest one I know."

"Surely they're gone now. Cop killers wouldn't linger around."

His eyes hardened, but he didn't say anything.

She leaned over. "You know something. Or suspect it?"

"I've already said too much." He took some money from his pocket and threw it on the table. "I have to go." He looked at her again. "Just do what I say. Don't go snooping on your own."

Then he was gone.

She didn't follow. She knew he wouldn't answer any more questions, nor did she want to press him. Not now.

She would wait. He would tell her more. She felt it.

*"I don't think they would stop at a nosy reporter."*

*Who were "they"?*

The press conference was as useless as she knew it would be.

There were "leads" but nothing that could be discussed at this time. The Georgia Bureau of Investigation had joined the investigating team. The medical examiner had given his pre-liminary report. One man had been beaten. All three died from a small-caliber bullet to the back of the skull. One each.

"Is it a professional hit job?" one electronic reporter shouted. Robin recognized him as an investigative reporter for the highest-ranking local news show.

A dumb question in her view. Of course it was a profes-sional job.

"We can't say that at this time," the sheriff said.

"How could the killers get the drop on three officers?"

"If we knew that, we would probably know who commit-ted this outrage," the sheriff replied.

"What about tire tracks?" asked another reporter.

"We don't discuss details of the investigation," the police chief said, regaining his place at the microphone.

"What *can* you tell us?" The last exasperated question came from still another television reporter.

"That we've formed a task force and we'll find the people who did this."

Bored with the expected answers, Robin glanced around. Her gaze caught a man standing about ten feet behind her. He didn't have the casual wear of most print reporters, nor the professional finish of television ones. Instead, he wore a pair of slacks and a blue shirt with the sleeves rolled up. But it was his face that captured her interest. She certainly would have remembered it if she'd seen it before.

She'd read of hawk faces but had never seen one before. A true definition of features: a lean, sharply angled face and profile. His hair was dark and well cut except for a cowlick that defied control and fell on his forehead. His eyes were deep-set and dark as navy coffee but it was the intensity in them that drew her attention. For a second it seemed as if her perusal drew his own. His gaze riveted on her face, and the intensity in it was so strong she fancied the ground shook. She felt an unwelcome surge of heat in her cheeks and hoped he didn't notice it as well. Then she thought she saw a flash of contempt in his eyes before he shifted his gaze away.

She felt judged without knowing why, but her gaze lingered on him as she wondered whether that impression had been her imagination. He was lean but not thin, and his foot tapped with an impatience that, like that cowlick, she sensed he couldn't quite control. A reporter? She knew she hadn't seen him before. She certainly would have remembered his face. But then she'd been away for nearly a year and had been out of the press mainstream since her return. She simply had not had the energy to socialize as she had before, not with the brace and crutches . . .

"There will be press conferences daily." The police chief's words jerked her attention back to him. He was obviously winding things up.

She glanced back toward the speaker, heard the fruitless additional questions that echoed former ones, then turned back to where the dark-haired man had stood.

He was gone.

She turned to the reporter next to her. She knew him from the Press Club.

"That dark-haired guy who was standing in the back . . ."

The reporter turned, then shrugged. "I don't see anyone."

"He must have just left. I just wondered if you noticed him. Dark-haired. Lean. In a blue shirt and dark slacks."

The reporter's eyes narrowed. "Why?"

"I just hadn't seen him here before."

"Sorry. Didn't notice anyone." He turned his attention back to the sheriff and police chief, who were going into the courthouse.

"Damned useless," the reporter muttered.

She nodded in sympathy, then smiled a good-bye. "I have to file my story."

The reporter moved away. She waited a few moments, then limped inside the courthouse when she felt no attention was on her. The image of the stranger went with her. He had been in back of the others, but she'd had a strong image of a man alone, that he had nothing in common with the others who'd stood poised with their pencils and recorders and cameras.

So why was he there?

Only an onlooker? Maybe an attorney from one of the many small law firms that surrounded the courthouse. But then why the intensity she'd felt even at a distance?

Had anyone else felt it? Or just her?

Or was her curiosity running away with her? She pushed the image away and strode down the hall of the courthouse to the justice of the peace's office. She would go over to the police department later and try to get some officers to tell her more about the three dead officers. But right now she wanted to talk to Graham Godwin, the courthouse historian and gossip.

Godwin was ancient. He admitted to being eighty but she suspected he was a decade older than that. The joke around the courthouse was that the only way he would leave was in a hearse. He was also a lecher who had, more than once, tried to grope her.

But he knew more than anyone about the county and the people in it.

"Ah, Miss Stuart," he said with a leer when she entered the

open door of his office. He pushed over a candy dish full of peppermints as his gaze undressed her. "Have one."

"Thank you."

"Been to the news conference?"

"Yep. It wasn't very helpful."

"Didn't think it would be."

"What do you think happened?" she said.

"Crime is coming to our peaceful little county," he said mournfully.

"Did you know the police officers?"

"Knew two of them. Their families, too. Third came from somewhere else."

"Families always lived here?"

"As long as I have." He chuckled. "Damn long time. Went to school with Jesse's grandfather." He leaned over. "Now I know that would surprise you but . . ."

His hand touched hers. She fought not to snatch it back.

"Good cop?"

He nodded.

"Why did he join the police department? Why not the sheriff's department?"

He drew his hand away and leaned back in his swivel chair. "Sheriff's department was closed."

"How closed?"

"Just . . . closed. Friends of the sheriff's." His eyes gleamed as he waited for the next question. It was obvious he enjoyed her attention, and he didn't have the fear that she'd sensed in Sandy.

"I hadn't heard that before."

"Not exactly something we talk about."

"You are."

"Sammons can't fire me. I have as many friends as he does. I also know where all the bodies are buried."

She sat up in her chair. "Now that's a provocative statement. Would you like to tell me about a few of them?"

He chuckled. "Thought that might get your attention. Maybe sometime . . ." He let the likelihood drift in the room.

She returned to something more substantial. "The sheriff's not your friend?"

His face didn't change, nor did he answer. He merely rocked again in his chair.

"He's not?"

Godwin only smiled at her. A Cheshire cat smile.

She tried again. "Do you think it has something to do with drugs?"

"Why would you think that?"

"I can't think of anything else that would be so valuable that someone would risk killing three police officers."

"I can think of several things," he said. "A love nest discovered that someone wanted to keep private." He leered again.

"Wouldn't killing cops to protect a love affair be rather extreme?"

He shrugged. "To some people, life is cheap."

"What people?"

"Now that's for the sheriff and police chief to discover."

He was playing games with her. He had done it before but she'd usually gleaned some kernel of truth from him. Otherwise he knew she wouldn't come back, and his game would end.

She took another candy and stood. "Thanks for the peppermints."

"Come back and see me."

"I'll do that."

She left, turning over his words in her mind. She stopped in the hallway and jotted down notes.

She glanced at her watch. It was nearly noon. Time to phone in her first story for the early editions. She would write the final in her office for the morning delivery. Hopefully.

She didn't really have anything new, certainly nothing that the other news media didn't have. But she did have some hunches.

Now if only she could get anyone—several anyones—to speculate . . .

She just had to find the right people.

# chapter four

*Ben knew he shouldn't have* gone to the press conference, but it was outside on the steps of the courthouse, and numerous onlookers were attending as well as the press. He would be lost in the crowd.

If not, if someone noticed him, Holland would be displeased. Maybe even more than displeased. But something in him just wouldn't let it go.

He hadn't wanted to wait for a personal invite to the investigation.

It was his day off, one of the few he willingly took. He had no private life. Working *was* his life, always had been, and it became even more so after his divorce. He couldn't afford romantic relationships even if he wanted one. And he knew now that another marriage probably wasn't in the cards for him. His childhood had been full of betrayal, and he'd learned early to trust only himself.

He'd broken that rule for Dani, and she'd betrayed him in more ways than he could count. Although he knew meth was responsible, he'd been wounded to the core that she hadn't trusted him enough to come to him when things might have been fixed.

Because he had never really let her inside?

Since their divorce, he'd turned reticence into an art form. Mentally. Emotionally.

Holland often accused him of not being a team player, and

he knew he wasn't being one now. He'd been told to take the day off, to forget about the murders.

Rather than taking that break, he found himself driving up the expressway to a slumbering town that had been thrust into the headlines. He'd tried to dress like a reporter. No tie. No suit. He stood in the crowd, but felt apart from it. He studied each of the participants and those who obviously were only onlookers, staying alert for anyone who looked out of place.

Then he noticed the woman. Judging by the notebook in her hand, she was obviously a reporter. Yet she was one of the few who wasn't trying to grab the spotlight, who stood quietly even as her eyes roamed over the crowd.

His gaze had been drawn to her mainly for that reason. He'd listened with disdain to what he considered inane and often stupid questions. He'd studied each of the onlookers, his mind cataloging anyone who looked out of place. Perps sometimes attended press conferences, though he doubted it would be the case this time. That was for amateurs. This was a professional hit. Still, he wasn't going to miss this. Then he noticed the slightly bemused look on her face. She was obviously puzzled by some of the questions as he was. He waited for her questions, but they didn't come. Instead, her gaze had continually moved, finally catching his.

Awareness jolted through him. In that second something passed between them. A shared amusement at the questions, perhaps. A connection that startled him.

And from the startled look on her face, he saw she felt it, too.

He forced his gaze away. The last thing he needed in his life was some absurd attraction, particularly with a reporter. He hadn't wanted to be noticed. This was not the relaxation Holland had in mind. Still, even as he turned away, her image stayed with him. Blue eyes the color of a summer sky at dusk. Short honey brown hair that was windblown rather than tamed and streaked with lighter colors he would swear came from the sun rather than a bottle. She wore a tailored short-sleeve sky blue blouse that was tucked into dark blue slacks. One leg of the slacks looked different, and he noticed she wore a brace on her left leg and heavy black shoes.

His most striking image, though, was not the leg but the vitality that radiated from her, even as she stood silent. He felt it even at a distance. He also realized she was soaking in everything. Not just the words being spoken, but the inflections in them, and, more than that, the crowd. She studied every face with the same concentration he did.

The press conference was drawing to a close. He finished his perusal of the crowd. Was the killer—or killers—there? If so, he saw no hint of it. Nothing that gave anything away.

Time to go.

He strode across the street and from there watched as she talked to another reporter and glanced to where he had been standing. Then she limped into the courthouse. Unlike the other reporters, she wasn't putting a phone to her ear or running toward a vehicle.

He watched as people dispersed back into the courthouse or into the several restaurants around the square. Nothing else to do here.

He had, though, memorized faces and reactions. He'd listened to the anger in the sheriff's voice and the police chief's, and shared it. He suspected from what they said, and didn't say, that they had zilch. Nothing.

It had to be a professional hit. Nothing else would be that clean. Bullets to the back of the head. One each.

Must have been tire tracks. Shoe impressions. They hadn't said anything about the ground being smoothed out. Or had too many locals trod over the scene? They wouldn't want to admit that.

Damn, he wanted in on the investigation.

How many perps had there been to take three cops down? More than one, certainly, to cuff three trained cops. At some point, they would have seen what was coming and tried to defend themselves. One man wouldn't have been able to control three trained officers. How many? Two? Three? More?

Multiple shooters didn't keep secrets that well. He suspected other bodies would turn up soon.

He returned to his car and started the air-conditioning. Yet he sat there several more moments. He'd never been in this town before and it was like a flashback to a classic '50s or '60s movie. A place where everyone knew each other. Wouldn't last much longer. Not the way Atlanta was spreading.

*Why here?*

Location, no doubt. Meredith County sat astride an east-west interstate. Although the first fingers of an ever-growing Atlanta were beginning to reach into the county, it was predominately rural with plenty of undeveloped land. There were probably private airports that would make it the perfect portal into Atlanta. He made a mental note to check on private airports or airstrips. Perhaps there was even one of those developments that seemed the rage these days, houses with their own private airfield where the owner could taxi to his own home.

Composing his mental list, he drove onto the street that led to the interstate. He was surprised that the image still remaining in his mind was the woman.

He'd been way too long without a woman if he was attracted to a reporter, for God's sake. She wasn't anything close to the type of woman who usually attracted him. He'd always been drawn to small, dark-haired women. This one, as well as being blond and blue-eyed, was tall and nicely rounded rather than slender.

And what in the hell did it matter? He had no use for reporters. Vultures, mostly, who fed off tragedy.

He pressed his foot down on the gas pedal. He had half the day left. A movie? A good meal?

None of it appealed to him.

*His computer.* Maybe it would tell him more about the history of this county, and the families who ruled it. There were always families like that. Then he would check real estate records. Who owned property around the scene of the killing?

It was a start. Maybe a piece of a puzzle. And puzzles had always intrigued him. Eventually the FBI would be called in. He had little doubt of it. He would have a head start.

Sandy woke to see his son, Mark, standing at the side of his bed.

He looked at the clock. It was four p.m. His wife would be home soon, and he would have a few minutes with her before going back to work. All deputies were on double shifts now.

"Mark?"

"I wanted to see you . . ."

*Alive.*

The word wasn't said but it lingered in the air.

Sandy sat up, then stood and hugged his son. He couldn't remember the last time he'd done that. Men in his family didn't do that. His father had never shown outward affection, though Sandy had known he cared. But in the Harris family, open affection was a sign of weakness. So was sparing the rod.

But now the uncertainty and fear in Mark's eyes reminded him of his own when his father had nearly died on a domestic call while with the sheriff's department twenty years ago. He remembered looking at his father in the hospital, tubes coming out of every orifice. His father had survived but been badly crippled. The sheriff had given him a desk job, but his father was embittered by his disabilities until the day he died.

Still, the family had been grateful that he had a job, and there had never been any question that Sandy—Hugh Harris Jr.—would join the sheriff's department. He'd practically grown up inside it. The former sheriff had been his godfather and the current one had been a friend of his father's.

"What about tossing a few?" he asked Mark, and guilt plunged through him as he saw the surprise in his son's eyes.

"Don't you have to go to work?"

"Not for another couple of hours."

A slow grin crossed his son's face, and Sandy realized how many Little League games he'd missed. He had to remedy that.

He pulled jeans over the briefs he'd slept in.

Mark disappeared and reappeared with a ball, bat, and glove.

The sight of his son's eager face almost, but not quite, took some of the worry from him. Perhaps a game of catch would replace the words that kept running through his mind. The words he'd heard the night before the murders.

He was making too much of them. But damn, he'd recalled them at the scene of the murders. They'd struck him like a sledgehammer.

"Come on, Dad," Mark said anxiously.

He followed Mark outside and paced off twenty feet. He pitched the ball several times, impressed at the sureness with which Mark caught the ball and the force with which he tossed it back. Mark was a natural pitcher, just as he'd been as a kid. He'd never done anything with it. His father thought baseball a waste of time. They'd owned a small farm, too small to support a family, which was why his father had been a deputy sheriff. It was large enough, though, to provide endless chores for a boy.

But Mark . . . maybe he was good enough to get a scholarship. The first Harris to go to college.

His cell phone rang, and he saw the disappointment in Mark's face.

This time he would let it ring. He waited until it stopped, then turned it off.

His kid deserved this time.

Jesse's kid did, too. And Zack's two teenagers.

He shut their image from his mind. He would think about them later. And the words that continued to nag at him.

*Later.*

Robin sat at her desk and stared at the computer, trying desperately to put more life into the story.

There was precious little new with the investigation. She reported the facts from the press conference, fully realizing they were on all the evening newscasts. Despite the police chief's statement that they had "leads," she knew from other sources that there were few or none.

She added personal vignettes of the three officers, as told by their fellow cops, and she did a community reaction sidebar. Crime coming to Mayberry.

That made her wonder about this more modern version of Mayberry. She went into the files to learn all she could about Meredith County. She'd done some background research when she was first assigned the beat, but now she planned to probe far deeper. She wanted to read everything she could about the police department, the sheriff's department, and the politicos that controlled the county.

Robin hadn't met the victims' families yet. Someone else from the paper was doing those stories. But she'd read about Jesse Carroll's Sarah and his son, about Zack and his teenage daughters, and young Kell who'd just gotten married. They were becoming real people to her now, and their deaths more personal.

She still remembered the phone call when her father was

killed in Iraq. It had devastated the family, especially Robin's mother, who had hated every moment of his military career. She'd been full of anger at the injustice of losing him. It would be so much worse to know that bad guys—and even someone the victims knew—had killed a husband or father.

She'd never had the chance to say good-bye to either of her parents before they died. Neither had the families of those officers.

She shook away the memories and thought again about the story. After talking to Godwin, she'd listened to the gossip at the courthouse and later at police headquarters, all off the record, about various reasons for the killings. They ranged from a personal vendetta against one of the officers to stumbling on a chop shop. She'd also heard even more about the contentious nature between the sheriff's deputies and the county police department.

She planned to write a story about the two agencies, and the fact that some residents were questioning the need for two law enforcement entities that basically did the same job. By state statute, the sheriff controlled the jail and served papers. Succeeding sheriffs had steadily expanded the size and scope of the department to include road patrols and a special drug unit which directly competed with the county police.

The county commission controlled the budget, but Will Sammons was popular, one of the last "good ole boys" who'd ruled southern counties like their own fiefdoms for years. His support usually meant victory or defeat for county commissioners, and thus he usually got what he wanted.

She'd recognized affection for Will Sammons in Sandy's voice when she had first ridden with him in his squad car. She recognized it in other voices yesterday when she asked questions.

She hadn't heard the same affection in the voices of the county police officers. One officer, off the record, said the police no longer informed the sheriff's department of raids for moonshine stills, which still flourished in some parts of the county. Many times when they informed the sheriff's office, they found the evidence gone when they arrived.

She hated not being able to use that tidbit, though she intended to find other sources to back it up.

She wondered how much Sandy knew about that particular rumor about his department.

Robin looked at her watch. After five thirty. Sandy had said he went to work at seven. She itched to call him again, still had to respect his reluctance about talking to her, even on his cell phone. She knew how easy it was for law enforcement to get phone records. Persistent calls from the paper to his home or cell phone could be noted.

After turning off her computer, she went to Wade's desk. "I'm leaving."

"Should've left long time ago," he mumbled, as he was wont to do. "But damn good job. You up to keep covering the story?"

Satisfaction flooded her. "Yes."

"What about the funerals?"

"They're the day after tomorrow."

"You want to cover them?"

She did and she didn't. She hated funerals, but if she let go of this part of the story, she might well lose it. She couldn't show weakness.

She nodded.

"Your leg holding up?"

"You forgot. I have the bionic leg. Plenty of good metal. Better than ever."

He looked at her dubiously. "No story's worth hurting that leg again."

His concern warmed her. It also worried her. She had been fighting that concern for a year, even before she came back. No matter how much the city editor, even the managing editor, might want to keep her, she knew the corporate mentality. She knew about insurance and worries about workmen's compensation and things that had nothing to do with her competence.

"Okay. Don't bother to come to the office tomorrow. Just go straight to Meredith and call in."

She tried to minimize her limp as she left the office and headed for her car, then changed her mind and went in the opposite direction. Two blocks away was Charlie's, a pub patronized mostly by the press. She'd been there only a few times since the accident. Usually by the end of the day, she was too tired for the walk, but she used to haunt the place. She'd loved the comaraderie of those who loved news as she did.

On the way, she went inside a building and used the pay phone. She called Sandy's cell phone.

He answered.

"This is Robin. I'm calling from a pay phone," she added hurriedly.

"I've said everything I'm going to say."

"You said some interesting stuff."

"I was tired."

"I just need to verify some stuff I've discovered."

"Can't do it. I told you the sheriff—"

"It's about the sheriff," she said.

A silence. Then, "We have orders not to talk to reporters."

"Just background stuff."

"The sheriff's a good man."

"I didn't say he wasn't."

"Damn it, Robin, I can't be seen with you."

"What about tomorrow?"

"I work until eight a.m. Then I go back on duty again at eight tomorrow night. I have to get some sleep and see my kid."

"What about meeting me just before you go back on duty?"

"You never give up, do you?"

"I can't stop thinking about those three officers," she said simply. "And *their* families."

He paused, then said wearily, "You know where Montcrest School is?"

"I'll find it."

"Be at the back of the parking lot at seven."

She hesitated. She didn't hesitate often. *But it was Sandy.* It would still be daylight. But she didn't like the cloak-and-dagger stuff.

"I may be late. I may not even be there," he added.

Then he hung up.

She didn't like the fear she thought she'd heard in Sandy's voice.

She didn't like the prickling down her spine.

There was no reason for it. This was a story like any other story. She was an observer, not a participant. But she knew that thought for the lie it was. It wasn't just a story to her. Not anymore. Not after seeing the three men through the eyes of people who worked with them.

Or, she was honest with herself, knowing what it could do for her career.

She wanted to know what happened two nights ago.

And why.

*Curiosity killed the cat.* Her mother's words echoed in her head.

She dismissed them. She was just a reporter, after all.

She only reported what other people told her. What she saw. What she felt.

She felt this story deeply.

She would keep picking at it.

She *would* meet Sandy.

In the meantime, she would stop at the pub. Perhaps the enigmatic man from the news conference would be there. He had remained in her thoughts all day, though she knew it was folly. He probably didn't even have anything to do with reporting, though he'd been no casual onlooker. She had become more and more certain about that. He'd been far too intent on the speakers, on those in the crowd, to be a mere curiosity seeker.

*Did he have something to do with the story?* He'd disappeared quickly enough.

She still felt a jolt down her spine at the memory of the way their eyes had locked, at the visual contact that had conveyed a momentary connection.

*Nonsense.* Imagination. He was probably married with eight children and, if not, why did she think he would be attracted to her? Males in her life had always considered her a buddy more than a date. She'd never been a beauty, and her ambition had driven her life. She hadn't had time to nurture relationships.

Still, the image of the dark-haired man lingered as she made her way to Charlie's. It was her darn curiosity again.

Nothing more.

# chapter five

*The pub was full. She* made her way to a table surrounded by *Observer* reporters, her eyes looking for the dark-haired man who'd stood behind her earlier.

He wasn't in the bar.

She recognized everyone at the table but a very good-looking man with sandy hair and quick smile he flashed as she neared.

She thrust out her hand. "I don't know you. You must be new at the paper. I'm Robin Stuart."

A sheepish look replaced the quick smile. "Afraid I'm not with the paper. I'm an interloper."

"A would-be reporter turned accountant," Bill Nugent, a features writer, said. "Smart man."

"Couldn't get a job," the man said. "Luckily I minored in accounting." A wry smile, then, "I'm Michael Caldwell. I'm auditing a company across the street and someone told me about this place. Bill invited me to join the table. We went to college together. Same dorm."

"He sprang for a pitcher of beer," Bill said.

Enough said. Bill was the biggest drinker at the paper, as well as the biggest freeloader for drinks. But his writing was sheer brilliance and it was impossible not to like him.

Michael Caldwell stood up and pulled out a chair for her, something the reporters never did.

Mama, the waitress who had been there forty years and knew everyone, greeted her with a chilled glass and the usual smile, and Michael filled it from the pitcher of beer on the table.

Robin took a sip and put it down. "You said you were auditing. Are you based here in Atlanta?"

He nodded.

"What company do you work with?"

He mentioned one she didn't know, but then she didn't know much about accounting and auditing firms.

He leaned over the table toward her. "I liked your story this morning," he said. "You really made those officers come to life."

"Thanks," she said.

"What do you think happened?" he asked.

"I wish I knew."

He had one of the nicest smiles she'd seen. That alone drew her to him. His dark blue eyes were an extra. "Did you major in journalism?" she asked.

He nodded.

"And minored in accounting? An odd combination."

He shrugged. "I've always been good with numbers. It was my fail safe option. Turned out to be a good one. Only job I was offered in journalism was with a weekly that didn't pay a living wage."

She sympathized. She knew how hard it was to get a decent-paying job, especially in print journalism. Too many papers had folded, too many others had merged with their competition.

He was well dressed, especially next to Bill, who loved to pretend he lived in a 1940s city room. He came into the office in an unpressed suit, a tie with the knot halfway down his chest, and a frayed white shirt. He'd been known to take people in off the street to stay in his apartment. He was also known to lose everything he owned in doing so.

"How long have you been with the paper?" Michael Caldwell asked.

"Nine years, including a two-year interlude," she said.

"Robin thought her car could fly," Bill said.

"It did," she said. "It just didn't have a good landing. The result is a bionic leg."

"Must have been difficult," Caldwell said, his eyes glancing down at her empty ring finger. Or did she imagine that?

"It had its good points. I stayed with my sister for part of the time. We became close."

"Must be a good sister."

"I'm lucky. I have two of them."

He lifted his glass. "To luck."

She lifted her own glass in response. She liked him. There was something inherently nice about Michael Caldwell.

She listened to the conversation for several moments, then stood. "I have to go."

Caldwell stood as well. "I'll walk you to your car."

"I'll be fine," she said, dismissing his offer. "I walk alone all the time."

"Her father taught her self-defense," Bill chimed in. "You don't want to fool with her."

Michael grinned. "I'll remember that. Anyway I'm ready to go as well. Two beers are my limit when I'm driving."

She didn't know how to say no. In fact, she didn't want to say no. She needed the company right now. Her emotions were still veering widely between the adrenaline of the story and the tragedy behind it.

He followed her out of the pub, his hand lightly touching her back as he opened the door. A courtesy, nothing more, but the human contact made her feel better.

She felt awkward with her leg, as she always did when she met someone, but he measured his pace to hers and seemed comfortable. "Are you from Atlanta?" he asked.

"No. My dad was military. Wasn't really from anywhere but army bases both here and overseas. What about you?"

"Born here. Went to school here. Then the University of Georgia."

Small talk. What new acquaintances did. But right now it warmed the cold parts of her.

She was sorry when they reached her car. She unlocked it, and he held the door open for her. "I would like to call you sometime," he said.

It was so old-fashioned. Everything about him was polite and correct. Yet oddly comforting right now.

"I would like that," she said.

She hated being so awkward in getting into the car with the brace, but he didn't seem to notice.

"Good night," he said and closed the door.

She started the car and drove off. In the rearview mirror she saw him standing there. Then she directed all her attention to the road ahead.

Robin arrived at the school nearly an hour early. She cursed her compulsion never to be late, but despite her assurance to Sandy she hadn't been exactly sure where it was.

She understood immediately why Sandy had selected the school as a meeting place. The beginning of the school year was still a month away, and the parking lot was empty. The weathered brick building had no ball fields to attract kids, and it was surrounded on one side by trees and on the other by a fenced and locked playground.

She drove around to the back and parked near some trees for shade. Then she left the car and studied the old building. It served the east side of the county, an area still rural in nature, where small farms were just beginning to be squeezed by new subdivisions spreading out from Atlanta.

There was something lonely about the empty old building. For a moment she thought she heard the spirits of generations of children who'd passed through its doors. She wondered when it was built, and how much longer it would last.

Or perhaps the loneliness reflected her own mood, even the small but growing seed of uneasiness she felt. She trusted Sandy but probably she should have told someone where she was going. The police officers might well have known their own killer or killers, and this spot was as isolated at the moment as the clearing in the woods.

She shivered. She no longer felt that safe in a county she had considered quaint, especially as far as many of the establishment went. The laid-back sheriff, the "good ole boy" commission chairman, the wily and lecherous justice of the peace could all have marched off the pages of a southern novel.

But now she was seeing something not nearly as benign as she had thought. She thought about calling Wade at the paper and telling him about the meeting with Sandy, but it might well come to nothing. Still, she should have told someone. She stared at her purse with the cell phone in it. Then turned her eyes away. Wade might well order her to leave.

Then she dismissed the discomfort as pure nonsense. Sandy was completely safe. It would still be daylight at seven. There was no reason to get spooked. Sandy's reticence was due to his job, and she would make it clear that a source was sacred. She would die before betraying one.

Or hoped she would.

She touched the small recorder in her pocket. She used it for all interviews since her fingers often didn't move as quickly as words. It was her protection against any charge that she misquoted someone. She usually threw the tapes out or reused them.

She looked at her watch. Forty minutes left.

If he came.

He hadn't wanted to meet her. He'd wanted to get rid of her. Yet she couldn't rid herself of the feeling that he had something inside he wanted to say.

She thought back over the day. It hadn't been that productive. She'd basically rewritten yesterday's story, staring with a lead saying the investigation was intensifying but that local officials were saying little. Neither the sheriff nor the police chief had been available today, and the only real news had been the funeral plans.

They were scheduled for tomorrow. Two of the murdered officers attended the same church and a joint funeral was planned. The third officer's funeral would be later in the day.

She'd talked to the pastors of both churches, learning even more about the two men with families and about the officer who had recently married. He and his new wife had had counseling sessions at the church before their wedding, according to the pastor. The bride was a longtime resident of the county, and he had relocated and changed jobs so she could remain close to her family.

An irony that ripped into her heart. She couldn't even imagine the guilt the woman might feel.

Another look at her watch. Fifteen minutes.

Would he come?

Then she saw an older-model sedan entering the lot. Sandy

usually drove a red pickup. For a moment, she felt a sudden chill although the temperature hovered in the midnineties. She switched on her miniature recorder in her pocket and went to the driver's side of her car.

She saw Sandy step out of the car and went over to him. His eyes were bloodshot, and he looked years older than his thirty-some years.

"Thanks for coming," she said.

"I just came to tell you not to contact me again," he said. "I could lose my job if anyone thinks I'm talking to you."

"You're not," she said. "You haven't told me anything."

"Just being seen with you . . ."

She waited for him to finish the sentence. When he didn't after several seconds, she tried to prompt him.

"I'm just asking about background. Stuff I could get from anyone."

"Then try 'anyone'," he said shortly. "Not me."

"Surely—"

"Look," he said, "you don't know what's involved here."

"No," she said, exasperated. "You won't tell me."

He was silent.

"You said before, or intimated, that a 'nosy' reporter could be in danger. It sounded as if you might have an idea who may have been involved."

"Anyone who kills three cops is dangerous."

"But wouldn't they be long gone by now? Unless someone is protecting them?"

His mouth tightened, and he wouldn't meet her eyes.

She tried a different tack. "Tell me more about the sheriff's department. Judge Godwin said it's a closed shop. What did he mean?"

"That crazy old coot." Sandy's voice was harsh. "You can't pay any attention to what he says."

"Is it?" she persisted. She hadn't really thought it was important before. Why wouldn't a local sheriff hire people he knew and trusted? She'd basically wanted a little color, a paragraph, but something about his reaction alerted her instincts.

"Is it what?"

"A closed shop? Didn't you tell me your father worked for the sheriff's office?"

He stared at her for a long moment. "I don't know what you're getting at."

"I'm interested in the differences between the sheriff's office and the police department."

"Why?"

*At least she had him talking.*

"It just seems strange to have two agencies covering the same area and responsible for the same duties."

"We do a heap more than the police. We serve warrants, control the jail, and take care of the courts."

"But you also have joint authority over crimes. What happens if you both turn up at the same burglary?"

"Whoever gets there first takes the case."

"And patrolling the county. Do you duplicate that as well?"

"We pretty much divide the county."

"Who patrols the area where the officers died?"

"We do."

"Then why were the county police there?"

"Probably so none of their own friends would see them drinking," he said.

"Drinking?"

"There was a container of 'shine at the crime scene." The moment he said the words, his lips clamped together.

"'Shine?"

"I didn't say that."

"Moonshine?" she persisted. "Illegal whiskey?"

"Damn it, Robin. I didn't say that. Swear you won't say anything. They don't deserve a cloud over their name."

She hesitated. He hadn't asked that anything be off the record. Then she nodded. "Unless it comes from someone else."

He owed her now. She wasn't above using it later.

"Does your department patrol that particular road on a regular basis?"

He was silent for a moment too long, then said, "Why should they? It doesn't go anywhere. It's private property."

"Kids, maybe. Drinking. Making out."

"I don't think so. There's only one way out. If anyone came . . ."

"Wouldn't that be true then for something illegal?"

He stared at her in dismay.

"Unless," she continued without a pause, "they knew somehow that no one would patrol that night."

His fists knotted. "Damn it, Robin, that's crazy."

"Is it?" she said.

She hadn't planned these questions but one had just led to another. It didn't make sense that the three officers would be found so readily on a road that everyone said was rarely used. Unless there was some kind of electronic way to keep track of the squad cars. She doubted that. Neither department seemed that advanced in its equipment.

"How were they found if no one went there?" She already knew the official version. She wondered if his would match.

"Because they didn't check in," he said. "The police put out an alert. Our department received it. Everyone was looking for them."

"But why look specifically in the woods?"

"Someone noticed the chain that usually blocks that road was down. They checked it."

"Who are the deputies who patrol this area?"

A muscle worked in his throat. "You'll have to check with the sheriff."

Suddenly she realized she should have checked the ownership of the property. No one had mentioned ownership, not any of the media. Not any of the law enforcement agencies.

"Who owns the property?"

He shrugged.

"I can find out from tax records."

He didn't reply.

"There weren't any signs posted," she persisted.

He still didn't answer.

"Sandy," she said with irritation, "surely you all know who owns the property."

"I told you, I can't tell you anything about the investigation."

She studied him. His tanned face had paled slightly.

"What are you really afraid of?" she asked suddenly.

"I'm not afraid of anything," he protested too strongly. "I need my job. My family has always worked for the sheriff's office. My cousin works for the department. Both me and my wife have family all over the county. I need this job, and if anyone thinks I might be talking to the press without the sheriff's okay . . ."

His voice trailed off. She was losing him. She took a wild stab, hoping it would cause some reaction. "Some people say the officers must have known whoever killed them. Others say it must have been committed by professionals. Do you think it could be a member or members of either department?"

Something flickered in his eyes before he uttered an oath. "Hell, no," he said.

"Then . . ."

"Doesn't have to be cops," he said. "There's gangs around here," he said, his eyes not quite meeting hers. "You don't want to rile them."

She was just about to ask who the gangs were when he turned almost violently and went to his car. He turned toward her again. "Do me a favor. Do yourself a favor. Just go with the press conferences. Don't poke your nose around, and I haven't talked to you. Not about anything."

Then he was in the car and tires squealed as he tore out of the parking lot.

She leaned against the car and took a deep breath. He'd obviously said much more than he'd meant to say, or wanted to say, and she was sure he wouldn't talk to her again.

She took the recorder from her pocket and balanced it in her hand for a moment, then kept it there as she opened the car door. She was more convinced than ever that he knew more about the murders than he was saying. And he didn't like what he knew.

She started the car. It was a long drive home, and she would listen to the conversation on the way.

Was there anything really there?

Or was it just the way he looked, moved, spoke? The way his eyes couldn't quite meet hers, the paleness of his face, the palpable fear as he spoke of his family? She couldn't get over the feeling that he knew something that frightened him.

Something that haunted him.

Or was it her imagination?

As she steered the car onto a main highway, she looked around. Perhaps some of Sandy's caution was infecting her as well. There was a steady stream of cars but none that looked as if they had any purpose other than getting to where they were going.

In minutes, she was on the interstate. She switched the recorder on and heard the conversation again. Nothing could be interpreted as definite. Just vague comments that could be construed in different ways.

She thought about sharing it with her editor, but he would want to know the source, and that wouldn't be fair to Sandy. He had been speaking to her as a friend, not a news source.

But she would find the owner of the property tomorrow, right after the funeral.

And perhaps tomorrow she could get another source to discuss the possibility of some kind of gang, or an internal connection. Two sources—even protected, anonymous ones—would allow her to explore possibilities in print.

She pressed her foot down on the gas pedal. A disgruntled Daisy would be waiting in front of the fridge. She would hear about her tardiness tonight. She smiled at the thought. Daisy made the cottage home.

And tonight, she had a story to write in her mind. One that, if she could confirm her suspicions, would put her back in the big time of journalism. No more endless city hall meetings of a rural town. No one then would think her bad leg an impediment.

Her mind wandered briefly to the intense man she'd seen at the press conference the day earlier, even as she wondered why. Reporter? Sightseer? Good guy? Bad guy? The very intensity that radiated from him had alerted her. So had the way he'd swept her with his eyes, as if he was searching the crowd whereas she'd merely been glancing around in frustration at the repeated questions.

It was said that sometimes criminals attended such events, that they took pleasure in the fact that they'd stymied authorities. Had the killer been present yesterday?

She arrived at the cottage and went inside. Daisy was, as she thought, standing in front of the fridge, the best background to appear neglected and abused.

As Robin started to open a can of tuna to the accompaniment of some rather pitiable meows, the phone rang. She quickly shoveled the contents into a dish and ran for the phone.

"Sis," her sister said, "I need your help. "Cal is suing for custody of the kids. I need you to testify for me. Next week."

"I can't believe he would do that."

"Well, he has."

"On what grounds?"

"That I'm careless."

"You've never been careless with them."

A silence, then, "Hunter disappeared last week when I was shopping. I turned around and he was gone. He apparently saw a puppy when we went into the grocery store. When I turned around, he'd gone back to the parking lot to find the dog. He went several blocks looking for it, before the police found him. They called Cal when I reported him missing."

"That could happen to—"

"He doesn't want to pay the child support," she said. "He never paid any attention to them when he was home, but now he's found a woman who has some money and wants to be a stay-at-home wife."

Robin was stunned. She'd never particularly liked Lark's husband. He was too good looking and knew it. He could never keep a job. He always felt that he was superior to any boss he had and eventually showed it. But she never thought he would try to take full custody of little Hunter and Kim.

"I'll do whatever you need," she said.

"There will be depositions. You will have to come up here to do it."

"When?"

"Next Tuesday."

That was seven days away. Robin hated to leave the story, to give it to someone for even a day or two, but her niece and nephew were more important. She knew how much Lark adored them.

"I'll be there. What about Star?"

"She'll be there, too, if the baby doesn't come before then."

"We'll have a mini-reunion."

"I wish it was under other circumstances. We haven't been together since Mom died."

"No one will take the kids away," Robin said. "I feel like calling Cal right now and—"

"It won't do any good. He's convinced he's right. It might dilute whatever you have to say at the hearing."

"Whatever you want. Are they with you now?"

"Yes. They're in bed now. The house is so quiet. I wish you were here now."

"Me, too. I'm pretty sure I won't have a problem getting the time off."

"Call me when you get a flight. I'll pick you up."

Her sister hung up.

Depressed, Robin turned on the television. It was about thirty minutes before the newscast. She would go from one to another to see which reporters were covering the story, and what they had. She prayed it wouldn't be what she did not have, or she would hear about it in the morning.

They didn't. The news was mostly about the funerals on the following day. She didn't see the man who had so intrigued her, but then she hadn't really expected it.

Daisy hopped up on the chair next to her and kneaded her claws into Robin's slacks, meowing softly in a demand for attention.

Robin scratched behind her ears, wishing with all her heart she could solve Lark's problem as easily as she could placate Daisy, who now purred contentedly.

And discover why it was that Sandy seemed so spooked by something.

Once again, his strange behavior haunted her thoughts, as did his vague warnings. A sudden prickling ran down her spine as the faces of the slain officers flashed on the screen.

It still seemed such an unfathomable crime.

She tried to brush the disquiet away. Tomorrow would be a long day, and her sister's voice worried her. She'd never heard that frantic note before.

She was asleep when the phone rang. She looked at the clock. Three a.m. Her heart clenched. Calls at that hour in the morning invariably were bad news.

"Robin Stuart," she said.

"It's Sandy," came a low voice.

She woke up immediately.

"What's happened?"

"I just wanted to make sure you won't repeat anything I told you. Nothing."

"You really didn't say anything," she tried to reassure him.

"Reporters protect their sources. That's right, isn't it?"

"Absolutely."

"You won't report anything I said."

"Not unless I can get someone else to say it. Even then, no one would know where it came from."

"Don't do it, Robin. Don't even try to find out who owns that property."

She was wide awake now. "I can't—"

"I trusted you, Robin. Don't betray me. Don't say hello to me. Don't call me." The connection went dead.

She sat on the side of the bed with the receiver in her hand, totally dumbfounded. Evidently he thought he had told her something he shouldn't have.

What in the hell was it?

# chapter six

*Ben took a sip of* what was called coffee in the office and read the morning edition of the newspaper with a jaundiced eye. He noted that there was nothing new in the *Observer*. He wondered whether he could get away for the funerals. One cop paying respect to another.

"Still chewing on the murders?" Ellis Mahoney asked as he peered over his shoulder at the *Observer*.

Ben folded the paper and tossed it in the waste can. "We should be in there. Now."

"Maybe they have more than they're saying."

Ben raised an eyebrow, and Mahoney shrugged. "The SAC is pressing as hard as he can."

"Not hard enough," Ben retorted. "Those were cops, damn it."

Mahoney was silent. He knew that Ben had lost a friend from the academy.

"They don't have any damn leads, and they refuse to ask for our help."

"It's their own," Mahoney reminded him.

"I did some looking on my own last night," Ben said. "That land is owned by a company that doesn't exist except on paper."

Mahoney raised an eyebrow.

"The officers are members of a law firm that filed incorporation papers."

"Not that unusual."

"Except when three murders take place there."

"Anything else?"

"There's a private airstrip fifteen minutes away from the murder site."

"Not exactly a smoking gun for a conspiracy."

"No, but convenient."

"Talk to Holland," Mahoney said.

Ben took another sip of coffee and looked at the paperwork in front of him. They'd just arrested a low-level drug suspect in a continuing case with DEA, and he'd hoped that arrest would lead to others. In the meantime, he had to make detailed descriptions of how he and Mahoney had obtained each and every piece.

He hated doing that, knowing the slightest mistake would be magnified to something that could be used against the prosecution at trial. He always checked and double-checked, then triple-checked.

But that could wait.

He rose and went down the hall to Holland's office.

"Is he free?" he asked the secretary.

"Is it the drug case?"

He nodded, knowing that would get him through the door.

"I'll check," she said. She lifted the receiver and punched a button. "Agent Taylor is here." Then she turned to Ben. "Go on in," she said.

Ron Holland looked up from a pile of papers and gave him a rueful smile. "And I thought I wanted this job."

Holland was a good agent who hated his desk job and obviously yearned to be back in the field. He was also new enough as a supervisor to be cautious.

"I'm taking you off the task force. The U.S. attorney says to wind it down. Too many dead ends."

"I don't think so."

"Unfortunately you don't make the decisions." Holland was clearly not happy with the decision. He picked up a file. "We have a money-laundering case. You'll be our lead agent."

"I'm not an accountant."

"You can have Robert Haver, and anyone else you want. It's preliminary. If you find anything, you'll turn it over to the Money-Laundering Unit."

Ben took a deep breath. "What about the Meredith County murders?"

"We haven't been invited yet."

"It wouldn't hurt to keep up with the investigation. That way we'll be ready when we do take jurisdiction."

"Sure of that, are you?"

"It wasn't just local. A rookie would know that. No one would take that kind of risk for anything that's penny ante."

"Maybe someone just doesn't like cops."

"You don't believe that's what it is, do you?"

"No, but it's one of the motives being bandied around."

"We need agents on the scene."

"We'll have one," Holland said with a wry smile. "That money-laundering case? There's a Meredith County connection."

"We're going in the back door?"

"As long as the locals try to keep us out."

Anticipation stirred in Ben. "What do we have?"

"Whispers that Hydra might be involved."

"Hydra?" The anticipation grew stronger. "That would explain the murders."

"Yeah, I thought so, too," Holland agreed with a gleam in his eyes.

Ben knew that name. God, he knew it. It seemed to have tentacles everywhere. No, not tentacles. Heads. Named by law enforcement agencies after the many-headed snake whose heads regrew as they were cut off, Hydra was a criminal network that covered at least five southern states, including Texas, Louisiana, Mississippi, Alabama, and Georgia. It was mythical in law enforcement quarters.

Hydra had taken over where another organization—the Southern Mafia—had ruled for thirty years until it was dismantled. But Hydra was far more sophisticated. Where the former had been a loose alliance, Hydra was, according to what they could discover, a very tightly ruled organization of cells, none of which knew—or were aware of—the other cells.

The FBI had few clues as to its leadership. They'd found one witness ready to identify some lower-level members, but he'd been killed, along with his family. Ben doubted there would be many more willing witnesses.

"What connection does this new assignment have?" he asked.

"It's an import business. Perfect cover for laundering money. One of the owners is a developer from Meredith County."

"Do we have enough for a search warrant?"

"No. It's your job to find enough."

"Who's the developer?"

"James Edward Kelley. The company is Exotic Imports."

Ben started. Kelley was one of the developers of a high-scale "fly-in" community near the murder site.

"Name familiar?"

Ben winced. Holland didn't miss much.

"I ran a search for 'fly-in' communities in Meredith County," he admitted. "Just a hunch."

"What else did you run?"

"The property where the murders took place."

"You were told to leave it alone."

Ben shrugged. "It was my off time. A mental exercise."

"And . . . ?"

"It's owned by a company called the Somerville Group, which in turn is owned by a shell corporation. Mahoney's following the trail."

"Officers?"

"Not Kelley. That would be too easy. Only names are members of a law firm."

"Who'll claim attorney client privilege if we request the officers' names. You think the locals know who owns it?"

"I would think someone knows."

"Find out who pays the taxes," Holland said.

Ben nodded.

"Be discreet. I don't want to step on toes. Not yet, anyway."

"I'm always discreet."

Holland raised an eyebrow but said nothing.

"I thought I might go to the funerals. See who's there." He didn't mention the fact he'd attended the press conference.

"Go ahead. There'll be hundreds of various types of cops. You can always say you're paying respects."

"We should have someone taking photos."

Holland shook his head. "A little too obvious. We can get the television raw film. They'll be out there in force."

Holland's phone rang and he gestured for Ben to go.

Ben paused. "I have a free hand?"

"I'll give you two weeks. Haver won't be available until then. Sniff around. But don't forget to be discreet. I don't want complaints that we're butting in without cause."

Ben nodded, exhilaration filling him. At last he had a chance of helping bring down a major crime ring, not to mention murderers.

A strike back for his ex-wife.

Robin was at the courthouse early. Her first stop was Justice of the Peace Graham Godwin.

She took him a cup of coffee and donut she'd bought at the crowded diner across the street.

"Ah, Miss Stuart," he said, a licentious gleam in his eyes. "Twice in the same week. I'm honored."

She set down the coffee and donut in front of him.

"A bribe?"

"Yep," she agreed.

"Don't get much for that. Of course . . ."

"That's as good as I can do today."

"There's always tomorrow."

She decided to ignore his last comment. "Have you heard of any gang activity here?"

"There's gangs everywhere these godless days."

"Kid gangs? Or adult gangs?"

He shrugged.

"Do you know who owns that property where the bodies were found?"

"Not anymore."

"Who did own it?"

His gaze fixed on her breasts.

"Judge?" she reminded him.

"Used to belong to old Ethan Morgan. Died in a house fire out there two years ago. Didn't have any kin."

"Who owns it now?"

"Records are in the tax office."

"But you know everything," she said, flattering him. "It would save me time."

"For a cup of coffee and a donut?"

"Lots of coffee and donuts."

He sighed in disappointment and his grizzled hands tapped a file folder in front of him.

"Who owns it now?" she persisted.

He shrugged. "Something called the Somerville Group. Don't know who they are. Mighty secretive, if you ask me. Locals didn't like it when it happened. A law firm represented the buyers. A corporation. Houston people, someone told me."

"How long ago?"

"Two years ago or thereabouts."

"And they've not asked for rezoning or building permits or anything?"

He looked at her with new respect.

"Not that I've heard."

And he would have. He heard everything. Knew more about the county than anyone. Too many people had told her that to doubt it.

"Wasn't there any curiosity that someone bought a large tract of land like that? Must be valuable."

"Nothing like the counties closer to Atlanta. It's coming, to my regret, but land is still cheap compared to that closer to Atlanta. They could have bought it for timber as much as lake development. Lots of that going on."

She had the oddest sense that he was rambling for a reason. She tried to steer the conversation back.

"And crime? Since I've been covering the county, I've heard of very little."

"Not bad."

"Drugs?"

"No worse than other places."

"Do you think someone in either department could have been involved in the murders?"

"Don't mention that around here, missy, unless you want a lot of enemies."

He had never called her "missy" before, and although she didn't think it was a good sign, she pressed on anyway. "Some say it would have to be someone they knew to take them down like that."

He leaned back in his chair. "Who are 'some'?"

"Common gossip," she lied. "Didn't it occur to you?"

"Can't say it did."

"Who do you think would murder three police officers in cold blood?"

"Can't say."

"No guesses?"

"Guesses ain't worth spit."

She knew she wouldn't get anything else. His voice had grown increasingly hard from the moment she'd asked whether some local cops could be involved.

She stood. "Are you going to the funerals?"

"Yep."

"I'll see you there."

He picked up the donut she'd brought, took a bite, and opened the file in front of him.

She'd been dismissed.

Robin hated funerals. She didn't want to attend this one. She felt as if she was intruding on others' grief. But this was one she could not avoid, not and do her job.

She'd come early because she knew as many as a thousand law enforcement officers would attend. Motorcycles and squad cars from a dozen states or more clogged the streets and roads of the county.

When she arrived, people were already milling about the simple white chapel. Two police officers stood ramrod stiff at the entrance. She went up and showed them her press credentials.

"No press inside, ma'am," one said. "Just the family and close friends."

She nodded. She'd already been inside when she'd talked to the pastor, but she'd felt she had to try. She looked around at the mourners who were already gathering, then for anyone she might know from the county. She wondered whether Sandy would attend.

There were several other reporters who'd come early for the same reasons she had. They'd hoped to get inside. She went over to where they had gathered in a small cluster. Two television cameras were already rolling.

Hank Conrad, the editor of the local weekly, headed toward her. "Good stories."

"Thanks. Do the police have anything yet?"

"Not that they're talking about."

She drew him aside, out of hearing of the others. "Have you heard of any particular gang or crime group operating in Meredith County?"

He shook his head.

"What about the sheriff's department or police force. Any corruption?"

"Nothing big. Just some DUIs that were covered up. Maybe tolerating a few stills."

"Do you know anything about the Somerville Group?"

He looked startled. "Who?"

"The Somerville Group? They own the property where the murders took place."

He shook his head and scribbled down the name. "Should have checked that myself."

"I didn't think of it myself until . . ." She stopped herself, then changed the subject. "I was thinking about doing a story on crime in the county. Gangs. Drugs. Et cetera."

"Nothing here that's not anywhere else."

"That's not what I heard."

"What have you heard?"

"That there might be a connection to one of the local law enforcement agencies, that the police officers stumbled onto something very big." It was a great exaggeration of what she had heard, but she wanted a reaction.

"A connection with the local law? You mean police killing police? Where in the hell did you get that?"

"Do you think it could be true?"

His gaze searched her face. "It would explain how three officers could be taken, but no, I haven't heard anything like that."

"You've heard nothing?"

"They're keeping everything very tight."

"Because they don't have anything?"

"Maybe."

Another reporter joined them then. She excused herself and went to her car and opened it. Her leg was aching and she needed to sit down.

She took out her notebook and jotted down some impressions of the church.

Her thoughts were interrupted by the roar of many motorcycles.

She stepped out of her car as what must have been more than a hundred officers on motorcycles roared up to a field just to the left of the church and parked their vehicles. They then lined the road, apparently in preparation for the arrival of the hearse.

Just minutes later, it arrived. Uniformed men went to the back of the hearse and carried first one casket in, then a second as two women, one holding the hand of a child and the other clutching the sleeve of an older man, watched. The child was sobbing.

A huge lump formed in the back of her throat. In defense, she stared around at the growing crowd. She saw Sandy standing with a group of deputies. Then her eyes moved to the right, scanning the crowd of people who followed the caskets into the church. *Family and close friends.*

She jotted down a possible lead to her story:

*An endless blue line united by grief and dedicated to memorializing three of their own filled the town today.*

*Police officers choked the streets of Benton, some having traveled as far as halfway across the country to pay their respects to three fallen comrades.*

*They came first to a small country church, a plain white chapel that overflowed with local mourners. A large screen and plain chairs from other churches were provided for those who could not crowd inside. Hundreds of uniformed officers sweltered in the above-100-degree heat and listened as family and friends eulogized police officers Jesse Carroll and Kell*

*Anderson. The service for the third officer, Zachary Palmer, was to be held later in the day at another church.*

She looked at her watch. Her first deadline was in an hour.

She continued jotting down sentences, forming an emotional backdrop for the story. When the time neared, she would go toward one of the loudspeakers.

She finished as much as she could, then stepped back out of the car. She started toward the cluster of people near one of the loudspeakers. The foot of her bad leg caught a rock, and she lost her balance. She felt a hand steady her, keeping her from an undignified plunge into the grass. She found her balance, then turned around to thank the good Samaritan.

Dark brown eyes met hers. She remembered them, remembered the lean body and arresting face of the man who had intrigued her as he'd stood on the fringes of the press conference two days earlier.

And his dark eyes were just as piercing and hard as they had been then.

# chapter seven

*"It's you," Robin blurted out* in what she immediately realized was not one of her more brilliant moments.

"I hope it's me," he replied with just the barest hint of a smile. "Are you all right?"

She tried to put some weight on the leg. A jolt of pain ran through it, and—for a second—fear struck that she might have injured it again. She grasped his hand for support.

The ache faded. She breathed again. She'd already started putting a small amount of weight on her leg without the brace. But very, very carefully. Another break could be crippling for the Humpty Dumpty leg, and she feared for an instant that she'd twisted it as she started downward.

She felt the strength in his hand, in his body, as one hand stayed at her elbow. Heat from his body darted through hers, and she seemed to absorb some of his strength. For a moment she found herself leaning into it, something that startled her. She'd worked damned hard to restore her sense of independence after the accident, usually spurning attempts to help. She could do everything herself, a resolve made especially strong after lying immobile and helpless for too many months.

"Miss? Are you alright?" he repeated.

She forced herself to reply. "I . . . think so. Except for feeling rather foolish. And awkward. Thanks for rescuing me."

Her gaze caught his. He was as attractive as she'd remembered, especially now that concern had replaced the disapproval that she'd seen in his face at the press conference. He really had very nice eyes when they weren't cold and wary.

She desperately tried to regain her dignity. His hand was still on her arm. He was close. Very close. She smelled the slightly tangy aroma of aftershave.

"You're welcome," he said in a soft drawl that was singularly sexy. "And you shouldn't feel foolish. This is rough ground." He released her hand, though he kept his left hand around her arm.

He'd neatly avoided reference to her leg.

"I noticed you at the press conference," she said. Still not very bright. But the words had popped out like a jack-in-the-box.

He merely nodded.

She felt like a fool. Worse yet, a besotted fool. She balanced herself and straightened, ignoring the fact that her legs, both of them, wanted to fold under her. Something must have shown in her face, because his hand tightened around her arm.

"I'm okay," she said, though she wasn't. She didn't know why she found him disturbingly attractive.

She met his gaze, then she tried to dismiss the impact of him. "I'm Robin Stuart," she said, reaching out to shake his hand. As she did, her purse went spinning off her arm. She closed her eyes as belongings went skittering over the ground. Her notebook. Wallet. Pencils and pens. *Lots of pencils and pens.* She didn't even want to think what other items had tumbled out.

She wished she could ignore the spilled contents of her purse, but her notes were on the ground. Along with her recorder. She couldn't risk them getting into wrong hands.

She backed away from his arm and did one of her inelegant balancing acts, dropping to her good knee and letting the one in a brace stretch out. She would have a devil of a time standing again, but she reached out and grabbed the two most important items.

Her companion stooped down and started gathering pencils and pens, dumping them into her purse before holding it out to her for the notebook and recorder. Then he reached down and pulled her to her feet.

"You *are* a good Samaritan today."

"I think that's the first time anyone has called me that," he said.

"Then who *are* you? Press? Law enforcement? Interested citizen?" She was pretty sure he wasn't the latter. But she didn't want him to disappear again. Not only because of the unprecedented effect he had on her, but because he'd appeared once more at an event related to the murders.

Another slight twist of his lips. So slight she thought she might have imagined it. "Ben Taylor."

"What is Ben Taylor doing here?"

"Paying respects."

"Are you law enforcement?"

He hesitated, then said, "Yes."

He was avoiding answers. Why? She was in full reporter mode now. "Local? State? Federal?"

"FBI," he said reluctantly. He didn't wish to identify himself. But then why not? He had as much reason to be here as all the other law enforcement.

"Are you here officially?" she asked.

He released her arm but the warmth of his touch lingered.

"No," he said softly. "As I said, I'm paying my respects."

"Why were you at the press conference?"

"Personal. It was my day off."

"Did you know any of them?"

"No, but they were fellow cops."

Her gaze locked on his, and she wondered whether he felt the same little jump in the stomach as she did. Lord, but his face was arresting. *Hard.* But the shock of dark hair that fell over his forehead lessened the severity. Didn't FBI agents have short, cropped hair? Or had those days passed?

He was wearing a dark suit, just like so many of the other mourners who weren't in uniform. His eyes were even darker than she remembered but every bit as flinty again.

She took a step back. His proximity was too disturbing, too intense.

She wasn't sure he felt it as well until she saw a sudden confusion in his eyes, a momentary awareness. Then his eyes shuttered. "Sure you're okay now?"

"I'm sure." She wasn't. She was altogether too confused

about how totally out of character she felt. She who prided herself on her professionalism and cool demeanor.

He studied her for a moment, then gave her a short nod and started to turn.

"Do you think the FBI will come in officially?" she asked before he could leave. Her mind had started functioning again, and the questions he'd aroused in her demanded answers. She started to see the lead of her next story in her head. *The FBI has taken an interest in the murder of three Meredith County officers.*

He turned back to her. "You don't give up, do you?"

"I've been told that," she admitted with what she hoped was a disarming smile.

He didn't respond to it. "I'm not here for any reason other than to pay my respects to fellow law officers."

"I would think the local police would welcome help from the FBI."

He shrugged again.

She didn't want him to go. For several reasons. One was a story. The other was more personal. He intrigued her in a way no man ever had before. "Thanks again. I would have hated sprawling across the ground in front of everyone. I'm not very graceful, right now."

That twitch of his lip eased the severity of his face.

"You do all right, Ms. Stuart," he said. Then he walked away, leaving an odd void where he had stood, a loss of energy, of presence. She watched as he walked away quickly, heading toward a group of officers. He didn't look back, but then why should he?

He probably hadn't felt the same warm sizzle that she had when he touched her and held her a moment longer than necessary, or was that just her imagination?

Other than those few seconds, he'd demonstrated a marked lack of interest in her.

She wondered whether it was her questions. She was not a police reporter. She'd not come in contact with the FBI before. Perhaps it had been a normal reluctance to talk to reporters.

Or maybe he wasn't supposed to be here. He'd certainly slipped away quickly from the press conference.

She scrounged through her purse and found the notebook she'd dumped into it. *Ben Taylor*, she scrawled in large letters. As soon as she returned to the office she would call the police reporter and see if he knew Agent Taylor, then she would do a computer search.

Robin placed a new tape in the recorder and turned it on. Dismissing the pain in her leg, she limped over to where the other media had been herded. She'd been standing much too long, but she feared she couldn't hear the service if she went to her car. The heat, too, was draining. There was no shade, and the sun beat down on them.

Music started inside the church and was broadcast outside. A hymn she didn't recognize. Then a strong, rich voice: "Dear friends, we join in grief to honor two . . ."

She jotted down some notes even as the recorder ran. Words that made an impact. Then she stopped. *Listened.* Remembered the words being read, "Any man's death diminishes me, because I am involved in mankind; and therefore never send to know for whom the bell tolls; it tolls for thee."

Then came the lonely mournful cry of the bagpipes with "Amazing Grace."

Tears welled behind her eyes. She hadn't realized it would hit her like this.

Embarrassed, she wiped a tear away. She glanced around. She saw a few other wet eyes among the media but not that many.

She watched the mourners leave the church for the small graveyard to the side. The graveside service was to be private, family only, and county officers started shepherding others away. She saw Sandy. He stopped when he saw her, and she noticed his red eyes as he stared at her for the briefest of seconds. Then he walked quickly to a squad car with another deputy.

She waited, though, until she saw Ben Taylor leave the church, glance at the media with a frown, then stride down the road, apparently to where he'd parked.

Emotionally drained, she limped over to her car. Perspiration trickled down her back. She turned on the air-conditioner and leaned back in the seat, letting the squad cars and motorcycles go first. She thought about Sandy and Ben Taylor and all the officers who attended the service.

Most of all she thought about the families. The wives who would have a lonely bed tonight and children who wouldn't have a father to tuck them in, and parents who wondered why their children died before they did.

Then she continued to write the story in her head.

*The plaintive sound of a bagpipe bade two Meredith County police officers a final farewell.*

*The familiar salute to fallen warriors followed a quote from John Donne's Meditations: ". . . I am involved in mankind: and therefore never send to know for whom the bell tolls: it tolls for thee."*

*They tolled proudly for Jesse Carroll and Kell Anderson, two of the three slain officers who were memorialized today at a small white chapel as hundreds of their fellow officers from throughout the country held quiet vigil.*

She would change that to three in the later edition.

One more funeral to go.

Ben Taylor cursed his luck as he left the church and saw Robin Stuart glance his way.

Damn but there was something about her.

He couldn't figure it out. He didn't trust reporters. He certainly didn't like them, especially pushy ones, and she was certainly that.

But there was something about the blush that reddened her cheeks and the subsequent quips when she fell that appealed to him. She was gutsy and funny and self-deprecating. And her eyes were so damn alive. They fairly danced with curiosity and energy and life. Something he hadn't felt in too long.

*Robin Stuart.* He'd been reading her stories.

She was good. Most reporters—print and electronic—had just repeated the ten versions of no comment that were coming from official sources. Not her. She obviously knew how to ask questions.

Surprisingly, she'd ruined his concentration, something few people did. He'd been studying faces, body language. But he hadn't seen anything that spiked his instincts.

And then out of nowhere she was next to him, stumbling, and he'd reached out to catch her, never expecting that quick contact would send a rush of need through him.

Sex. That was all. He'd been too long without a woman. He had no intention of ever letting anyone get close to him again, or for himself to get close to another woman. He'd destroyed one. He wouldn't do that to another.

He decided not to attend the second funeral. As Holland said, they could get raw film from the television stations. He wanted to track down the owners of the property.

Sympathy wouldn't do a damn thing for the dead cops and their families.

Only results would. Only justice.

Racked with guilt and fear, Sandy left the second of the funerals.

It could have been his widow standing with her arm around their son.

*It could still be.*

He'd heard something he shouldn't have heard. He didn't think anyone knew he'd been listening when he overheard Danny Evans, the dispatcher coming on duty, and Deputy Brett Schroeder talking about something taking place that night at the old Morgan place. *"If any calls come in from that area, call me. Don't call in any of the other deputies."*

"How much this time?" Evans had asked behind the half-closed door to the locker room.

"The usual. The boss always takes care of us."

Sandy had walked away then, not wanting to hear more.

*The boss.*

Could have been the sheriff. Could have been any number of people.

Hell, he'd been around long enough to know that the sheriff took care of his friends. Some people just didn't get tickets. Bootleggers who still existed in the county were warned before the feds reached them; the feds knew if they wanted to catch anyone not to tell the sheriff first. Some kids got away with almost anything as well, because their folks were prominent or monied or politically helpful. He knew that some deputies took payoffs to look the other way when bars held poker games in back. He'd taken a few dollars himself. Nothing major, he'd told himself. Just a little extra to look away when he found a small marijuana patch.

But murder? Of cops?

The sheriff's department had been the first to arrive on the scene of the murders. He'd been among them when the call came in. He'd seen the carelessness with which they handled the crime scene. He wasn't sure it was completely due to ineptness.

If he said anything, he knew his career would be finished. The sin of betrayal would not be overlooked. He could never get a decent job again.

*If* he lived beyond the telling.

Three other cops were already dead. Fear in the past few hours had become a growing, poisonous vine inside, strangling the human parts of him. He knew now that men he worked with had been at least partially responsible in some way for the murders.

Perhaps even the sheriff.

He didn't know how long he could continue working there. Yet an abrupt resignation would be too dangerous. And what would he do for a job? He had a family. He had a high school diploma and nothing more. He loved police work.

Move? If he quit, the sheriff would want to know why; he didn't like losing people. Would he get a good reference, or would the only job he knew be closed to him forever?

And his family? Cleo would not want to leave the county. Her mother was here. Her sisters. Her job. His extended family. She loved family, lived for it.

Yet how could he live with himself if he didn't speak up? The crime scene was virtually clean of any evidence and what there was had been destroyed. The team of investigators from the police department and sheriff's office had no leads, not as far as he knew, and they were not bringing in the FBI.

His head ringing with doubts and guilt and questions, he checked in with the dispatcher. He looked at his watch. He had just enough time to go home, have dinner with his family, and return in time for roll call.

• • •

That evening, Robin returned to Charlie's Pub. It was after eight. She was emotionally drained from the funerals and the story she'd just completed. It had some of her heart in it, and the city editor said he would run it on page one.

*Some of her heart?*

*Too much of it.*

She'd felt much too much today to be comfortable. Reporters were supposed to be onlookers, neutral observers.

But too many memories clouded her view.

Drained. But she couldn't relax. Along with the emotional overload, there was also adrenaline surging through her as it always did on a big story and after the rare occasion of knowing she'd written a good story. She usually never thought a story was good enough.

Tonight she needed company, human rather than feline. Friends. Other reporters.

She maneuvered her way next to the police reporter and ordered a beer, the beverage of choice during these after-hours sessions, and listened as the others discussed the upcoming governor's race.

She turned to Bob Greene, the police reporter. "Do you have much to do with the FBI office here?"

"It doesn't have much to do with us," he replied. "There's the occasional press conference when they want to brag about something. Other than that, it's nearly impossible getting anything from them."

"Have you ever met a Ben Taylor?"

"Doesn't ring a bell. Why?"

"He was at the press conference the other day and then at the first funeral today."

"That doesn't mean anything. Cops from half the country attended those funerals. They do that. By the way, that was a great story today." He said the last as if it pained him. She knew he wanted the story himself.

"But at the press conference?"

"You think they're in the investigation?"

"If they're not, I think they might be trying to nose their way in."

"I'll check around," he said.

"Thanks."

She listened for a while, finished her beer, and headed for her car. She'd made a rule a long time ago. One drink if driving. Preferably one over a very long period of time.

Daisy would be waiting.

It was ten when she reached home. She unlocked the door and went inside. She looked for messages on the answering machine and heard several hang-ups. She didn't recognize the number that went with them. She flicked off the machine for the night. It answered at two rings and it usually took her longer than that to get to it.

Daisy was the world's most abused cat, to hear her tell it. She meowed plaintively and refused to rub against Robin's leg as she usually did. Eager now to rid herself of the brace, Robin quickly filled the food dish, refilled the water dish, and went into her room.

She unbuckled the brace and pushed the heavy, ungainly apparatus into a corner, then rubbed her leg. She needed an hour in a hot tub, but she also needed sleep. Without the protection of the brace, she used crutches to get to the bathroom and ran the hot water.

When the tub was full, she moved onto the edge of the tub and used her arms to lower herself down without putting weight on the leg. Just a few more weeks, the doctor promised, and she could discard it. How she awaited that day!

Once in, she sat back and reviewed the day, the sorrow of it still haunting her. Daisy finally entered and sat on the toilet seat and stared at her with rebuke.

The phone rang and she groaned. She should have left the machine on.

It kept ringing.

She finally managed to get out of the tub and onto the crutches, very aware that by the time she reached it, the caller would likely have hung up. But she tried anyway; maybe it was one of her sisters. Maybe the baby had come early.

As she expected, the phone was dead when she reached it. Then she thought of the hang-ups on her answering machine. Her first thought had been telemarketers. But now . . .

She left the water in the tub. She wasn't going back for that. She'd take care of it in the morning. Whoever had called apparently was persistent. They would call back. She wanted to be near the phone.

Daisy jumped onto the bed but took the far corner to continue to sulk. Robin turned off the light and stretched out on the bed. Her leg ached, but not as badly as before the bath. *A few more weeks.*

She would always have a limp, the doctors said. A small price to pay to keep the leg. The initial call was to amputate. Thank God there were second thoughts.

She had just dozed off when ringing pierced her consciousness. She reached for the phone.

"Robin?"

She was instantly awake.

"Sandy?"

"Is it true that reporters won't give up their sources?" There were no preliminaries, and she heard the strain in his voice. He'd asked the question before, but now there was new urgency, a frantic need for reassurance.

She took a deep breath. "Yes."

"No matter what?"

She paused then, trying to think of a scenario where she couldn't keep that promise. "If someone told me they were going to commit a crime . . ."

"No other reason?"

"Not if I promise . . ." She was wide awake now, looking at the clock. She thought she'd just dozed off, but it was three in the morning.

"You'll swear to it."

"Yes," she said again.

"Can you meet me tomorrow morning? Not here in Meredith County."

"A coffee shop?"

"No. Someplace where no one can listen."

"My house?"

A silence, then, "No."

She tried to think of a place on his side of Atlanta. "Kennesaw Park. The battlefield. The picnic area outside the visitors' center. I'll bring coffee."

"I won't be able to get there until eight, maybe later."

"I'll be there," she promised.

The phone went dead in her hand.

She stared at it for several moments.

She'd been right about him wanting to tell someone something. A mixture of uncertainty and exhilaration surged through her. She couldn't forget the stark fear that had been in Sandy's voice.

And despite her words, she didn't know legally how far she could go to protect a source. She did know there was a state shield law. But she wasn't sure how much protection it gave her.

She did know, though, that when she made a promise she would keep it. Whatever Sandy said would stay with her unless he gave her permission to share it.

*I'm getting ahead of myself. He might not have anything of real importance.*

It could also be the biggest story of her career. One that would be a ticket to the best newspapers in the country.

She turned the light off.

But she couldn't turn off the chill of apprehension that snaked up her spine.

# chapter eight

*"I want your word that* you won't say you talked to me." Sandy's fists clenched. "I want to be sure I can trust you."

No breeze ruffled the leaves of the oaks around them. Nothing broke the stillness of the hot summer morning except his ragged voice.

"I might have to tell my editor, but I won't do it unless he agrees to keep it confidential."

He turned to go.

"Sandy, I won't say anything to anyone until you tell me I can. I promise you that. Tell me what's bothering you, and we'll go from there."

He walked over to a cannon and put his hand on it. "I should have gone into the army. I'd planned to. But then Pop got shot and I stayed home."

She waited.

"The sheriff has been good to me. Me and my family."

She didn't try to force whatever he was reluctant to say. Reluctant, but obviously he had to say it or he wouldn't be here.

"I knew those guys," he said. "Not well, but I knew them. They didn't deserve that."

"You know something about it?" she finally asked after another long pause.

"I don't know who," he said.

She waited again.

"The patrol guys had orders to avoid that spot the night of

the murders," he finally said. "I overheard several of them talking about it."

"Who ordered it?"

"I don't know. I can't ask. No one knows I heard anything."

"There's no one you trust?"

The silence was deafening.

"The FBI?"

"Proof? I have none. Just what I overheard. And if anyone knew I did . . ."

His words trailed off.

"Someone in the sheriff's department killed those officers?"

"Or knew something was going down. Those guys must have wandered into something they shouldn't have. Maybe they saw some lights. But someone didn't want to be seen there."

She was stunned. But she wanted him to put into words what she had to hear. "What do you want me to do?" she prompted.

He shrugged. "I don't know. I thought maybe you could write something that might get the Feebies involved. They can do it with official corruption. Someone needs to know where to start looking."

"Why me? Can't you give an anonymous tip?"

"My voice would be on tape. A letter? I thought about that, but . . . that could lead back to me, too. You've been talking to a lot of people. It could have come from anyone."

Stunned, Robin stood there. Nine years as a journalist, and she'd always been an onlooker, an observer. A role she took pride in. Now she was being asked to become a participant. And it could be one of the biggest stories in her life. Excitement exploded inside her until it was tamed slightly by the fear in his eyes.

If he was afraid, shouldn't she be?

"Why would your guys kill their counterparts?"

"Something big would be involved. Bigger than I know how to handle."

"Any ideas as to who?"

He hesitated. "Rumors. There's been rumors the Hydra Network been inching in."

"Hydra Network?"

"Ever heard of the Southern Mafia?"

She nodded.

"What was left of it was gobbled up by a bigger group that operates in a bunch of southern states. Hot cars. Drugs. Prostitution. They're crowding out all the local dealers. Two locals have been killed in Meredith County. No big deal made of it. They were dung."

She tried to make sense of it. Mainly why she'd never heard of it before, though she'd heard tales of the old Southern Mafia. "No one was arrested?"

"Not a trace of evidence. Just like at the crime scene here."

"You mean this . . . Hydra is in Meredith County?"

"I didn't put much stock in the rumors. But I can't get that warning out of my head."

"Did the deputies mention this Hydra?"

He shook his head. "But I can't think of anything else big enough that they would bring this much heat here."

"What deputies were they?" she asked.

He shook his head.

"You don't know—or won't tell me?"

Silence.

"How can I do anything if you don't want to get involved?"

"You guys always use anonymous sources."

"What would this anonymous source say?"

"That patrol officers were told to avoid the area at the time of the . . . murders."

"Then why did the county police go there?"

"We don't share information," he replied bluntly. "We have our territory. They have theirs. Those guys never should have been there."

"Why do you think they were?"

He shook his head. "Everyone's been asking that."

"Could they have been involved in some way as well?"

He shook his head. "They would have been more careful." His eyes met hers. "I just want to send the Feebies on the right trail." He paused. "I really hate their arrogant guts but it's the only way the truth might come out."

"What about the state investigators?"

He just shook his head. "Everyone knows everyone."

"I can't promise anything until I talk to my editor. He might have to tell the attorney. Otherwise the paper can't afford to go with it."

He hesitated.

"I won't give him your name unless he swears not to use it."

"I trust you. You've haven't let me down. I don't know *him*."

"I do. If he gives me his word . . ."

He stared at her. "The Feebies will want to know where you got it."

"They can want."

"They will pressure you. They're damn good at that." He paused. "You swear on your sisters' lives?" He had asked about her family, as well as her nonexistent romantic life.

"I swear that I won't tell my editor unless he gives me the assurances I need. If you like, I'll call you and tell you what he says about withholding it, before I give him your name."

"I don't like someone else having it."

"They won't go with an anonymous source unless they know who it is."

"What will you write?"

"I'll read it to you before it goes to press."

"You can't call me."

"Then you call me."

He ran his hand over the cannon again. "I don't like doing this."

"I know."

"They can't kill cops and get away with it." His voice was fierce. Scared yet fierce.

"No," she agreed softly.

"My . . . the people I work with. They know. Several of them know." His eyes glazed with tears.

She knew she should look away, but she couldn't. Sandy was one of the most macho guys she'd ever met. For the first time, she saw the demons eating at him these past few days.

"What would the anonymous source say?" she asked.

He hesitated. "You can say it better than me. Something about patrols being told not to go to the area that day."

"I'll talk to my editor today. Call me on my cell phone from a pay phone."

"I'm betraying them," he said.

"If anyone from your office was involved, they betrayed themselves. You're the good guy here."

"The hell I am. I don't have the guts to do what should be done. But I've heard . . ."

"Heard what?"

"They don't just go after people they don't like, they go after the families."

"There's witness protection.

"For the immediate family. Not sisters and aunts and grandmothers. My wife's life revolves around her family."

Fear stabbed through her then. The story meant everything to her. Justice as well. But did she really know what she was getting into? If they killed three police officers . . .

His eyes were intent on her.

"I'll talk to my editor," she said again, her voice more unsteady than she would have liked.

"When should I call you?"

"This afternoon."

He turned then and left, his steps dragging, his normally straight shoulders slumped.

She felt sympathy and something else. Pity. Even a slight contempt.

He had just dropped a bomb in her lap, a bomb he'd refused to defuse and was handing to her.

Wade Carlton read the transcript of the conversation Robin gave him.

"My God," he said when he finished.

She merely nodded.

"Who is he?"

"I promised I wouldn't tell you unless you promised to protect his identity."

"You have the tape?"

"Yes."

"We'll need it."

"I promised him I wouldn't give you any information until he has assurances, and the tape is mine. If I have assurances, I'll let the attorney hear it."

"The investigators will come after you."

"I know."

"Do you? It sounds noble to protect your source until you get squeezed. Believe me, it's not when they come after you." He paused. "And you said this source is afraid. Have you considered that whoever murdered those officers might want to know who gave you this?"

She took a deep breath, then nodded. She wasn't going to let fear kill this chance.

"Write your story. I'll take it to the attorney, along with the transcript."

"We can protect him?"

"We have a shield law in Georgia," he agreed. "They can't compel you to testify if they can get the information some other way. And they can do that by interviewing all the sheriff's deputies. Until they've exhausted that . . ."

She just nodded.

"Go write the story."

"Hey, Ben, you seen the *Observer* yet?"

Ben cradled his cell phone against his ear as he navigated an intersection. "No. Why?"

"Get it."

He'd spent a late night trying to crack the mire of companies sprouting from the one owning the property where the officers were killed. One led to another to another until he reached an office in the Seychelles, an island group off Africa. He knew what he would find then. A dead end.

Frustrated, he'd finally gone to bed, mentally seeking his next step. It didn't come.

"Don't play games," he told his partner. "I'm not in the mood. What is it?"

"Ah, grumpy this morning. Late night?"

"Spit it out, Mahoney."

"You have to read it for yourself. But basically she's claiming the Meredith County Sheriff's Office was involved in the murders of its sister agency's people."

He nearly choked on the coffee. "Say that again."

"Get the paper." Mahoney hung up.

Ben stopped at the first convenience store. The story was at the bottom of page one. It started benignly enough.

*The investigation into the murders of three Meredith County police officers resumed after emotion-filled funerals.*

*While official sources say there is no new information, a source close to the events suggested that officials look specifically at the Meredith County Sheriff's Office. The source said that patrols in the area were warned away from the murder site the night of the murders.*

*The source also said there could be a connection to the Hydra, a criminal network that has allegedly engaged in drugs, car theft, and prostitution throughout the Southeast.*

*Sheriff Will Sammons labeled the charges "pure fiction" and categorically denied any connection to his department.*

The byline said Robin Stuart.

He took another sip of coffee. He remembered her face. Expressive. Pretty. A smile to kill for. A natural warmth that was hard to rebuff.

What in the hell was she thinking?

An oxymoron. Reporters didn't think. He'd almost let himself think otherwise. He stared at the headline again. She knew something he needed to know. She also knew something that others with less than good motives needed to know.

He uttered an oath under his breath, then called his boss. He was turned over to Holland immediately.

"I saw the article," Holland said. "I think it's enough to bring us in, or at least interview that reporter. You want it?"

"Hell, yes."

"Take Mahoney with you. And I want everything on tape."

"If she doesn't cooperate . . ."

"I'll ask the attorney general to call her in to a grand jury. She'll be forced to give up the name."

"I'll pick up Mahoney at the office."

"Let me know what she says immediately after you leave her."

"Do I have the authority to get a search warrant for her home?"

"Not yet. Play it by ear. If she refuses to cooperate, then we'll go to a friendly judge."

"I have the feeling we'll need that search warrant."

"You know her?"

"Met her at one of the funerals."

"Well, sweet-talk her. Duty. Responsibility."

"I'll do my best."

"I'll get people working on the search warrant."

Robin read the story over her coffee. Sandy had called yesterday afternoon and she'd given him the editor's promise and her own. She'd also read the story to him.

He'd paused, and she knew he was second-guessing himself yet again. But at the end he told her to go ahead.

But as she read it in black ink, she wondered whether she'd done the right thing. He couldn't be identified from the story, not if no one realized he'd overheard the conversation. And she'd talked to enough deputies and other people to make it difficult for anyone to narrow in on one specific person.

But she read the story with a jaundiced eye, wondering how she could have made it better. Too many unanswered questions.

The phone rang and she picked it up. After several seconds of silence, the caller hung up.

She checked the caller ID. It reported "unknown."

In disgust, she replaced it back in the cradle. It wouldn't have been Sandy. He would have used her cell phone.

The phone rang again. She waited until the ID reported another "unknown."

She picked up the phone and slammed it back down as loud as she could. She would buy a whistle later today.

But that resolve didn't quiet the sudden anxiety that knotted and writhed in her stomach.

She quickly dressed, took one more slug of coffee, said good-bye to Daisy, who looked forlorn, and went to her car. She was to meet with Wade again this morning, along with two other reporters now assigned to work the story with her.

One was Bob Greene, the police reporter, the other Cleve Andrews, an investigative reporter. They were to work as a team from now on, but she was to be the lead reporter.

She was no longer the Outer Siberia reporter. She was back in the big time with a huge story that belonged to her.

But she found herself looking in the rearview mirror as she drove, something she'd never done before.

Had that black sedan been there four blocks back?

She turned a corner, then another. She looked back again. No black sedan.

She was becoming paranoid. The calls were obviously a wrong number, or a computerized sales pitch.

*Get over it.* Sandy's fear had infected her. Reporters weren't harmed for reporting.

Her cell phone rang.

She hated that when in traffic.

The light ahead was red. She looked at the number.

The paper's.

She punched the talk button. "Wade?"

"Are you on the way?"

"Should be there in ten minutes or so, depending on traffic. The meeting's at ten, isn't it?"

"Yeah, but there's a complication."

She waited.

"The FBI is here. They want to talk to you. I've contacted our attorney. We don't want you to talk to them without him."

Her heart thumped unsteadily as she switched the phone off, and the traffic started moving again.

Sandy had warned her this would probably happen. So had the company attorney.

She looked down at her hand and saw it tremble slightly. Like most people, she found the idea of talking to the FBI a little off-putting, even as a reporter. It was one thing to ask questions, quite a different one to answer them. Or not answer them.

Was she really ready for this?

She had to be. She'd consciously grabbed the tiger's tail, and now she would have to hold on till the end.

# chapter nine

*Robin sat in one of* the private offices on the management floor of the paper and tried to ignore the nervous tingling in her chest. Not only were her editor and the newspaper's attorney present, but also the executive editor of the paper.

She'd received flowers from the latter immediately after the accident two years ago, but she'd never actually had a conversation with him.

Richard Reese greeted her warmly, though, and she knew Wade must have already discussed the story with him.

"You might be in for a hard time," he said, "but the paper will stand behind you."

"Thank you."

The door opened, and two men were ushered in by Richard Reese's secretary.

Her gaze went immediately to the taller of the two, and her heart quickened. She'd been occupied since the funeral with the story, with meetings, but Ben Taylor had lurked in her thoughts.

Taylor led the other man into the room. As on the day of the funeral, he wore a dark blue suit with a striped tie and his hair, which had been unruly that day, was neatly combed. The flinty look in his eyes was the same.

He nodded at her, his gaze holding hers for a fleeting second. "Ms. Stuart."

Richard Reese was already standing. "You know Ms. Stuart?"

He turned to Reese. "We met at one of the funerals. I'm Agent Ben Taylor. This is Agent Ellis Mahoney."

Reese introduced the others at the table. Wade. The attorney, Mason Parker.

Ben Taylor frowned as his gaze moved from one to another. He was clearly displeased. "Gentlemen."

"Please sit," Reese said.

Taylor obviously didn't want to do that but he chose a chair at the end of the table where he could see everyone's faces. His partner sat next to him. Reese was at the other end, the attorney on his right side, and Robin had been placed on the attorney's right side. Wade was seated across from her.

Ben Taylor didn't waste any words. "We want to know the name of your source for the story." He addressed her directly.

Mason Parker interrupted. "Is the FBI officially involved now? It's my understanding that it's not."

"Ms. Stuart's story, if true, indicates official corruption as well as involvement by an organization that operates across state lines." Taylor's voice was clipped, with none of the southern drawl Robin had heard earlier.

She felt heat rise in her cheeks at the "if true" in his statement. Mason Parker gave her the smallest shake of his head, as if warning her not to react.

Taylor's gaze didn't leave her. The intensity she'd felt in him before had reached storm level. Storm, heck. Hurricane force.

She started to answer when the attorney cut her off. "Until it's an official federal case, Ms. Stuart is protected by the Georgia shield law."

Ben Taylor didn't move his eyes from her. "You want murderers to go free?"

"Her source wouldn't have spoken if he, or she, had not been assured of privacy," Mason Parker interjected.

"The Georgia shield law isn't absolute, and there is no federal shield statute," Taylor said. "Ms. Stuart just gave us reason to enter the case."

Mason Parker shook his head. "Ms. Stuart is not obligated at this point to reveal her source."

"Then you will release it at some point?"

"That's up to Ms. Stuart."

"She can be subpoenaed."

"I think this conversation is over," Mason Parker said as he stood.

Taylor leveled a stare at her that would have frozen hell. "Murder. Drugs. Prostitution. Corruption. Do you really want to protect that?"

"If I did, I wouldn't have written the story," she said, ignoring the attorney. Anger seethed deep inside.

"Good intentions or not, you're impeding an investigation," Taylor said sharply. "Someone else might die because of it."

A suffocating sensation tightened her throat, but after a few seconds she defended herself. "There would have been no story if I had not promised," she shot back. "Then you wouldn't have what you might have now."

"Ms. Stuart," the attorney cautioned.

"If someone didn't think they could hide behind you," Taylor retorted, "they might have come to us."

That, too, could be true. She'd watched Sandy's personal agony.

"We're through here," Mason Parker said sharply. "If you have any more questions, bring them to me."

Robin saw the anger in Taylor's face, the frustration. But he rose with his partner. "We'll keep in touch." Then he walked out with the easy grace she'd noticed before, a grace that made her feel that much more awkward.

After the door closed, Richard Reese turned to her. "We'll support you in whatever you decide, but I think they'll try to compel you to talk. You could go to jail. Be aware of that. We wouldn't be able to help you there except to continue your salary."

Mason Parker tapped his pencil on a notebook. "Try to get your source to come forward. Talk to the FBI about giving him protection."

"He already said that wasn't an option. He said the bad guys go after families, and both he and his wife have large extended families in the county."

"Ask him to think about it again."

She stood, her legs as unsteady as the first time she'd stood after the accident. Still, the adrenaline was back.

"One more thing," the attorney said. "We've been notified

that the sheriff's department might file suit against us. You are no longer welcome in their offices."

"They can't ban me. It's public space."

"You won't get anything," Reese broke in. "Wade, maybe you should put someone else with the sheriff's department. Ms. Stuart can work the county police department and other aspects of the case."

"That's giving in to them," she protested. "They shouldn't be able to decide what reporters—"

"Perhaps not, but unlike Atlanta, where politicians worry about public reaction, I don't think Meredith County people give a damn." Reese shrugged. "I'll leave it up to Wade." He grinned conspiratorially. "I suspect most of them hate our guts already. The liberal Atlanta press. Might as well give them more heartburn."

Ben swore as he slammed down on the brake as the traffic light changed.

"That went well," Mahoney quipped. "What do we do now?"

"Get her away from her minders."

"You think charm will do it? Then better me than you," Mahoney said with a sly smile.

"Holland indicated the same thing," Ben said dryly. "I lost my temper. I'm so damned tired of reporters thinking they're above the law. They twist what you say, they cast blame without knowing what the hell they're talking about, then they sit snug and safe after they start their damn fires."

"She was right, though. We wouldn't have even as little as we do without her story and anonymous source."

"It's not enough. Her story doesn't officially put us on the case. It could be nothing but one person's suppositions or paranoia. Damn it, we need to interview that source to know whether the report is credible."

"I'll start an extensive background check on her. Maybe our boss got the okay for a search warrant."

"I'm not sure the U.S. attorney has the balls to take on the press."

"He wants to take down Hydra as much as we do. It would be damned good for his career." Mahoney didn't have to add what they all knew: that Joseph Ames would do almost anything to promote his own career. And right now press credibility wasn't that great.

"She's kinda pretty," Mahoney added with a leer.

"Haven't noticed," Ben lied. "Don't forget you're a married man."

"I'm thinking about you," Mahoney countered. "It's time you started thinking about women again."

"I do think about them, but I'm too poor to do anything about it," Ben said. "Every extra penny I have goes for Dani."

"It's not just that, and you know it. You shouldn't feel so damned guilty."

Ben silenced him with a look. "I'm content as I am. And if I were inclined to seek female companionship, I sure as hell wouldn't go after a reporter."

"She's got a thing for you," Mahoney said as the car slowed. "Betcha a beer."

"You're wrong."

"I know you hate the press, with good reason, but they're not all like Ceci Walker."

"They're all a bunch of jackals," Ben replied.

Mahoney grinned and spread his hands. "Okay. But you research her while I talk to U.S. Attorney Ames. He likes me better than you. We'll compare notes tonight. Over a beer."

"Your wife approves?"

"She understands," Mahoney corrected.

"Don't ever believe that, pal. You think they do. They think they do. Then one day you wake up and realize it's all been a myth."

After the meeting with Wade and the other reporters, Robin went into the restroom and splashed cold water on her face.

The combativeness was gone. The adrenaline had faded. Mason had made it clear what she faced. And Ben Taylor's anger left its mark. She resented the contempt in his voice, but it struck home. Was she really doing the right thing?

She'd just defied the FBI. That was a big thing for the daughter of a man who lived for duty, honor, country. She didn't think he would approve.

Jack Ross would. She used her cell phone to call him.

He picked up immediately.

"Jack, this is Robin."

"Great stuff, kid," he said.

Some of the uncertainty left her. Jack Ross had been her mentor, a Pulitzer Prize winner, when she'd first joined the paper. He'd been the political editor and had taken her under his wing. It was one reason she'd moved up so quickly. It had been friendship only. She became part of his family, as close to his wife as she was to Jack.

She'd learned writing, and reporting, and regret from him. Years earlier, he'd authored a series on prisons, using a number of anonymous sources. He gave one up, and that person was killed in prison. He'd never completely recovered from it, and he'd started drinking heavily, a habit that eventually forced him from the paper.

"Whatever you do, kid," he told her over and over again, "never give up your source. In this business, if you don't have trust, you don't have anything."

"They say they're going to subpoena me," she said.

"They won't keep you long. Public pressure's too strong. Hang in there, Robin."

The words were a balm, an affirmation.

"Another thing," he said. "Make sure your notes are safe. That's what got me."

After she ended the call, she weighed how to protect and preserve her notes and the tape she had. She considered destroying them, but if the paper were sued or she needed proof of the conversation for some reason . . .

She couldn't use a safe-deposit box. If she refused to answer questions, they might try to subpoena her notes. She couldn't send them to one of her sisters, not without drawing them into this. Same thing, friends. She could try to bury them somewhere, but she didn't like that idea, either.

She compromised. She left the office and stopped at a pay phone in a convenience store. She called information and found the number of a former classmate and friend. A mutual acquaintance had told her he had a law practice in Santa Rosa, California.

In minutes, she'd found him and even got him on the line.

"Shelby, this is Robin Stuart."

"Robin—God, it's been years. Where are you?"

"Atlanta. The *Observer*."

"What you always wanted."

So he remembered. "Yes."

"Is this a hello call or something else?"

"Something else. I would like to hire you."

"In California?"

"Particularly in California."

"Okay," he said softly. "Am I to ask any questions?"

"No. But it's nothing illegal. What would you suggest as a retainer?" A retainer would establish the attorney-client relationship.

"What services do you need?" he replied cautiously.

"To hold on to a package."

"That's it?"

"Yep."

"Then five dollars will do. A bargain-basement price for you."

"Thanks. I'll send the package along with a five-dollar bill."

"I'll need your signature. I can e-mail you the document."

She thought about that for a moment. "Not here."

"Where?"

She thought a moment. "I'll call you back as to where to send it. What's your address?"

He gave it to her.

"Keep it safe," she said. "It could be important."

"It's a pleasure serving you," he said with mock humility. "When are you going to be in town?"

"I don't know."

"Robin, it's good to hear from you." His voice turned serious. "I don't know what you're involved with, but be careful."

She drove home, gathered her tapes and written notes, and put them into a large, padded envelope, adding a five-dollar bill. She carefully wrote Shelby Mann's address on it. Then she erased every address from her computer address book, as well as most on her cell phone.

On her way to the office, she slipped the envelope into a post office collection box. Once back at the office she started calling all her sources for the next day's story. She quickly learned her earlier story had made an impression. The sheriff refused to take her call, as did every other source she tried. Some just hung up on her. Others explained they could no longer talk to her.

Bob Greene was working all his police sources. The investigative reporter, Cleve Andrews, was trying to trace down the ownership of the land where the officers were killed.

She wrapped up the report at six after being on the phone for four hours. She led with the blanket denial from the sheriff's office that it had any connection to the shooting, or that any deputy was told not to go by the crime scene the night of the murders.

Much of the rest was a retelling of facts.

Her phone rang.

"Hi, it's Michael. We met a few nights ago at Charlie's."

"I remember."

"I was hoping I could take you to dinner tonight. To celebrate the story."

Surprised, she considered the offer. She hadn't had a real date in two years. Since she'd returned, she tired much too quickly at night.

Michael Caldwell. She'd liked him. He hadn't made her heart jump or raised the temperature when he was in close proximity, but she was comfortable with him.

"Sorry," she said with real regret. "I'm really beat."

"Tomorrow?" he asked hopefully.

"I'm not sure. Depends on the story."

"I'll check with you again soon."

She hung up. Part of her regretted the refusal. It would be nice to be normal. But she desperately needed some sleep. Perhaps tonight she wouldn't see the bodies in her dreams, or nightmares.

Bob Greene approached her desk. "Great job. What about a beer?"

She stretched. "I'm heading home."

"This source," he said, "you're sure of him?"

"Or her," she corrected. "Yes, I am."

He waited, obviously hoping she would share more information. She wanted to. She didn't want to keep this to herself. It was becoming a far greater burden than she'd envisioned when Sandy had extracted his promise.

"Be careful," he said. "If your source is right and it is

Hydra, they'll want to eliminate anyone who might know something about them. They thrive in the dark."

"Tell me more about Hydra." She'd researched it on the computer, but there was very little of substance.

"Nobody knows much. Neither the locals nor the feds have been able to penetrate the organization. At least that's what I've heard. No one really knows how big it is. The rumors are out there. Fear's out there."

"Then every crime could be attributed to it," she said. "The myth grows."

"Could be. Could also be it's all true."

"It could corrupt a whole sheriff's department?"

"Corrupt some members. Scare others."

"What do you think?"

"I think three dead policemen say someone is real serious about concealing something."

"Thanks."

"It's an important story. I'm glad to be working with you."

She didn't believe a syllable of it. His eyes said he wanted the story himself.

She wasn't going to let go of any of it.

Ben turned off the computer. He looked outside. It was nearly seven and daylight still streamed in through the windows.

Mahoney had already left. He had received a "maybe" on a subpoena from U.S. Attorney Ames in Atlanta after explaining what breaking the Hydra would do for his career. But Ames wanted to talk to the woman himself before making a decision.

Ben had spent the last several hours finding out everything he could about Robin Stuart. He'd brought up all the articles she'd written for the paper, finding an astounding cross section. The one that interested him most was a story about an autistic child. There was compassion in every word. Then there was a series on autism and lack of facilities for its victims. She'd parlayed a story into a front-page series.

There were some investigative stories: an organization that bilked the blind; a driver education firm that basically sold driver's licenses with the assistance of several state licensing officers.

He saw a passion in each of the stories. Some were the basic who, what, when stories, but most went far beyond that with the why. He partly envied that passion. His own had died years ago . . .

Then he came across the story of her accident. Nearly eighteen months passed before the next byline. That explained the brace.

He stood, glanced at his jacket with disgust. It was hot as hell outside, and he hated the suit-and-tie culture that was still expected at the FBI. He pulled the knot of his tie down.

Home. He should go home. But that was so damnably empty. It was a roof over his head. Little more.

Instead, he decided to ride by Robin Stuart's house. He knew he couldn't ask her any questions, but maybe, just maybe, she would hear him out. It was worth a try.

Her house was an even more welcome sight than usual.

Robin felt her moral compass was going awry, the needle swinging back and forth without any clear direction.

Protect Sandy? Protect the law? And herself? She didn't like the fear that both Ben Taylor and then Bob Greene had planted inside her. They both had reasons to do it. Taylor wanted a name. Greene wanted the story.

She drove into the driveway, picked up the groceries she'd just purchased, and sprinted for the door with her keys in her hand. Another car drove in behind her.

She immediately recognized Ben Taylor, as he unwound his long body from the front seat of the dark sedan. Still angry at his words during the meeting, she turned back to the door, unlocked it, and stepped inside.

"Ms. Stuart?" His voice was soft but compelling.

She turned around. "I thought our attorney told you everything had to go through him."

"I'm not going to ask you any questions. But I thought you might like to know more about Hydra."

That stopped her. She had done some research on the Internet, but he would know much more.

"No questions?"

"No. I swear. I might try to persuade, though." Charm oozed through the last words.

"A few moments," she conceded. "And no persuasion. Just Hydra." As angry as she was with him, she wanted to know as much as she could about the mysterious organization.

He gave her a wry smile. "Fair enough."

She opened the door and went inside, leaving him to follow.

She expected Daisy to run to her, then to the kitchen. No Daisy.

"Daisy," she called out.

Still no cat.

Her heart started thumping. It was unlike Daisy not to greet her, not to be sitting in the window looking out, not to be meowing for her treats. She couldn't remember when it had happened before.

She started looking through rooms, even awkwardly mounted the stairs, though she lived mostly downstairs. She planned to change that once her leg was fully operational again.

"Ms. Stuart?"

She spun around. She'd almost forgotten about Agent Taylor.

"Who's Daisy?"

"My cat. She's usually perched on the window seat and runs to the door when I come home. I didn't see her at the window but I thought she'd already jumped down . . ."

Robin went into the kitchen. Everything looked the same except for the absence of Daisy, meowing for her supper. She checked every room. Then, her heart beating faster with every second, she went into the small laundry room and looked behind the washing machine. She'd found Daisy there before, once when the cat was ill, and another time when she was recuperating from a dispute with another cat. It was her "cave."

Daisy was lying there now, on an old towel Robin kept there, first for leaks, then for Daisy's occasional foray.

"Daisy?"

Daisy didn't move. Didn't respond in any way. Robin squeezed next to the washer and balanced herself as she tried to lean down. Damn brace! She inched down and, finally, her finger touched the soft fur at Daisy's neck. She was alive, thank God. Then she saw Daisy's front paws. They were bloody.

*What had happened?*

She looked around but nothing seemed to be disturbed.

She picked Daisy up and wrapped the old towel around her. The cat still didn't respond. Her breathing was barely audible. Robin bolted toward the front door and slammed into Ben Taylor.

Once more his hands kept her from falling. His eyes slid over the cat, the blood on her claws.

"I have to get her to the vet," she said.

"I'll drive you," he said.

She hesitated, then nodded. She wanted to keep Daisy in her lap, and calm if she woke.

"The name of the vet?" he asked.

"The phone number is on the fridge."

Faster than she could blink, he had the clinic on the phone and told them they had an emergency on the way.

Gratitude erased any misgivings she had about him. She didn't care who he was or what he wanted or his motives. She wanted the "juice" he had as a federal officer and, for Daisy, she wasn't above accepting it.

In seconds, he shepherded her out to his car and opened the passenger-side door so she could slide in with Daisy.

She held Daisy close to her as he ignored the speed limit and drove fast, and expertly. She glanced at the set expression on his face. Somehow, he hadn't seemed the animal type. But at the moment she was accepting any help she could get.

Seven minutes later, they arrived at the emergency clinic. In seconds, they were ushered into an examining room. A woman who identified herself as Dr. Lori Hammer entered immediately and took Daisy.

"What happened?"

"I came home and found her unconscious. There was blood on her claws but I didn't see any open wound," Robin said.

Daisy moved slightly, mewing softly, as the vet gently probed. "She's hurting. She seems to be bruised. It doesn't look like anything is broken but I should take some X-rays to be sure." Robin nodded, gratitude pooling inside.

"Can you save a sample of the blood on her claws?" Taylor said. From his pocket he took what she recognized, from the Meredith County crime scene, as an evidence bag. "Mark and sign it with your name and date, and return it to me?"

The vet looked startled.

"Ben Taylor. FBI." He took out his credentials and flashed them, then added, "The cat may have attacked someone who was in Ms. Stuart's house."

The vet glanced at Robin.

Robin nodded. "It's . . . it could be a possibility."

"All right," the vet said. "I'll get some blood off those claws, then take the X-rays. Shouldn't take long." She turned to Ben. "You probably want to go with me."

Robin started to follow, but the vet shook her head. "It's better if you stay here."

Robin thought about protesting, but she wanted all the vet's attention on Daisy. Instead she paced the small examination room.

*Had someone come into her house?* She hadn't added an alarm system, mainly because she simply hadn't had time, and it was a rental house, not hers. She made a vow to herself she would contact the owner the next day and have one installed.

In the meantime, a chill ran through her. Just thinking of someone prowling through her house.

Maybe not. Maybe Daisy had been hurt in some innocent way.

*Please don't let anything happen to Daisy.*

Taylor returned to the room then, the evidence bag in his hand.

"Do you always carry those around?"

"Yeah, usually."

"How's Daisy?"

"Complaining loudly." He smiled slightly. "If her meowing is any sign, she should be fine."

The rare smile reassured her.

"I misnamed her," Robin admitted. "When I got her, she was thin as a rail and mean as Satan. I hoped the name would help her personality."

He chuckled. It came from deep in his throat and rumbled through her. She was aware he was trying to distract her. Her mind told her to resist, but an undeniable magnetism was building between them. She felt it in every fiber of her body. *Bad. Very bad.*

"Did it work?"

"Well, she's no longer as thin as a rail."

"What about mean as Satan?"

"Depends on whether she likes you."

"I'll remember to stay on her good side."

She raised an eyebrow. "You think you'll be around?"

"Ouch."

"You can go," she said, disgruntled by her growing awareness, by the sparks she felt every time she looked at him. "I'll wait until I know more."

"You don't have a car."

"I have friends."

His gaze didn't leave her face. "I want to be there when you get home."

"You really think someone was in my house?"

"I think it's a distinct possibility."

She didn't protest more. He was doing his job. And if he was right, she didn't want to go home alone. Now, though, she wasn't sure what was the most dangerous. Going home alone, or going with him.

She moved away from him. Proximity was far too dangerous.

He moved away, too, and leaned against the wall, that energy she always felt in him radiating in the room. His was not a peaceful presence. She wondered whether it ever was.

"How long have you been with the FBI?" she asked.

"About fifteen years." His eyes met hers and they were as dark and enigmatic as they had been before. Yet in the moments after she'd found Daisy, she'd experienced the same protectiveness she had when he'd helped her at the funeral. It was a warmth he evidently took pains to hide.

"Have you ever had a cat?" Inane chatter, but better than a silence that heavy with tension.

"No."

"A dog?"

"No."

"Why? You seem to care for them."

He hesitated, then said in a flat, inflectionless voice, "Not practical in my profession. I'm gone most of the time."

"Your wife?" There. She'd asked it.

His eyes shuttered then. "There isn't one."

*There isn't one.* She wondered whether that meant he'd never been married or was divorced. But his tone this time didn't invite any additional questions. Yet an invisible web of attraction was enveloping them. She knew from the dismay in his eyes she wasn't imagining it.

"When you were a kid? You didn't have a pet then?" she persisted.

"No," he said simply. "I moved a lot." But she knew voices. She suspected it wasn't simple at all.

She had a habitual disease of asking questions. Couldn't seem to stop them. She always wanted to know everything about everyone. But Ben Taylor didn't seem like a man who revealed much.

"I didn't have one as a kid, either," she said. "My dad was a sergeant major in the army. We moved from one post to another and we couldn't take pets overseas. He said it wasn't fair to get attached to one. Daisy is my first. And dear to me. Thank you."

She was talking too much. He wasn't talking at all. For her, it was part anxiety. The thought of someone having been in her house and hurting a helpless being was becoming a huge weight in her stomach.

The door opened, and the vet reappeared.

"The X-rays looked fine. No broken bones, but there might be internal injuries. I would like to keep her here overnight. I'll call you if there's any change. Otherwise you can pick her up in the morning."

"Thank you," Robin said.

Taylor opened the front door for her and guided her to his car, opening the passenger's door for her. She watched as he strode around to his side and got inside. The interior suddenly felt even warmer than the temperature justified.

*Business.* Concentrate. "Were you really at my house to talk about Hydra?"

He shrugged. "That was the intent."

"Nothing more?"

"Perhaps I had hoped . . . a little persuasion might help." He made the admission with an odd quirk to his mouth that was more self-mockery than smile. It was unsettling. He didn't seem a man to show any vulnerability.

She glanced over at him. He'd left his jacket somewhere and his tie was gone. His sleeves were rolled up to his elbows, and raw masculinity radiated from him.

*He wants something from me.*

But at the moment she wanted something from him as well. She wanted to know about Hydra. And she certainly didn't want to go into her house alone.

He glanced at her, then down at her hands, which were pressed into her lap. She quickly moved them.

"Daisy will be all right," he reassured her.

"An empathetic FBI agent?" she asked with more bite than she intended.

"I don't think anyone has mentioned that word in connection with me before."

She ignored that comment, along with that damn warmth that started to creep up her spine again.

She tried to shake it off. "So you had only persuasion in mind?"

"Yep. For now." He paused, then added, "But we have asked the U.S. Attorney to subpoena you. Then you'll have to testify."

"I won't, not without permission."

"Ms. Stuart . . . these people don't fool around. You wrote something that leads both the perps and us to believe you know something we need to know. Besides being downright stupid, it's also irresponsible."

Her spine went rigid. She wanted to attack back, then she realized he was probably baiting her for a purpose. Instead, she tried to swallow her anger, only to discover that her breath was already trapped in her throat.

"Was there anything in your house identifying your source?" he asked suddenly.

"No," she said.

He turned and looked at her. "Nothing?"

"No."

"Damn it, you're playing with a life. You're not doing your source any favor. They will find him, and he'll die. It's as simple as that. If we get to him first, he'll get protection."

"I didn't say it was a him."

He ignored that. "Don't you care about anything but your

damned story?" If he'd been kind and cajoling just a moment earlier, his voice was pure, icy anger now.

"I care about justice. I care about the person who trusted me."

"As long as you get a headline."

"That's unfair."

"Is it? God save me from reporters and their righteous stupidity."

Her back stiffened. "You're an arrogant ass."

"Been said. At least I concede my shortcomings."

Her mouth clamped down before she said something she would regret.

"We're talking about murder, Ms. Stuart," he continued. "Capital murder of three police officers. You think these people would stop at searching a reporter's house? Hell, you're lucky they didn't burn it down with you and that cat in it."

He drove up and parked in front of her house. She looked around. The lights in Mrs. Jeffers's house next door were still on. No one occupied the house on the other side.

She stepped out of the car, her keys in her hand. His fingers brushed hers as he took them from her, and once again anger and attraction warred with each other. She had to wrench herself away from her ridiculous preoccupation with him.

He took the keys from her as she reached the top of the stairs and steered her to his side. He took out his gun before turning the key in the lock. Then stepped in as he opened it.

"Wait out here," he ordered.

He was back in several minutes and opened the door wide. Then he inspected the lock. "Doesn't look tampered with."

She went inside. Everything looked as she'd left it earlier today.

She went to her office first. Everything of value to her was in there. Her notebooks. Her computer. Her research ranging over several years. This was her life far more than the bedroom.

The desk looked the same. So did the computer. She looked at the top of the desk, and her heart skipped. Although her desk was always covered in piles, she knew exactly what was in those piles. She had gone through them hours ago to make sure she was erasing all traces of Sandy and the attorney to whom she was sending her package.

The notebooks were out of place. She'd stacked them, according to date, starting with the oldest on the bottom. Now they were reversed.

With increased panic, she checked her top drawer. She'd left her address book there along with a credit card, tucked inside the book next to the cover. She always kept it there because she did a lot of research and sometimes had to pay a fee for a certain article. The card was in the book, but not in its proper place.

She turned to the computer and turned it on. Then she saw a smear on the rug beneath. It looked as if someone had tried to clean something, but couldn't quite do it. Blood from scratches? She turned to Ben Taylor, who was regarding her with intent interest, as if he realized she'd found something.

"Someone's been in here," she said.

His eyes asked the question.

"Notebooks are out of place. So is a credit card. And there's a spot on the rug."

"Do you have any valuables?"

"Not really."

"Check the rest of the house. See if anything else is missing."

It didn't take her long. She didn't have much. A few inexpensive pieces of jewelry. The computer. A large television set and VCR.

She reported back to him. "Nothing."

"It looks like someone didn't want you to know anyone was here. Your Daisy spoiled their plans. Once your intruder bled on the floor . . ." He pulled out a cell phone and called the local police.

"They'll be here shortly," he said.

She pictured an intruder snooping in her office.

And became sick to her stomach. She also realized in that moment that all her mother's clichés had a root of truth. *Don't catch a tiger's tail.*

*Curiosity killed the cat.*

She'd just barely escaped killing the cat and now she feared she had the tiger by the tail.

Or was it the devil?

# chapter ten

*The Atlanta police and crime* scene technicians swarmed Robin's apartment like a horde of locusts.

It was nothing like the first time she'd been burglarized five years ago. Then a lone police officer came over, told her to make a list of missing items and take it to the local precinct. End of interest. She'd been highly irate at the time.

She suspected the mention of FBI and Hydra had drastically increased their diligence.

After Ben Taylor had called the police, she'd conducted a more comprehensive search, but everything outside her office seemed to be in place. The fact that nothing—apparently—had been taken was even more frightening than if it had been a common burglary.

She'd barely gotten started when the police arrived. She was aware of their incredulity when she said nothing was missing. The locks on the doors and windows looked undisturbed.

"If someone entered here, they knew their business," said one officer. Robin didn't appreciate the "if" and started to say so when Taylor interrupted and took the officer to one side.

The officer was more polite when he returned. "We'll start in the kitchen."

"Can I go into my office?"

"No. Let us do our job."

Ben Taylor nodded and turned to her. "We'll just be in the

way. It's eleven but I noticed your neighbor's lights are still on. Maybe she saw something."

"That would be Mrs. Jeffers. She and Damien stay up late. She's probably dying of curiosity about the police cars out here. She's just too well mannered to come out and ask."

"Damien?"

"Her guard dog," Robin said. "I think Mrs. Jeffers would be delighted if you questioned her."

He arched an eyebrow. "Would Damien have alerted her if anyone came around your house?"

"Maybe," she said.

It was amazing how at ease she felt with him, even after his harsh condemnation an hour earlier.

"Let's go," he said. The two of them walked to the house next door. It, too, was an old Victorian, one that looked like an aging dowager.

She rang the bell.

Mrs. Jeffers immediately appeared at the door as if she'd been sitting next to it. The inside door opened and her neighbor peered out the storm door, then opened it.

Damien wriggled out of Mrs. Jeffers's arms and tried to jump into Robin's arms. Being less than a foot tall, he didn't make it. Robin caught him halfway down and scooped him up before he fell to the ground.

"I swear that dog likes you better than me," Maude Jeffers said.

"He doesn't see me as much as he sees you," Robin mollified her. She kept Damien when Mrs. Jeffers was out of town. "Mrs. Jeffers, this is Ben Taylor with the FBI. My house was broken into earlier, and Daisy was hurt. I wondered whether you saw anything unusual today."

"FBI, you say," Mrs. Jeffers said, her eyes narrowing. "You have credentials?"

"Yes, ma'am," Taylor said, whipping them out even as he stared at the aged teacup poodle that frantically licked Robin's face.

Mrs. Jeffers examined them closely. "Always wanted to do that," she said as she handed them back. "I can scratch that off my list now," she added with satisfaction. "What's the FBI doing investigating a burglary?"

Ben Taylor looked taken back. Apparently he wasn't accustomed to such questions from feisty ladies in their eighties.

Robin thought about letting him answer, but that would be too cruel. And he *had* been kind tonight. "Mr. Taylor thinks it might have something to do with a story I'm covering," she said before he could utter a word.

"The murders," Mrs. Jeffers said with delight. "Come in, come in. It will take me only a moment to make some tea." She opened the door wide and stepped back.

They had no option but to follow.

"No tea for me, ma'am, thank you," Taylor said. "But can you tell me if you saw anything unusual earlier?"

"Just a cable truck."

"When was that?" Taylor shot back.

"About six. I thought they were working late. Can't get my cable fixed when it goes blooey. Takes weeks. Dratted cable company never works late. Should have known it was strange. Especially when Damien barked. He doesn't bark at everyone." She paused. "You said Daisy was hurt?"

"She was unconscious. Blood was on her claws. She probably jumped on whoever came in."

"Brave as my Damien. He's a good guard dog, you know."

Robin had to smile at the picture of a brave Damien. The only danger to an intruder was being licked to death.

"She's going to be okay?" Mrs. Jeffers asked.

"I think so. The vet is keeping her for observation."

"Poor Daisy. She was just beginning to trust me."

"Can you describe the cable truck?" Taylor broke in.

"Just like every one. White with blue lettering. I only saw one man."

Ben Taylor turned back to Robin. "Any cable service scheduled?"

She shook her head.

"Can you describe the man?" he asked Mrs. Jeffers.

"Tall and skinny. Blond. Wore a hat but his hair was longish."

Taylor was looking at Robin's elderly neighbor with admiration. "Would you be able to help a police artist sketch him?"

Her face lit again. "Dear me, I think so. Wouldn't swear to it, though." She whispered to Robin. "That's on my list, too."

Robin saw that rare smile play on Taylor's lips.

"I'll ask a sketch artist to come by in the morning. He'll call first."

"Oh my, that's exciting."

"Thank you for being so much help," he said. "You and Damien."

Mrs. Jeffers beamed. "Anything for the FBI." She looked at Robin. "Such a nice young man."

Robin winced. Mrs. Jeffers had been trying to fix her up with men friends since she'd first moved in.

Ben Taylor's usually somber eyes glittered with amusement he no longer tried to hide. "It's been a pleasure, Mrs. Jeffers."

He went out the door. Mrs. Jeffers put a restraining hand on Robin and whispered, "Oh he's a lovely one. You should set your sights on him."

*Lovely, indeed.*

Robin muttered to herself as she followed Ben Taylor down the steps.

Ben didn't usually enjoy interviews, but he'd been captivated by this one. Usually people were nervous, even when there was no reason to be. Mrs. Jeffers was irrepressible as well as observant, and he saw a side of Robin Stuart he hadn't seen before. He made a mental note to send an FBI artist to the house.

"I like your neighbor . . . and her guard dog."

"Damien is very protective," she said defensively.

"I don't doubt it for a moment."

She gave him a suspicious look, then walked faster than he would have thought possible with the brace.

He caught up with her. "What's the list she mentioned?"

"Everything she wants to do before she dies. It's a very long list. She'll have to live to a hundred and fifty to do it all. Diving out of a plane is one."

"At eighty?"

"Eighty-two to be exact. She saw an ex-president do it. She figures that if he could, she could. She's saving her money."

"And the FBI is on the list?"

"No accounting for taste."

She was obviously still irritated with him about several of his earlier observations about her good sense. Damn it, he was right. She was being foolish to the extreme. So why did she get under his skin, and why was he beginning to like her so much?

Why, for God's sake, had he wanted to lean down and kiss her when that dog jumped into her arms? Maybe that quick grin and delighted laughter that warmed him in places that had been cold.

The woman he'd taken to the vet and then to the eccentric neighbor was not the same hard-headed, stubborn, story-at-any-cost reporter he'd expected. There was a naturalness and caring about her that appealed to him in a way no woman had for a long time.

*Don't even think about it.* Even if he didn't have a lousy record with women, he spent nearly his entire salary on his ex-wife.

More important, Robin Stuart was protecting information he wanted. Hell, had to have. Not only for his investigation but for her own safety. That was becoming increasingly important to him.

Disturbingly important.

The crime scene technicians were still working when they returned.

"We'll need Ms. Stuart's fingerprints to compare with the others," the senior officer told them. "We'll also need the names of people who've been in the house."

She nodded.

"We cut out the section of carpet where you found the stain. We'll check the DNA with what Agent Taylor has. That wraps it up." The officer hesitated, then added, "Strange thing about the doors. Doesn't look like anyone tampered with the locks. You sure they were all locked?"

"I'm certain of it."

"Then it was a real pro. Take my advice, miss, and get a good security system."

"I plan to."

Ben watched her face. He wished he saw more fear there. Not for fear's sake, but she was taking everything too lightly.

She had no idea of the rat's nest she'd just disturbed. The fact that nothing was missing told him they were looking for information. And if they didn't get it one way, they might well try another.

He needed it before the bad guys got it.

If only he could convince Robin Stuart of that.

When the police and technicians left, Robin headed back to her office. "I want to check the computer," she told Ben.

She sat down in her chair and turned it on, then checked the log. "Someone started opening files at 6:08 p.m.," she said.

"Did they need a password?"

"No."

She went through the computer files in her head. Some e-mails from her sisters, even some random thoughts for a novel someday. Much too much of herself were in those files. She suddenly realized she was shivering.

She felt his hand on her back and she stiffened. She didn't want to show fear. Not to him. Yet he didn't drop it, and she felt its assurance and warmth flow through her. Darn it, she wanted to turn around and throw herself in his arms and tell him she was scared.

She forced herself to concentrate on the screen in front of her.

Whoever had paid her a visit had opened a number of recent files. Had he copied any of them?

"They were looking for a name. Is there any chance they found one?"

"No."

"Are you sure?"

"Yes. I checked this afternoon. I removed anything that could lead to the source." She didn't add that she'd done it because of his visit this morning, but the implication hovered in the air.

*Thank God she had.*

He noticed, though. He raised an eyebrow. "Removed?"

"Yes," she replied a little defiantly.

"Nothing in your computer files?"

"Nothing concerning the story except some research on Hydra."

"Can I read it?"

"There's nothing that hasn't already been in the newspaper."

His gaze didn't leave hers.

She sighed, found the file, and brought it up.

He leaned in and read over her shoulder. She scrolled down the document. He paused when he saw a note she'd made to herself to check into a multiple murder in Rome, a city north of Atlanta. A family. Husband, wife, seven-year-old son. The father had been arrested in a drug case. A local law official said in the paper he believed it was linked to a large drug investigation. There were several articles. Then nothing.

She looked up at him. "A family? An entire family?"

"Yes." His voice had hardened. A muscle throbbed in his cheek.

"Was it Hydra?"

"We think so."

"And you want me to give you a name?"

"The dead man wouldn't accept protection. He thought it would mark him."

"He was going to testify against them?"

Silence, then, "Yes."

She stared back at the screen.

"That's what they do, Ms. Stuart. They kill people and they do it in such a way that no one else will talk. That's why we need the name of your source. It's obvious he knows something that can help us. And he's safer with us."

"My source doesn't agree."

"At least talk to him."

She nodded. "When my source contacts me."

"You said an address book was out of place? Did you also have one in the computer?"

She nodded. "Just e-mail addresses."

"Was your address book personal or business?"

"Personal mostly."

He frowned.

She questioned him with her eyes.

"They may have photographed the pages."

He saw the implication register in her eyes. "Then they may have the names of people close to me."

He nodded. "What other documents were opened?"

"An idea for a novel I'm playing with. Several letters to my sisters. Some features I wrote here."

She stood awkwardly, only too aware now of the brace, her lack of grace. He was standing near the chair. Close. Too close. The aroma of a very male aftershave was seductive. Darn it, everything about him was seductive, particularly those enigmatic dark eyes.

"I need a cup of coffee." She hesitated, then asked warily, "Would you like one?"

He nodded.

It was little enough to offer after he'd taken her to the vet.

That's what she told herself. She didn't want to admit his presence was reassuring, that a fragment of fear had lodged inside.

Nor did she want to admit he had a charm that was insidious. Mrs. Jeffers certainly thought so. But then he hadn't condescended to her. It had been obvious he liked her.

Mrs. Jeffers liked to think of herself as a "tough old broad" and Damien as the world's best protector, dismissing the reality that Damien was an ancient, five-pound, snaggle-toothed poodle.

Ben Taylor had ignored the obvious, and she liked that about him. She liked it very much. She found she liked other things about him as well.

She led the way to the kitchen and quickly readied her electric coffeepot.

"Can I do anything?" he asked.

She shook her head. "I warn you, it's navy coffee. I can't seem to make any other kind."

"Strong?"

"Some say so."

"Good."

She gathered cups and saucers, grateful for the activity. She didn't want him to notice the fear she'd been trying to keep at bay.

As the coffee brewed, she turned around, only to bump into him. Darn, but he filled the kitchen with his presence. His eyes met hers. She knew their intensity now, but it still stunned her.

"Ms. Stuart, . . ."

"Robin," she corrected.

"Robin . . . surely you know this break-in could be only the beginning. You could have been here when—"

"But I wasn't, and I suspect he knew I wasn't."

"If they didn't get what they wanted, they could go after you next. Damn it, you're in danger. Not to mention your source. How can I make it more clear?"

"Clear for you, maybe. Not so clear for someone who trusted me."

The coffee stopped brewing. She was glad for the excuse it gave her to change the subject, even momentarily. She poured them both a cup. "I'm afraid I don't have cream or sugar."

He took the cup and took a sip. "Don't use either. It's good."

"Why didn't you bring in your people?" she asked.

"We're not officially on the case yet. I'll ask for copies of their reports." He took another sip of coffee. He hesitated, then asked, "Do you have a weapon?"

"I have a gun in a safe-deposit box."

"That's not much help."

"I'll get it tomorrow."

"Do you know how to use it?"

"My father was military. He insisted that his daughters know how to protect themselves." She didn't add that it had been years since she'd used the gun he'd given her. She kept it because he'd given it to her, but she'd put it in her safe-deposit box the last time Lark had visited with her kids, and she'd never gone back for it.

"You're no competition for Hydra."

"Are you trying to scare me?"

"No, I want you alive. I don't think you have any idea what you may be dealing with."

"I'm learning, Agent Taylor," she said, forcing a coolness into her voice. She didn't like being treated as if she were a child. Even by someone as damnably attractive as Ben Taylor.

"Not fast enough," he muttered.

She bit her lip. "I can't trade my safety for his." She didn't even try to imply it may not be a "he" now. She'd only narrowed it to fifty percent of the population.

He took a gulp of coffee, his eyes willing her to comply.

"Tell me about Hydra," she said. "I found out what I could but it's not much."

"They work like a terrorist organization with cells, one unaware of the others. If one is destroyed, the members can't implicate anyone else. It's very sophisticated and very dangerous."

"Why haven't you—the FBI—been able to break it?"

He hesitated. "We can't get witnesses to talk."

"Because witnesses die?"

"Those that won't accept protection," he countered.

"What about extended families?" she asked.

He was silent.

"That's what my source said. He can't leave with just his immediate family."

"We'll see what we can work out."

"Including lies?"

"Damn it, don't you know both your lives could be at stake? They didn't hesitate to kill three cops. You think they'll stop at killing a reporter?"

She met his glare. "I'm not a fool. I know I opened a Pandora's box. But I promised, and it doesn't have anything to do with a story. It has to do with integrity."

"One thing to remember. They know who *you* are."

She'd already realized that. She didn't like the menace that was settling like a boulder in her stomach.

"I'll be careful."

"You can ask for protection."

"Without giving a name?"

"I don't know whether my boss will approve it under that condition. But I'll sure as hell try."

She wasn't sure she wanted it. How could she do her job with FBI agents trailing behind her?

"We don't even know whether the burglary is connected—"

"You're smarter than that," Taylor interrupted, frustration clouding his eyes.

She stood there, her coffee cooling as she thought. She wanted a way out. She wanted to warn Sandy, tell him what had happened, transmit Taylor's offer. But the only way she knew to reach him was to call him, and she couldn't call his cell phone. Not now. That might lead both the good guys and the bad guys to him.

He paced the floor of the kitchen, then turned to her. "There's a federal grand jury already impaneled. Chances are you'll be subpoened. It would be much easier if you told me now."

She'd known it might come to that. "Is that a threat?"

"It's a reality." His voice was suddenly cool.

"The . . . person wanted to give you enough information to start looking in some corners," she said. "You can do that now. Isn't that enough?"

"He obviously knows more. A lot more. Including names. We need that information."

"No."

His lips thinned. "You could have been here today. The same thing that happened to Daisy could have happened to you."

The image of Daisy lying so still came back to her. *She will be all right. She has to be.* She bit her lip.

And then his hand was on her cheek. Gentle. Very gentle. It was disarming. More than disarming. Alluring. Irresistible. She leaned into that hand. There was something so solid about him and at the same time . . . challenging. Her heart pounded an erratic rhythm.

She balanced herself on wobbly legs. His touch sent streams of sensation through her, and a warmth that overtook the chill of fear she couldn't shake, despite her brave words.

She lifted her eyes to his and his dark eyes seemed to smolder. Electricity sparked and sizzled between them. Sex. Fear. Adrenaline. She felt she was standing in the eye of a storm. Quiet. Even breathing seemed to be trapped. Yet the calm was deceptive. She felt the surrounding storm raging out of control.

*Step away.*

She couldn't.

They moved at the same time, each taking a single step toward the other. Then she was in his arms.

With a muttered oath, he tightened his arms around her.

Her head came to rest against his chest, and she heard the quickened beat of his heart.

She should move away, yet her legs wouldn't obey. Instead they inched closer to him until she felt the swelling within his trousers and knew a yearning so deep and needy that she thought she would die of it.

His mouth pressed down on hers. There was nothing gentle about the kiss. It was demanding and challenging and angry.

Her lips moved against his, responding with a need that seemed to spur his own, and his tongue played inside her mouth, searching, awakening every nerve ending. Streams of heat surged through her.

She trembled as his lips gentled, caressed rather than plundered. His hands ran up and down her body as if savoring every curve. Then he pulled her so tight against him that she felt every muscle of his body, spreading a fiery craving throughout her body. Her arms went up around his neck, her finger playing with tendrils of hair.

He stiffened for a moment. He groaned, and then she heard a catch in his breath as he stepped back. He dropped his arm and let her go. *"Damn it,"* he muttered. His gaze met hers. "I'm sorry. That shouldn't have happened."

But it should have. She knew exactly what she'd been doing. She sensed he wasn't going to accept that, though.

"I should go," he said.

She nodded soundlessly. She was still numb from the kiss, the sea storm of emotion.

She forced herself to take a step back instead of forward. "Thanks for helping me tonight." She prayed her voice didn't sound as trembling to him as it did to her.

But she took some satisfaction in the fact that he'd been affected as well. She saw it in his eyes. They weren't wary now. They were as full of fire as she thought hers must be.

His eyes raked her. "Think about what I said."

"I will. I'll be careful."

She looked up at him again, and the face wasn't as hard as it had been days ago. Worry lines crinkled around his eyes, and she saw a caring she hadn't noticed before.

She suddenly wanted to know so much more about Agent

Ben Taylor. Natural journalistic curiosity, she told herself, but she still couldn't tear her gaze from him. It was as if they were locked in some prolonged mating game. She had to fight her overwhelming need to move close to him again, to feel those unexpectedly gentle hands skimming over her body.

But if he stayed . . .

She walked him to the door, suddenly, desperately, not wanting him to go, not wanting to be alone.

He turned as he went out the door. "Good night," she said.

His gaze lingered on hers for a long moment before he turned and headed for his car.

She locked the door, realizing again that someone had gained entrance earlier. She placed a chair against the doorknob, did the same with the kitchen door. *A professional.*

The word was cold. Unsettling.

Perhaps she should go to a hotel.

But then she would be giving in to fear. She wasn't going to do that. Otherwise she would spend the rest of her life writing about small-town budgets.

She went to the kitchen and fetched a knife to place on the night table next to her bed. Tomorrow, she would retrieve the gun, as much as she was loath to do so.

A plan of action in place, she headed for bed. She doubted she would sleep, though, and she bitterly resented the aching need in the pit of her stomach.

It had been the fear. The invasion. Nothing else. It couldn't be.

Still, as she left a light on in the bathroom and living room, she wished he'd lingered.

# chapter eleven

*Robin jerked awake, startled by* the ring of the telephone. She glanced at the clock. Three a.m. Her breath caught in her throat and her heart pounded.

*The vet?*

*One of her sisters?*

*Sandy?*

She grabbed the receiver and heard a falsely gravelly voice invade her senses. "Bitch. Your reporting could get you hurt. Bad." Then a dial tone.

She sat on the edge of the bed, staring at the phone as if it were a cobra. No one had ever called her a bitch before, at least not to her face, though she imagined some of the subjects of her stories might well have thought it. But it was the pure malevolence of the voice that terrified her.

They'd been meant to terrify her. She knew that.

They'd succeeded. Her whole body had tightened, and fear writhed in her stomach.

*Don't let him succeed.* She took a deep breath, then checked the caller ID. *Unknown.* Probably a throwaway cell phone. Not surprising.

Knowing she wouldn't go back to sleep, she grabbed her robe at the end of the bed and struggled into the brace. Only a little over two more weeks now before she saw the doctor. There would be X-rays and hopefully she would leave the office limping but without the heavy brace.

Even that prospect didn't quiet her screaming nerves. She

checked the doors, then peered out the window. Nothing unusual. She made some coffee and turned on the television in the living room. She needed the noise, the company. She especially needed Daisy cuddling against her.

And a weapon. For the first time, she was glad she'd applied for a gun license when she'd moved to Georgia even though she'd never intended to use it. Nevertheless, she was a stickler for the law, and she owned the thing.

She retreated to the bedroom where she'd taken the knife before going to sleep. She felt foolish carrying it with her, but it gave her just a smidgen of control back. It was better than nothing.

She considered calling the police, but the caller hadn't really threatened her. It had been the disembodied voice that was so frightening.

Damn it, but she wanted to call Ben Taylor. She wished for his acerbic presence. For those rare seconds of tenderness that had been so surprising. She'd felt safe with him. She glanced at the top of the table. His card was there. But the last thing she wanted to show was weakness.

She would tell him tomorrow about the call, just as she would tell the police, but she wouldn't let him see her panic tonight.

She fetched a cup of coffee and sipped it. *Work.* She needed to work.

She limped to her office and turned on the computer and wrote down the few words that had spewed from the phone, then recorded her feelings on another document. This time, though, she established a password for her files, one she knew no one could decipher except perhaps her sisters.

Her life had changed today. She hadn't realized how much until that phone call. For the first time in her life, she felt evil touch her. She shivered and pulled her robe closer around her.

God, what in the hell had he been thinking?

Simple fact: he hadn't been thinking at all. He'd just reacted to those damn blue eyes, and that intense physical awareness between them. Maybe it had been that transparent mixture of emotions in her: the concern over the cat, then the gentle humor during their encounter with Mrs. Jeffers and her Damien.

Or maybe it was too-long abstinence from female companionship. He hoped to God that was all it was.

Ben continued to berate himself as he watched Robin Stuart's house from down the street where he was parked, positioning the car so he could see the house but she was not likely to see him. She may not totally appreciate the fact, but he felt to the marrow of his bones that she was in danger.

*Damn that kiss.* He sure as hell knew better. He could be taken off the case for that stupidity. And he didn't want to lose this case. He'd been waiting for it for years.

Kissing a witness. More than kissing. He'd nearly consumed her. What in the hell had got into him? He'd never done anything like that before. Not with someone involved in an investigation. And especially not with someone so determinedly headed for trouble.

*He hadn't been able to stop his wife's headlong rush into disaster.*

All the pain resurfaced as Dani's face appeared in his thoughts. Unlike Robin's blue eyes and short honey brown hair, Dani's eyes were dark like his own, and she had long dark hair. Young. Eager. Intense. And, like Robin Stuart, consumed with ambition. Ambition that had killed the person Dani once was. Her soul, if not yet her body.

He couldn't do that again!

He would be taken off the case if Robin Stuart reported it. Hell, if he had any integrity, he would report it himself. But he didn't want off this case. If they closed down Hydra, he could make one hell of a dent in drug trafficking in the Southeast. Payback for Dani . . . something he could do for her he'd been unable to do as her husband.

And Robin Stuart? She had no idea of what could happen . . . what might well happen. He didn't want to leave her standing alone, but he doubted that his boss would provide the protection she needed. The FBI had manpower shortages; a burglary and uncooperative witness wouldn't qualify for its limited resources. Not yet. Probably not until it was too late.

He saw a light go on in a room, then another. A figure paused at a window. Then the shutters closed and all he saw was diffusion of light. He fought his instinct to go to the door. He suspected if he returned, he might not be able to leave again.

He took out a thermos, full of coffee he'd bought at a convenience store. The thermos was with him always. Then he settled back, thinking both of how he could get her to cooperate and how to ensure her safety. How could he convince her that one relied on the another?

He suspected that until tonight protection of a source had been a moral and intellectual decision on her part. He needed to take it to a more primal level.

And do it before she stumbled into depths she didn't comprehend.

The voice on the other end of the phone was cold. "I told you to find the name of her source and do it without her knowing. The place was crawling with cops tonight."

"It must have been the damned cat."

"What cat?"

"Goddamned cat jumped on my arm and clawed the hell out of me. I tossed it off and it ran. I tried to find it but it just disappeared. I couldn't hang around to try to find it."

"What did you get?"

"I have photos of her address book and files from the hard drive from her computer. I also photographed some notes about Hydra."

A silence. Then, "Didn't I tell you never to use that name over the phone?"

"It's safe. I have a disposable phone."

"I don't care what you have. Understand?"

"Yes."

"Leave the film at the usual place. There'll be a sum of money there. Take it and leave town."

"But . . ."

"I don't tolerate clumsiness. I told you what I wanted. I wanted discreet. You were not discreet. If I hear you're still around, or that you said anything to anyone, you're a dead man."

The phone went dead and the man, still holding the receiver, swore long and hard. He had a girl here. A house. He didn't want to leave. He thought about trying to go underground in the city, then changed his mind. He knew only too well what happened to people who irritated the Hydra.

He would get the hell out of town.

Robin called in the next morning, said she would be late and told Wade about the break-in.

He paused, then asked: "What do the police think?"

"At first, I think they thought it was my imagination since nothing seemed to be stolen. Daisy apparently injured herself. But then Ben Taylor—"

"Taylor? The FBI agent who was here yesterday?"

"Yep, that one."

"How in the hell was he involved?"

"He came to my house. He said he wanted me to know about Hydra, and what we were dealing with."

"Officially or unofficially?"

"Unofficially."

She heard him muttering under his breath.

"It's okay," she said. "He was there when I found Daisy, and he called the police. They wouldn't have paid any attention if I had called."

"He was told to go through our attorney," Wade said.

"He didn't ask any questions. He was there when I found Daisy injured and he took me to the vet, then called the police." She hoped that none of her other, more personal, reactions reflected in her voice.

Silence. "Did he ask you for your source?"

"He implied it would be safer for the source, and for me, if the FBI had it."

"What do you think?"

"He's probably right," she said. "But he also admitted that a recent witness and his family were killed. That's what my source fears." She paused, then added, "There's something else. I received a call in the middle of the night. It was . . . threatening."

"What was said?"

She repeated the words. She'd memorized them.

"The voice?"

"Metallic. Like someone on a television show that uses a gadget to mask the voice."

"Have you told the police?"

"Not yet. I called you first."

"Call them. Call that agent. I think you should have protection."

"I don't think they will give it unless I become a witness. Besides, it might have simply been a crank call. Someone offended by the story."

"We'll talk about it when you come in. Do you think you can make it by two?"

"Yes. Probably by noon."

"Take your time. Call the police, the FBI. Get a security system, for God's sake. We'll pay for it."

That jolted her. The paper was notoriously tight-fisted. "I will."

"We can send a car for you."

"Thanks, but no need."

"Anytime you want off the story . . ."

"I don't," she replied and hung up.

She went into the bathroom and took a shower on crutches, then stared at herself in the mirror. Her eyes were bloodshot, her hair a messy tangle of curls. She brushed it, and slipped on a casual pair of slacks and cotton shirt. That accomplished, she called the veterinarian. Daisy was ready to return home. No apparent permanent injuries and they would be happy to see her go home. She had become a demon.

Robin reluctantly pulled on the brace, made a pot of coffee, poured some into a travel mug, and loaded the cat caddy into the car. She looked up and down the street with eyes even more aware than in the past. It was seven thirty.

As she searched the street, she saw a vehicle she recognized from last night. A dark gray sedan. A man got out and leaned against it. Ben Taylor. *Has he been there all night?*

He was wearing the same shirt and slacks, and he needed a shave. His hair looked as if it had been combed by fingers.

She walked over to him. "Been here all night?"

"Pretty much. I thought I would be gone before you got up. I saw the light on all night."

"Are you here officially?"

"Not exactly."

Warmth flowed through her. He'd cared enough to stay all night. She only wished she'd noticed the car last night. She might have slept.

Or not.

"Want some coffee?"

"I'd sell my soul for some."

"I don't think I'll ask that price. Not now."

"Have you heard anything about Daisy?"

Not "the cat." *Daisy.* He earned a few more points. He already had too many points for her peace of mind. His actions were not entirely altruistic. She had to remember that.

"She's good. You can have a cup, then I have to pick her up."

He followed her inside. She poured coffee into a cup and handed it to him. "I got a call last night," she said. "Around three."

He stilled.

"The voice was disguised and the comment brief." She repeated the message.

"Nothing more?"

"No."

He frowned. "You should have called the police. Or me."

"I was going to call later today."

"You checked caller ID?" Not a question. An assumption.

"Unknown," she said. "But why?"

He shrugged. "I don't know. Intimidation, perhaps. They might well come after you, particularly if they didn't find what they needed."

"They didn't."

"You say that with such assurance," he said dryly.

She clamped her lips together. He was baiting her. Still, he fascinated her. With the overnight beard, he looked more like a bandit than a lawman. Masculinity exuded from him. She met his flinty gaze directly, and shafts of electricity coursed through her. She silently cursed them. She needed her wits about her, not to fall victim again to that magnetism.

She tried to ignore it. "Can you get the number from phone records?"

"Yes, but won't do any good if he used a throwaway

phone. Phone records would show you've received a call, but I would guess the other number is no longer in existence. I'll check it, though. Could be just an unhappy deputy or even a crank."

"But you don't think so?"

His eyes gentled. "I don't know." His fingers brushed back a lock of her hair. "Did you get any sleep last night?"

"No. And I have to call the police, get Daisy, then go in to the office."

"Are you going to write about the break-in?"

"I don't know."

"Don't say anything about Daisy."

"Why?"

"Just don't."

"Why?" she insisted.

"Hydra's good at finding weak points and utilizing them."

"You're trying to frighten me again."

His fingers touched her cheek. His touch burned all the way through her. "I honestly hope so." His gaze locked on her again. "Do contact the police about the call. You need to compile a record."

"I will."

"And get that gun."

"Second on the list after Daisy."

"Tonight you're on your own. I would recommend sleeping at a hotel or a friend's until you get a damned good alarm system." His eyes were steady on her. "If Hydra is responsible for the Meredith murders, they'll be relentless in hunting down anyone that might provide a lead to them. They won't draw a line at you, reporter or not. I'm afraid you haven't understood that fully."

A hardness had crept into his voice again. Damn it, he was treating her as a wayward child rather than a responsible adult. What *he* didn't—wouldn't—understand was that someone had trusted her with his life, and it was a trust she couldn't betray and live with herself.

She also resented his condescending attitude. Still there was a maddening inability to break free of his gaze. "You've made your point," she finally retorted. "Several times. I assure you I understand."

"Robin . . ."

"Whatever you think, I'm not your responsibility. I'm grateful for your help yesterday, but—"

Two of his fingers stopped the stream of words.

"I don't want gratitude," he said softly. "I want you to stay alive."

His eyes were anything but granite now. They were smoldering. She felt the whisper of his breath on her cheek.

All the air in her lungs expelled in a gasp. She found herself edging toward him and his arms went around her.

His lips touched hers and explosions rocked her to the toes.

# chapter twelve

*Ben was stunned.*

Stunned that he had just vowed not to repeat his mistake, and now he was doing exactly that.

Even more stunned as he wallowed in the kiss, in her response to it. The way her body melded into his, and her lips opened to his, and the passion that blazed between them.

God, she felt good. And looked irresistible. It was that smile that lit the day despite the circles around her eyes. She had that "damn the torpedoes, full speed ahead" view of life. Bound by a code he thought stupid, but she abided by.

But it was that very naivete, the conviction, the assault on life that stirred something in him that had been dormant. He felt flutters of anticipation again. How long since last he experienced that?

It shocked the hell out of him. Especially the fact that he couldn't get enough of her. His hands explored her back, worked their way to her neck and the hair that smelled like roses and felt like silk.

She tasted good, too, like fresh peppermint.

She slipped her hands around his neck and drew even closer. His body responded accordingly. With a groan he released her lips and studied her face. This was a no-no. A very big no-no. A career-ending no-no.

Yet he was befuddled by longing, locked someplace between disbelief and enchantment. Her face was flushed, telegraphing a need as strong as his own, her body fitting his perfectly, her eyes no longer open and honest but smoky, sultry.

*Move away.* His brain commanded but his body didn't obey. Her body aroused every masculine instinct, and he wanted to take her then and there. Against the wall. On the table. Hell, anyplace. It had been there since the beginning. The whiff of attraction. The second look. The awareness. Then last night . . .

He felt caught in a whirlwind he couldn't control. There were only those blue eyes, and vulnerability mixed with uncertainty and desire. She was—or should be—as untouchable a woman as he could ever encounter. Still he couldn't quite force himself to move. She felt too good, too damn good, and he was so damned lonely for that kind of warmth.

Her breath caught on a sob, and she stared up at him, her eyes dazed. Hell, his probably were, too. This had been the last thing he'd expected. She was the last woman he would have thought to . . .

She moved suddenly, then faltered and he caught her as she almost fell. Hell, he'd forgotten about the leg. He steadied her and saw a flash of embarrassment in her eyes.

"What just happened?" she asked.

"You almost fell."

She took a long, deep breath. "That's not what I meant."

"I man, you woman," he said wryly, hoping that was the end-all of it, though knowing it wasn't.

"Is that it?" she said doubtfully.

"You're too damn pretty when you're angry." He regretted the words the moment he said them.

But she gave him a smile that was blinding, one he hadn't seen before. "You're too damn seductive when you're angry."

"Don't think anyone ever noticed that before."

He told himself he was holding her so she wouldn't fall. But she had gained her balance seconds ago. Or was it minutes? Time seemed to have stopped. He knew he needed to break out of this . . . spell . . . and yet he couldn't quite force it.

*Was that what addiction was?*

Those eyes were his downfall.

He'd never seen any quite as blue. Quite as expressive. Quite as inviting even as they challenged.

His cell phone rang.

He dropped his hand from her arm and took the phone from his belt. The time flicked. Eight thirty. He should have been at the office by now.

It was Mahoney. "Where are you? The boss wants to see you."

"Ms. Stuart had a visitor last night," he said. "I'm with her now. I'll be there in an hour."

He hung up and turned to her. "I have to go. Be careful. Always keep your cell phone with you. Call me anytime if you feel threatened. And get that alarm system installed today. If you can't, stay in a hotel." He paused, then added, "We can put a tap on your phone in case you get any more calls."

She shook her head.

He wanted to shake her. "At least contact me."

It wasn't so much a question as a command.

She hesitated long enough that he knew she didn't want to make any promises she may not keep. She finally nodded. "Any threats," she agreed.

He wanted to touch her again, but that would be fatal. He'd already gone so far beyond the bounds of professionalism that he should be sacked. She was a witness. An uncooperative witness, and he may well have a part in compelling her to testify. And sending her to jail.

She could charge him with all kinds of inappropriate conduct. And the bureau was all he had left.

He went out the door without any additional words.

Robin limped to a chair and sat down.

All the energy left the room with Ben Taylor.

He infuriated her. He enthralled her.

No one had ever told her she was pretty in the way he had. She really wasn't.

Unconsciously she rubbed her bad leg, her hands feeling the metal underneath her slacks. She looked at the clunky shoes she had to wear. She thought of the ugly scarring on her leg.

She wouldn't know for weeks how well her leg had really healed, whether she would be able to run again, or dance again or . . .

*Where was this all coming from?*

Months ago she'd come to terms with the injury. Grateful that she hadn't lost her leg. She'd come so close to that reality that she gratefully accepted every surgery, every inconvenience that came with them. She hadn't allowed it to interfere with her career. She'd fought with all her heart to regain her job despite management's doubts.

Now she was so close to proving herself all over again.

And, damn it, she wasn't going to destroy it by falling for someone who obviously had his own agenda.

*He couldn't fake that look in his eyes.*

And he'd left like the devil was after him.

She couldn't quite accept that he was swept away by her, that he was indifferent to her career choice and the fact that she might well have a permanently bum leg.

*Daisy.*

She had to get Daisy. Then to the paper.

No time to daydream. To moon over someone who was worlds away, and should be.

She stood, her legs still unsteady and her body too warm. She truly hated losing control as she had. She hated the lingering effects of his touch.

*Daisy.*

She grabbed her purse and left the house.

Robin turned off her cell phone during the meeting as a matter of office protocol. She wouldn't have done it had not Richard Reese, the publisher, been present, as well as Wade Carlton, Bob Greene, and Cleve Andrews.

She'd picked up Daisy two hours earlier and left her with Mrs. Jeffers, who promised to spoil her. The cat had licked her hand, then settled into her bed, which Robin had brought with her. Damien hovered around her.

They'd always liked each other, but now Damien was at his protective best.

"That FBI artist was over here this morning," Mrs. Jeffers said as Robin left. "She said I was real observant, had real good eyes."

"I always knew that, Mrs. Jeffers."

After arriving at the paper, the meeting was moved up to

one p.m. The sheriff had scheduled a news conference at four p.m., timed, she thought, for maximum impact in the electronic media.

Her paper had not received a notice, but they had picked up the news from a television news alert.

Wade told the others about the break-in and phone call. Since nothing was taken, it was decided not to do a story on those two events. Crank calls were not that unusual for reporters, and there was no proof that it came from anyone other than an irate reader.

"The paper has agreed, though, to hire protection, starting tonight," Reese said. "We'll play it by ear as to how long or until the FBI agrees to provide it."

She nodded. "Thanks."

"You sure you want to go to the press conference today?" Wade asked. "Either Cleve or Bob can catch it."

"I'm going," she said.

"Okay. I'm sending a photographer as well. I've asked for Kevin McConnell. Bob will work the Hydra angle, and Cleve, you keep working on the ownership of the property."

A surge of adrenaline ran through Robin. She'd feared they would take the story away from her. And Kevin was one of her favorites in the photo department.

He was a great photographer, and he was also big. Very big. No gentle giant him. He protected reporters. He'd once bounced a camera off the head of the high wizard or whatever of the Ku Klux Klan when the man took exception to a reporter and tried to attack him.

"I like that idea," she said.

"I thought you might."

"You can go with him in a company car."

She hesitated at that. She wanted to do a little poking around of her own. What she really wanted was for Sandy to try to contact her. She didn't want anyone around when he did.

She should be safe. It was daylight, after all, and any number of people would be around the courthouse square.

"I'll meet him at the press conference," she said.

Wade looked dubious. "I would prefer someone accompany you."

"Would that be true if I were a man?"

He looked uncomfortable.

"I *will* be careful," she promised.

He agreed reluctantly.

After the meeting, she went to her desk and checked her cell phone. A text message. The rate of her heartbeat speeded.

*Meet me at the school. Seven p.m. tonight. Alone or you won't see me. Don't tell anyone.*

No name, but it had to be Sandy. He was one of very few people who had her cell number. And the warning sounded like him. She checked the number. It wasn't Sandy's, but then he couldn't use his own cell phone. Too easily traced.

*Alone . . .*

*Don't be stupid. Tell Wade. Tell Ben Taylor.*

*Alone . . . or you won't see me.*

She had to talk him into going to the FBI, and she didn't know how to reach him herself without leading the bad guys to him. He'd just given her a way.

She'd picked up her gun this morning. She would have that, and her cell phone.

*The stupid heroine syndrome.* How many times had she thrown a book against the wall because the heroine had done something utterly dumb.

*Perhaps my only chance to get the story of a lifetime. And convince him to go to the FBI.*

Why had she turned off the phone, even for an hour?

She thought about telling Wade but she knew he would say no, at least alone. She couldn't betray Sandy by taking someone with her. He wouldn't trust her again.

She hadn't been hurt yesterday.

She had already arranged for an alarm system for her house. It would be installed in two days. She'd picked up the gun from the safe-deposit box this morning.

And she trusted Sandy.

Ben stopped at his apartment long enough to put on a clean shirt, slacks, and dark sports coat as well as a different tie. He wasn't in the mood to take any jokes about wearing the same clothes as yesterday. As the only bachelor in the office, he was too often the butt of wishful thinking.

When he arrived at the office, he reported to his boss, telling everything—almost everything—that had happened the previous night and asking that his evidence bag be sent to the lab. To his surprise, Holland listened intently and agreed readily.

"You seem to be making points with Ms. Stuart."

"Don't know I would say that. But she did listen. I think she'll try to get her source to come to us."

"Good. Very good. Our esteemed U.S. attorney doesn't want to go through a First Amendment battle."

Ben didn't want to disillusion him at this point. He'd definitely gotten the idea that it would take more than him driving her cat to the vet for Robin Stuart to reveal her source.

"There's a press conference this afternoon in Meredith County," he said. "I think they'll probably try to refute her story."

"You have a hearing this afternoon. Judge Becker won't tolerate a postponement."

Ben nodded. The hearing was an appeal on bail for a particularly vicious thug who'd committed several carjackings, usually targeting older people and leaving them badly injured. He didn't want the guy back on the street.

"Then Mahoney should go in my place. He wasn't with me when I made the Carson case so he can't fill in for me there. I'll ask him to keep an eye on Ms. Stuart."

"You think you can get her to give us her source?" Holland asked.

He hesitated, then said, "I think she will be willing to go to the source and try to get him to agree to our protection. I doubt if she will give him up if he doesn't agree."

"I'll go to a judge and see whether we can get a GPS unit on her car. It's for her own protection. In the meantime research her. See if there's anything we can use to get her cooperation."

"I've already done that. She's as clean as a whistle. In ten years, one traffic ticket for speeding. That's it."

"Keep looking."

Ben nodded, though he knew any such search was probably useless. Robin Stuart was the epitome of a law-abiding citizen. She was impulsive. Stubborn. Infuriating. But obviously law-abiding.

If only he could convince her . . .

He wouldn't be able to do that if he continued to pant over her like some adolescent.

"What about protection?" he asked.

"Because of a simple break-in and call? Maybe if she were to give us a name, but now . . . you know how tight our manpower is." Holland hesitated, then said, "Keep working on her."

Ben had the tacit permission he needed. He left Holland's office and went back to his desk. Halfway there, he stopped. Then took out his cell phone and punched a number. A too familiar number.

"Roseview Clinic."

"Ben Taylor. I'm checking on Dani Taylor."

"I'll see if the doctor is free."

In another moment, Dr. Meadows came on the phone.

"How is she?" Ben asked.

A pause. "She's cooperative. I think we're gaining some ground. But you know there are no guarantees."

He felt the same hopelessness that had haunted him these last eight years. "At least she hasn't left."

"She needs at least another month."

Ben's heart sank. The clinic already took nearly half his salary.

"As long as it takes," he said.

"I'll let you know if there's any changes."

"Thanks."

He replaced his cell phone and made his way back to Mahoney.

"You go to the Meredith press conference. Keep an eye on Robin Stuart. Don't let her out of your sight."

Mahoney questioned with his eyes.

Ben told him what had happened last night.

"The phone call doesn't make sense if they were trying to keep their visit secret."

"Yeah, I know," Ben said. "That worries me. It could mean they have someone watching the house."

"Or," Mahoney suggested, "it could be a deputy or a member of a deputy's family. She put the onus on the entire department. Every one of them is probably mad as hell."

"Except maybe one. Her source."

"Does she have any idea what she's done?"

"I tried to tell her. But damn it, she thinks she's doing the right thing. She's given her word. It's her integrity at stake. God help us from reporters, particularly idealistic ones."

"How long were you with her last night?"

Ben shrugged. "I took the cat to the vet's, then slept outside. She doesn't even have a home alarm system."

"Above and beyond, I would say. Is she getting to you?"

"A reporter? Hell no."

Mahoney raised an eyebrow. "How's Dani?"

Mahoney was one of the few people who knew about Dani. And that only because he had to cover for Ben once when Dani had disappeared from the hospital.

Ben shook his head. "You know the odds, but she's trying. She's really trying this time."

"It's time you met someone."

"I meet lots of people."

"You know what I mean. Terry has some ideas . . ."

"Can't afford it right now," Ben replied. "Besides, I don't have time now that we have a lead on Hydra." He paused. "Just keep a close eye on Robin Stuart."

Mahoney nodded his head. "I'll be her guardian angel."

"You'd better be."

# chapter thirteen

*Robin saw Kevin leaning against* the company car almost immediately after she arrived at the courthouse. He gave her a broad grin as he shouldered his camera gear.

"Lead the way," he said.

"I have to warn you, they might not like anyone from the *Observer*."

"I was already warned. I doubt anyone will try anything with all those TV types around."

He had the print photographer's disdain for TV cameramen. They were technicians. He was an artist, with several awards to prove it.

She looked at her watch. Fifteen minutes before the conference and the courthouse steps were crowded. TV cameras were already in place and reporters were huddled in the usual groups.

She looked around for Ben Taylor, but he wasn't there. Disappointment rushed through her. She did see his partner, though, who stood a short distance away.

Hank Conrad from the local paper rushed over to her. "You've really stirred a hornet's nest. The sheriff is mad as hell. Talking about suing you and the paper."

"I know."

His eyes narrowed. "Was that story for real? Do you really have a witness?"

She stared back at him, refusing to dignify the question with an answer.

"Every deputy feels he is being accused," he said after an uncomfortable silence. "Not only accused of murder, but murdering fellow officers."

"No one was accused. It was merely pointed out that officers were steered away from the area that night."

"Same thing in their eyes. Be prepared for a hit during the press conference."

"I thought as much. Our paper was told I was no longer welcome at the courthouse."

"You're definitely persona non grata." He paused. "You don't really think anyone in the sheriff's department was involved, do you?"

"Just think, Hank. What is so big that three cops would be killed, and killed so dramatically? Whoever did it could have dragged the bodies off somewhere, even buried them in those woods back there. Let the county look for them. Maybe forever. There was a message here. Someone doesn't want interference and doesn't mind if everyone knows it. There's a certain arrogance there."

"It's all supposition."

"You write your story, and I'll write mine."

"I'm surprised your paper let you get away with it."

She was, too. But she wasn't going to admit it.

The sheriff, Chief Deputy Paul Joyner, and the county police chief appeared on the steps and moved to the podium. Kevin moved away from her and took several shots of the three, then the crowd. His eyes, though, kept returning to her.

Sheriff Sammons stepped to the podium. "I have a statement."

He paused, waited for dramatic emphasis, then continued. "The *Atlanta Observer* printed a story, under the byline of Robin Stuart, in yesterday's editions intimating that someone in this department could be involved in the murders of three Meredith County police officers.

"I categorically deny the accusation and I have instructed our county attorney to begin legal proceedings immediately."

He looked out, his gaze settling on her. "I see Miss Stuart is here, although our legal counsel advised her paper that we would prefer another reporter. Evidently the *Atlanta Observer* doesn't care about truth and accuracy."

She tried to keep her face masklike. However, she felt the heat in her cheeks as everyone, including the television cameras, turned toward her like vultures eyeing a particularly tasty mouse. Of all of them, though, the glare that came from Chief Deputy Joyner was the most malevolent. She shivered under its impact.

Kevin moved closer to her. She also saw the FBI agent, Ben Taylor's partner, head in her direction.

"Are you saying it couldn't have happened?" one reporter yelled out.

"What happened last week was like losing a brother, a family member, no matter which department we work for," the sheriff said. "Any suggestion that one of us would have anything to do with it is a stain on all of us."

"What about the Hydra?" yelled out one reporter. "Is there any indication Hydra could have been involved?"

"We think our officers interrupted a drug deal. We think it's out-of-state people."

"How would they know about this particular piece of property? The place where the bodies were found?" another reporter asked.

"There could be a local connection of some kind," the sheriff said reluctantly.

"I heard it was a clean crime scene," one reporter said. "Can you tell us what progress you've made?"

"Now, you folks know we don't discuss details of an investigation, but we do have some good leads."

"Are you saying the *Observer* made up the story?" one television reporter yelled.

"Made it up or talked to someone who was making it up. We would certainly like the name of whoever it was."

"You going to subpoena her?"

"I'm not going to talk about what we will or will not do."

It went on that way for thirty minutes. The same questions were asked over and over again. The only offered information was that the *Observer* and Robin Stuart were bad, and progress was being made.

The press conference finally broke up.

Kevin turned to her. "I'll walk you to your car and follow you into the city."

She shook her head. "I have a few stops to make."

"I have to get the photos back."

"I understand. You go on. I'll be fine."

He gave her a dubious look. "There's some angry people here."

"I'll be careful," she said. "I have my cell phone with me. I'll call my story in."

He frowned. "I don't like it."

"If I were a man would you worry as much?"

"Damn square I would. It's poisonous here."

So he'd felt it, too. It hadn't just been anger or righteous indignation. It had been pure hatred.

But the message today had made it clear she was to come alone. Sandy had not been visible today, and she knew that he would not risk a phone call.

"Go," she said.

"At least let me see you to the car before they try to lynch you."

"That sounds reasonable."

On the way, she stopped Hank Conrad, who was walking toward his office.

"See that guy in the blue suit?" she said. "He's FBI. You might ask him why he's here."

She saw him head toward Ben's partner, Agent Mahoney, and engage his attention.

She hopped in her car, turned on the ignition, and darted into the traffic. As she looked back, she saw Mahoney running for his car. She turned down a side road, took a left, then a right, and parked behind a grocery store.

Guilt filled her. She knew he was probably there to watch her, but she couldn't lead him to Sandy.

She looked at her watch. Almost five p.m. A couple of hours before meeting Sandy.

Glancing often at the rearview mirror, she headed for the east side of the county, even as she kept an eye on the speedometer. She planned to stay at least five miles under the speed limit. She had no doubt that the sheriff's office, and possibly the police department, would love to give her a ticket.

She wasn't going to lead anyone to Sandy. Not the FBI. Not the bad guys.

She stopped at a chain restaurant and ordered a hamburger only because she knew she had to. She'd had only a cup of coffee for breakfast and a package of crackers for lunch, and she didn't do well without food. But the burger tasted like sawdust. She couldn't shake the apprehension that had been hovering in her since last night. Not only for herself but for Sandy.

She had to convince him to go to the FBI.

Robin left half of the burger on the plate, paid the bill, and went back outside. She had more than a few second thoughts about this. But she didn't feel she had a choice. He had more information for her, information he obviously didn't want to give to the FBI. She wanted the story but even more she wanted Sandy to go to the FBI.

Thank God for the daylight that lingered far into evening. It would still be light when she met him.

When she got back in the car, she checked her glove compartment. Her gun was there. Then she called Wade and told him she was going to meet her source.

"Alone?"

"That's the only way he'll show."

"Where?"

Reluctantly she gave him the name of the school. "If you don't hear from me before seven thirty, call the FBI. Not the locals."

"Are you sure you know what you're doing?" Wade said.

"I trust my source," she said. "The school's safe."

Still, a hard fist of fear grew in her stomach even as her adrenaline level started to rise. This could be the biggest story of her career. A major crime organization brought down. Corruption in the sheriff's department.

And justice. There would be justice for three slain police officers.

She drove three miles and turned down a two-lane road. She glanced at the clock. Twenty to seven. She remembered the road. The school was about five miles away.

Something made her glance in the rearview mirror.

A dark SUV was behind her. She tensed. Then tried to relax. Nothing to worry about. She hadn't seen it before; it couldn't be following her. She turned her attention to the winding road ahead. It was empty. She glanced at the rearview mirror again. The SUV had closed on her car.

She speeded up, trying to keep an eye on the mirror even as the winding road demanded her attention. The SUV moved even closer. Her car lurched at the same time she heard the clash of metal in back. She jerked in her seat, grateful for the seat belt.

She pressed down on the accelerator. A whisper of terror shot through her. She'd seen enough movies to guess at what was happening. She also knew how much damage metal could do to a body.

Her left hand clamped around the steering wheel. She picked up her cell phone and pressed the button to ring the paper. Another jarring bump. Harder than the last. The cell phone flew from her right hand as she grabbed the steering wheel with both fists.

The next crash almost sent her into a ditch. The phone bounced to the floor.

She managed to straighten the car and accelerate. The vehicle behind was more dangerous than the winding road ahead.

Then the SUV passed. She saw a man on the passenger side. Despite the fact that he wore dark glasses, she knew she'd never seen him before.

She pressed down on the brake, hoping that the SUV would go ahead as they reached a blind turn. Instead it also slowed, then turned in to her car, striking it on the driver's side. She was jerked against the seat belt by the impact and frantically tried to keep on the road. Her car veered off the pavement, but she managed to turn it in a half circle and get back on the road going in the opposite direction.

Where was other traffic?

*Her gun!* The gun was in her glove compartment, but she needed two hands on the steering wheel to keep the car on the road.

She looked in the rearview mirror. The SUV had also turned and was bearing back down on her again.

Her heart pumped and she fought to keep a scream down. Too many memories. Car going off a cliff. Her leg barely hanging together by muscles. The bone protruding and blood spreading in a pool. Months of operations and pain.

She accelerated again, but the SUV overtook her. She glanced to the right and saw the ground falling away on her right side. She pressed the pedal as far as it would go, but her car was no match for the SUV. The roar of its engine grew louder, and dread whirled inside her. Dread, but not acceptance.

She steered her car to the middle of the road to block her opponent, but the SUV rammed her again and this time the force of the impact sent her car careening off the side of the road.

Another accident. Another car going off the road. A scream clawed in her throat. Two years ago she'd flown off the road. Now someone else was re-creating the horror.

*Did they know?!*

She stomped on the brake as the car tumbled down a ditch and sped toward a clump of trees.

A hammer slammed into her chest. A cloud of powder nearly suffocated her. Glass flew over the seat and she felt pinpricks of pain on her left arm. Dozens of small slices leaked blood over her clothes.

Struggling to keep conscious, she was vaguely aware that someone had approached the broken window. A face under a baseball cap, eyes shaded by dark glasses, peered at her.

God, she hurt. She could barely breathe. She tried to move but the brace was caught by the crushed dashboard. Ignoring the stabbing pain in her chest she tried to lunge for the glove compartment—and the gun—but the seat belt and trapped leg put it a few inches too far away.

To her horror, she smelled gas.

"Miss Stuart?" The words were innocent enough, but the voice reeked of malice.

"Who are you?" Stupid question but she couldn't come up with anything better.

"Who was it?" the man asked. "Who talked to you?"

The words sank in. She shook her head.

He looked down at her.

"A match. That's all it would take to send this car into a fireball."

She heard the sound of a cell phone ringing. It was close. Very close. The man's face disappeared and she struggled against the seat belt still holding her firm. She smelled smoke.

Then she heard another voice. "Gotta get out of here. Someone's coming."

Cursing. Words she'd never heard spoken before. The meaning, though, was clear. "Fire," the man whispered. "It's so easy. A name? Just a name."

But she knew if she gave him the name there was no reason to keep her alive.

She dropped her head as if unconscious.

The smoke became more dense. "I'll see you again, sweetheart," the voice said.

Silence.

She opened her eyes. No one was there.

She struggled to release the seat belt again. Finally. She tried to get out of the open door, but her brace was still caught under the dashboard. Every movement felt like someone was pounding against her chest, and she could barely breathe.

She was going to die.

Because of a name.

Ignoring the pain, she scrambled to get out of the car. She pulled her leg but a piece of dashboard had caught the metal. She felt blood on the leg and prayed there was no more damage.

But it wouldn't matter, if she couldn't get out. She screamed even though she knew it was probably hopeless, then the smoke filled her throat and she heard the crackle of flames.

Hands grabbed her and started to pull.

"Her leg is caught," a voice said.

Someone leaned over and pulled on her leg. New pain streaked through her. But she felt herself moving. Then she was dragged outside.

"Come on, lady. We got to get the hell out of here."

She tried to stand, but she couldn't. Her chest hurt too badly. She couldn't catch her breath. The men pulled her away from her car and up the embankment.

The flames flared and she felt intense heat.

An explosion rocked her, and flaming pieces of her car flew in a hundred directions.

# chapter fourteen

*Camouflage print pressed against her* body. The odor of gas and burning and stale sweat filled her nostrils as a wave of heat blew over them.

The man covering her body was big, and his weight didn't help the stabbing pain in her chest as they waited for the last of the debris to rain down.

Then the man rolled off her and she realized from their heavy camouflage clothing that they were hunters. She noticed the man next to her had several burns and cuts, and several places on his trouser legs were smoldering. He quickly doused them with dirt.

"You're hurt," she said, overwhelmed by what he'd done.

"Ain't nothing. We'd better get you to the hospital, little lady," he said. "Good thing we came by."

"Did you see anyone leaving here?"

"Sure didn't. Just smoke from the car." He stared at her. "You mean someone just left you like that?"

"Two men. Forced me off the road."

"Hell you say. Pretty thing like you. Like to get my hands on them."

Pretty thing. She'd never felt less like a pretty thing. She looked down at herself. Everything in her ached, stung, or burned. Her voice was hoarse with smoke, she had cuts over her body, and her chest hurt like all the devils in hell were pounding on it. She touched her left leg, but it seemed to be the one limb that survived without much trauma. *Thank God.*

*Thank God and these two men that I'm still alive.*

"I don't know how to thank . . ."

"Hell, weren't nothin'. Thank the fact that Ernie decided to ignore that detour sign," said one of the men. "Figured someone left it there by mistake."

"Detour?"

"Down the road some."

"It wasn't . . . there when I passed."

He looked puzzled, then scowled. "You saying someone put it there so they could run you off the road?"

"I just know it wasn't there. Someone rammed me off the road. Two men came down, threatened to blow up the car . . ." She stopped. It was hard to believe, even for her.

"Now stop those questions, Bobby Joe. Ain't none of our business. She needs to go to the hospital," the man called Ernie said.

The other one nodded. "I'm Bobby Joe, this here's Ernie." He looked at her, waiting for a name.

"I'm Robin Stuart. And I'm very grateful."

"Ain't no need for that." Bobby Joe looked down at her left leg and the brace, and frowned, then turned to his larger companion. "Can you carry her up the hill?"

"I can . . ." She started to get up, but slid back.

Before she could say another word, Ernie gingerly picked her up and carried her to an old pickup truck and put her in the front seat. "I'll ride in the back," he said. "Bobby is driving."

Sitting upright hurt. But then so had lying down. To divert her mind from the pain, she looked around the cab of the truck and saw a rack of rifles. She'd been right. They were hunters. Illegal probably, since the season hadn't started. At least they didn't seem to be hunting humans. She was pathetically grateful for that.

The blessed numbness of shock was wearing off. Waves of emotion flooded her. Gratitude. Anger. No, fury. *And fear.* The man who'd threatened to light the match had made it clear he was not finished.

• • •

Twenty minutes later, Robin sat on a table in a cubicle of the county hospital. She wore only a hospital gown while her bloodied clothes lay in a pile on the floor alongside her brace.

Ernie and Bobby Joe had let her out at the emergency room door. She'd asked for their last names, but they took off without giving them to her.

Once inside she was besieged by questions, mostly about insurance. She tried to tell them her insurance card was burned to a crisp. As were, she added to herself, her car, cell phone, her purse with her credit cards and identification, and her gun. She assured them she had very good insurance, gave them the name of the insurance company, and told them if they had questions they could call the *Atlanta Observer*.

Then she waited. And waited. No phone. No money. Scenes kept flashing in her mind. The voice. The dark glasses that hid eyes. The menace that exuded from her attacker. The panic of being trapped in a car filling with smoke.

The terror at leaving the road again.

She couldn't quite control her trembling. She'd come close to dying two years ago. Now a second time. Like Daisy, she might be running out of lives.

She wanted someone. But who? No boyfriend. No sister within five hundred miles. She had some friends at the paper, but none she felt she could impose upon. Bob Greene. No. He wanted her story.

*Her story.* Was it really that important now?

A grandmotherly-looking woman popped in. "I'm Jane Perkins. Patients' advocate. Fancy name for volunteer. Can I call someone for you?"

She thought, but not rapidly. Her mind seemed to have gone into slow motion.

Wade. She had to call Wade. It was after seven thirty—he would be frantic. But after that. There was no family close by. No one to rush to her side. She certainly didn't want to alarm her sisters and disrupt their lives over a few scratches.

Before she could answer, two Meredith County deputies came through the door. One took a notebook from his pocket.

"Miss Stuart?" he asked with no little insolence as he examined her, his gaze going through the cotton gown and lingering on her scarred leg. "Heard you had an accident."

"It wasn't an accident. Someone forced me off the road."

The deputy raised an eyebrow. "You got any witnesses to that?"

She realized she hadn't. Ernie and Bobby Joe hadn't seen the SUV or the two men. They had seen a detour sign. Even if they had seen something, she didn't have their last names. She realized they hadn't wanted to wait for the police. She didn't care why.

She told the deputy what had happened, and he shook his head. "No names for these so-called heroes?"

"Bobby Joe and Ernie. That's all I know."

"For a reporter?" the deputy said. "I would have thought better of you. But then after reading your story yesterday . . ."

"Sure you weren't speeding?" asked his partner. "Maybe drinking a little? Imagining little green men?"

She was being baited and she was determined not to let them see her sweat. "No, I wasn't speeding," she said calmly. "Not in this county. As for drinking, you're welcome to take a blood sample."

"You can be sure we'll do just that."

"What about the men who tried to run me down?"

"We just have your say on that, Miss Stuart."

"The men who helped me said there were detour signs."

The deputy shrugged. "I'll check but I don't know of any detour."

"An SUV rammed my car several times. When I went off the road, I was trapped inside. One of the occupants of the SUV threatened to light a match and blow up the car."

"Now why would he do that?"

"He wanted the name of my source for a story."

"Oh, that piece of fiction you wrote. This sounds like another to me. Another big story at our expense."

She moved, swallowed a gasp of pain. She'd become used to pain after the accident two years earlier and the succeeding surgeries. She prided herself on having a high pain threshold. But this took her breath away.

"I'm not saying anything else," she told the deputies, one of whom had a malicious smile on his face. "Not without an attorney present."

"We'll investigate your charges, but it looks to me like you just made up a story to cover your own negligence. Or wanted another story."

"I don't care what it looks like to you," she said, not even bothering to defend herself further.

"There might be charges. Reckless driving. Speeding."

"Try it," she challenged them, too angry now to hold her tongue.

"The facts will speak for themselves."

They turned and left. The patients' advocate's gaze followed them out the door before turning back to her. "Can't say I like their attitude."

"You asked if you can contact someone for me?"

Mrs. Perkins nodded.

"Two people?"

"I can do that."

"Wade Carlton." She wrote out the *Observer*'s number. "If he isn't there, ask to speak to the night city editor. He'll contact Wade. Also Ben Taylor." She realized she'd lost his private number in the fire. "You'll have to call the FBI and ask them to contact him. Please tell him where I am."

Mrs. Perkins looked disconcerted by the requests but nodded.

The doctor came in then. He looked at the cuts and wanted to take X-rays. "Air bags have been known to crack a rib," he said. He looked at her leg. She was covered by the infamous hospital gown, the brace attached to her shoe obvious. So were the scars from the injury and surgeries.

She tolerated the next hour of waiting, X-rays, then waiting again. A nurse came in and swabbed, treated, and bandaged the cuts, including a small one on her face.

She was just finishing when Ben Taylor appeared.

The nurse blinked twice as he pushed aside the curtain. Maybe it was the deep scowl on his face.

"She had someone call me," he said and showed his credentials. Then he turned to her and she saw a flash of real concern in his eyes before they turned cold. Furiously cold. "How is she?"

The doctor returned then with X-rays in hand. He looked curiously at Ben Taylor. "Mr. Stuart?"

"No. A friend."

The doctor—Bruns, she remembered—turned back to her. "Nothing appears to be broken, but your ribs are going to hurt for the next week or so, probably several weeks. Doesn't seem to have injured your leg. Keep the wounds clean." He scribbled something on a pad and handed her two prescriptions. "One's for pain. Take it as needed. There's also one for an antibiotic for those cuts." He looked to Ben Taylor. "You're taking her home?"

He nodded.

"She needs to stay in bed for the next few days."

"I don't think . . . ," she started.

Ben Taylor quelled her with a look. "I'll wait outside until you get dressed."

She returned his hard stare even as she felt vulnerable in the shapeless and faded hospital gown with her scarred leg hanging down, and much of her skin covered with bandages. Her hair was probably a fright.

His frown didn't help.

He stepped outside and the nurse returned, fitting the brace back on her leg and then helping her dress in the bloody clothing. As she stood, the pain in her ribs made her breath catch. She swayed and caught the edge of the table.

Then Ben returned, and his hand steadied her.

"They tried to run me off the road," she said, wondering if she made any sense.

"You can tell me about it in the car," he said. He put an arm around her and steered her toward a wheelchair an orderly had brought.

"I don't need . . ."

"I know you don't," he said, "but there are hospital rules."

"Thank you for coming. I couldn't think . . ." She stopped again as she fell into the chair. She wasn't making any sense. And she certainly didn't want him to think she didn't have one person she could call after an accident. "It was just someone tried to kill me, and they're trying to make it my fault."

She was babbling. She never babbled.

He didn't say anything until he had helped her into the front seat of his car. Then he turned to her. "Someone tried to kill you?"

"Yes. No. Not exactly. They wanted to know who my source was."

"Who?"

"Two men—I think it was two—in an SUV. They tried to run me off the road. No. Not tried. Did. Kept hitting my car, first in the back, then on the driver's side. Pushed my car off the road. I was trapped inside. I couldn't move. Couldn't reach my gun. Then a man—he wore dark glasses—appeared at the door. My leg was trapped. I couldn't move, and I smelled gas. He threatened to light a match and explode the car if I didn't give him the name of my source."

"Did you?" he said in a level voice but she saw a muscle throb in his cheek.

"No. Then he *would* have killed me. I saw it in his face. The only thing keeping me alive . . . was he needed that name."

"What happened then?"

"A cell phone rang. He cursed. Apparently . . . told someone was approaching. He left but not before saying he could reach me. Anytime. Anywhere."

"Who came along?"

"Hunters. Bobby Joe and Ernie. They pulled me out just before the car exploded."

"Last names?"

She looked at him helplessly. How to explain she hadn't gotten the last names? "I don't know. They just brought me in and disappeared." She felt stupid and terrified and out of her depth.

He swore. "Mahoney was supposed to look after you. He called me and said he'd lost you."

"It's my fault. I tried to lose anyone who was following."

"Why?"

"I . . . thought I was meeting the source. I didn't want to lead anyone to him."

"Where were you going to meet?"

"Montcrest School."

"Where's that?"

"The eastern part of the county."

He glared at her. "Do you have any idea how completely stupid that was?"

She met his gaze. "Yes." She hated the trembling in her voice. "But I don't know how they followed me. I was careful." She paused, then added, "Or I thought I was."

"Your source asked to meet you there?"

"I thought it was my source. There was a text message on my cell phone. Only a few people have that number. He just said to meet him at the school at seven p.m. We'd met there before. I assumed—"

"Where was your car earlier today?"

"In a parking garage near the paper."

"You park there every day?"

"Yes."

"It would have been easy enough to plant a GPS tracking device in your car. Maybe a bug as well. Looks like they were trying to find a good place to get you alone. They could track you without your seeing them. When they found their opportunity, they took it."

"The hunters said there was a detour sign. They couldn't figure why it was there, so they went around it."

"Which means there were several people involved. Once they had you on a lonely road, they could call for help to detour traffic on both ends."

"Isn't that convoluted?" She didn't want to believe anyone had that kind of power. Then she remembered the smirk on the deputies' faces. Had they been involved in her attempted murder? She shivered. "Why not go after me more directly?"

"An accident on a lonely road?" he asked. "They would have the name they wanted, and no one would be the wiser. An explosion. A bottle of alcohol. You were drinking. Then they could go after whoever talked to you."

"You believe those deputies who were at the hospital were involved?"

"Maybe. Maybe they were just giving you a hard time because they feel you blackened their department. Did you get those names?"

"Yes," she said. "They had name badges. Staples and Murray."

"I'll check them out." He started the car. "Where to?"

"Home."

"Not alone. You don't have the sense God gave a billy goat." Fury accompanied every word.

At the moment, Robin couldn't deny it. Her hands still trembled. She'd come close to being burned to death because she thought she was smarter than the bad guys. She swallowed hard, then said softly, "You're right."

He looked startled at the admission, but didn't amend his characterization. Instead his jaw clenched.

She gritted her teeth, then asked, "Can I use your cell phone? Mine was in the car. I think it's probably cinders now."

He detached the phone from his belt, handed it to her, then pulled out of the parking lot. Even that movement sent pain pounding against her ribs. She looked at the numbers, blinked as she tried to concentrate.

She didn't have Wade's phone number with her. She dialed the night city editor.

"Robin, where in the hell are you? Wade and I have been going through hell since a nurse called from Meredith General Hospital. I tried to call back but they wouldn't put you through. Then they said you were being released. What the hell happened?"

"A car accident. Planned, I think, but I'm okay."

"What kind of accident? Where are you?"

"On the way home. Can you give me Wade's home number? I'll explain everything to you tomorrow."

Then Wade was on the phone. "Robin? Thank God. I've been worried sick."

"I'm sore, but whole," she said. "Someone is taking me home. My car is a total loss. It exploded. I don't think I'll be in tomorrow, but I'll phone the story in."

"Damn it, Robin. How badly were you injured?"

"Just some cuts and bruises," she said. "County deputies are claiming it was my fault." She realized she wasn't making much sense. "An SUV forced me off the road. It rammed me. Then someone threatened me . . ."

Silence. Then, "I don't know who's the bigger fool. You for going, or me for letting you go."

"I made the decision," she replied.

"Do you need our attorney?"

"Not now, but I might later."

"Give Greene the story tomorrow morning."

"I can write it."

"No," he said. "You've become part of the story."

"They're going to deny it."

"Who?"

Robin tried to put her thoughts in order. They didn't want to cooperate. *I will not panic.*

"The sheriff's department. Deputies. They claim I was reckless. Drinking. I wasn't." She hated the defensiveness in the statement.

"You say you're going home. You have a safe ride?"

"I . . . yes."

"We've hired an agency to watch your house. They should be there now. I'm coming over."

"No. I'm fine. Truly I am. I just need to get home."

"Tomorrow then. I'll stop over before going in to the office."

She ended the call, returned the phone to Taylor, and tried to think ahead. She didn't want to think about the last few hours. She didn't want to relive the terror.

So many things to do. So much lost. Notes. Transportation—her beloved car. Insurance. Finding another car. Then the thought she'd been avoiding. Someone wanted to kill her. Or was willing to risk killing her in a most unpleasant way to obtain a name from her.

Taylor was silent, a fact she appreciated. Outside of the comment about her stupidity, which she agreed with, there was no "I told you so." She needed to think, to process everything that had happened. She was surprised, though, that he didn't take this opportunity to ask her for the name of her source.

She suddenly started shaking. She opened her eyes and looked at her hands. Willed them to stop moving. She clasped them to stop it.

Taylor reached out a hand and put it over hers. Just the touch was enough to stop the shivering. His hand was warm. Strong.

"I'm sorry," she said. "I'm not usually this . . ." Wobbly? Weak? She didn't want to admit to either.

"I don't know a cop alive that hasn't had a reaction after an experience like that."

"I remembered two years ago when my car went off a cliff. It was happening all over again . . ." The shaking resumed.

"Can you give us a sketch of the face?"

"Yes . . . I think so. He wore dark glasses, though, and a cap."

"I'll have one of our artists come over in the morning."

She wanted to go home. She didn't want to go home. She wondered whether she would ever feel safe there again.

She considered blurting out the name that Ben Taylor wanted. That the bad guys wanted. But how could she exchange her life for Sandy's? She knew now why she'd heard the fear in his voice.

Ben moved his hand back to the steering wheel as they entered the interstate. He stepped down on the pedal and just that acceleration increased the aching pain in her chest.

"Why did you call me?" he asked.

"I don't know."

But she *did* know. She had friends at the paper, but when she had to call someone his was the first name that came to her. She'd felt safe with him last night. She'd desperately wanted to feel safe again.

He didn't say anything else until they neared her neighborhood. He stopped at a drive-through pharmacy for the prescriptions. She realized she didn't have any money—or credit cards—to pay the bill.

Minor concern, considering she was still alive. And yet worrying about minor things diverted thoughts from bigger ones, about the absolute terror she'd felt just hours ago.

She'd thought she was going to die when her car had spun out of control and tumbled down the incline. But a malicious attempt to do her harm was far different from her own carelessness.

They waited in silence until the order was filled and came through the window.

Then he drove her home. The house looked the same from the outside. A car with two men was parked in front.

"My editor said he would hire someone to watch the house," she said.

Ben parked behind it and took out his gun. "I'm leaving the key in the ignition. If you see anything suspicious, take off for the nearest station." He didn't wait for her assent, but got out and went over to the driver's side of the other car.

Thank God, it was a bench seat. Easy enough for her to slide if necessary. She watched as he leaned over and talked to the driver. She saw him hand over his credentials and look at others. Then he made a call on his cell phone.

He returned to her side of the car. "They're legit. Decent enough agency. Mostly ex-cops."

The lights were on next door.

"I want to get Daisy," she said. "She's with Mrs. Jeffers."

"I'll get her after you're inside."

Robin shook her head. "I don't have a key. It was in the car."

"Wait for me here, then, while I get the cat and key."

Every muscle in her body ached. Too much to protest.

He sprinted across her lawn to Mrs. Jeffers's. The door opened almost immediately, and she knew that Mrs. Jeffers had watched them drive up. In seconds, Ben Taylor returned to the car with a key in hand.

He opened the car door for her. "Mrs. Jeffers is bringing Daisy and her bed over. I asked her to give us a few minutes to get inside."

He offered his hand, and she took it as she stood. Every bone and muscle in her body ached. She forced a step. The next came easier.

"Stay behind me when we go in," he said.

"You don't think . . . ?"

"I don't think anyone is there, but those hired guys didn't check inside your house. I don't think you can take anything for granted."

She nodded. Her heart pounded even as she yearned to be inside. In her own bed. In the nest she'd created for herself.

Except it was no longer a sanctuary. No longer invulnerable to the outside.

The numbing fear lingered. She kept remembering that instant when she'd lost control of the car. The certainty that she would die . . .

She waited as he opened the door. "Wait here," he ordered.

He went inside, just as she had watched cops in movies do. Pistol in hand. And fast.

Several minutes—a lifetime—later, he reappeared. The gun was holstered in his belt.

"It's clear," he said, opening the door and moving aside as she walked in.

The lights were on. Her living room looked the same. She headed for the big overstuffed chair she loved.

*Home.*

Yet she didn't feel the satisfaction she usually did. She wondered whether she would ever feel it again.

A knock. Ben peered out the door, then opened it. Mrs. Jeffers appeared, carrying Daisy and a cat bed. Damien followed behind.

"Oh, my." Mrs. Jeffers stared at her. "Mr. Taylor said you were hurt, but . . ."

"That bad?" Robin said.

Her silence answered that question eloquently.

Robin explained the best she could, though she feared her words were running together.

Mrs. Jeffers hovered over her. "You should be in bed." She cast a reproachful glance at Ben. "I'll turn the covers down and make some hot cocoa. It will help you sleep." She turned on Ben. "How did you let this happen?" She didn't give him a chance to answer. She was on her way down the hall, presumably to Robin's bedroom.

Robin tried to stand and couldn't stifle a groan. She couldn't remember feeling that kind of pain before. Not even through the long medical journey with her leg. Then it hurt to laugh when they took a piece of her hip for a bone transplant. Now it hurt to breathe.

Mrs. Jeffers was back. "You help her into the bedroom while I make some cocoa."

Robin was bemused at the way Mrs. Jeffers ordered an FBI agent about, but that thought was quickly replaced by the fact that she would soon be alone tonight with a bum leg and a chest that ached every time she took a breath.

He obediently helped her stand. His arm stayed around her until they reached the bedroom. The covers were turned down and she sat down on the edge of the bed. "You haven't asked me about my source."

"Would you tell me?"

"No."

"Then it wouldn't do any good, would it?"

She studied him through narrowed eyes. "I'm not sure I trust this new, understanding you."

"You've been hurt. I don't kick hurt kittens."

"I'm not a kitten."

"Okay, bad analogy. You're definitely not a kitten."

She started to lean down to unzip the left leg of her slacks. A sharp ache stopped her midway. "I . . . my ribs . . ."

He kneeled on the floor and unzipped the pant leg, then his hands quickly unbuckled the straps of the brace.

She didn't want him to do it. The leg was still badly scarred, though the white puffiness was gone. But he finished before she could protest. He placed the brace next to her bed and his fingers massaged her leg.

Gentle. His fingers were gentle and they felt so good. She leaned down on the pillows, easing some of the strain on her ribs, the stiffness in her leg. She closed her eyes and savored his touch.

He caressed the leg as if it were a thing of value, even of beauty, not the scarred, ugly limb she saw each morning. She'd thought her leg would repel him.

Warmth started filling her. Warmth and an odd contentment. The terror of the earlier hours faded.

"I see you're in good hands," Mrs. Jeffers said, and Robin opened her eyes. Her neighbor was carrying a mug and placed it on the night table. "I'll be on my way."

"Those two men in front—"

"Ben told me all about them," Mrs. Jeffers said.

*So it was "Ben" now.*

"You need me, you call me," Mrs. Jeffers said. "No matter when." She left, casting an approving look at Ben Taylor.

Robin wasn't sure she wanted Mrs. Jeffers to go. She was comfortable with Ben Taylor. Entirely too comfortable. There was something else, as well. A raw ache, a rush of heat that burned her body inside out.

Once Mrs. Jeffers had left, Ben took two bottles from his

pocket and took one pill from one and two from the other and handed them to her.

She wasn't sure she wanted to take them. The one for pain undoubtedly would also help her sleep. She wasn't sure she wanted sleep.

"I'll stay on the couch tonight," he said as if reading her mind. "Also, I would like to call someone from technical and sweep your apartment for bugs."

"You think . . ."

"It's just a precaution. But I need your permission."

She nodded her head. The last thing she wanted was for her assailants to listen in on her personal conversations. Dear God, it was overwhelming in its implications. Everything was.

She nodded and took the pills with a sip of cocoa. She didn't realize until this morning how much she'd wanted, needed, someone with her.

"What do you sleep in?" he asked.

"T-shirt," she said. "Second drawer."

He was back in a second with a large T-shirt, one of several in the drawer, and handed it to her, then sat on the bed next to her. Gently again, very gently, he unbuttoned her shirt and her slacks.

"I can do the rest," she said primly. As tired and sore and emotionally sapped as she was, she didn't want to be dependent. She didn't want him to see any weakness.

*He already has.*

Yet he'd not taken advantage of it. Not asked questions she knew he wanted to ask. Instead he turned away while she took off her shirt and bra and pulled on the T-shirt. She was sorry then she hadn't let him help her. How could such a simple thing as removing a shirt hurt so much?

She couldn't stifle the cry when she tried to take off her slacks. In seconds he was at her side, gently sliding them down.

Something shifted inside her. His touch warmed all the cold, frightened places in her. Despite the burns and cuts and pain in her chest, she still reacted to him in ways that astonished her.

Then he finished. He pulled a sheet over her, his hand lingering at the base of her throat, then her cheek. She made a sound deep in her throat. Or was that Daisy, lying next to her? Now she knew why cats purred.

She looked up at him. "I'm usually very independent," she said, knowing she was babbling again. It was the painkiller. Had to be.

"I know," he agreed with that half smile that went straight to her heart. "Get some sleep. We'll talk in the morning."

"Cabbages and kings," she said drowsily. "Talk about cabbages and kings."

"And a bit more," he promised.

She wasn't sure she liked that "bit more."

She *was* sure she liked the notion of him being there.

Her eyes closed. As long as he was here, she was safe.

# chapter fifteen

*Ben woke to a moan* from inside Robin's bedroom.

He sprinted from the couch in the living room. She had a guest room upstairs, but he'd preferred to stay closer. She'd been in shock last evening, and he'd suspected sometime during the night she would need company.

He'd stayed awake for several hours after she went to sleep. He opened the door to a "sweep team," which found bugs in the telephones in her office and living room. None in her bedroom. The intruder, or intruders, probably hadn't had time to do a more comprehensive job. According to Mrs. Jeffers, they hadn't been inside more than fifteen minutes the night before last.

Damn it, he should have had the house swept yesterday morning. He should have realized the entry had had more than one purpose. He was slipping. Losing focus. Becoming more concerned about Robin Stuart than his job. The fact that her bedroom wasn't bugged was one of the few pluses. He hadn't acted very professionally there.

Robin hadn't awakened during the sweep. The painkiller had been strong, and she'd lost blood. After the team left, he'd kicked off his shoes and folded up on the sofa. He'd slept on much worse.

He'd expected nightmares, a quick awakening. Fear. He'd experienced all after his first shooting.

He went into her bedroom and turned on the light.

Robin was thrashing in the bed. No danger other than the

demons in her own dreams. He knew, though, how real those could be.

He sat down on the bed and touched her.

She shouted, then woke suddenly, flailing her hands.

"It's all right," he said. "A nightmare."

Her eyes, when they opened, were wild, frightened. He took her hand and squeezed it. "Hey, it's okay," he said.

She gradually relaxed, then embarrassment flooded her face. "I don't usually do this."

"Do what?"

"Have nightmares."

"I think you have reason to have a nightmare."

"The crash . . ." Her voice wavered slightly.

He was silent.

"Do you think they knew that I'd had an accident before?"

"Probably."

She shivered. "As soon as I was physically able, I got into a car. It was the hardest thing I've done." She was going back. Remembering. She hadn't intended to admit it. That was clear in her face. "When that SUV rammed me, it was happening all over again . . ."

She shuddered.

He touched her shoulder. Her body was tense. The smooth skin of her cheek was marred by a small white bandage. There were too many others scattered on her body.

He wanted to hurt someone for doing that. Hurt them very badly. He could only imagine how she must have felt trapped in a car with someone threatening to light a match.

He saw the recurring terror in her eyes. He should use it. He should ask questions.

He couldn't. Not now.

"What happened with the first accident?" he asked.

"I was going home. My mother had had a stroke. I was going too fast, it was raining and the road was slick. I flew off the cliff. Not one of my finer moments."

Her wry smile went straight to his heart. Her strength was one of the things he liked about her. Though he'd seen the fear in her last night, she hadn't allowed it to diminish her. No suggestion she would abandon the story, nor give up her source.

He admired that strength, and he rued it.

The strength could be the death of her.

"What happened exactly?" he asked as he sat on the bed, and she propped herself up on pillows.

"I was lucky. I was thrown out but my leg was mangled. Some very good doctors did bone grafts and muscle transplants and any number of other doctor tricks. It won't be as good as new, but can be *almost* as good as new. I could have lost it, so nothing seemed very bad when I didn't."

"That would have been a tragedy. It's such a pretty leg."

"It's a mess."

"No. It's damn shapely."

He saw the doubt on her face and realized then that she was far more sensitive about it than she wanted anyone to know.

She struggled to sit and he sat next to her. He started gently massaging her neck.

"Ummmmm," she murmured with obvious pleasure.

"How are your ribs?"

"Sore."

"It's only five a.m. You should get more sleep. Do you need another pill for pain?"

She shook her head. "I don't like pills. Had too many of them in the hospital. Started to like them too much."

His hand stilled. *Shit.* Memories hit him like a sledgehammer. Dani had liked them too much, as well. As well as other drugs. Only she hadn't started in the hospital.

He closed that door in his mind. "You said something earlier about 'cabbages and kings.' "

"Did I?"

"Yep."

"From *Alice in Wonderland*. She shrank and slipped down a rabbit hole and found herself in a peculiarly strange and sometimes dangerous place."

"Sounds apt. How did Alice extricate herself?"

"You'll have to read it to find out."

She leaned against him and heat shot through him. He fought the need to put his arms around her. He'd been unprofessional enough in the past few days. He also knew that probably every bone in her body hurt at the moment.

"I'm glad you stayed," she said.

He didn't answer. He couldn't answer. He feared he would say the wrong things. "Why did you call me?" he finally asked.

"The other night . . . with Daisy, you knew exactly what to do."

"Anyone would."

"Maybe," she said. "But you have the weight of the FBI behind you, whether they want to be there or not."

He chuckled. She kept surprising him. She was a complex mixture of street smarts and innocence. A living oxymoron. "And I thought it was my sparkling personality."

"I don't think so."

"Ouch," he said.

She grinned. "I do appreciate your staying here tonight."

"Far better than some other places I've slept." He paused. "Want some more of Mrs. Jeffers's cocoa?"

She shook her head. "Just . . . talk to me for a while."

"I can manage that."

"Why did you join the FBI?"

He was always startled by her questions. Sometimes they seemed to come out of nowhere. But he was learning that questions were as much a part of her as a smile was to others.

"Why not?" he asked simply. "I'm good at puzzles."

"Family?"

"None."

"Siblings? Cousins?"

"No," he said shortly.

Her hand caught his. "I'm sorry."

"Don't be. Good for self-reliance."

Daisy meowed and Robin reached over and buried her hand in the thick fur.

"Get more sleep," he repeated, changing the subject. "I'll have a sketch artist here in the morning. Have you remembered any more?"

"Just how intimidating those dark glasses were. Like the ones bad cops wear in movies." She cut her eyes toward him. "They're very effective."

"Maybe I'll have to try them."

"I don't think they would flatter you." The sparkle was coming back into her eyes.

"You think they were cops?" he asked.

"Not like the ones I know in the sheriff's department. There was a . . . professional hardness about him. A northern accent."

"You didn't mention that before," he said.

"I didn't think of it until now . . ."

"Anything else?" he asked tightly.

"No. I don't think so."

"Keep picturing every moment in your mind. Sometimes it's startling what you will remember."

She was silent, her face a study in concentration. Empathy swept through him as he surveyed the bruises on her face and body. He realized from her comments on their drive from the hospital that it wasn't the story that compelled her to keep her source's name from him, but her feeling of right and wrong and the need to keep her source safe. Even at her own expense.

The question was how long that determination would last, given the legal pressure from his side and the more violent pressure from the bad guys.

"He really intended to kill me." Her voice cracked slightly as the words blurted out. "I saw it in his face."

She shivered again, and he took her hand, rubbed it with his own. He had no right to touch her, didn't want the right. God, he'd already gotten more involved than he ever intended. He just hadn't been able to force himself to leave last night.

He tried to tell himself it was all to gain her trust, but that was a crock, and he knew it. The kisses they'd shared had knocked him for a loop. The call earlier tonight had jolted him. He'd broken every speed limit to reach the hospital, and one look at her made his knees buckle with gratitude that she was still alive.

"Give up the story," he said.

"I can't. I've worked too hard for it. It's mine."

"Is it important enough to die for?"

Her face paled slightly but her jaw jutted out. "I'll be more careful now."

"I don't think you know the meaning of the word 'careful,'" he said. He hesitated, then added, "You're not doing your source any favor. They're going to find him."

"It won't come from me."

He thought about telling her about the conversation he'd had with his boss after she'd gone to sleep. He'd asked for protection. Private cops were okay in some instances, but most didn't have the level of expertise of trained agents.

He'd been turned down flat unless she agreed to cooperate. He also learned that she would be subpoenaed to appear before a grand jury Tuesday, the day after tomorrow.

He decided to change tactics. "Did many people know your cell phone number?"

"No."

"Did your source?"

"Yes."

"He could have sent the text message, then?"

"I think it was. It sounded like him."

"Could he have set you up?"

"No," she said vehemently.

He thought about other possibilities. The privacy of cell phones wasn't that great. An expert hacker could probably find it. The sophistication of the attack worried him.

"Think about it. Who else would have it? How do you get in touch with him?"

"I don't."

"If there's an urgent need for you to contact him?"

She shook her head.

"Is there any way he can be connected to you? Were you friends?"

Something flickered in her eyes. "More like acquaintances."

He hesitated, then said, "I had someone here checking on bugs. There was one in your telephone in your office, another in the living room."

"None on this extension?"

"No."

He saw her face screw up in thought, trying to remember every call she'd made.

"Any to worry about?" he asked.

"I don't think so. Are they still there?"

"No."

"Then they'll know we—you—found them."

He nodded.

"You thought they might be watching the house?"

"Not now. Not with so much interest in it. Those two guys in front are good. There's another car that keeps circling the area, looking for anything that looks out of place."

"So I don't need you."

"Probably not," he said wryly. The comment didn't do much for his ego.

"You must have better things to do than nursemaid me."

"I can't think of one. But the bugs mean the bad guys are definitely serious about you, though I would have expected a higher degree of competence." He paused, then added, "You shouldn't go to Meredith County again. Not without someone with you."

"Do you think everyone will believe me, that I was run off the road?"

"I do." He paused, then asked, "Did they take a blood sample?"

"Yes."

"You agreed?"

"Yes."

"Don't be surprised if it's positive."

"You think they might tamper with it?"

"It's possible. It's to their benefit to discredit you. You inferred the sheriff's department might be involved in murders. I don't think many deputies were happy with that."

"I shouldn't have given them permission for a blood test," she said dejectedly.

"Then they could imply that failure to take it meant you were guilty."

"So it didn't make any difference if I had or not. They could get me either way. That makes me feel a little better. Maybe."

He grinned inwardly. Those little spurts of wry humor always surprised him. "That's supposition at this point. I just want you to be prepared."

"That would mean the whole department is involved."

"Maybe not in the murders. Maybe salvaging its reputation. I've been doing some research on the department. There's lots of rumors."

"The JP—the justice of the peace—said it was a 'closed' shop. You either had to be a friend of the sheriff's or the son of a deputy or a longtime resident."

"The name of the JP?"

"Godwin. He's about ninety years old and a gossip, but there's always a grain of truth in what he says."

"He's not . . ."

"No. He's not my source." She moved and gave him a wry smile. "You never stop trying."

"I don't want you dead. Or in jail."

She looked up at him. Her blue eyes were shadowed. "The attorney at my paper said jail was a possibility . . . but it rarely happens. Do you really think . . ."

"Decisions like that are above my pay scale. They're made by the U.S. attorney for this district."

"Do you think they should try to force me to reveal my source?" she asked intently.

God, her eyes were blue. The exact shade was difficult to describe. Somewhere between sapphire and the sky at dusk.

"Ben?"

He wasn't going to lie. "Yeah, I do." He told her about the conversation he'd had with his boss. "We have to know what you know. It's not just your source, Robin, it's hundreds of kids that could be hooked by the drugs peddled by the organization."

"I'm trying to help bring it to an end. You wouldn't have what little you have without my source."

"It's not enough."

"It has to be."

Ben had already said more than he should. He could be putting the case in jeopardy. "Think long and hard about what you'll tell the grand jury. Judge Davenport is not known to be sympathetic with the press."

"I have to go to South Carolina that day to make a deposition for my sister."

"I would suggest you postpone it."

"I can't. It has to do with the custody of her kids."

He didn't say anything, but the silence spoke for him. He'd started the ball rolling on the subpoena. If he had the guts he would tell her that. But it was out of his hands now, and into those of the U.S. attorney. It was his job to keep her alive so she could testify. Maybe he hadn't been told that specifically, but now, by God, it was what he intended to do.

She closed her eyes. He wanted to fold her in his arms and tell her everything would be all right.

But it would be a lie. Nothing was all right. As long as she clung to the name of her source, he was her adversary. And the undeniable magnetism between them made that fact more painful.

He touched her shoulder, ran his arm down it, stopping at one of the bandages. Lust and tenderness cascaded through him, clashing against each other.

Hell, he had to get out of here.

He stood, then watched as she lay back down.

"Good night, Agent Taylor."

He was gone when Robin woke later in the morning to the ringing of her phone. It frightened her for a moment, remembering the earlier call that woke her. She cautiously sat up and answered it.

But it was Wade's voice. "Robin?"

"Yes."

"How are you?"

"Honestly?"

"Yes."

"I'm alive."

"Up to a visitor or two?"

"Uh-huh."

"Ten okay?"

She looked at the clock. It was eight. Long past her usual wake-up time.

"That's fine."

"Have you had breakfast?"

"No."

"I'll bring something."

He hung up before she could protest.

She put her good leg on the floor and reached for the crutches. She wasn't sure she wanted to use the brace today. She longed for a hot bath to soothe the bruises, but she had too many bandages for that. Plus she was unsure she could ease herself into and out of a bath.

Where was Ben Taylor?

She went into the living room. A blanket was neatly stacked at the end of the sofa. Otherwise it was empty. She knew the guest room upstairs was, as well.

She went to the window. Ben's car was gone. Another car, much like the one parked in front of her house last night, was there. She went into the kitchen for coffee.

The pot was hot, and a clean cup had been placed next to it.

A note rested on the other side.

*Robin . . .*

*Had to go into the office. I didn't want to wake you. I'll call later.*

It was a very unsatisfactory note, and obviously hastily scrawled. Well, what did she expect? He had already gone far and beyond the call of duty.

Or had he?

Had she been his duty? She poured coffee and sat down at the table. Her ribs hurt even more today than last night. Every breath she took was painful. She gave the rest of her body a cursory look. She resembled a mummy more than a living person.

She took a sip of coffee. It was a small thing, his preparing the coffee, but a big one for her at the moment when it hurt to move. She flinched at the idea of getting dressed, or even going outside to get the morning paper.

Several lights were on, and she knew he'd purposely left them that way. Still, the house that had always been full for her was suddenly very empty.

She went over everything that had happened since the press conference. Her mind wasn't quite as fogged. A sketch artist. Ben said a sketch artist would be over. She concentrated on the face from last night. Knew she would never forget it.

Her car. She had to call the insurance company and get a rental. A driver's license. Replacement credit cards.

She hadn't thought she would be called before a grand jury as soon as Ben indicated. She'd thought she would have more time to convince Sandy . . .

She tried to remember everything she'd said to Ben Taylor during the last days. Anything that could be used against her in a grand jury room? She wondered whether she'd been wrong in trusting him so quickly.

She didn't even know how it happened, how in just a few days he'd wormed himself into her confidence. Nor why she'd called him last night when she could have called someone else.

She'd needed that sense of confidence in a world that was spinning out of control, where she didn't know whether she was right, or whether in trying to protect Sandy she was condemning him.

She still hurt, and she desperately wanted another pain pill, but she'd learned in the hospital how dangerous they could become. When it got to the point that she couldn't wait for another operation to feel the euphoria of morphine, she went without.

Darned if she was going to give in to it now. She had to think straight.

She especially had to think straight when she thought about Ben Taylor.

"Sorry, Ben, I shouldn't have lost her."

Ben stood at the door. They'd both been called in to meet with the agent in charge despite the fact it was Sunday. It was the reason he'd had to leave before Robin Stuart woke.

"You had no reason to think she might try to lose you."

"An amateur," Mahoney exclaimed with disgust. "An amateur got away from me. It's humiliating."

"Now that you put it that way—"

Mahoney threw a crumpled piece of paper at him. "Holland wanted to see us as soon as you got in." He looked Ben over. "You look like hell."

"That's what happens when you're forty and don't get any sleep. Let's go."

He already had his tactics planned. He hadn't discussed his plan with Mahoney, who was none too happy with Robin Stuart at the moment.

Once in Holland's office, he told both what had happened the night before.

"She called you?" Holland said, raising one of his bushy eyebrows.

Ben nodded.

"You stayed all night?"

"On the sofa."

"You aren't getting involved?"

"Only as part of the case." God might well smite him for that lie.

"No name yet?"

"No."

"Can you get it without the subpoena? Ames really doesn't want to rile the press."

"I don't think so. She thinks she's protecting the source."

"She knows she could go to jail?"

"I told her it's a possibility. It's rather minor after what she went through last night."

"Tell me in detail."

Ben had reported in after Robin went to sleep, but it had been a fairly brief call. Now he gave Holland all the details, including the fact he was sending an artist over this morning.

"They actually threatened to charge her with drunk driving?"

"I think 'implied' is a better word."

"And you're sure they're not right."

"There wasn't the slightest sign of alcohol. And the fear was very real."

"She knows she can get protection if she cooperates?"

"She knows."

"Damn it."

"I think we should provide it now."

"You know we can't. We can't justify it."

"They went after her once," Ben said. "Twice if you include the break-in. They used a lot of resources to do it. I don't think they'll give up now. It may be to our advantage to be there."

"You mean use her as bait?"

"Something like that."

"You want to let her in on it?"

"No."

"Okay. It's your baby. But if this goes south . . ."

Ben kept his face emotionless. It was what he wanted. She would get her protection. "What about the subpoena?"

"Ames received approval from the Justice Department. He didn't much like it but I convinced him the public disliked the media now more than us. He's having it approved as we speak." Holland met his gaze. "You wanna give it to her?"

"I'm the good cop on this one," he said. "Anyway, shouldn't we go through her attorney?"

"More shock the other way. She might say something."

"I don't think so. I've been trying. She doesn't frighten easily."

"Okay. Go home and get some sleep," Holland said.

"I won't argue with that. When will you have agents over there?"

"You said the paper has some guards there now."

"Rent-a-cop. One of the better agencies, but still . . ."

Holland cast a wary glance his way. "I'll have a team start today, see if they can't find an empty house nearby to keep an eye on her house." He paused, then said, "I don't want this to go bad. Jailing a reporter is bad publicity. A dead one is worse."

"I realize that." He certainly didn't intend on that happening.

Holland speared him with his gaze. "Don't get personally involved, Taylor."

"I never get personally involved. You know how I feel about reporters."

"Just keep feeling that way."

Ben turned and left.

Damn it. Just what had Holland noticed?

# chapter sixteen

*The phone rang as Robin* hobbled into the bathroom for as good a wash as she could manage with the bandages.

*Ben.* Maybe. She hurried as fast as she could to the bedroom phone, plopped down on the bed, and stared at it as it continued to ring.

It *could* be Ben, and that possibility tightened her stomach. Then again it could be her anonymous caller. Or Sandy.

She grabbed the receiver.

"Hi," came a lazy voice.

She recognized it immediately.

"Michael?"

"Mike," the voice corrected. "Thought I would try again for dinner. Hope you don't mind."

Michael from the pub. A date. Normalcy.

Some time away from thoughts of Ben Taylor. How much of the attraction between them was real? How much was his job? How much came from adrenaline and danger? How much just plain sexual attraction?

She still didn't know why, of all the people she knew, she'd chosen him to call after the wreck. He'd been the first person who came to mind. The only one.

But now she was filled with doubts.

"Robin?"

The question jerked her back to the moment. How long had she been lost in thought?

"I'm sorry. This has been a rather strange night and day."

"Bad time? I can call back some other time."

"No," she said. "When?"

"Tonight?"

If he came, Ben Taylor wouldn't. Then again maybe he wouldn't come anyway, and, heaven help her, she needed time to get her senses under control.

But she knew today was not the time. She had a meeting with Wade, a session with a FBI sketch artist. Her head hurt, her chest ached, and all she wanted was to go to bed and pull up the covers around her.

"I had an accident last night, and I'm pretty stiff. I'm supposed to stay home tonight."

"An accident? Was it bad?"

She liked the warm concern in his voice. "Bruised ribs. Some cuts."

"What happened?"

She didn't want to go into the story now. "I'll tell you when I see you."

"Tomorrow?" he persisted.

"Yes," she said, "unless something happens on the story." She had no intention of obeying the doctor's orders to rest.

"Tomorrow it is," he said, though she thought she heard disappointment in his voice. "I'll call you for a time. Anyplace special you would like to go?"

"Depends on my ribs."

He hung up and she wondered what she'd just done. Made a date with a normal guy. An accountant. Her mother would have been ecstatic.

Or maybe it was simply to show Ben Taylor that someone was interested in her. Someone who had no agenda.

The phone rang again.

"Robin?" Unlike Michael's voice, Ben Taylor's was clipped. None of the warmth from last night.

"None other," she said flippantly.

"How are you?"

"Alive."

"Above and beyond that?"

"Still sore. Thanks for making the coffee."

Silence, then, "The sketch artist will be there at noon. Okay?"

Her day was rapidly filling. And she still hadn't called her insurance agency about the car. She had no transportation. If she needed anything . . .

"Okay," she agreed.

"His name is Allen Cruise. Make him show his credentials before you open the door." The phone went dead.

Her heart sank. His voice had been cool. Reserved.

So much for any wild fantasy.

She went back into the bathroom, looked in the mirror, and winced as she surveyed the ruins from yesterday. Her eyes were red-rimmed. Bruises covered her body and were particularly colorful across her chest. Her skin was punctuated by bandages. Every step jarred something inside.

She washed her face, sponged the rest of her body, and pulled on a T-shirt and altered pair of jeans. She added some lipstick and a bit of makeup to conceal some of the bruises. Just as she finished, the phone rang yet again.

*Damn.* She should have brought it into the bathroom with her. She limped as quickly as she could back to the phone.

"You got out," a voice said. "Maybe your sisters won't be so lucky."

She froze as she recognized the voice. She would never forget it.

*I'll see you again, sweetheart.*

"Think about it," the voice continued. "We want the name before the cops. Think about your family. I will be calling back. You'd better have an answer."

Before she could respond, the phone went dead.

She stood stunned. Terror, stark and vivid, swept through her. She could deal with fear for herself far better than for her sisters.

*What to do?*

Call Lark and Star?

*Lark's hearing for custody was pending.*

She looked down at the phone clutched in her hand. It was shaking. Ben Taylor had left his phone numbers on her night table. She dialed his cell number.

He answered on the second ring. "Taylor."

"It's Robin." Even she heard the panic in her voice.

"Robin? Something wrong?"

"I had another phone call. He threatened my sisters."

A mumbled curse came across the line, then, "What was said?"

She told him the exact words.

"Would you agree to a tap on your phone?"

She paused. What if Sandy called? But since the story had come out he always used her cell phone.

"I'm . . . not sure."

"I'll be there as soon as I can," he said.

She wanted him there more than she thought possible. Much more than she should.

She broke the connection and called Lark.

In short sentences, Robin explained what had happened and that in any event she may not be able to make the deposition.

Lark's silence was painful.

"I want you to be aware. Careful."

"The kids? They wouldn't go after the kids?"

"I don't know. I'm talking to the FBI later. I'll call you after I talk to them."

"Give that caller the name of your source," Lark said, and Robin heard the panic in her voice.

"I can't."

"Who's more important? Someone involved with corruption or your own flesh and blood?"

The words were like a lance through her heart. Her niece, Kim, was seven and a beautiful little towhead. Kim's brother, Hunter, was a precocious five-year-old. Robin loved them both dearly.

"I'll call you back tonight," she told Lark.

Her conversation with Star was as excruciating. Star had taken care of her in between hospital stays. It had been painful for both of them, Robin being so helpless, and Star in the unexpected role of caretaker. Robin owed her more than she could say. Now Star was expecting her first child, and Robin had unwittingly dragged her into danger.

"I know you, Robin," Star said. "I know how important your word is. But now we're involved. It's no longer just you. Or your job. You should go to the FBI."

"If I do, the bad guys might go after you."

"And if you don't, they may, anyway. I would prefer the FBI on my side rather than homicidal maniacs."

If she did reveal her source to the feds, then someone else's family might die. Heartsick, Robin said good-bye and dropped the receiver. Daisy jumped up next to her and meowed softly.

Robin held the cat for a moment and scratched her ear.

Her doorbell pealed.

She gently dislodged Daisy and headed for the door. She looked out the glass storm door she was keeping locked these days.

Wade stood there, holding a bag and a laptop.

She opened the door and he stared at her.

"Christ," he said, his eyes roaming over her with concern.

"It's not that bad," she protested.

"You look like you belong in the hospital."

"Not in Meredith County." She stood aside for him to enter. She led the way to the kitchen. "Coffee is in the pot. Cups are in the cupboard above it."

In seconds he placed two cups on the table and opened a bag full of donuts. "There's a bit of everything in there."

She wasn't hungry. "Something just happened."

His hand stilled. "What?"

She told him about the telephone call.

"My God," he said.

"I've called Ben Taylor. He's coming over. I'm not sure what to do. Maybe they're bluffing."

"How would anyone know about your sisters?"

"My address book. After the break-in two nights ago, I found it out of its usual place. Ben said they might have photographed the pages."

"Ben?" Wade's eyebrows raised.

She felt her cheeks warm. Probably turned red as a beet.

"Ben Taylor. The FBI agent who helped me after the break-in. He . . . stayed here most of the night last night after the attack."

Wade's brows knitted together and he hesitated for a moment, then said, "Keep in mind he's the opposition right now." He paused. "Unless you want to change your mind now. No one would blame you if you gave the FBI the name."

"Now the bad guys have threatened my sisters if I give it to anyone but them. They want the name. I don't think they'll stop at anything to get it."

"I'm sorry, Robin. I didn't see this coming."

"Neither did I."

"Mason Parker has been in contact with the U.S. attorney's office. He's been told to expect you to be subpoenaed."

She looked down at the coffee.

"Robin?" Wade's voice brought her back to the present.

"I don't know what to do."

He opened his laptop and put it on the table. "Let's start with what happened last night. Tell me everything."

She recounted every moment. Up until she arrived home. She was a reporter, had trained herself to remember details. The color of the SUV, the shape of the attacker's face, the voice. Every word. Then the deputies at the hospital.

His fingers moved rapidly over the keys. His expression grew increasingly grim as she spoke.

When she finished, he shook his head. "I never thought it would go this far."

"Neither did I," she agreed.

"You and Greene take time writing the story tomorrow. I want it right. No need to do it today. It has to go through Mason first, anyway, and he's out of town this weekend."

She nodded.

"We'll keep the protection. Everywhere you go."

"My sisters?"

"I don't think the paper will do that. I'll try."

She looked at her hand. It was trembling. She'd accepted the danger last night. For herself. Not for anyone else.

Now she was caught between loyalties. To Sandy, to her sisters, and, to a lesser degree, to her story.

"You don't need to keep the story," Wade said. "God knows you've done a great job. No one would fault you if someone took it over. Take time off. Go somewhere with your sisters."

"The subpoena?"

"It hasn't been served yet," he said, his jaw setting.

Stunned, Robin thought about what he was saying. Running to avoid testifying. The idea was tempting. She and her sisters could disappear for a few weeks. But what of Lark's children? Their school? Their friends? Their father? If Lark took them, it could mean loss of custody. And Star was expecting after years of disappointment.

Wherever she turned, she seemed trapped.

"I don't think I can do that," she said. "I started this. And endangered people in doing so. I can't run away now."

"From what you say, they might try to charge you with some traffic violations, maybe even DUI. That could mean the Meredith County jail."

"I know. I might be the only reporter in the history of the paper to go to both a local and a federal jail."

The small joke provoked a smile, but then his expression turned serious again. "You can stop this now. If you won't leave the city, go talk to the FBI. Get protection for your source, yourself, your family."

"I don't think they protect extended families. Even if they did, how can I ask my sisters to give up the lives they have now?"

"Whatever you decide, the paper will support you."

"Everyone at the paper?"

"Management certainly. I would think everyone else."

"Thanks for convincing them to give me bodyguards or whatever they are outside."

"I was afraid you would object."

"I'm not usually an idiot," she said, "though I suspect I acted like one last night."

"You had every reason to believe the text message came from your source."

"I'm still not sure it didn't. They might have followed me any place I went, especially if they could track the car."

"No way you can get in touch with him?"

"Not without possibly leading someone to him." She paused, then added, "Ben Taylor thinks they might have planted a device in my car that they followed. He had someone come over last night and sweep the house. They found two listening devices in my phone. One in the living room and one in my office."

"You didn't tell me that."

"I am now," she said.

"That's it. You're off the story."

"That's not going to help, Wade. The problem of the source will still exist. That's what everyone wants, whether or not I cover the story. So I might as well continue."

"I'll see if we can't double the protection."

She nodded.

The FBI sketch artist followed Wade's visit, and twenty minutes after he left, a florist truck arrived. She watched as one of the bodyguards approached it, apparently asked for identification, then allowed the delivery man to approach the house after checking the vase of flowers he carried.

After thanking the delivery man she took the vase. It was huge and filled her arms as she took them to the table. They were lovely, an intricate mixture of colors. Not roses but an exotic arrangement of blue and purple blooms she couldn't identify.

She tore open the card. *Hope you're feeling better. Looking forward to dinner. Michael.*

She stood there and stared at them. She'd received many, many flowers when she'd had her accident. But she'd never received flowers just as a token. Under other circumstances, they would be a pleasant surprise. Now all she could think about was her sisters.

She put the flowers on her coffee table. An uneasiness stirred inside. She'd instantly felt comfortable with Michael and at any other time would have no qualms about dating him. Now, though, she wanted to know more about him before inviting him in. She would call him tomorrow at the company he said he worked for, as well as check out the company itself.

The last few days had made her extra cautious.

She wished she had been that cautious yesterday. She'd thought then she had been. She didn't plan to take anything for granted again.

Ben talked to the two men in front of Robin's house. They were different from the ones last night. He tried to assure himself of their competence. Both were ex-cops, better than untrained rent-a-cops. Then he went to the door. He'd been chafing all morning, ever since the phone call, since she'd told him about the threats to her family.

He didn't know what they meant for the case. Or for the plan. The bad guys had upped the stakes, and he didn't know if he had anything better to offer. He very much doubted that the FBI would protect the families of Robin's two sisters.

She must be going through hell.

He wasn't altogether prepared when he saw her face as she opened the door. The light in her eyes was gone. The dancing mischief. "Thanks for coming," she said. Gratitude was etched in her face.

He tried to ignore the rumbling of guilt inside. "The sketch artist been here?"

"Came and gone. I don't think I was as much help as I hoped. Those sunglasses . . ." Her voice faded off, and she looked as taut as a telephone wire.

He had vowed not to touch her again. It was all he could do not to.

She held the door open and he went inside, trying to avoid brushing against her. God, what had happened to his self-control?

"Have you been up all day?"

She nodded.

"You don't submit to authority very well, do you? The doctor told you to rest."

"It's been a little busy."

He glanced around the room and couldn't miss the huge bouquet of fresh flowers. The card was still among the stems.

Her eyes met his, and a fine warmth ran through him. It was as if he was coming home, not just visiting a subject involved in an investigation. He should hand the case to someone else. He'd known it since he'd taken Daisy to the vet's. But he'd told himself he could control it. Now he knew he couldn't.

"Back to bed," he said, knowing he sounded like a stuffy old uncle.

She didn't protest. That told him a lot.

He accompanied her back into the bedroom and found a T-shirt for her. "What about food?"

"A donut for breakfast."

He shook his head, then left, closing the bedroom door behind him. He went into the living room and stared out the window. It was still midday and the sun shone on the street in front. The dark sedan with the bodyguards stuck out like a sore thumb. He only hoped that someone was watching the back as well. There should be an FBI team in the neighborhood tomorrow. It couldn't be too fast for him.

He went into the kitchen, looked in the fridge. Like his, there wasn't much there. Milk. Cheese. Two eggs. A stick of butter. A jar of peanut butter. Bread. He spread some peanut butter on the bread, poured a glass of milk, then went to the bedroom with it and knocked.

"Come in."

She was in bed, propped against several pillows. Daisy was on her lap.

He put the plate in front of her and the milk on the bedside table. "Have you called your sisters?"

"Yes. It wasn't easy to tell them that I've put both of them in danger."

Now was the time to pounce. "We can provide protection for them," he said, hoping it was three.

"If I cooperate?"

"Yes."

"For how long?"

He didn't answer. He couldn't answer. If they chose not to go into witness protection, there would be a limit, and he wasn't at all sure that the witness protection program would take extended families. Her source had been right about that. They could only hope they scooped up the Hydra leadership.

"I haven't heard from my source. I can't give anyone his name without at least talking to him," she said after a prolonged silence.

He'd feared that would be her response. Hell, it would have been his, as much as he hated to admit it. He'd had a similar decision to make years ago, and he'd made it with his heart, not his brain. The consequences had been disastrous, but he wouldn't listen then, and he doubted she would listen now.

"Where do your sisters live?"

"Lark's in South Carolina. She's just gone through a divorce and is involved in a custody case. She can't leave, or she might lose her children. Kim and Hunter. Star is just a few weeks from having a baby. She's in Richmond, Virginia. Her husband has a one-man law firm that's just being established."

Though her tone was normal, he felt the tension in her, the barely restrained fear. But then any normal person would feel the same.

"I'll alert the FBI offices there. See if they can't keep an eye out."

She looked at him directly. "Thank you." She released a long breath. "I want to be released from my word. Dear God, I want it."

"You may never get it. What then?"

This time, she didn't answer.

"What about a tap on your phone? We can get voice prints on your caller."

She shook her head. "The voice is metallic. He's using something to disguise it."

His cell phone rang. He damned it, but answered.

Mahoney's voice was clipped. "A sheriff's deputy has been killed in a traffic accident."

"Are you sure it's an accident?"

"No, that's why I'm calling you. Holland wants you and me to come in. He wants us to research this guy's background and the facts of the accident. Discreetly," he added ironically.

"Who is it?"

"Edwards. Richard Edwards."

"How did it happen?" he asked.

"Looks like he went off the road and the car burned. Coincidental, wouldn't you say?"

"I'll be in shortly." He hung up and fixed his stare on Robin. "Your source couldn't be a deputy named Richard Edwards?"

"No."

The puzzled look on her face told him Edwards was not her source. "Do you know him?" he asked.

"Edwards? Richie? I've met him. He was bailiff for the court, and we had coffee several times during a recent trial. Why?"

"He just turned up dead. A traffic accident and explosion."

"No . . ."

He watched her.

Her face crumpled. "It wasn't him," she said. "He wasn't my source."

"Then they may be systematically going after anyone in the department associated with you."

She closed her eyes, then after a second opened them as if she'd made a decision.

"Thanks for coming," she said.

It was an abrupt dismissal. Any hope that she might give up the source died.

He also realized she had a plan of some sort forming in that creative mind. Unfortunately most of her plans had gotten her in trouble.

"Robin?"

"I'm really tired," she said.

"If you are planning to do anything, you'll let me know? No more secret meetings on your own?"

Her eyes didn't meet his.

"Damn it, Robin."

"I won't do anything foolish. But I do have to get my life back in order and do a few simple things like get a car, a checkbook, and a credit card."

He pushed back a curl that had dropped on her forehead, willing her to trust him.

Her eyes did not change, nor did the stubborn set of her chin.

He dropped his hand. "You'll contact me if you need anything? If you get any more calls?"

"I will," she said, the earnest blue eyes meeting his. "I promise. And thanks."

He hated the helplessness that washed through him. Thanks for what? He'd been able to offer little comfort or advice about her sisters. But he had limited options. He was constrained by his own job, by his orders.

He gave her one last glance, then reluctantly left.

# chapter seventeen

*The front door clicked behind* him.

Robin locked the door, then went into the bedroom, sat on the side of the bed, and tried to ignore the bone-chilling weariness. The one person she wanted to confide in was the one person she couldn't. Not yet.

She *had* to get in touch with Sandy. By now she suspected he would know about the ambush in Meredith County. Why hadn't he tried to reach her?

But how? Her cell phone was a molten shell.

It was up to her. And she could do nothing without a car.

She reached for the brace and buckled it on, then pulled jeans over it and slipped into the T-shirt she'd worn earlier. Then she went to her office.

She looked at her watch. Nearly four p.m. Time to get a rental car. She went through her Rolodex and found her insurance agent. In minutes she had provided information to the agent and received authorization for a rental car. Now to get to the rental car company and convince them to give her a car without a current driver's license in hand.

She took a handful of quarters from the large jar that held her spare change, then located her expired driver's license and the credit card she kept in her desk, as well as her latest car insurance bill. She tucked them all into her jeans. Tomorrow, she promised herself, she would get a replacement driver's license. She was not about to go into Meredith County without one. But she had to go out tonight.

Being afraid for others was far more terrifying than being afraid for herself, and God knew she was afraid. Four men dead, and she had come close to being the fifth victim. She had walked into this knowing the risks, but she would never forgive herself if her sisters were injured or killed because of her.

Now she wasn't only terrified for them, she was mad as hell. White hot rage filled her.

Sandy had to release her from her promise. But even if he did, and she told the FBI, the bad guys had sworn to go after Star and Lark. She wasn't at all sure she believed the FBI would put teams of agents on them for weeks, maybe even months.

Therefore it was up to her to trump the bad guys.

Ignoring the lingering pain in her ribs and from other assorted bruises, she went into the kitchen, fed Daisy, made herself a cup of coffee, and formulated a plan.

First objective: reach Sandy without anyone knowing. It would not be easy to leave her house alone. Not only were the private investigators outside, but she wouldn't be surprised if the FBI, or even the bad guys, was following her.

Mrs. Jeffers. There was nothing Mrs. Jeffers liked more than a good mystery unless it was conspiracy.

She called the older woman. "Mrs. Jeffers?"

"Oh, how are you, my dear? I've been wanting to come over, but you had a stream of visitors and I thought you might be worn out."

"I need company," she lied, unsure whether someone was listening. "May I come over?"

"I would love it."

She checked the locks on all the doors, left on lights in the bedroom, living room, and kitchen, picked up a complaining Daisy, and left through the front door.

She stopped by the two men in the car. "I'm going next door for supper," she said.

"Yes, ma'am. We'll keep watch. There's someone in the back as well."

*Good to know.*

She wished every step didn't jar the still wounded ribs. She had a long walk ahead of her. But there was no help for it.

The door opened as she gained the porch. Mrs. Jeffers clucked over her face and showed her inside.

"That nice FBI agent left you?"

"I chased him away."

Mrs. Jeffers cocked her head like a curious bird.

"I have to get away from prying eyes. I need your help."

Her sharp eyes caught Robin's. "Will it put you in danger?"

Robin shrugged. "I hope it will take me out of it. It's the only way."

"What can I do?"

"I would like to use your phone to call a cab, then I need you to distract someone who's watching the back of my house."

"Are you sure you should do this? That Agent Taylor . . ."

"He has his own agenda," she said. "I have to talk to my source without anyone knowing who it is." She hesitated, then added, "They threatened my family. You might be in danger, too, if they knew . . ."

"Hush, child. I have a pistol in my night table, and I'm a crack shot."

Another surprise about her neighbor. The thought of plump Mrs. Jeffers going after someone with a gun blazing was mind-boggling. The last thing she wanted, though, was to draw someone else into the line of fire. After this, she would keep a distance from Mrs. Jeffers.

"If I can use the phone . . ."

Mrs. Jeffers pointed toward a phone on a table next to a big, overstuffed rocker.

Robin had already found a taxi that operated in her area. She called and asked that she be picked up at a deli, three blocks away. "Twenty minutes," she promised.

She hung up the phone and turned to Mrs. Jeffers. "Can you take a cup of tea to the guy watching the house out back?"

Mrs. Jeffers's worried face creased into a smile. "An investigator?"

"Yep. Private."

"It will be my pleasure. My dear, I haven't had this much excitement since I ran away with my first husband. Then I discovered he was a rounder."

"It could be dangerous," Robin warned again.

"I look at your poor, sweet face, and I realize that," Mrs. Jeffers said. "I don't tolerate people who do such things, and

I'm old enough not to worry about whether death comes tomorrow or next year."

"But I do, Mrs. Jeffers."

"Maude," Mrs. Jeffers said softly. "If we are to be conspirators, it must be Maude."

"Maude then," Robin agreed. "One day you have to tell me about your first husband."

"Maybe the others as well," Maude Jeffers said with a twinkle in her eyes.

Robin restrained a giggle. She hadn't known there was a giggle left inside her.

Or perhaps it was a touch of hysteria.

Mrs. Jeffers made a cup of tea and carried it outside.

When Robin saw Mrs. Jeffers adroitly turn the man away from her, she slipped out the back door. She moved across the lawn as quickly as her bad leg allowed her, then through a yard to a side street. The effort winded her. Her breath came hard, and her ribs ached, though not as badly as last night.

Three more blocks. She turned left, then right, keeping to the shadows. She finally reached the deli. The cab was already there.

Thankfully, she sank inside the back seat, then checked the street. She saw no other cars going in their direction. And there could be no tracking device.

For a moment, she was proud of her subterfuge. It fled as quickly as it came. She'd also been proud of herself yesterday afternoon. She was a novice to this, and her only weapon, she hoped, was the unexpected.

An hour later she had her rental car. It hadn't been easy, not without a current driver's license in hand. It was even more difficult to explain why. That the last car she drove was a smoldering ruin. Explaining bad guys were after her didn't seem a good idea. Instead she pretended she didn't know it had expired.

"Oh dear," she said. "I didn't realized it expired. I'll have it renewed in the morning." She'd given him a game smile and asked him to speak to her insurance agent if he had a problem. Fortunately the company did not want to lose the business of that particular insurance carrier. She was finally given keys when she promised to stop back the next morning with a copy of a new license.

She got into the car and put the key into the ignition. It caught immediately and she hesitated. The image of a car on fire, of her leg caught under the dashboard flicked through her mind. The terror came back, paralyzing her . . .

*Get a grip.* She only had a few hours. Someone would check on her when she hadn't returned to her cottage. That someone would, most likely, call her boss, who, in turn, would probably call the FBI. She hadn't used her credit card, since the insurance agency would pay the fee, but she feared Ben Taylor was beginning to know how her mind worked. He would probably charm Mrs. Jeffers into telling him everything. He would find the cab, then the car rental agency.

He would be mad as hell.

The late Sunday traffic was light for Atlanta. She took several detours through the city streets, always checking behind her until she felt no one was following.

She stopped at an ATM and used her one credit card to take out a cash advance, then drove to a large drugstore, where she purchased a small voice recorder and billfold.

Then she went to the Varsity, Atlanta's most frequented hamburger emporium, and used one of its multiple pay phones.

Sandy answered immediately.

She tried to deepen her voice. "You said you'd call." She tried to sound like a distraught girlfriend if anyone was listening.

A silence, then, "I tried the number you gave me."

She heard the stress in his voice. "I lost the phone. I have to see you."

"My wife . . ."

"When can we meet again?"

"My wife is suspicious. Is there a number I can call?"

She gave him the number of the public phone.

He hung up.

She hovered near the phone. Her stomach rumbled. The aroma of frying onions and chili and burgers beckoned to her, but she couldn't chance losing the phone.

Finally the pay phone rang.

"What happened last night?" he asked. "I waited for you."

"I was ambushed on the way," she said. "You sent the message, then?"

"Yes. What do you mean, ambushed?"

"A SUV pushed me off the road. A man threatened to burn me alive if I didn't reveal your name."

She heard him swear. "Did you?"

"No. Someone came along." She told him the rest.

Then there was a silence.

"Why did you want to meet?" she asked.

Silence again.

"I heard they found a dead deputy," she prompted.

"It might have been an accident."

"I don't think you really believe that." She paused, then said, "They've called me at home twice. This morning they threatened my sisters and their families if I don't give them a name."

"You can't!" Panic raised his voice.

"You have to give me something I can use for barter. I need something strong enough that I can use as a threat this time."

"I don't have anything."

"Find it," she said, ice in her voice. She owed him, but he owed her as well. He had used her to do something he was afraid to do. She sympathized with his motives, and his fear, but her family was involved now. If there was a way she could protect both of them she would. If not, she would bargain with the FBI to protect all of them.

"There may be something . . . ," he ventured.

"What?"

"A photo . . . maybe it could be useful."

"I need it tonight."

"Where?"

"There's a church in north Atlanta." She gave directions. She'd done a lot of thinking about the "where." She'd attended a wedding there, and it had a huge parking lot with more than a few exits. Not only that, it was on a busy road. Not easy to be trapped there. She sure wasn't going to return to Meredith County.

"It'll take a while. I'm at my brother-in-law's house with my kid. I told them I had to get out to get cigarettes."

"No one is following you?"

"No."

"You might check for a GPS. I think that's how they found me."

Silence, then, "I'll see you in about two hours."

She hung up the phone. *Two hours.*

Robin suddenly realized she'd had only a piece of bread and peanut butter since morning. She went to the counter, ordered a cola and two chili burgers and carried them to one of the many rooms, each featuring a television and furnished with school-type chairs. She found a chair in a corner, where she could look out over the room. An almost hysterical giggle rose in her. Wild Bill Hickok used to do that a hundred years earlier: choose a chair in a corner of a room. She never thought she'd have to emulate him. She hoped she didn't end up the same way.

She ignored the churning in her stomach and tried to enjoy the food. Apprehension and, she admitted to herself, cold hard fear had dulled her usually healthy appetite. She knew she was an amateur playing in a field of professionals. All she had were books and movies to give her guidance. She did know Ben and whoever else wanted to could quickly find the car rental. But what good would it do them? Hers was one car among hundreds of thousands in Atlanta. Even the license plate wouldn't help unless there was a BOLO, a Be On the Lookout notice, and even then it was unlikely the police would spot her car. She just had to stay out of Meredith County.

Had anyone noticed she was missing yet?

Her bodyguards? Ben?

Had he tried to call her?

Part of her wished he had. She couldn't believe how much she wanted to hear his voice, to feel his arms around her. She had never thought she would feel that way. She'd always yearned to be one of those journalists who traveled the world. No attachments.

Now she had a story that might take her to that exalted level. The price, though, was climbing.

If Ben Taylor knew she'd left her house, he would be furious. But she couldn't live in a bubble, knowing people were outside wanting to burst it, and her unable to do anything about it.

She finished the food and glanced at the television. She had selected an all-news room, not particularly because of the station that was on but because the room was closed in. Most of the other occupants at this time were students, some studying despite the noise from the television. There was one older man. Alone. Reading a newspaper. He occasionally looked over toward her. She studied him. Work pants. Work shirt. Hair graying. Tired looking.

Still, apprehension ran through her. She wondered if she would ever go anywhere again without searching a room for someone suspicious.

Probably he was only curious about the bandages on her face and arms.

She looked at her watch. Time to leave. This was one meeting she couldn't miss. Since she didn't have a valid driver's license, she couldn't risk getting stopped.

Robin wished she still had that gun. Buying a new one would be a high priority. Fortunately she had neglected to take the permit with her to the press conference, so that was still safe at home.

She got up stiffly. As the day progressed she was finding new aches. She limped outside to her car, turning every few seconds to see whether anyone was following. She took a labyrinthine path through the parking lot. When she reached the rental car, she drove out the quickest exit and drove through the Georgia Tech campus before heading for the expressway.

The final Sunday service over, the church parking lot was empty except for a couple of oversized vans with a church logo. She drove around to the back and moved into a space between two exits. She was prepared to race out one of them, horn blowing.

As minutes passed, she clenched her hands together to keep them from trembling. Every headlight on the road made her heart speed.

She didn't know whether he would show or not. Whether he might lead someone to her. But she had nowhere else to go.

This wasn't a good idea. She'd known it since she left her house. Her mother would have called it stubbornness. Maybe that was part of it. No one was going to terrorize her. But it was also the only way she might protect her sisters.

A car appeared at one of the entrances and cruised around before stopping a short distance from hers. She didn't recognize it. She stayed in hers, but started the engine. She remembered the first time she'd met Sandy, when everything had started. She wished now she could erase those moments. Not so much for herself. More for her sisters. Her niece and nephew. She'd never wanted to bring evil into their lives.

Sandy stepped out of the car and walked over to her. He held a flashlight in one hand, his pistol in the other.

She nearly stomped her foot on the gas, but forced herself to wait as he flashed the light into her face and along her bandaged arms. He was silent for a moment, then put his pistol in its holster. "God, I'm sorry, Robin."

"You're alone?"

"Yeah, and I'm driving my brother-in-law's car. Told him I was having a bit of trouble with mine and asked him to look at it."

He went around to the passenger's side and got into the car. Reluctance was in every move.

He sat awkwardly, his gaze roving over the parking lot. "No one checks this place?"

"A church parking lot? I doubt it."

He opened a pack of cigarettes.

"I didn't know you smoked," she said.

"I quit years ago." His hands trembled as he lit one. "Just started again." His eyes were haunted.

She decided not to mince words. "Do you have something for me?"

His eyes pleaded with her, then he tried with words. "Damn it, you don't know who or what you're dealing with. You go to the FBI, and we'll all die. You. Your sisters. My family. I wish to hell I never said anything to you. But I did, and I'm sorry, but you swore . . ."

"There's something more important than my word now. How many people will die before they find you?" She was harsh out of desperation. "You started this by giving me information you knew—a lot better than I—was very dangerous."

"I never thought they would come after you," Sandy defended himself.

"They went after cops."

"They thought they could control the investigation. Threatening—hurting a reporter—would bring nationwide attention to them, even more so than three rural cops. I misjudged that. I'm sorry, Robin. If I'd thought I was putting you in danger, I never would have said anything. It was a mistake. I knew the families of those cops. I wanted their murderers caught. But I can't come forward."

"They'll find out I went on patrol with you."

"I never told anyone. It was against the rules."

"We had coffee."

"In out-of-the-way places."

"My family's involved now," she said, trying to make her voice more cool and sure than she felt.

"And mine. My son. My wife."

"At least talk to the FBI about witness protection."

He looked at her as if she'd grown another head. "Damn it, the moment I talk to them, I'm a walking dead man. Not to mention my family."

"They can protect you. Even your extended family. I've been assured—"

"You just don't get it, do you? There's a damn good chance they've been penetrated."

Stunned, she could only stare at him.

"There's been talk, rumors that there's a mole in the FBI as well as other local police agencies. If they learn I'm the one who has been talking to you, I wouldn't live long enough to testify. That's why I wanted to talk to you."

Stunned, Robin stared at him. "The FBI? Who?"

"I don't know. I just know what I've heard. That the local FBI has been penetrated."

"I don't believe it. They've talked to me. They've made it clear how much they want Hydra. They promised protection to my source."

"They can promise anything they want," he said bitterly. "But if there's an informer . . ." He stopped and she saw his hand tremble.

After a moment, he continued, "If the rumors are right, and either you or I talk, our lives wouldn't be worth a nickel. Not mine. Not yours. Not our families'."

# chapter eighteen

*Robin froze. A thunderbolt of* disbelief, then horror, tore through her.

She knew that corruption could be found everywhere, and she'd heard of the case of FBI corruption in Boston—agents who'd sent innocent men to prison to protect their mafia sources—in years past, but she'd felt safe with Ben Taylor. She'd had confidence in the FBI.

Just because Sandy speculated there was a mole in the FBI didn't mean it was Ben Taylor.

But unwelcome thoughts rumbled through her. Why had he been at the press conference before the FBI had reason to enter the case? Then the funeral?

He'd certainly been attentive to her, even though he disdained her occupation and sense of ethics. She hadn't even liked him in the beginning. There had been that weird attraction but, except with Mrs. Jeffers, he certainly hadn't been the epitome of charm.

*No!* Not Ben. She prided herself on being a good judge of character. But she had liked Sandy, and now his white hat was turning a very muddy shade.

"You didn't say anything about that before," she said, doubt in her voice. It occurred to her that he was making the accusation to keep her from going to them.

"Why do you think I came to you? No fed made a move until your article ran."

"There were jurisdiction problems."

"Hasn't stopped them in the past. They usually find a way."

"I don't believe it," she said.

"Why not?" he said bitterly. "If Hydra can . . . take over a sheriff's department, why stop at a few agents?" The questions were asked with self-condemnation.

Her reporter's mind logged the combination of guilt and fear and self-disgust, and yet he'd given her that one glimpse of the truth.

"How certain are you that someone from the FBI is involved?"

"After your article appeared, I was told personally we didn't have to worry about the feds. It was under control. Others were told as well."

"But no specific agents named?"

He shook his head.

"What about the Atlanta police?"

"Look, I wouldn't vouch for anyone right now."

"Not everyone in the FBI could be involved."

"No, but I wouldn't trust any of them."

"Damn it," she said. "Why did you talk to me?"

"You came to me, remember. You wouldn't leave well enough alone. Then I thought maybe you could be the answer, that the publicity would force federal authorities to dig deeper."

"You could get caught in the net."

"I'm a very small fish," he said.

"You didn't tell me how far it goes," she countered.

"I didn't know myself," he said. His gaze locked on hers. "Would you have done anything differently if I had told you?"

She honestly couldn't say she would have done anything differently. The story had meant everything to her. And even now she couldn't quite believe the scope of what he was saying. She surely wouldn't have believed him then.

Foolish to the extreme. She knew it now. But she was neatly trapped. Only more information would give her power. "At the very least, I need a bargaining tool," she said. "I need *them*—whoever they are—to believe I know enough that they have to leave my family alone." She paused, then said, "If I don't get it, I'll have to take my chances with the FBI."

He hesitated, then took an envelope from inside his shirt.

He held it for a moment as if weighing what he was about to do, then held it out to her. She took it gingerly and opened it. It contained a photo of a boat, a luxurious fishing boat from the looks of it. A group of men was gathered in front of it. She recognized some of them, including the deputy who had accused her of drinking, at the hospital.

She looked at Sandy, a question in her eyes.

"On occasion deputies are taken on fishing trips," he explained. "I took the photo after a trip last year."

She waited.

"It's one of the ways they ensure loyalty," he said bitterly.

"To whom?"

"Loyalty to the department. To each other. To the sheriff."

"Who owns the boat?"

"I don't know. No one seemed to know. We were always told it was a friend of the sheriff's."

She looked at the picture dubiously, unsure as to what good it would do her.

"Why is it important?"

He was silent for a long time, then said, "I asked a few questions. Innocently. Kinda like I wish *I* had a friend like this. I was told real quick never to mention the boat to anyone or the sheriff would get in trouble."

"I still don't understand . . ."

"The trips started at the same time we were told to avoid patrolling around private airfields and certain properties."

"Tell me more about the trips."

"After a year in the department, everyone is invited at least once a year, usually twice."

"Are the wives invited?"

He looked at her as if she'd sprouted wings. "Are you kidding? The attraction's booze. Women. Gambling. There's also a beach house in Fernandina Beach. I went there once with a group about two years ago. I don't know if anyone else has."

She was quite aware of the good ole boy syndrome, but somehow she hadn't thought of Sandy like that. He'd talked about his son, baseball, his wife.

"Everyone participates?"

"Some more than others. There's pressure . . ."

A chill ran through her despite the heat. How could this

have gone on without anyone noticing? Raising a protest? But she still wasn't sure how that helped her. "How does this affect the murders. And me?"

"Imply you know everything about the boat and beach house, that you know who owns them and how they are used. That you know the department has been told to avoid certain locations on patrol. That you have names. They can't risk the fact that you might really have them."

"It won't narrow possible sources to you?"

"There's nearly two hundred men in the department. More if you include the jail. They've all been on the trips. There's people who know more than me." He looked at her.

She stared at him with dawning horror. "How deeply are you involved?"

He sighed. "When I first joined the department, there were minor favors. We always knew there were some people in the county we couldn't touch. Some gambling joints we should ignore. Some stills to avoid. There was an extra ten dollars, or fifty sometimes. But things changed three years ago. Then the trips started. The 'bonuses' got larger. We knew we weren't supposed to get curious about small aircraft landing at night in small airfields."

"Why didn't you leave?"

"You don't leave the sheriff's department." He said the words in a flat, hopeless voice.

Blood ran through her veins like cold needles.

"How can I find out more about the boat and beach house?"

"You don't want to find out more," he said. "Just drop the bomb on them, then get out of the story. Maybe they'll let you alone."

*"Maybe?"*

He avoided her gaze and looked away.

They wouldn't let her alone, and she knew they wouldn't. So did he. She might delay them a bit. Unless she could checkmate them in some way. The more information she had, the more protection she had.

"What's the name of the boat? I don't see it in the photo."

"I don't know. It wasn't important. I don't even remember if there was a name on it. But we got on it in Brunswick."

"Where's the beach house?"

"Fernandina Beach in Florida."

"What's the address?"

"I don't know. We went down in a van loaded with booze. Spent most of the time drunk."

"Where is it when you get on the island?" she persisted.

"Couple of blocks off the main road."

"What does it look like?"

"Robin?"

"What does it look like, Sandy?" she repeated.

"Big Victorian-type house. Three stories, I think. Maybe a few blocks from a restaurant with a net in the window. Directly on the beach. I remember it had a pelican mailbox. That's all I know."

"I need names of the two men you overheard."

He shook his head. "No. I doubt they knew exactly why they were told to avoid that area. They didn't have anything to do with the murders."

"But they would know who told them," she countered.

The stubborn set of his jaw told her he wouldn't say anything more.

Perhaps she had enough. At least she had enough to start digging.

"That's it," he said. "That's as good as I can do." He jerked open the door and spurted toward his own car. With her bad leg, there was nothing she could do to stop him. She drove out behind him onto the highway that led to the interstate. The taillights of his car turned north while she turned south.

Time to go home.

She felt numb; her feelings were paralyzed.

*The FBI might be involved.*

Ben Taylor might even be involved. She didn't believe it, but neither could she take a chance that she was wrong. He'd been everywhere she turned since the murders. Despite the admonition from the paper's attorney, he'd pressed her for a name.

Or Sandy could be a liar of the worst sort.

Both thoughts were painful. She'd risked her career, possibly her life, on Sandy's truthfulness.

Think! Think about the next move!

She certainly didn't have a smoking gun, but Sandy seemed to think that mention of the boat might draw a reaction, might help protect them both.

As much as she wanted to flee Atlanta and head south to investigate the information Sandy had given her, she had to return home. She had to get her driver's license. She couldn't risk being stopped without it. She needed to get a new cell phone and reactivate her number. She had to be available for the call she'd been told was coming from the bad guys.

That latter thought caused her to exit the expressway. She couldn't delay reactivating her cell number. In fact she needed two cell phones. A permanent one to replace the one she'd lost, and a disposable prepaid phone that couldn't be traced to her.

She found what she was looking for: a twenty-four-hour discount store. In minutes, she had two new phones and a prepaid card for one of them. She paid for all in cash.

As she left the store, she studied the nearly empty parking lot, looking for anyone, or anything, that might be out of place. Nothing suspicious. The people going into the store were obviously coming off late shifts, or hurrying in for some essential item. Normal. Her keys in her hand, she hurried to the car and got in, immediately locking the door.

Then she sat back. The adrenaline that had carried her this far was fading quick.

Now what?

She really didn't want to go home. Her home was no longer a refuge. She suspected her watchers had discovered she was gone. She also suspected Ben would be called.

Would he be there? Demanding to know where she'd gone? Or looking at her with those inquisitor eyes?

She was too tired and heartsore to confront him tonight. She could go to a motel but she suspected she didn't have enough money to pay in cash, and she didn't want to use her credit card.

She started back home, trying to focus on her next step.

More digging. More investigation.

Thoughts roiled in her head. How much time did she have? She had slipped away this time. She didn't think it would be as easy to slip away again. From either the Hydra or the FBI.

She'd almost decided to tell Ben everything before she met

with Sandy. Now doubts nagged her. How well did she really know him? She thought she had rightly judged Sandy, but she hadn't.

And if not Ben, could his partner be involved with Hydra? His superior? If she gave them Sandy's name, he could die.

Just as her mentor's source had died. It had destroyed him. She had no doubt it would destroy her as well.

She couldn't take the chance.

The only thing she knew right now was that she couldn't trust anyone.

Ben was furious. Furious with himself. Furious with Robin.

She'd disappeared.

He shouldn't have left earlier. He'd sensed she was planning something, but he knew how badly she hurt. She'd never admitted it to him, but he couldn't help but see the pain in her face when she moved. Anyone else would be flat on their back.

He'd thought he had time to coordinate FBI teams to watch her house. He had resources now that his superior accepted the idea of live bait. He'd hated to do that, but it had been the only way he thought he could get her the protection she needed.

He should have heeded that gleam in her eyes, and the determination that he reluctantly admired.

He'd gone home for a shower and clean clothes, then called his boss's home to tell him about the latest threat to Robin. He was told then to put protection in place.

"The sisters?"

"I'll contact our offices in their cities, but I can't promise anything. You know how shorthanded we are."

After hanging up, he'd shaved, then prepared to go in to the office when the phone rang. "Wade Carlton," the voice announced. "I just received a call from the security detail at Robin's home. She's disappeared."

He wasn't prepared for the way his heart plunged.

"How?"

"She must have planned it. She went over to her neighbor's. The neighbor went out and talked to one of the detail watching the back of her house, allowing Ms. Stuart to leave without being seen." He paused. "We couldn't have stopped her anyway, but apparently she didn't want to be followed."

*Mrs. Jeffers!*

*God, didn't Robin realize yet the danger facing her?*

Or had she gone to persuade her source to release her from the promise?

He could only hope so for her sake.

He could only pray she made it back safely.

How did she get away from trained professionals? Especially with that limp and bruised as she was.

He left his apartment and drove back to her home. Lights were on inside. Two men were standing on the porch. He ignored them and headed toward Mrs. Jeffers's home.

Damien barked frantically as he took the two steps at a leap.

Mrs. Jeffers opened the door.

He tried not to glare at her.

"How good to see you, Agent Taylor."

He wasn't up to niceties. "Where did she go?"

"I don't know."

"How?"

"She called a taxi to take her to a car rental place," she said. "She needed a car."

"And you agreed to help her?"

"It seemed reasonable. She needed a car."

He gritted his teeth. "She shouldn't have gone alone."

She didn't reply.

"What cab company?"

She shook her head. "I didn't ask."

"The car rental company?"

"I don't know."

He stared at her with frustration. Then he saw Daisy. "She left the cat with you?" That worried him as much as anything had. Was she afraid she wouldn't return? Damn it.

He turned away and called his office. There were several agents on duty. "Call all the car rental agencies within a four-mile radius of here and see if anyone has rented a car to Robin Stuart. I want to know the model and license number."

He started pacing the room.

"She's a bright girl. She'll be all right," Mrs. Jeffers tried to assure him.

"She's an amateur who's playing in the big leagues. I can't seem to make her understand this isn't a television show."

"I think she knows that," Mrs. Jeffers said quietly.

He looked at her sharply, his opinions of her shifting. He liked her two days ago but thought she was more than a little eccentric.

Now he realized there was much more to her than he'd thought. Just as there was a lot more to Robin Stuart than he'd thought.

He worried now that he would never know how much more there was.

# chapter nineteen

*He was sitting under the* porch light on her doorstep when Robin returned.

Robin's stomach clenched when she saw Ben Taylor, red-eyed with lines of exhaustion etched around his mouth. She'd been dreading the confrontation since she left the church.

She really needed to hone her skills as a liar. He could see right through her.

He stood as she drove up and parked. She locked the car and tried to ignore the various aches and pains, including her leg, which was stiff and complaining. He visibly stiffened as she approached the door.

"Where in the hell have you been?" His voice was low, almost a whisper, yet the anger in it lashed at her. "It's almost midnight."

She was too tired and heartsick to be diplomatic. "I didn't realize I had to report to you," she retorted. "I'm not under arrest. Or am I?"

"Your editor called me. He was worried sick when his so-called protection informed him you were missing."

"I'm sorry about that, but I'm not used to having every movement monitored."

She moved ahead and fitted her key into the lock. Despite the anger, her heart pounded at his nearness. She wanted to feel his arms around her, to shoo away the new fears that plagued her and made her blood run cold. But even if he were honest, someone else in the FBI may not be.

She couldn't even ask him about it. What if he *was* the leak?

Too many lives now, including her own, depended on her not making a mistake. She was terrified his mere presence would cause her to make that mistake.

He tried to follow her inside. She didn't give him a chance. She turned to him. "I'm really tired."

His eyes turned to black ice at the dismissal.

Then he left without another word. She saw him talk to the two guards in front. Then he strode down the street to his car. He glanced back, got into the driver's seat, and drove off.

She stood there for a moment. Had she done the right thing? She didn't know. She just didn't know. But she couldn't trust anyone now.

She went down to where the men stood guard.

"I'm sorry," she said.

"Next time just let us know," the older man said. His name was Ted, she remembered.

"I wasn't sure you were the only ones watching."

"We haven't seen anyone else," Ted said.

"I hope I didn't get you in trouble. I'll tell my boss it's my fault."

"Just let us know next time," Ted repeated with some emphasis.

"If we're still here," mumbled his partner.

Robin tried a small smile. She might well need them in the future. "I'm really sorry," she said again. "Can I get you some coffee?"

The two men looked at each other. They had been embarrassed big time. She understood that. Yet she hadn't wanted questions, hadn't wanted anyone to guess what she was about.

"No, ma'am," he said. "We brought coffee with us."

Mrs. Jeffers's light was on. Probably anxiously waiting for her to get home, even at this late hour. Robin walked over to her house.

The door opened before she could knock.

"Saw you drive up, dear. Are you all right?"

She nodded.

"Agent Taylor was upset."

Robin thought that might be an understatement. "I know."

"He really is a nice young man," Mrs. Jeffers said. "Even if he is a little . . . testy sometimes."

Another understatement.

Daisy meowed plaintively and rubbed her body against Robin's slacks. Robin reached down and picked her up.

"Thanks for keeping her."

"Anytime, you know that."

Robin took Daisy home and fed her. She washed her face. Her eyes were as red-ringed as Ben Taylor's had been. She had gotten some sleep the night before because of the painkiller. Yet she knew she couldn't sleep. She kept seeing Ben's face. His anger had been stark. So had frustration. But there had been something else, something like disillusionment.

She poured herself a glass of wine, turned on the classical music station, then went into the bathroom and ran hot water in the bathtub. She didn't think she could sleep without its soothing comfort. Hopefully, it would take some of the stiffness from various abused parts of her body, and soften the hard edges of tonight.

After undressing and thankfully taking off the brace, she sank down in the bath, not bothering to take off the bandages. She would redo those as necessary when she got out. She leaned back, took a sip of wine, and listened to the music, allowing the hot water to soothe the hurting muscles.

Daisy jumped up on the edge of the bathtub and meowed.

Robin didn't want to move, but she knew she must. She pulled the plug, then used her arms to get to the ledge and get out. Then she stood on both legs. No brace. Just legs.

She had tested her bad leg before. A moment now and then in the past two weeks. But she hadn't wanted to push it. Now she did.

It felt good. So very, very good to place equal weight on both legs, to do it without a contraption of metal and leather. She took a step, keeping a hand on the wall and ignoring the crutches she usually used when she'd taken off the brace for the day. Another step.

She hadn't done her exercises in the past few days. Too much had happened. But though a little unsteady, the leg felt good. Solid.

She took a deep breath and slowly walked to the bed. She thought about calling Wade but it was far too late now. *An excuse.* She knew it. She should have called him much earlier but she hadn't been sure what, or how much, to tell him.

Would he and management demand, at this point, that she go to the authorities?

Daisy leaped onto the bed and Robin turned out the light. She was tired, too tired to think, but she also thought she might have trouble sleeping.

She didn't. She was asleep as soon as her head hit the pillow.

Sunlight streamed through her windows and the telephone jolted her awake.

Heaviness weighed on every move as she reluctantly picked it up.

"'Ello," she mumbled.

"Robin, this is Mason Parker." The attorney's voice was clipped. "A subpoena was served to me this morning as your attorney. You're directed to speak to the federal grand jury tomorrow at ten a.m."

That woke her up. She struggled to sit up. She drew in a breath as her ribs complained about the sudden movement.

"Robin, are you all right?"

"Not exactly," she said honestly.

"I heard about the explosion." He paused. "But we have to talk about a statement for the grand jury tomorrow. Can you come in today? Or should I come over?"

How could she say no if he learned she'd been running all over the city last night?

"I planned to come in. Bob Greene and I are writing a story about the attack on me."

"Just let me know when you get in."

She looked at the clock. Seven thirty. "I should be there by noon. I have to get a replacement driver's license this morning. Mine was burned in the car explosion."

"That's fine. Just ring my secretary when you get in."

"Mr. Parker . . ."

"Yes?"

"Does it make a difference that the subpoena wasn't served to me personally?"

A pause. Then, "You mean not appearing as ordered?"

Her silence answered the question.

"I told the FBI that everything was to go through me. The service to me is the same as service to you, except the paper is now involved."

She said good-bye and hung up. She stood, again testing her leg. She wanted to disregard the brace altogether. Maybe she could reschedule the final appointment earlier. Like this week.

Or maybe nothing could be scheduled at all.

Subpoena. Grand jury. Jail. For how long? Weeks? Months? She would have to talk to Mrs. Jeffers about keeping Daisy.

As those thoughts bounced in her brain, she did the much neglected exercises, then went to the kitchen to prepare coffee. Obviously feeling neglected, Daisy darted in and out of her feet.

"You may have to stay with Mrs. Jeffers for several days," she told the cat, praying it was only several days if at all. Perhaps the federal judge wouldn't force testimony.

Daisy meowed, whether in objection or approval Robin wasn't sure. She gave Daisy a feline treat, and then brewed her coffee.

She turned on the radio and sat down at the table with the coffee and her new disposable cell phone. She took a sip of the coffee, then called Lark, hoping that the music from the radio would mask her words if anyone was listening. She wasn't taking anything for granted today.

Lark answered her call immediately.

"Lark, can you go to a public telephone and call me back on my cell phone?"

"Robin?"

"Just do it. Please," she added, realizing how she'd sounded.

Then she called Star's husband at work. She doubted that phone would be tapped. Jeff had been a police officer, then a private investigator while working on his law degree. She told him to take Lark's family and Star somewhere safe.

"The baby is due in two weeks," he protested.

"I hope you can come back in a few days, but if not you're going to have to find a new obstetrician."

"I can't just up and leave."

"You have to," she said. "I can't tell you how vicious and dangerous they are."

"The FBI?"

"My source says they might have some agents involved."

A loud groan came over the phone.

"I'm sorry," she said. "If I'd known . . ."

"I'm a one-man law office. I can't afford to leave."

"Then send my sisters away. They both have a lot of friends. Just be careful of the communication between you."

"If anything happens to Star or the baby . . ."

He didn't have to finish the sentence. She was already sick to her stomach with fear for them all.

"What about you?" he asked. "Star will want to know."

"I've been ordered to testify tomorrow."

"What are you going to do?"

"I can't give them a name. Not when I know there might be a leak in the FBI."

"Hell, he should have the guts to go himself. He started this." The phone slammed down on the other end.

Robin pressed the "end" button, feeling more desolate and alone than ever. Her choices could destroy her family. Her word meant little to them. It meant everything to her.

But even if she was willing to give up the name to the FBI, she feared the bad guys would still go after her sisters.

Lark called then, and Robin told her to contact Star's husband. She should leave for a few days.

"The depositions!" Lark wailed.

"Get a postponement. I'll help with any legal expenses." Robin paused. "I'm so sorry, Lark. But even if I went to the FBI now you wouldn't be safer. I'll tell you about it later."

Her heart ached as she ended the call. Her life was one thing. But she'd had no right to bring harm to her sisters and their families. It was up to her to try to right things.

She forced herself to return to the bedroom and dress, reluctantly lacing the brace. She went to her guards outside and asked one of them to take her to get a driver's license. With her luck—and decisions—lately, she would be stopped by the police on the way to getting the license.

Two hours later, she emerged with the driver's license and asked her bodyguards to take her to the office. She would get a ride home. Going in to the office, she stiffened her shoulders. She sensed the next few hours were going to be nearly as bad as those this morning.

Ben sat in on the newly organized task force meeting. He and Mahoney had been supplemented by four additional agents. Two members of the Drug Enforcement Agency had joined them.

"The subpoena was served on Ms. Stuart's attorney this morning," Ron Holland said. "It requires her presence tomorrow."

"Fast work," Mahoney said, glancing at Ben.

"Time is of the essence. The current grand jury session ends in a week. There won't be a new one until next month." Holland looked at Ben. "What will she do?"

"I don't think she'll give you what you want," he said.

"Not many reporters hold out when faced with jail."

"I think she will," he said. "Then we'll have to protect her in jail, along with her family outside."

Holland glanced at him. "You haven't changed her mind?"

"I don't think anyone can change it."

"Any other suggestions?"

He didn't have any. He could only hope he was wrong. He'd made a mistake last night, lashing out at her. But he'd been eaten alive by worry. He'd imagined any number of scenarios, all of them bad.

Robin's face had been lined with fatigue and pain when she'd finally appeared. He'd wanted to put his arms around her, but there was something in her eyes . . .

Something had happened, and she wasn't going to tell him about it.

The pain of that sudden and certain knowledge ran unexpectedly deep.

He had been a damn fool caring in any way but professional. He'd lost his wife to ambition. He wasn't about to let his heart get involved again.

Holland continued to blister him with his eyes. "I thought you might be getting through to her."

"She thinks she's doing the right thing."

"You said her family has been threatened. Any leverage there?"

"She doesn't respond well to leverage."

"Assistance then."

"Assistance might help."

"Do what you can to help. Call the bureau offices in those cities."

Ben nodded.

"You tell her. You can be the hero."

"I'll try." He wasn't going to say he didn't seem to be her hero last night. Not with the suspicion he'd thought he saw in her eyes.

"Also explain to her what jail means," Holland continued.

"I imagine her attorney is doing that."

Holland turned to the others. "Okay, what do we have on members of the sheriff's department? Deputies living beyond their means, et cetera?"

"We don't have much," one of the other agents said. "We're halfway through the list. No big expenditures or change of lifestyles on any of them."

"The sheriff appears clean?"

"Lives in the same farmhouse where he was born. Drives a five-year-old pickup. Kids going to county schools. Vacations are mostly hunting or fishing trips."

"Keep trying. What about ownership of the property where the cops were killed?"

"The trail starts with the Somerville Corporation and ends in an offshore island. We've had Washington trying to hack into government files there. Also the banks. No luck."

"Okay, keep working on the sheriff's department. Nothing on the murdered cops?"

"Nope," said a woman who was with the DEA. "Same as the sheriff. Looks like they were just struggling to get by."

"What about the deputy who was just killed?"

"Nothing again," Mahoney said. "Recently divorced and

lived in a small rental house. A few days late on two credit card payments. Certainly doesn't live beyond his means."

"Check the divorce settlement and talk to the ex-wife," Holland said.

"Ex-wife moved away, but I'll call her," Mahoney answered.

Holland tapped his fingers on the desk. "So all we really have is one reporter and her informant."

"One stubborn reporter," Mahoney interjected.

Holland looked toward Ben. "Maybe faced with the subpoena she'll listen. Try again. She called you from the hospital. She obviously trusts you."

She *had*. He would have sworn that. But early this morning he had more than a few doubts. Was it that explosive anger he'd displayed? Or something else? In any event, he doubted that the subpoena would help the trust level.

But Holland rarely changed his mind, and Ben wasn't about to voice the reasons he knew would separate him from this case. He'd learned last night how much he was beginning to care for her. He'd have to learn now to damn well control those feelings.

# chapter twenty

*The day passed rapidly once* she arrived at the paper.

First the meeting with the attorney.

Together they forged a strategy for the next day. It was short. Asked to reveal her source, she would plead First Amendment rights. If the judge rejected it, then Mason would announce intent to appeal and ask for a stay of any contempt of court judgment.

Failing a favorable ruling, he would go directly to the Court of Appeals.

Neither of them were optimistic of the outcome. Recent decisions were not favorable.

After that demoralizing meeting, she and Bob Greene met to do the story on her attack.

"A bit late," he said.

"Mason wanted to read it before it goes."

"They really threatened you, those deputies?"

"A little more subtle than that."

"Have you considered giving up the source?"

"Hah. Many times." She looked at him. "What would you do?" she asked him.

"I would like to say I would do what you're doing," he said. "But I'm not sure I would go to jail for someone who doesn't have the guts to come forward himself."

"It's not that simple," she said. "He didn't have to say anything at all. He's scared to death for his family."

"It still isn't right to make you pay."

They went back to the story. He did the actual writing, but she described the experience. It all came back in the telling. The face. The threat. Then the flames. The helplessness.

Bob called the sheriff's office about the attack and was told officially that the department had found nothing to indicate an attack. No witnesses. No physical evidence. The incident was being filed as an accident. Blood tests had been taken. Charges might be filed against Ms. Stuart.

After he'd finished the story, which included the official pronouncements, a number of *Observer* staffers asked that she join them at Charlie's for—in their gallows humor—a wake for her. Just in case she went to jail the next day.

She agreed. She needed to relax. More than she'd realized. Especially with people who understood.

It may be the last time she could do that for a while.

Some staffers had left the newsroom earlier; several others waited to go with her, and they walked together. Their intent was clearly support, and she needed it. When she arrived, she saw Jack Ross as well as some other former reporters who'd left the paper. Jack gave her an okay sign as an *Observer* reporter pulled out a chair for her with a flourish. "The seat of honor. The only *Observer* reporter ever to go to jail."

"Lord, I hope not," she said to laughter.

"You got guts," the city hall reporter said. "Don't know if I would risk jail."

"You would," she assured him.

He didn't look convinced.

Then Michael walked in, greeted the reporters he knew, and was introduced to others. He took a seat on the fringes. "Bob told me about the party. Hope you don't mind."

Robin suddenly realized she'd had a tentative date with Michael. He'd even left a message at the city desk and she had forgotten about it.

Filled with remorse, she shook her head. "I'm sorry, Michael. I should have called you. The day has been . . . crazy," she paused, "but the flowers were lovely, and I needed them right then. Thanks."

"Don't worry about it," he said with a smile. "After hearing about the subpoena, I figured that you wouldn't have much time."

"Thanks. I don't. I just came here for a few moments," she said, trying to explain how she had time for a beer at Charlie's and not enough to call him.

"Just promise me a subpoena check," he said. "Rather than a rain check."

"You have it. Unless I'm in jail."

"Anytime," he said, and she thought again how easy he was to be with. Nothing like Ben Taylor.

Michael's eyes twinkled. He was all charm, and she had never trusted charm, but there was something impishly attractive about him that made her smile.

She needed a smile.

She mentally compared it to Ben's glower, then decided to enjoy the party. One glass of beer from the pitcher. No more. She had to keep her wits about her. So much to do tonight. So much to do tomorrow if she wasn't in jail.

She wanted to investigate the leads Sandy had given her, and she wanted to do it alone. She hadn't told Wade about the possibility that the FBI might be involved, nor had she told him about the boat. Then she would have to admit she'd met with Sandy, and she knew what he would think of that. She could lose her job for withholding the information.

She'd promised herself that if there was any hint that her family was in continuing danger she would tell both her editor and the federal authorities everything. But she hoped her silence would ensure the safety of her family, and herself. In the meantime she might be able to unravel pieces of the puzzle. But tonight . . . tonight she wanted to spend an hour or so with friends, with fellow journalists who understood what she was doing and why she was doing it. Despite what Bob said, she suspected most of those here would protect a source all the way.

She finished her one glass of beer, then announced she had to go.

Jack looked at her. "Do you need a ride?"

She shook her head. "I'll have Charlie call a cab."

Michael stood. "I'd be happy to drive you home."

She hesitated.

"I won't ask to stay."

She nodded. It was just a ride. And she needed one. She really didn't want to call her bodyguards, who were watching her house. Better there to make sure no one got in again. And Michael was safe.

"Thanks."

Ten minutes later they were on the road. He kept darting looks at her. "You would really go to jail?"

"If I have to."

"It could be dangerous."

"Right now, Meredith County is probably more dangerous."

"You think they really meant to kill you?"

"Yes," she said shortly.

His jaw set. "Bastards."

"Apt description."

"You shouldn't be alone."

"I'm not. I have a couple of watchdogs, courtesy of the newspaper."

"I would think the FBI would provide protection."

"I haven't asked for it. I can't work smothered by agents."

He took his eyes from the road long enough for a quick glance. There was respect in them, something that had eluded Ben Taylor.

Then his gaze returned to the street ahead as she gave him directions. The bodyguards were there waiting in the same car that had taken her to the office.

She didn't wait for Michael to go around and open the door, but got out herself. He was instantly at her side.

One of the private guards came over. "You going to be here tonight?" he asked.

"Yes. And I promise to let you know next time I leave."

"We'd appreciate that."

Michael followed her to the door.

She suddenly didn't want to be alone. "Coffee?"

"I would like that."

She opened the door to him and went inside. Daisy was there immediately, rubbing against her ankles.

He followed, and she noticed him glancing around the living room, at the overstuffed furniture and bookcases, the table loaded with books. "I like it," he said.

She went into the kitchen, got Daisy some cat food, then

prepared the coffee. Almost immediately she wished she hadn't invited him inside. He wasn't Ben. *Damn it.*

"Milk or sugar?" she asked him.

"Both."

Ben took it black. Like she did.

"Wish I could help in some way," he said.

"Just being here is a help."

He sipped the coffee. Ben had gulped it.

*Don't make comparisons.*

Michael leaned down and scratched Daisy's ear. To her surprise, Daisy allowed it, even purred. A plus for him.

He straightened and took another sip of coffee before setting it down. "Thanks for the coffee. I promised not to stay." His gaze held hers steadily. "I'll be rooting for you tomorrow," he said softly. "Maybe when this is over . . ." She liked that. No demands.

"Call me," she said.

He left, the scent of a very sexy aftershave lingering in the house.

She closed the door behind him.

She'd started for her office when the phone rang. Her stomach clenched. She hurried to the nearest phone and looked at the caller ID. *Unknown.*

Reluctantly, she picked it up. Before she could say anything, the menacing metallic voice came over the line.

"Did you have a good time at Charlie's tonight?" the voice asked.

"Yes," she said defiantly.

"I wonder if your sisters are having as good a time."

Did he know they had left, or were leaving? No indication. She was being followed, but did they really have the resources to do the same to her family?

"I'm glad you called," she said. "I have a message for you."

"The name we want?"

"A warning. I know about the boat in Brunswick. I know who went. I know who owns it," she bluffed. "I know a great deal more than that, and I think the federal government would love that information. Public corruption is very big with them."

A silence met her declaration. Had she really taken them by surprise?

"It's stalemate now," she continued. "I won't say anything about what I've learned to the paper or the feds if you don't hurt my family. But if anything, anything at all, goes wrong and one of them is hurt in any way, I'll have statements sent to Washington. Not the local FBI. Not the local police. I've already mailed three packages to people who will forward them to various agencies if anything happens to me or mine."

A metallic laugh. "You're bluffing."

"Try me." She slammed the phone down so hard she hoped she injured an ear.

It was risky, she realized. More than risky. But it was the only card she had. The phone didn't ring again. Had she won this round? Or had she made them more persistent in tracking her and those she cared for?

She wished fervently she could call Ben, tell him what she'd done, but she dared not.

The phone rang again. Her hand inched toward it, drew back, then grabbed the receiver. The only ID information was "private number."

That was also what showed when Ben Taylor called.

She didn't trust herself to answer. Sandy's warnings kept echoing in her head. Was Ben a mole, or was it one of his friends? Or in the office hierarchy?

The phone continued to ring.

She punched the "talk" button.

"Robin?"

Heat crept in her at the sound of his voice. "Yes."

"I overreacted last night," Ben said. "I want to apologize."

"I accept."

"Can I come over?"

"Because your superiors want you to?" she asked.

"Because I want to see you."

"I'm really tired."

"I'm close by."

"Now why am I not surprised by that?" She wanted to keep him at arm's length. No, much farther than arm's length. Arm's length, and she was a goner.

"I don't know. Why aren't you?"

"Because every time anything happens you're there." Even she heard the hard note that had crept into her voice.

"That's bad?"

"Convenient."

A short silence, then, "Good night, Robin," and the signal went dead.

She put the receiver down. His voice had grown cool, even cold.

Her soul turned even colder. There was no one she could trust now, except herself.

Ben turned off his cell phone from the vantage point of the attic of a house five doors down from her own. Earlier in the day, the FBI had convinced the salesman who lived here alone to move in with a friend for a few days.

He shouldn't even be here. He was not part of the surveillance team, but he'd stopped by and offered to fill in for an hour or so while one of them went for take-out. Something had happened yesterday that affected the way Robin thought of him, and he wanted to know what—or who—had caused it.

His foot crunched on an empty bag of potato chips that the previous watcher had used as he scanned the area around the house. Robin's rental car was still parked in front. He knew that the bodyguards had taken her in to work.

He also knew from an agent following her that she'd left the paper and stopped at a pub named Charlie's, then left with someone. Twenty minutes later, a tall, well-dressed man accompanied Robin Stuart to her door and went inside. Feeling like a voyeur, he watched a light go on in the kitchen. He was stunned at the jealousy that knotted in his gut.

It had seemed like hours, but the visitor left within thirty minutes, and a light went on in her office.

He scanned the two yards. He saw the private bodyguard's car in front. He knew another private detective was at the back of the house. He shifted his glance over to Mrs. Jeffers's house. Why, he didn't know. Just instinct.

He saw a flicker of a flame in back.

He didn't wait. He started running down the stairs and yelled at the other agent in the house to call the fire department. Then he raced out of the house and down the street to Mrs. Jeffers's house. Flames rose into the sky.

The men guarding Robin's house joined him. He reached the porch and rang the doorbell, even as he used his foot to try to break the door down. No luck. Then two other men were there. Between them they broke the door, and he rushed in.

The back of the house was in flames and smoke filled the interior. He heard frantic barking from upstairs and took the stairs two at a time. Mrs. Jeffers was on the bed. He tore a piece of cloth from a sheet and wrapped it around her nose and mouth, then another around his own. Then he scooped her up and told one of the men following him to take Damien, who still barked madly.

They both raced for the stairs. The house was rapidly becoming engulfed. Fire licked at the bottom of the stairs. It had been only minutes since he'd seen the first flicker of flames. Something was feeding the fire.

Heat embraced him. Heat and smoke. His feet felt as if they were burning.

*Outside.* He was outside. He lay Mrs. Jeffers on the ground, then collapsed. His chest gasped for oxygen and he was aware of someone breathing air into his mouth. He tried to focus. *Robin Stuart.*

He shook her away.

"Mrs. Jeffers?" he asked.

"Someone is giving her CPR," she said. She looked anguished against the wall of flames behind her.

The high-pitched wail of sirens came first from a distance, then neared. The street filled with flashing lights as firemen spilled out from trucks and manned their hoses. He struggled to sit up while a team of paramedics approached him. "Mrs. Jeffers first," he rasped, pointing to the woman. One paramedic went to her, and the other approached him.

Then several more appeared. One pulled an oxygen mask over his nose and mouth, and Ben took deep breaths, his lungs filling with air. Robin sat next to him, her bad leg spread out on the ground. No brace. She wore a robe over a T-shirt.

The sky was blood red with flames, and he felt the moisture of steam as streams of water mixed with fire.

The air felt good. He took several deep breaths, then took the mask off and asked the EMT, "How's the lady?"

"The older lady?" the paramedic asked. "Alive. She's on her way to the hospital."

Ben closed his eyes in relief.

The paramedic looked at his legs. "You have some burns there. Not bad, but they should be treated."

"No hospital," he mumbled. He breathed in the fresh air. His throat was scratchy but he didn't think real damage had been done, but Mrs. Jeffers's age went against her.

"Your lungs should be checked as well."

"Go," Robin ordered. She held Damien now, the dog squirming in her arms.

He realized he should. He wouldn't do anyone any good if his legs became infected. They were beginning to burn like the furies. But he would do it on his own terms, not in an ambulance.

A fire department captain came over to him. "Understand you're FBI?"

Ben nodded.

"Anything our fire inspector should know?"

"It moved fast," he rasped. "I saw a flicker, then it seemed the entire house went up in flames."

"He'll want to talk to you."

"I'll be available tomorrow." He gave the captain his card.

Something nagged at him. The fire had spread too rapidly not to be arson. So why the house next door to Robin's, unless someone thought Mrs. Jeffers had helped her? Unless, of course, they wanted another lesson.

Or a diversion.

He turned toward another man who'd received oxygen. He was the private bodyguard—Burt Stanley—who'd grabbed Damien in the house. "Is anyone still watching Ms. Stuart's house?"

"Campbell was watching the front. He's here now, watching Ms. Stuart. Berryhill was at the back." He looked around, then got to his feet and started toward the back of Robin's house.

Ben went after him. He was aware that Robin was trailing behind. He turned. "Stay here with Campbell."

She started to protest.

"Damn it, Robin, just listen for a change . . ."

She stopped, hesitated. Then nodded.

He followed Burt Stanley to the back. He saw a body lying on the ground and hurried over to it. The man still had a pulse.

Stanley disappeared and returned with two paramedics and a uniformed officer, who was already talking into his radio.

"Looks like a concussion. He was hit pretty good," said the paramedic who was examining him.

"Maybe he saw something," Stanley said hopefully.

"If he had he would be dead," Ben said flatly.

He turned and Robin was standing there, still clutching the tiny poodle. "What . . . ?" she started.

"Someone knocked one of your guards senseless."

"He's not . . ."

"No."

"Why?"

"They probably didn't want to take a chance he might see something. He's lucky he's not dead."

A myriad of emotions crossed her face. Realization? Fear? Definitely sorrow and guilt.

Her eyes went over the burns, then to his face.

"They're not going to stop," she stated as fact.

"No," he agreed. His leg burned and his voice was hoarse. He looked around, signaling to the FBI agent who'd been watching the house. He was standing on the fringes of the crowd, eyes intent on Robin. "Check out the house before the lady goes back in. Look for bugs or taping devices. Then don't let her out of your sight."

The agent nodded. "Damned if I know how someone got by us."

"Maybe after he started the fire. You were calling 911. I was running toward the house."

An EMT interrupted to say they were leaving. "You really need to go with us."

"No," he said but agreed to sign a statement waiving any liability or responsibility. He looked up from the papers and saw Robin standing straight. The robe she wore left little to the imagination.

"I think you'd better go home," he said, his gaze running over her.

Her face blazed, realizing the robe was plastered to her body. It was the first time he'd seen her face that particular color. Or maybe it was the emergency lights that sent red blasts of color through the darkness.

"I'm going to get dressed and drive to the hospital," she said. "Mrs. Jeffers doesn't have anyone." She hesitated. "Do you want to go with me?"

He wanted to accept. Perhaps those few moments had dulled that suspicion he'd seen earlier. But there were still questions in her eyes, and he needed his car. He needed privacy to make necessary phone calls and he had to go by his apartment to get some clothes. His slacks were burned and his shirt was covered with soot.

Robin still lingered. "Thank you for saving Mrs. Jeffers."

"Not necessary," he said. He hesitated, then added, "Thanks for the breaths of air."

"Not necessary," she echoed his words with a slight smile. Then it disappeared as her gaze moved to the gutted house. The blaze had been quenched, though embers drifted through the air. Robin's house had been hosed down as had been the house on the other side. The fire department would probably stay through the night until there was no more danger of the fire spreading.

She'd dodged another bullet.

Or maybe not.

It depended on what the perps had wanted to accomplish.

One thing he knew. The quicker she went into jail, the safer she would be. Especially if they planted an agent in a cell with her.

Now she stood there with her damp hair curling and bare feet, trying to hold a tiny poodle while clasping her robe. She looked even more appealing to him than she had before.

"You'd better dress if you're going to look after Mrs. Jeffers," he said, "and put on that brace."

"You're right, of course." She fixed him with an unblinking stare. "Are you always right?"

"No."

"I think that's comforting."

"Think?"

"I don't know anything, anymore," she said sadly and turned back toward her house, Campbell behind her.

He wanted to go after her, but her earlier words stopped him. *Because every time anything happens you're there.*

Now they hit like a sword in his gut.

Obviously she'd considered the possibility that he was involved in some way.

He'd been there again tonight. She would remember that soon. What trust he thought he'd built was gone.

He was startled at the dismay he felt, and not because it was his job.

Trust, once gone, was difficult to mend. No one knew that better than him.

He would recommend that another agent be assigned to her.

With that in mind, he walked to his car. He called his boss and told him what had happened, asked for additional agents to protect Robin Stuart. "She'll be at Eastside. A private bodyguard will be with her, but I want more."

Then, ignoring the pain in his legs, he pressed down on the gas pedal and headed for his apartment to pick up clothes, then to the hospital.

All the way he remembered her face. Damn it, she'd looked more angry than frightened. And that scared the bloody hell out of him.

# chapter twenty-one

*Robin found Mrs. Jeffers in* a cubicle in the emergency room, her mouth and nose covered by an oxygen mask.

She went over immediately and clasped Mrs. Jeffers's hand, which tightened around Robin's fingers.

Pain squeezed Robin's heart as she rested her huge purse on the bed. Mrs. Jeffers looked so small in the bed with an IV seeping its magic into her veins.

Dave Campbell, the bodyguard who had driven her to the hospital, waited outside. She had asked him to tell her when Ben Taylor came in—if he came in.

Her purse wriggled and she put a hand inside, praying Damien wouldn't bark.

She knew, though, that Mrs. Jeffers could not rest unless she was assured that Damien was okay.

Through the oxygen mask, she heard Mrs. Jeffers's labored breathing but those bright, sharp eyes were undaunted.

The older woman tried to say something but Robin couldn't catch the words. Mrs. Jeffers pulled the mask off with one hand. A nurse in blue scrubs tried to stop her, but Mrs. Jeffers turned to Robin. "Damien?" she asked in a barely audible voice.

"He's fine," she said. The purse moved.

Mrs. Jeffers apparently caught the movement and she tried to smile but it was more grimace and she started to cough.

Robin quickly lowered the purse to the floor and caught

Mrs. Jeffers's hand with her free one and squeezed it. "He's safe," she said.

"A fire wasn't . . . on my list," Mrs. Jeffers said in a hoarse voice.

"I wouldn't think so," Robin said, squeezing the plump hand tighter.

Then Mrs. Jeffers's lips quirked upward. "But a handsome man saving me was. They told me in the ambulance Agent Taylor carried me out."

Robin chuckled. Mrs. Jeffers had just lost everything, and she'd found a silver lining. Like the Unsinkable Molly Brown.

"I imagine *that* was high on your list."

"Right in there with finding a husband for—" A spasm of coughing interrupted her words. The nurse replaced the mask, then asked Robin, "Are you a relative?"

"A friend."

"Do you know if she's allergic to anything?"

"I don't know."

The nurse repeated the question to Mrs. Jeffers, who shook her head.

"Any relatives?" the nurse asked.

"I don't know," Robin replied, realizing how little she really knew about Mrs. Jeffers. She'd never spoken of family members. All the photographs in her home were old ones.

Mrs. Jeffers evidently heard the question because again she shook her head.

Terrible regrets racked Robin. There apparently was no one but herself who cared.

So much was gone. All of Mrs. Jeffers's treasures. Her photographs. Keepsakes memorializing successes on her list. A ticket from Carnegie Hall. A stuffed bear she won at a carnival. A record—not a CD—from a play she'd seen. Letters from a child she sponsored in Chile. They'd meant so much to her. Those small symbols she treasured when she'd crossed off a goal on her list.

And it was her fault.

Robin had no doubt she was responsible. Whether it was another warning, or a diversion, she didn't know. She only knew she was responsible for the pain of someone she cared deeply about.

And she didn't know what to do about it. Except expose the people who'd committed the act.

A woman who identified herself as a patients' representative appeared at the door. "Are you a relative?"

"Friend," she said again.

"I need some information."

"I can't help you much. Name. Address. Phone number. That's it."

"Age?"

"Eighty-two and proud of it."

"Next of kin?"

Robin shook her head. "She never spoke of anyone."

"Insurance?"

Robin shook her head. "I imagine Medicare. But I'll be responsible for what isn't covered."

"What happened?"

"A house fire. She lives next door."

"Your name?"

Robin gave her name, address, and phone number. The purse wriggled at her feet. Robin leaned over and put her hand inside as if looking for something. She soothed Damien with her hand.

A doctor appeared, looked at the chart, asked some questions, then ordered that blood samples be taken. He added that she should be fine, but he wanted to keep her at least overnight for observation and probably several days longer to make sure her lungs weren't damaged.

Robin followed her up to a room and watched as she was moved to a bed and the oxygen adjusted. When the last staff person left, she took Damien from her purse. He'd been amazingly good, as if he knew he had to be still. Once out, he frantically licked Mrs. Jeffers's hand.

Mrs. Jeffers looked at her gratefully, though the oxygen mask was still in place. Then her eyes closed.

Robin tucked Damien back into the bag as a male nurse came in to check Mrs. Jeffers's vital signs.

The room looked stark and empty. No personal possessions to personalize it even a little. No clothes. Not even a pair of slippers or a hairbrush. Robin swallowed hard. She knew how she felt when her car had exploded with so much in it.

Mrs. Jeffers had lost so much more. Every piece of clothing. Every personal belonging.

And where would she go after being released by the hospital?

Robin would ask Mrs. Jeffers to stay with her until her insurance money came, but her home was no safer than her neighbor's had proven to be.

A dark, terrible rage filled her. She could take whatever was thrown at her. She'd grabbed hold of the tiger's tail and accepted the consequences, but to hurt an innocent old lady and her beloved, harmless dog . . .

What did that mean for her sisters and Lark's kids? Had they done as she'd asked? Had they left their cities? Had they been careful enough?

Had her own threat ensured their safety or infuriated the Hydra into burning her neighbor's home? She had no way of knowing. No way to find out. She had to wait for her sisters to contact her. And Hydra.

And she had to be in front of a grand jury in a few hours. Maybe go to jail.

The magnitude of what was happening momentarily stunned her into paralysis.

*No! They won't win.*

She took out the notebook that was sharing her purse with Damien. He had nestled down in a wool scarf she'd provided for him.

Make a list. She thrived on lists.

First on the list: Find a safe place for Damien and her own Daisy. She knew an animal-loving friend who would probably take them for several days. Robin glanced up at the clock on the wall. Three in the morning.

She would call at seven.

Second: Find Ben Taylor. Make sure he was all right.

Third: Fax Star's husband's office. He would probably maintain contact with it. She had to tell him what had happened.

Fourth: Have a friend get some clothes and personal items for Mrs. Jeffers and keep her company. If Maude Jeffers was released, find her a safe place at Robin's expense. Try to find a relative or friend.

Five: Grand jury appearance at ten a.m.

Six: Call her boss and Mason.

She concluded the notes with large bold letters. GET THE BASTARDS!!!!!

When she looked at Mrs. Jeffers again, her friend's eyes were open. She pulled down the oxygen mask again. "That FBI agent . . . Ben Taylor . . . is he all right?"

"I think so. He had some minor burns."

"Is he at the hospital? Can I thank him?"

"I'm not sure where he is."

"He's . . . a hunk."

Robin couldn't suppress a smile. The words coming from the tea-drinking, dignified Mrs. Jeffers were incongruous, but then her neighbor frequently surprised her.

But then guilt settled over her. "I'm so sorry," she said. "The fire was my fault."

"Did you burn my house down?"

"No, but . . ."

"No 'but' about it," Mrs. Jeffers said. "Don't you fret. Nothing but things. Damien is safe. You're safe. That's what matters."

The fact that Mrs. Jeffers worried more about her than her own losses made her blink back tears. Surely Mrs. Jeffers must have friends. A relative somewhere?

If Robin went to jail later today, who would look after Mrs. Jeffers? She leaned over. "Are you sure there isn't anyone I can call?" she asked. "A relative?"

Mrs. Jeffers's eyes clouded. Then she shook her head.

"No sisters or nieces or anyone?"

She hesitated, then said reluctantly. "A . . . sister in Memphis. We haven't talked in years."

"What's her name?"

Again a reluctance, then, "Evans. Mrs. Jason Evans."

Not a first name. Just the married name.

But at least it was something.

Then Mrs. Jeffers started coughing again, and Robin replaced the mask. A few moments later, she closed her eyes.

Robin stood stiffly. She wrote a note, placed it on the table next to the bed, grabbed the purse containing Damien. She was near the door when it opened and she faced Ben Taylor.

He wore a denim blue shirt and jeans, and he was clean shaven.

There was little friendliness in his dark eyes. None of the warmth she'd felt days earlier, or even hours ago when he'd thanked her. It was as if a spigot had turned off. Or summer had changed into winter.

"Robin," he acknowledged. But he might as well have called her Ms. Stuart for all the warmth in his voice. Or lack of it. She was left with an inexplicable sense of emptiness.

"You didn't wait for me," she said.

"No," he said without explanation.

He went over to Mrs. Jeffers, who was sleeping. He didn't look at Robin as he asked, "How is she?"

"Holding in there." Her voice broke. "And more gracious than I deserve. She should be okay physically, but she's lost everything but Damien. I'm trying to find a relative."

He turned to her, his eyes dark and forbidding. Tension coiled between them.

She ached with the need to touch him, to feel his arms around her, to see that rare smile and know that he understood her desperate attempt to make things right.

Instead, his lips thinned. "How many more people are you going to hurt while playing Brenda Starr?" His anger was palpable.

She had decided to tell him everything. She'd decided in the past few hours with Mrs. Jeffers that she had to trust someone, that altogether too many lives had already been taken or risked. And surely he couldn't be involved if he'd risked his life for Mrs. Jeffers.

She owed him for that. A lot.

Her cell phone vibrated.

She tore her gaze away from his. "My cell phone . . ."

She went out into the hall, walked down the corridor to a window, and answered it.

"You're spending a lot of time in the hospital," came the metallic voice. "And with a certain FBI agent."

She froze. How did he know that? Was the caller here now? Was he down the hall?

"The grand jury meets in a few hours," the voice said.

"Testify, and your sisters will die the way your neighbor almost did. They're not very good at hiding."

A suffocating sensation tightened her throat. Did they know where Star and Lark had gone?

"You shouldn't have burned down Mrs. Jeffers's house," she said, trying to keep her voice level. "That was a deal breaker."

"Alas, it was too late to stop it."

"You admit—"

"This is your last warning," he cut her off. "Talk to the grand jury and people will die. We have someone who will know, someone . . . close to you."

"What do you mean?"

"You should be more careful about your friends."

Then the phone went dead.

She stared at it for a moment. Did they mean Ben Taylor? Were they telling her he was involved. That he was their mole inside the FBI?

Or did they just want to separate her from him?

She started back down the hall to Mrs. Jeffers's room. She would ask Ben about the fire. How had he happened to be there so quickly?

He was standing over Mrs. Jeffers.

She panicked for a moment, then reassured herself. He'd saved her neighbor. He wouldn't harm her now.

He turned and must have seen something in her face because a muscle throbbed in his cheek. "Robin?"

"How did you happen to be at Mrs. Jeffers's house?" she asked directly.

He stiffened.

"If you really want to know, I was keeping an eye on you."

Just then a nurse knocked and came in. Damien chose that moment to complain with a loud bark.

The nurse raised an eyebrow.

"Toy dog that barks," Robin explained.

"Heard that one before. Won't work," the nurse said, eyeing the bag, which was moving.

"I just . . . wanted her to know her dog is okay."

The nurse smiled. "Good thing I'm a little hard of hearing, but you'd better leave now."

Clutching the bag, she headed for the door. Any idea that she would confide in Ben had vanished. It was not only the disdain when he looked at her, but the call, the warning, that had been damning. Who else was close to her? Who else would know what happened in a grand jury room?

Who else would know where she was nearly every moment?

Saving her neighbor could well be a clever trick. Or, as he said, a diversion.

She was out the door before he could ask a question. Dave Campbell, her bodyguard, was there waiting for her.

She leaned against the wall for a moment, trying to focus. For several moments she'd thought—really believed—she could tell him everything and somehow the two of them, together, could end her nightmare.

What if she had been wrong about him being a good guy?

Blindly she walked with Campbell out of the hospital to his car. Not dawn yet, but it shortly would be.

With dawn came decisions that had to be made.

Ben knew he could have handled that better.

But the moment he'd looked at her earnest face, he'd known he was no longer an objective investigator. He saw entirely too much in her. She was suffering intensely about what had happened.

He didn't want her to suffer at all.

He'd seen something else. A silent plea for understanding.

But he *didn't* understand.

He didn't understand the plea when obviously she didn't trust him. For a moment, he'd thought . . .

But then her cell phone rang.

Her face had changed when she returned. Instead of anguish, there was suspicion again. Suspicion and determination. No more plea. No more gratitude.

He wondered whom he would trust if he were in her position. Probably no one.

He stood next to Mrs. Jeffers. In her hospital gown she looked small, like a broken sparrow. He doubted whether she knew anything, or had seen anything. She had been unconscious in bed when he'd found her, her miniature guard dog beside her.

"Agent Taylor?"

The words were barely audible within the oxygen mask.

He leaned over. "You're going to be just fine, Mrs. Jeffers."

She pulled the mask up off her mouth. "They say you . . . carried me out."

"I had that privilege," he said, taking her hand. "It's been a long time since I've carried a lady downstairs. Or upstairs for that matter."

"I wish . . . I'd been . . . awake. My . . ."

"List," he finished when her words died off.

"Doesn't count," she struggled to say. "I don't remember it."

"Do you remember anything?" he said.

"No. Damien went outside to water the bush. I looked out, like I always do. Those nice men were in front of Robin's house. I felt safe. Then we went to bed. I woke up with someone breathing into me."

She looked up at him. "I don't think I left the stove on."

"You didn't. The fire started outside."

"There's nothing . . ." She stopped. "That's why . . . Robin was so upset. She thought it was her fault."

"We think the same people who broke into her house might have set your house on fire."

"But why?"

"Because they like to hurt people. To scare them."

Mrs. Jeffers's face grew even older, the lines deepening. "They used me to scare her?"

"I don't know. Maybe it was a diversion of some kind."

"You . . . will look out for her?"

"I'm trying. She doesn't make it easy."

"She's . . . like a daughter to me." The woman's hand gripped his with unexpected strength. "She brought my Damien to me." A faint smile creased her lips. "Broke rules."

"I know," he said, smiling at the vision of Robin's wriggling purse and weak but valiant explanation to the nurse. She'd known Maude Jeffers wouldn't rest until she'd seen Damien for herself.

"That's why . . ." A fit of coughing interrupted the words.

He replaced the mask over her face. He leaned down. "I'll take care of her," he said.

Her mouth formed the words, "Thank you."

He squeezed her hand and reluctantly went to the door. He looked back. Her eyes were closed.

He was surprised at the heaviness centered in his chest. He'd never had a mother. Or father, for that matter. None he knew, anyway. There had never been anyone but Dani, and that had been enough for him to keep other relationships at bay.

You didn't miss what you never had. He'd told himself that repeatedly. But he did, and with an ache that tore through him.

Heaven help whoever had caused Mrs. Jeffers's pain. And terrorized Robin Stuart. Because he meant to make them pay.

# chapter twenty-two

*Dave Campbell drove her home.* They arrived a few minutes before five a.m.

The air still smelled of smoke as she stepped out of the car. Her eyes were drawn to the blackened skeleton of Mrs. Jeffers's home.

She closed her eyes for a moment, remembering it as it once was. Damien sitting up in the window. Mrs. Jeffers peering out at the world from a place she thought safe.

Tears welled up behind her eyes. Damien ran over to his old home and sniffed. Then stood there, looking confused.

"Come on, Damien," she called and he pranced over to her as only poodles can do. But he kept looking back.

Two men stepped out of a dark sedan and approached her and Dave Campbell.

"FBI," he said. "We've been assigned to look after Ms. Stuart."

She remembered one from last night. He'd been at the scene of the fire. So they'd been on duty earlier, just without her knowledge.

"I'm Agent Bill Maddox," he continued. "And this is Agent Jerry Markum."

"I have some guards."

"We know," he said. "The more the better. I've been assigned to take you to the courthouse," he said. "Jerry will stay here."

"Afraid I'll skip?"

He smiled but there was little humor in it. "No, ma'am. It's strictly for your protection."

"I'll be inside for about an hour," she said. "Then I'm going to get some breakfast before going to the courthouse."

He nodded. "I'll be in front. Agent Markum will be in back."

*In other words, no sneaking out.*

Damien growled and started toward Maddox with his ears standing up as much as a poodle's ears could.

Maddox ignored him.

Robin picked him up and took him inside. Daisy immediately joined them, meowing. Robin fed them both.

Leaving both munching contentedly enough, she went to her room, found a plastic cosmetics bag. She filled it with her toothbrush, toothpaste, some cosmetics, and a hairbrush. She put the case in the purse vacated by Damien along with her two new cell phones. Then she found her gun permit and placed it, and her one remaining credit card, in the zipper compartment of the purse.

What to wear to a grand jury hearing? Then possibly jail?

She chose a dark blue pants suit. She thought about wearing the silk blue blouse but that may not be practical for what she had in mind. If, that was, she wasn't in jail. Instead she chose a washable cotton shell.

Finished, she regarded herself in the mirror. She still had a bandage on her face. Her eyes looked bloodshot.

She looked at her watch. Six ten.

She went into her office and made copies of the photo Sandy had given her. She blew up several aspects, zeroing in on faces, then printed them out. The last copy jammed in the machine. She tried to fish it out, but the page was jammed internally. A glance at her watch again. She was already late. She replaced the top, then turned the computer off. She tucked the other copies in her purse, which was already beginning to bulge.

"I'm ready," she said to the FBI agent waiting outside next to his car.

She directed him to a pancake restaurant two blocks away. Agent Maddox went in with her. She told him to order bacon and eggs for her while she went into the restroom, her purse clutched in her hand.

She knew this particular restroom. It had only had one

large room, and a door that locked. She turned on the water, then started making calls on her new disposable phone.

Four of the six calls were successful. She found someone who promised to look after Daisy and Damien, and someone to tend to Mrs. Jeffers's needs, including finding her a furnished apartment and purchasing some clothes. Then she called on a friend she hadn't seen in a while but was the same size as herself. After explaining her need, there was a gasp, then a certain excitement. Done. Finally, she'd called Jack Ross, her mentor, and asked the biggest favor of all.

Then she made her way back to the table and a worried FBI agent who obviously had spent the entire fifteen minutes staring at the door and tapping his finger on the table.

Robin approached the grand jury room, Maddox in tow. The bacon and eggs had not settled well in her stomach. Perhaps nothing would have, but for Maddox's sake, she had forced herself to eat every bite.

Bad move. Her stomach was a mass of writhing nerves.

She, who had so respected the law, been taught by her father to honor it, was about to defy it.

Dear God, but she was scared.

It was her against the force of the United States government. Not only the government, but something so evil she couldn't totally comprehend it. She didn't have much hope she would prevail.

Not having any rest didn't help.

Nor did seeing Ben Taylor outside the courtroom help. His back was to her, but she recognized the lean body and dark hair, the impatience that was obvious even when he stood still. As if sensing her, he turned. Their gazes touched for a moment. Then he turned again back to the man standing with him, as if she didn't exist.

No wishing her well. No quirky smile. But then she had tried to tune him out, afraid to trust him. Afraid to trust anyone at this juncture.

The hallways filled. A cross section of America entered the room before the door closed and a bailiff took his position next to it. The grand jury was to meet at eight. She was scheduled to testify—or not—at ten. A large number of men and women, all in suits, including Ben and his partner, waited outside as well. Some sitting on benches. Some leaning against the wall. She took the wall. She was too edgy for a seat.

To her relief, she saw Mason hurry down the hall. He approached her with a smile, then steered her down the hallway, out of earshot from others apparently waiting to go inside the room. "Heard about the fire last night. I'm sorry about your neighbor."

She nodded.

"How is she?"

"Angry at the bad guys," she replied.

"Good for her." His gaze bore into her. "Did it change your mind?"

She shook her head.

"As I told you, I can't go in with you. You're on your own. But you can ask to come out and talk to me."

"Do you really think they'll hold me in contempt?"

"I don't know, Robin. I know the U.S. attorney said he intended to ask that you be held for contempt if you don't tell them what he wants to know. But that might have been a ploy. Judges, even federal judges, are notoriously loath to send reporters to jail."

"What about this judge? Do you know much about him?"

"I've asked around. He's tough," Mason said. "Defense attorneys don't like coming before him. But on something like this, I just don't know." He paused, then added quietly, "No one will think less of you if you tell them what they want to know. Grand jury sessions are secret. No one will know what you said."

"Not according to the phone call I received."

"What call?"

"Early this morning after the fire. The caller said they have someone on the inside, that they will know exactly what I say."

He stared at her. "Did you report it?"

"To whom?" she asked. "He claims they have someone who will know what went on in the courtroom. That could be a U.S. attorney, his assistants, FBI agents. Even members of the grand jury themselves. He threatened to kill my sisters if I said anything."

"You should have called me. I could have gone to the judge."

"It just happened hours ago. After the fire. And why would anyone believe it? The U.S. attorney could claim I was making it up to avoid obeying the court."

"The fire gives you credibility," he said. "So does the attack in Meredith County."

"The *accident* in Meredith County, according to the sheriff's department."

"I think I should take this to the judge."

"And he would have to take it to the U.S. attorney. I can't afford to take the chance that he might say something to the wrong people."

"Be careful of that tightwire you're walking," he said.

"I don't know what else to do," she said, hearing the uncertainty in her voice and hating it.

"Tell me everything."

She told him about the earlier threatening call. But she didn't tell him about the meeting with Sandy, nor the photos. He was the paper's attorney, not hers. She didn't know his legal obligations. Were they to her? Or to the paper? If she told him, would he tell her editor? The publisher? Would they try to force her to drop the story? Without the newspaper behind her, she had no chance against Hydra. But if she was able to get evidence . . . hard evidence . . .

"You believed them?" Mason said. "About an insider?"

"They seem to know too much about me," she said. "They said they knew where my sisters went to hide. Yeah, I believe them."

"Ben Taylor." His name seemed to echo through the corridor as an officer of the court announced it. She turned and watched as he moved toward the door. His gaze met hers, but it was as indecipherable as it had been the first time she saw him.

Mason watched her face. "You don't think *he's* involved?"

"I don't think so. But I'm not sure of anything now."

Just then Mason's cell phone rang. He looked at the number. "I have to take this. I'll be back." He went down the hall.

Twenty minutes later, he returned. "I talked to Reese. We'll go ahead as planned today," Mason said. "If there is a contempt citation, we'll appeal immediately and talk to the judge."

Ben left the grand jury room then. He glanced at her, his

face softening slightly, then he approached her. "We have someone guarding Mrs. Jeffers," he said.

His eyes met hers but she couldn't read them, any more than she had read them that first day she saw him. Had he just recommended that she be cited for contempt? Or had he fought against it?

Or was he a conduit for someone else?

"Thank you," she said, hoping he didn't hear the pounding of her heart.

"How is Damien?"

"Missing his mistress." Her voice broke slightly. She hated to hand Damien over to someone who was a stranger to him. Daisy as well. And she hated the uncertainty she felt about Ben.

She turned away, back to Mason.

"Robin Stuart." The same man, the same sonorous voice that had called Ben earlier, called her.

Mason reached out and squeezed her arm. "Remember . . ."

"I know," she said. "The paper will support me. Thank you." Then she turned, stiffened her back, and went inside.

She'd been in the federal courthouse before and had covered several civil and criminal trials. But this room was different. It was meant for the members of the grand jury, not spectators and certainly not anyone on her side.

She was directed to the witness chair and sworn in.

A cold knot formed in her stomach.

Joseph Ames, the U.S. attorney, approached her.

"Miss Stuart. I have an article you wrote." He handed it to her. "Who gave you the information in that article?"

She thought she was prepared. She wasn't. Still, she parroted the sentence Mason had suggested. "I believe that information is protected under the First Amendment and therefore I cannot answer."

"I'm going to ask you again."

She repeated the statement.

"Judge Davenport, I ask that you direct the witness to answer the question."

The judge turned to her. "Ms. Stuart, I'm sure you've been advised there is no such legal privilege in withholding information. You are directed to answer the question."

Robin hoped her voice wouldn't waver. She believed in

what she was saying, what she was doing. Someone trusted her. Regardless of the threats, she was not going to betray that trust.

She repeated her answer.

The judge's gaze bore into her. "Ms. Stuart, you know the penalty if you do not comply. I can find you in contempt of court and send you to prison until you comply."

U.S. Attorney Joseph Ames spoke up. "I would recommend to your honor that Miss Stuart be given six days to reconsider her answer."

"This grand jury has only seven more days of its term."

"Yes, your honor. There's time. I would rather have an answer from this witness than send her to jail."

Robin tried to hide her surprise. And elation. Six days of grace. Six days to discover what Hydra was trying so hard to cover. Maybe all her efforts this morning would bear fruit after all.

Federal Judge Davenport looked to the foreman of the grand jury, then back to her. "I agree. I don't enjoy putting reporters in jail. But I will, Ms. Stuart. You have six days to reconsider. You will return here next Monday at nine a.m. Be prepared to go directly into custody if you don't comply."

"Yes, sir," she said.

Relief flooded her. She didn't care why Judge Davenport had relented. She only knew she had six days. Six days to find answers. Six days to make the identity of her source irrelevant.

Now if only her plan would work . . .

After the hearing, she went to the newsroom. All the staffers gathered around her to hear what had happened. Though the proceedings were secret, *she* could tell what she'd said, and what the judge had ordered.

FBI Agent Bill Maddox had accompanied her there, although the building was well protected and had been since 9/11. Guards checked badges and went through personal belongings as if it were the courthouse.

Then she and Bob Greene wrote the story of the grand jury session together. When they'd finished, she looked at the clock. Two p.m. Traffic would start to pile up in another hour.

"I'll take the story to Mason," she offered, though it was

unnecessary. He could read it on his computer. "I have a few questions," she added.

She started for the elevator up to the executive offices. The agent followed her. She shook her head. "I'll be right back down," she said.

"Ben will have my head," he said.

She shrugged. "Your choice."

Once on the sixth floor, she got out and headed toward the restroom. "I'll be several minutes. I have to put some makeup on."

She saw him eye the men's room next door. Just as she had hoped. If he hadn't, she would have had to find another way to escape him.

"Don't leave the restroom until I knock on the door," he warned.

She agreed and went inside.

She waited about eight seconds and looked outside. He was gone. The stairs were around the corner. She headed for them and went down to the floor below and hit the "down" button, hoping that the agent had returned to his post outside the restroom.

He wasn't on the elevator. She pressed the button for the ground floor, biting her lip while it stopped at two other floors. She wanted to rush out the door, but she didn't want to draw any attention. Instead, she waved at the building's guard, who was signing someone in, and walked out onto the street.

She left the building, went down an alleyway, then into a large bank building and out the back way, exiting on a different street. *One more block to go.* She walked as quickly as she could, trying to make her stride as normal as possible. She passed two more buildings, then entered the third.

She called the friend she'd talked to earlier, a member of the Press Club who'd left a competing paper for public relations. "I'm free for six days," she said. "Were you able to bring some clothes?"

"I heard. It's all over the television and radio. Yep. One skirt. Two blouses. Two pairs of jeans. And the other things you asked for. All in a big duffle bag, the one we took rafting that weekend."

"Perfect. I'm in the lobby."

"I'll leave it in the second-floor restroom. It's to the right when you get off the elevator."

"You'll never know how much I appreciate it."

"Anytime. You were there when I needed a friend. Just be careful."

She took the elevator up and found the restroom. The duffle was in the handicap stall.

She locked the stall door, then took off the brace. It was a sure way to identify her. She looked at it for a moment. She had less than two weeks to go before removing it. *If*, the doctor told her, the bones had thoroughly healed. They were. They had to be.

She removed a long peasant skirt and blouse, then a pair of dark pantyhose and flats from the duffle. A pair of dark glasses. A Braves baseball cap. Patty had done her proud.

She hurriedly undressed, then pulled on the pantyhose. They would help hide the scars on her legs. Then she buttoned the blouse and slipped on the skirt.

She put the pants suit in the duffle, along with the brace. She had to work to fit it in but finally she was able to zip it up. She put on the sunglasses and baseball cap, and opened the stall. She looked at herself in the mirror.

No more businesswoman. She looked like a free spirit in town for a baseball game. Not perfect. But hopefully she'd eluded both the FBI and the bad guys.

Freedom from the brace felt wonderful. Nothing else did. She was taking chances no reasonable person would. Holding on to the railing, Robin took the stairs going down to the street floor.

Then she was on the main floor and out the door. She forced herself to stride casually, trying to correct her limping gait. She tried to look like every other woman walking swiftly down Atlanta's streets.

She reached the underground parking lot where she'd asked Jack Ross to park the car. She knew the size and model and had memorized the license plate. She wanted nothing in writing.

Robin found the car. The key was in a magnetic holder on the underside of the car. She unlocked the door and slid inside. Then she sat there for several moments, wanting to make sure she'd not been followed.

She started the car finally. The parking ticket was in the compartment between the two front seats. She rolled out of the parking facility, paid the parking fee, and turned down the street. Instead of getting on the expressway, she drove two miles east and stopped at a branch of her bank. Ten minutes later she'd taken out six thousand dollars, nearly everything in the account. She didn't want to use her credit card on this trip.

By now, Betsy Meeks, who she knew from an animal rescue group, would have picked up Daisy and Damien, and Naomi, her friend from the Food section of the paper, would have purchased a nightgown and other items for Mrs. Jeffers and be making sure she had somewhere nice to live until Robin returned.

She made her way onto the expressway, and headed south toward Macon and the Georgia coast. If she could find the boat, perhaps she could trace the ownership to Hydra, or to someone who could lead her to Hydra. If the fishing trips were as frequent as Sandy implied, the boat probably had a permanent mooring in Brunswick.

The car she was driving was a twelve-year-old model but Jack had kept it in excellent shape. He had expected to give it to his grandson when he graduated. Instead, he attended a funeral when his grandson and three other students were killed on their way home from spring break.

It had been sitting in Jack Ross's garage since then.

She knew about the car because he'd offered it to her after her first accident. She declined because her insurance would replace her vehicle and she knew exactly what she wanted.

When she had called him this morning, he'd readily agreed to lend it to her. "You know I've always liked your instincts," he said. "But you're in over your head. I'll go with you."

"No," she said. "I've already nearly gotten one friend killed and put my sisters in danger. No one else. Just the car. That's all I need. I know how to dig. You know that."

"What if the boat isn't there?"

"Then I'll try the ownership of the beach house, but I expect that, like the property in Meredith, it'll be owned by some corporation on an island in the Indian Ocean. But if I can find that boat, and hang around, maybe someone will lead me to an actual person."

"I don't think . . ."

"I've gone over and over it," she said. "They seem to know everyone I talk to, everywhere I go. My source says law enforcement people are involved, and I have to believe them. I'm using a disposable phone, and I'm in a public restroom with the water running. I know how to avoid them, but I must have a car that's not traceable."

"I still think someone should go with you."

"Everyone in Atlanta knows you," she said. "If you drop out of sight, someone will put two and two together. The only thing that works is if I get a car no one knows about."

A pause on the phone. "Okay, baby girl," he said gruffly, using his nickname for her since the first day she entered the newsroom. "I've done stuff that would curl my innards these days. Do you have a weapon?"

"I will. I have a license."

"I don't want you killed," he said. "I sure don't want to contribute to it."

"This is the best way I know to keep alive," she said.

"There's no cop you trust?"

"Even if there was one, he would have to report to his superiors, and I don't know who there can be trusted."

"No one knows where you're going?"

"No."

"That scares the hell out of me."

She made her strongest shot. "You would have gone under the same circumstances. You would have wanted the story."

Thank God, he didn't.

"I'll never forgive either of us if anything happens to you," he said. She knew, though, he'd conceded.

"I'll call you."

"And if you don't?"

"Call this number," she said. She gave him the well-memorized number of the attorney in California. "I'll keep him posted."

"Tell me where you want me to leave the car."

She told him where she wanted him to park it

"It'll be there. For God's sake, be careful, baby girl."

She would have been insulted by that term if anyone else had said it, but Jack, a legend in Georgia newspapering, was a force of his own.

She looked in the rearview mirror for the umpteenth time but saw nothing familiar, only a constant stream of trucks. An exit was coming up. One that led into a small town called Jackson that had the world's best barbeque sandwiches.

Robin twisted around the small town, then stopped for some sandwiches and coffee to go. When she got back into the car, she glanced around. Only local county license plates. She pulled out and took a county road that would eventually hook back up with the interstate ninety miles south.

It was a road that ran through tiny hamlets, towns left to die when the interstate went through. There was no other traffic.

She'd traveled it years ago as a rookie reporter covering the local spelling bee contests.

She stopped at an overgrown roadside park and ate in the car. A lumber truck rambled past, then a pickup. That was all.

The car clock said eight p.m. It would be dark soon, and she'd never cared about driving in the dark, especially since the accident. She would stop at the next motel.

On this road, it would probably be the Bates Motel, complete with a resident psychopath. Couldn't be worse than the passel of psychopaths she was facing now.

Could she do what the FBI hadn't been able to do? Was she tilting at windmills but with a far deadlier consequence than Don Quixote faced?

# chapter twenty-three

*Ben quietly raged inside.*

He never should have suggested someone else handle the surveillance. He'd known how creative she could be. She'd managed to outfox everyone just two nights ago.

Her seeming acceptance of FBI protection, though, misled the detail. She knew, and they knew, that she was not a suspect, and no restrictions had been placed on her by the federal judge. She probably also knew that if she hadn't accepted FBI protection, they would have provided surveillance she couldn't control as well.

He'd underestimated her resourcefulness several times. He couldn't blame the agents. He *could*—and did—blame himself.

But he'd realized he had to get away from her before he did something really stupid. And in doing that, he'd probably committed the biggest blunder of his life.

Maddox was both humiliated and defensive. "She wasn't in custody."

"She might have been kidnapped."

"No. She meant to lose us."

"How do you know?"

"That newspaper building is as tightly secured as ours," he said. "A guard saw her leave. She was alone. She waved to him."

"And you were where?"

Maddox winced. "Bathroom. She said she would be in the

ladies' room for several moments putting on makeup. I needed to take a leak. I have a wife. I know how long putting on makeup takes."

Not Robin Stuart, Ben wanted to say. But Maddox may want to know how he knew that.

"She has an incredibly creative mind," he said. "Unfortunately it's not always tempered by caution. I should have warned you."

"You did."

"Apparently not enough," Ben said.

"I'll probably be sent to Alaska," Maddox mused woefully. "My wife will not be happy."

"See if you can help find her," Ben said. "Before the bad guys do. Check with her friends. See if she borrowed a car."

Maddox nodded. "You?"

"I think I should check her house."

Maddox started to say something, then snapped his mouth shut. "I'll question the other *Observer* staff members."

"You do that."

Ben drove over to her house. *Daisy.* She wouldn't have left Daisy alone, nor Damien. Were they with her? He knew from Maddox that they had been in the house when she'd left this morning. That meant she had to leave a key somewhere for someone to get inside.

He still didn't understand what had turned her against him. His attitude? Granted, he'd never been very diplomatic, but for a while he thought they had connected on several levels. He should have known that lawmen and reporters were like oil and water.

Hell, he *had* known it.

He tried to think what she would do. He doubted he could get a search warrant this soon, especially since she left on her own accord. The one thing he did know was she wouldn't leave the animals alone. Therefore someone would be coming to fetch them.

He could always plead concern for Mrs. Jeffers's dog, but he could also claim there was reasonable cause to suspect foul play since she'd been attacked earlier and threats had been made against her. It wasn't as if he were gathering evidence to use against her.

*Damn it!*

He'd decided not to involve Mahoney. He was willing to risk his own career. He wasn't going to do the same to Mahoney, who was nearing retirement. Instead, he called his partner and told him what had happened. "Maddox is going to talk to staff members. See if you can get the names of other friends. Talk to them."

Then he ignored every traffic law speeding to her house. He supposed that the agents were still parked in that house down the street. The private investigators, though, were gone, dismissed when the FBI took over.

Maybe a bad decision.

They couldn't do any worse than his own people. Or himself. Maybe *he'd* sent her running.

Or maybe she was on the trail of something.

If so, she was in more danger than before.

He was going to sift through everything in that house. A name on a pad. Something on her computer.

To hell with rules.

When the straight road started wavering, Robin knew she was in trouble.

Her eyes no longer focused. She pulled off the road and turned on the overhead light to read the map. The road led to a small town. Hopefully there would be a motel. She wished she had bought a couple of bottles of water and a cooler full of ice.

How much farther could she go without sleep?

She turned the air conditioner to full force, and the radio to music she hated. No mellow jazz now. More heavy metal. She drove the car back on the road.

*Concentrate!*

How ridiculous if she were to be killed in another auto accident while seeking so desperately to avoid a bunch of interstate killers.

Finally speed limit signs indicated a town ahead. She slowed, not wanting to capture the attention of any small-town police officers who supported their town with traffic tickets. She didn't want questions.

On the outskirts she saw a motel. Old. Half the lights on the sign gone. But it still said "Vacancy."

She turned in and went to the office. A teenager manned it. He asked her name.

"Mary Murray," she said. "I'll pay cash."

He didn't blink. "Most of our customers do."

And she had her room.

Ben found the key after scouring the front porch. It was hidden in a small metal box and barely concealed under some loose soil. Not the best hiding place.

He knew he was in the sights of the FBI detail in the house. They most likely assumed he had a right to be there.

He unlocked the door and went in. Damien greeted him with a frantic bark. Daisy was probably hiding in the laundry room. He leaned down to pet the poodle, wondering whether he should take the animals with him. Unease settled in his gut. He knew she wouldn't leave them alone. Either she planned to return or . . .

He went to her office and quickly surveyed the room. He had a good mind for crime scenes, for capturing individual details. Nothing appeared different. He went to the wastepaper basket. Ashes. So she'd burned something. He turned on the computer. She had e-mail but it was protected and he had no idea what the password was. He tried several possibilities. Daisy. Her sisters' names. Her birth date. Nothing came up. He checked the last time she logged in. This morning.

He checked the computer printer. Jammed. He opened the side of the printer and dug out the offending piece of paper, or the several pages of paper. The first apparently had been stopped during printing by a second page that was caught in the feeding mechanism. He took out both pieces of paper. One looked like a folding fan. The other contained half a photo of a boat and five men holding their catches. From the quality, he knew it had been enlarged and possibly other people had been cropped away at the edges.

One man in the photo seemed familiar, but he couldn't place him right away. He wasn't worried, though. He knew it would come to him soon.

He peered at the boat for a name. It was blocked, though, by the fishermen.

He sat back in the chair. He'd never been on a fishing trip, but he judged this was an oceangoing boat. It appeared rigged for deep-sea fishing. And who were the other men standing there, beaming with pride as they held sizeable fish?

More important, why was it in Robin's printer, and what did it mean to her? Was that the reason for her disappearance?

He made several copies of the photo. He'd finished when he heard Damien bark just a second before he heard the doorbell ring. He hesitated, then decided to answer it. Perhaps whoever it was had some answers.

He stuffed the photos in his shirt, then went to the door and opened it. A thirties-something woman with warm brown eyes stood there, looking frazzled. She held a cat carrier.

Startled, she stared at him. "Hello?" she said, a question in her eyes.

"Hello," he replied. "I'm Ben Taylor, FBI."

Her lips pursed into a big O.

"Why are you here?" she blurted out.

"Ms. Stuart appears to be missing."

"Oh, that. She decided to take several days' vacation," the woman said. "She asked me to look after her dog and cat."

"That's kind of you, Mrs. . . ."

"Meeks. Betsy Meeks. Do you mind if I see your credentials?"

He took out his badge and watched as she examined it closely before handing it back to her.

"I'm trying to find Ms. Stuart," he said. "There's been several attacks on her and I'm afraid she could be in danger."

Mrs. Meeks blinked several times. "She didn't say anything like that. Only that she needed a few days rest."

"Why did she call you about picking up the animals?" he asked.

"I work with an animal rescue group. Robin knows how much I enjoy animals. She's written several stories about our organization. Our guardian angel, I call her. She's brought in enough donations to keep us going. This is the least I could do for her. I would have been here sooner but we had an emergency . . . and, well, I'm late." Mrs. Meeks said it all in nearly one breath.

Guardian angel? He wouldn't have suspected she would take that much interest in a story that wasn't going to lead the front page. But then he'd been wrong about her from the beginning. About everything. "Did she say where she was going?"

"No. Just that she needed to get away."

"And she didn't say how long she'd be gone?"

"Just 'several days.' "

"When did she call?"

"This morning. About six thirty. I've been keeping up with the story, and knew she might go to jail. She asked me to foster the animals for several days, and said that if she didn't go to jail, she would take a few days off. She sounded tired and stressed . . ."

Her voice faded off as if she knew she'd said too much.

"Did she mention a special place, a location she particularly liked?"

"No. She just said she really didn't know where she was going. She was just going to imitate a wild goose and go where instinct took her."

That sounded like her. Instinct and impulse ruled her. Yet instinct told him the photo had something to do with Robin's abrupt disappearance.

He stood aside. At least something was being done about Daisy and Damien.

He waited, hoping to learn more as the woman went in search of Daisy, finally finding her in the laundry room.

"Robin told me Daisy might be here." Mrs. Meeks scooped up the cat and put her in the carrier. Daisy complained loudly.

Then she picked up Damien, who trembled. With a few soft words the dog settled in her arms.

"Do you know anything else? Anything at all?"

"I don't think I should be saying anything. She would have told you if she wanted you to know." She turned and bulldozed her way past him.

He watched as Betsy Meeks returned to her car. She had looked meek in the doorway. Now he knew there was nothing meek about her when protecting her charges.

Just as Robin was.

He left the house, copies of the photos folded and tucked out of sight.

It was dark when Ben went to the home of Wade Carlton, Robin's editor.

The door opened to him immediately when he rang the doorbell.

The editor's face was lined with worry. "Have you heard anything from Robin?"

"I was going to ask you that."

Accusation was in Carlton's face as he said, "You said the FBI could protect her better than the people I hired."

"I thought they could. I didn't bargain on the fact that she would try to evade them."

"Maybe you should have."

Ben wanted to retort that Wade Carlton might have been able to stop her as well. But that wouldn't solve anything. He needed an ally, not an enemy.

"What exactly did she tell you?"

"She didn't tell me anything. She left the office after finishing a story with Greene, then the agent with her rushed in and said he couldn't find her. When I arrived home, I found a message on my answering machine that she had to get away for a few days. I'd already offered to give her the time, but I would have appreciated a warning."

"She's not on assignment then?"

"No. Greene's taking over the story temporarily."

"She didn't say anything about new information?"

Carlton's surprise was evident. "No."

"I think she met with her source the night before last. I think he, or she, gave her some lead she's pursuing."

Carlton narrowed his eyes. "And not tell me? Or you?" He seemed to emphasize the last word. "Are you sure?"

"She disappeared for hours Sunday night. You know that. She said she just wanted to get a rental car, but she was gone a very long time and said very little when she returned."

"That doesn't mean she met with her source. And maybe it's just as she said. She needed to get away after the hearing today. She knows you want to send her to jail." The editor's voice had turned harsh.

"I don't want to send her anywhere. I want to help her, damn it. She's going to get herself killed, as well as others."

"Have you thought that maybe she doesn't trust you?" Carlton said bluntly. "Apparently the Hydra has its tentacles in more than the Meredith sheriff's department. Are you sure the FBI isn't penetrated?"

Ben stared at him for a moment. And Robin's words came flooding back about him being there whenever anything had happened. "Has Robin learned anything . . . ?"

Carlton's silence said it all.

So that was why she'd suddenly shut him out. He tried to put himself in her place. So much had happened in a period of a few days. She'd almost been killed, her family threatened, her neighbor burned out. Trust must be running pretty thin. Still, the lack of it hurt more than he thought possible.

The ice man was no longer that.

Carlton was still watching him, seeking his own truth.

*Was he sure the FBI wasn't penetrated?*

No, he wasn't. It had been penetrated before. And close to home. His home.

He knew how destructive distrust was. Knew it only too well.

For all the friends Robin had, he knew that right now she must feel like the loneliest person on earth.

# chapter twenty-four

*Despite her exhaustion, Robin hadn't* thought she could sleep.

She'd suffered that kind of wakefulness before. When she was just too tired to sleep. Too many questions in her head.

But the moment she laid her head on the pillow, she knew nothing else until light streamed through the cheap curtains.

It took her a moment to remember where she was. Then it all came flooding back in terrifying detail. The fires. The threats. The grand jury hearing.

Most of all she saw Ben Taylor in her mind. He would be angry. Puzzled. Frustrated.

Because he'd lost her.

She went to the window and searched around the parking lot. Nothing looked suspicious. In fact, it was mostly empty now that it was daylight. She took a quick shower, then pulled on a pair of jeans and the shell she'd worn yesterday.

It felt good walking without the brace. The exercises she'd done religiously had made her left knee as flexible as the right one, but it didn't yet have the strength. Or perhaps it was her caution.

She longed for coffee, but there was no little coffeemaker in the room. Probably wouldn't be any in the so-called lobby, either. In any event, she didn't want anyone to remember her face.

She looked at the photos again, praying that she was right, that the answer to her questions lay somewhere in them. Sandy had said Brunswick. Would the boat still be there?

Could she find the registration or had it been registered someplace else?

*If* it was in Brunswick. *If* she was lucky.

She looked out the motel window again before opening the door. Still nothing. Clutching her purse and duffle, she left. She would get some coffee and breakfast somewhere, then head for Savannah. She was certain she could purchase a weapon there. Then she would drive to Brunswick. Anyone who owned a boat like that would probably be a member of a yacht club, or at the very least be moored at one of the marinas.

That first. Then she would start looking for ownership records of the condos on the beach. Sooner or later, she would find a common denominator.

The question was how long she could search without being noticed and becoming the hunted rather than the hunter. Again.

She reached Savannah at midmorning.

First order of business was a weapon. She found a gun shop, showed her permit, and paid for the pistol in cash. She spent another hour at a shooting range, recapturing long-ago skills her father had drilled into her.

She found a discount store and purchased some underwear and a few other items she needed. She also purchased a prepaid credit card for a thousand dollars. No name necessary.

She desperately missed her laptop, but she hadn't figured out a way to put that in her purse and she couldn't afford a new one. Instead, she stopped at a Kinko's in Savannah, and used one of their computers to log on to the Internet, then she linked to the city of Brunswick.

In minutes she had a list of fourteen marinas in the Brunswick area. What she didn't know was whether the boat was docked in Brunswick permanently or merely sailed there for the various outings. But it would have had to be docked there at least temporarily.

She wished she had a name for the boat. But it could be easily changed in any event. It was the registration number that might lead to the owner.

She used a public telephone to call her attorney friend in

California. He'd heard from Star's husband, who reported they were all safe. They didn't say where, but it didn't matter. It was enough that they had evidently gotten away.

Then she checked her voice mail service, since she'd turned off her cell phone when she left Atlanta. She didn't know if someone could trace cell phone signals even when she wasn't making a call. She made a mental note to propose doing a story for the paper on the traceability of cell phones when her life returned to normal. *If* she still had a job.

There were ten calls, including two from Ben Taylor, three from her editor, and others by various friends indicating concern. She wished she could call them all back, but she couldn't risk it. Wade would ask too many questions and probably tell her to return.

And Ben . . .

She thought how safe she'd felt in his arms, in his presence after the attack in Meredith County. Could it have been fool's gold? Could she have been that wrong? Were her instincts that awry?

*Forget it!* Even if he was gold of the purest kind, his superiors may not be. The result could be just as deadly.

The list of marinas in hand, she got back into her car and turned south.

Ben arrived at the office at eight the morning after Robin's disappearance. He'd tried to grab some sleep. There had been none the night of the fire, and precious little the night before that, and he knew he couldn't function any longer without some. He slept a little, but it had been restless sleep, and he woke early. He ran a mile, trying to clear his head. The only clue he had to Robin's whereabouts was that photo. A boat. Some men. He had no idea where it was docked or why it was important.

The fishermen in the photo. He thought one had seemed familiar last night but he hadn't been able to place it. When he returned to his apartment, he looked at it again. Now it tumbled into place. Ben had seen him at the press conference. He'd been standing at the side of the sheriff.

He had a place to start. Mahoney and several other agents

were already doing extensive investigations on every deputy in the Meredith County Sheriff's office. They would have photos of them. He wanted to see if more officers were in that photo. Then he could learn where the boat was.

And he planned to do it fast.

He took a cold shower, the icy water thoroughly waking him as his mind raced ahead.

Once dried and dressed, he tried to call Robin again, but her cell phone was off. He didn't try to leave a number this time. It was his third call. He grabbed the photo and drove downtown to the office.

Mahoney was already there. "The U.S. attorney called. Wants to see you at his office."

"He's in this early?"

"Apparently."

"Me alone? Not us?"

Mahoney shrugged. "You've been the Lone Ranger lately. I don't think he's happy."

"What about Holland?"

"Holland wants what Joseph Ames wants. And Ames is feeling the heat. He doesn't really want to send a reporter to jail. Bad press might hurt his chances on his climb to the top."

"I'll call him later," Ben said. "I have something that might help the case." He pulled out the photograph. "I don't want Holland to know about this yet," he said. "Not until we know if it pans out."

Mahoney glanced at the photo, then looked puzzled.

"You've been going over the backgrounds of the deputies," Ben said. "Do any of the men in this picture look familiar?"

Mahoney looked again and slowly nodded. He picked up a file on his desk which included photos and information on members of the sheriff's department. Twenty minutes later, they had matched all five of the men in Robin's photo to photos in the file.

Four were currently with the department. The fifth had been killed at a traffic stop seven months ago.

Ben seized on that information. "Did they catch the perp?"

"I checked on that. No. It's a cold case. The officer—Mark Boatright—he called in to report he was stopping a car. Gave a license number that later turned out to be stolen. There was nothing else."

"Another death in Meredith law enforcement. Obviously not a good place to be a cop," Ben said. "Was he married?"

"Yep."

"I think someone should talk to the widow."

*Not just someone.* He damned well was going to do it. He wanted to know whether she remembered a fishing trip, and where it was.

"Do you have an address?"

Mahoney went back to work and came up with both an address and a phone number.

Ben debated calling or visiting. He decided a call would forewarn her. Surprise always trumped warning. If she wasn't there, they should be able to find out from neighbors where she worked.

"Let's go," he said.

"What about Ames?"

Ben shrugged. "That can wait."

"You know what you're doing?"

"I know we have a missing witness who might be running hellbent into trouble."

Mahoney groaned. "My pension . . ." But he got up and followed Ben out the door.

Fifty minutes later, Ben drove up in front of a modest frame house. A bicycle leaned against the porch and a tricycle was nearby. The grass looked ragged and untended, but the house was newly painted.

He and Mahoney went together to the door. He took out his badge and held it in his hand, then rang the bell.

A dog barked inside, but no one answered.

He rang a few more times, then Mahoney went to the left and he to the nearest house on the right. Two homes down Ben found a woman home. She stood behind a locked door while he showed his badge, then she opened it.

"I'm Special Agent Ben Taylor. Mrs. . . ."

"Allen. Jean Allen." She paused as she opened the door wider, inviting him in. "Wouldn't have been this cautious two weeks ago," she said. "This was always a real peaceful place."

"We're looking for Amy Boatright."

"No. We're just following up on her husband's death. Do you know where she might be?"

"She works at the school cafeteria. I'm keeping her youngest now. She should be home at two."

He looked at his watch. Almost eleven. He didn't want to wait until two. Every minute counted. Robin Stuart was out there on her own, probably thinking she was smarter than the perps. Always a big mistake. He'd disabused himself of that a long time ago. Despite the television programs, there were smart bad guys out there, and he'd discovered that whoever led Hydra was very smart indeed.

He didn't want to show the woman the photo. He didn't know where Robin had received it, and he couldn't be sure that her source wasn't in it. He sure didn't want to get someone killed because of carelessness. Instead, he planned to ask Amy Boatright details surrounding her husband's death, his moods prior to the attack and activities around that time. He wanted to throw in the fishing trip as an aside. Something unimportant.

His gut was telling him there were entirely too many accidents around the Meredith County sheriff's department.

He asked the neighbor a few more questions. How long had Boatright lived in this home? What had she thought of him?

The woman looked at him shrewdly. "Does this have anything to do with those murders?"

"I can't really say, ma'am."

"I hope you find whoever did it. Mark was a good man. A real good man. Helped everyone. Took care of all the single women in the neighborhood. Fixed their plumbing. Repaired roofs. Mowed their lawns. His death broke Amy's heart. Sheriff's department gave her a good settlement, though. That was a godsend."

"But she works at the school?"

"Mainly because she wants to keep near Mark Junior. MJ is the image of his father and I think she's terrified of losing him too."

"What about her daughter?"

"Merry? Bright and sunny. A real joy to be around. Both are good kids."

"A good marriage then?"

"I wish mine had been one-tenth as good. I wouldn't be keeping other people's children to support my own."

"Was he from Meredith County?"

"Sure was. Grew up not far from here."

"Ex-military?"

"Yeah. Think so. How did you know?"

"Lot of cops come from the military."

She looked at him curiously.

"Thank you, Mrs. Allen."

"I hope you find his killer, but general opinion is he's long gone from here."

"General opinion could be right," Ben acknowledged. "Thank you, ma'am." Ben handed her his card. "If you think of anything that might help, call anytime. That's my cell number."

Mrs. Allen walked to the door with him. As he reached it, he asked for directions to the school where Amy Boatright worked. She gave them to him.

He hesitated, then said, "I would appreciate it if you didn't tell anyone about this visit."

She looked surprised but nodded her agreement. "Anything that will help catch the killer. It would ease Amy."

Once in Brunswick, Robin rented a room in an inexpensive motel on the outskirts, this time paying with the recently purchased credit card. She tried not to take offense at the leering look of the proprietor.

Then another shopping expedition. She'd decided during the trip from Savannah to Brunswick that she couldn't just wander around asking questions without attracting attention.

But if she was a freelance writer researching a story on the Georgia coast, she would have reason to be snapping photos and asking questions, especially if she was researching a story for a yachting magazine.

She went to the local library and found a phone book from Chicago. She turned to the middle, to Murphy, found a phone number and address. Then she made a trip to a small printing company where she ordered business cards that should be ready in an hour.

While waiting, she bought a camera and notebooks, then matched the locations of local marinas to a map of the area. She hoped she would be lucky enough to spot the boat. If not, she would start asking questions.

Start with the small ones. If the owners were trying to escape notice they would dock in the smaller marinas. At least that was one theory. Another could be to hide in plain sight in the largest ones.

Time was at a premium.

*Flip a coin. Heads.*

Smaller ones first.

Ben decided against going to the school. He was only too aware of what happened to those who might be conceived as a danger to Hydra, or whoever was involved in the killings of the deputies. He didn't want to put Amy Boatright in danger.

Instead, he and Mahoney grabbed some lunch, then discussed what Mrs. Allen had told Ben.

They compared the records of deputies. There were very few women in the department, and those were dispatchers and support personnel. Nearly all the deputies were lifelong residents of the county. Some were second- and third-generation members of the department. That wouldn't be odd in a smaller department. But this one was large enough that it rang some major bells. There had also been an unusual number of fatalities, most of them automobile accidents. One a hunting accident.

Ben looked again at the photo. How many more fishermen had been in the original photo? Probably another five.

Camaraderie was obvious. Several of them had arms slung around shoulders. Big grins on faces.

Robin Stuart had found something in that photo. What in the hell was it? And was one of the men her source?

He tried to call her cell phone. Received another "out of service" message. He left another message, even knowing—or at least suspecting—she would ignore that one as well.

"We should tell Holland about this photograph."

"Robin Stuart changed toward me in the past day or two. I

think she met with the source Sunday night, and he told her something that made her stop trusting us."

Mahoney's brows drew together. "You think he told her someone with our office is involved?"

"Or implied it."

"I don't believe it!"

"It happened in Boston. I can't see any of the people in our office being involved, but . . . hell, I guess you never know."

"We can't keep vital evidence quiet," Mahoney objected. "Holland will want to know where we've been."

"Just checking out recent deaths in the sheriff's department."

"You know what you're asking me to do? Withholding information from my boss?"

"That photo could possibly point to Ms. Stuart's source. I don't want to be responsible for his death if we don't get to him before the perps do. And if someone in our office leaks it . . ."

Mahoney didn't give him a promise, and Ben wondered if he should have told his partner about the photo. But he needed Mahoney's help. Time was too important right now, and he needed another mind to reason. He didn't want to think he was too involved with Robin Stuart to make sound decisions but neither could he preclude it.

He looked at his watch. "It's nearly two. Let's go back to the Boatright house."

They were parked in front of her house when she drove up. She looked at them curiously as she drove into the driveway, and a boy jumped out and ran inside. The woman took more time in getting out.

He and Mahoney walked up to her and introduced themselves.

She was a pretty woman with tired eyes. Her smile was more automatic than real.

She invited them inside when they said they were reviewing the circumstances of her husband's death. She asked if they would like a soft drink, and both said yes.

She introduced them to her son, then told him to go into his room and do his homework. He looked rebellious for a moment, then took one look at his mother's face and reluctantly went down the hall. When the door closed behind him, she turned back to them.

"Why now?" she asked.

Ben didn't pretend not to understand. "There's too many deaths in the sheriff's department. Your husband's as well as a number of accidents. Could be a coincidence, but we wanted to find out why."

"Six," she said. "Six in two years. I've been to the funerals."

"That's high for a rural sheriff's department," Mahoney said.

She didn't respond.

"How long did your husband work for the department?" Ben asked.

"Ten years."

"And he was happy with the job?"

"I don't think happy describes it. He'd always wanted to be a law officer. He liked helping people."

"He enjoyed working with the sheriff's department then?"

"Up until a few months before his . . . death."

"And then?" Ben asked.

Amy Boatright's hands clasped together tightly. Her gaze went to the door, then back to him. "In the last months before his death, he was angry about something. Retreated into himself."

"Did he usually patrol alone?"

She nodded. "We don't have two-officer cars. Not enough violent crime. Most of the stuff was traffic stops and domestic violence. Mark hated those most of all. He couldn't understand how a man could hit a woman." Her eyes filled with tears.

"I'm sorry, Mrs. Boatright. But this is important."

"You think someone in the sheriff's department is responsible for those deaths, don't you?" she replied.

"I think it's a possibility." He paused, then added, "I understand that some of the deputies took fishing trips together."

She looked surprised, then nodded. "Usually two a year. Mark always looked forward to them. He liked most of the guys."

"Did you ever go?"

"Boys only," she said dryly. "I wasn't that happy about it,

but Mark said it didn't count against his days off. And he did bring back enough fish to feed us for a month."

"Do you remember where they went?"

She nodded. "Mark liked it so much he took me and the kids down there several months later. Jekyll Island."

"You said he was upset before his death. Did he tell you why?"

"No, but he started having bad dreams. I thought it might have something to do with Gary's suicide."

Ben dredged up names in his memory. *Gary Sutler.* He'd shot himself three months before Mark Boatright died.

"A friend of his?"

"Got him into the department. Last man in the world you'd think of killing himself. It shook Mark terribly."

"Can you do something for us?" Ben asked.

"I'll try anything to get his killer caught," Amy Boatright said.

"Draw us a time line. When he joined the department, when Gary died, when your husband started to get angry. Anything he might have said, no matter how insignificant you might have thought it was."

Her gaze was steady. "You think all this might be connected?"

"All what?" Ben asked innocently.

"The recent murders of the police officers. Maybe Gary. Maybe even Mark." Ben noticed the odd lack of surprise in her voice.

"I don't know, Mrs. Boatright. We're only asking questions."

"If he was killed by his own . . ."

"We don't know that." Ben got up. "Mrs. Boatright, I'm asking that you don't mention this conversation to anyone. Anyone at all. Not to your family. Not your closest friends."

Her face paled, but she nodded.

He handed her his card. "I'll check with you in a few days on the time line. Call me or Agent Mahoney if you think of anything you haven't told us."

They left.

"What now?" Mahoney asked. "Jekyll Island? We'll have to talk to Holland about that."

"No," Ben said. "I'm going to take a few days' leave."

Mahoney got that despairing look back in place. "Never happen. Not with the investigation ongoing."

"Never a better time. A week before the next grand jury session. We're still not officially on the case. Not much we can do before then. Besides, Holland's been pressing me about taking vacation time."

"What do I tell Ames? He wanted to see you, remember?"

"You told me. It's my problem now."

"You really do want to end your career."

Ben shrugged. "If I find Robin Stuart, he'll be happy."

"Finding her won't be easy."

"If that's where she's gone, she'll be checking out marinas. That will take time."

He used his cell phone to check on flights to Brunswick, the closest city to Jekyll Island. As he waited for a reservations agent, he thought about the city. He knew it well. He'd spent a few months there a while back as part of another joint task force that was investigating a drug ring.

The agent came on the line. There was a flight to Brunswick in two hours.

It would take at least ninety minutes to reach the airport but once there he could use his credentials to get through security quickly. It was worth a try. He could be in Brunswick in three hours. He made the reservation.

"What about Holland?" Mahoney asked. "What if he says no to a few days off?"

"I'll figure that out later. Just get me to the airport. Fast."

# chapter twenty-five

*Lou Belize didn't even try* to keep his voice calm as he talked to the obviously nervous accountant. "You said you were making progress. Mr. Kelley doesn't tolerate liars."

"I *was* making progress," Michael Caldwell responded. "The fire scared her off. You didn't warn me about that."

"It should have sent her into your arms."

"I need more time. I told you that. I couldn't force myself on her."

"You must have some idea where she's going."

"We were to get together tonight . . . The fire . . ."

"Talk to her friends. Talk to the old lady. Find out where she went. Get what I want, or your services will terminated."

"She's not going to say anything. She's made that clear." Fear was in Caldwell's voice. And desperation. "I've done everything you've asked me to do."

"Not everything. Someone knows where she is. Find that person."

"Her sisters . . ."

"They are none of your business." Belize slammed the phone down. He wasn't going to admit to Caldwell that he'd lost the sisters as well. He hadn't thought they could move that fast, not with one sister caught in a court battle, and the other near delivery time. An error on his part. He didn't like errors.

He particularly didn't like a damn reporter getting the best of him. Mr. Kelley would like it even less.

He should have stopped her days ago. He'd thought the

attack in Meredith would get him the name Mr. Kelley needed. Then a quick disposal. When the two bumblers came along, he'd hoped threats would prevail.

Not that he was adverse to violence, but her informer would still be out there, a ticking time bomb.

And if she went to jail she would tell the grand jury everything she knew. The feds would find her source and make him talk. Which could be very bad for Belize, as well as his boss.

Another failure, Belize knew, and he would have his own explanations to make.

Or he would have to leave town hastily. That idea did not sit well. He and Kelley had spent years setting up this network, and the protection they needed to survive. No bitch was going to ruin it for him.

He picked up the cell phone and made another call. He would make as many calls as necessary. He wanted Robin Stuart's sisters found. He wanted the woman herself found. And he was going to get the name of the rat who'd talked to her.

Robin picked up her business cards and decided to junk her first thought of visiting the smallest ones first. Instead, she would check the closest marinas first and move outward. She wanted to see as many as possible before their offices closed.

She found the first on her list and wandered down the docks looking for a luxury fishing boat similar to the one in the photo.

The first marina she visited was small and obviously catered to small pleasure boats. The office was closed, as were the gas pumps. A quick glance told her there were no boats that resembled the one in the photo.

The second was a larger marina. A young man—a college student wearing a University of Florida T-shirt—tried to be helpful but said he didn't recognize the boat. He suggested it might run out of one of the two largest marinas, both of which advertised fishing charters.

It was nearing dusk when she stopped at the third on her list. The marina advertised showers, a restaurant, and fishing gear. She went into the office, grateful for her newly minted business cards. Strange the way everyone accepted them as they would accept, say, a badge.

She asked for the manager, and an older, bronze-faced man came from another room. She handed him a business card. "Mary Murphy," she said. "I really hope you can help me."

Deep-set green eyes twinkled. "Well, I hope so, too, miss. What can I do for you?"

"I'm doing a story on marinas in Georgia," she said.

"For who?"

"I'm a freelancer. *Yachting World* is interested."

New interest came into the manager's face. "In our part of the world?"

"It's a look at yachting on the Southeast coast. Off-the-beaten-track destinations. Number of slips, amenities, area attractions," she said. "Who sails here now. Vignettes on people who come here on a regular basis and why."

"We get business from all over the world," he said. "Our fishing's some of the best."

She took the notebook from her purse. "So you get foreign-registered boats as well as U.S. ones?"

"Not a lot. Maybe ten percent. We would like more. Maybe your article will help."

"How do they hear about you?"

"Word of mouth, mostly."

"Any of those have permanent leases?"

He shook his head. "Most belong to local residents."

"What about charter boats? Do any of them lease slips from you?"

He shook his head.

Was the boat in the photograph a charter boat someone rented for those trips? If so, she probably wasn't going to discover much. Someone could use a foreign corporation to pay the lease costs.

She took the photo from her purse. "This is what got me interested," she said. "One of the men on this trip raved about it. Said the boat was the best he'd sailed. He fell in love with Brunswick and the Golden Isles."

He took it. "A fine-looking boat. Looks like a sixty-four-footer."

"Do you know it?"

He shook his head. "Don't know if I've seen that exact one. That's some expensive equipment. There's several charter boats that size around here."

"Where would I find them?"

"Probably the Jekyll Island Marina. Or the St. Simons Marina. Most of the charters run from those two marinas."

"Thanks," she said.

"I'll contact a couple of owners who might talk to you."

"I'd be grateful. Call me when you do." She gave him her card and scribbled down the temporary cell number. She didn't want him to phone Chicago and find out there was no Mary Murphy. Not until she discovered what she wanted to know. She vowed silently that once back she would write a story for the travel section. That way it wouldn't be a total lie.

She left that marina and stopped for a bite while she analyzed her performance. She wished she knew more about boats.

She had no more luck at the next two marinas, both rather small with little or no security. She walked down the docks. Most of the boats were small. There were several small cabin cruisers, but nothing the size of the boat in the photo.

Enough for now. The last few days were catching up with her. She was tired. She wanted to call the hospital and ask about Mrs. Jeffers, but she feared the FBI could track the call. Instead, she called Jack Ross from her temporary cell phone.

"Make your getaway, kid?"

"I think so. Has anyone contacted you?"

"Nope. Not yet, anyway. I hear the FBI is questioning the news staff, though. But as long as you're not wanted, they can't do much."

"Can you do another favor for me? Call Eastside Hospital and ask about Mrs. Maude Jeffers."

"Okay," he said.

"I'll call back in a couple of hours."

"Are you all right?"

"Perfectly." She paused, then added, "Maybe not quite perfectly. Haven't found what I need. Not yet. But I will."

"Go to it. Let me know if you need any info on anyone. I'll use some of my old sources."

"I don't want you involved."

"I already am. Sorta good to have my fingers in a good story again. By the way, I ran into someone named Michael Caldwell at Charlie's. Asked about you. Apparently he knew that I knew you from the other night, at your send-off for the grand jury."

She stilled. Why would Michael Caldwell go to him? Why was he looking for her?

"You said no one contacted you."

"Casual conversation. That's all."

She wondered whether she'd just made a grave mistake by calling Jack. "What did you tell him?"

"That his guess would be as good as mine. Now that much is true. So is the fact I have no idea where you are."

"Be careful, Jack," she said, her heart in her mouth. She didn't want someone else she cared about hurt.

"I am," he said.

"I'll call you back in a couple hours. Will that give you enough time to check on Maude Jeffers?"

"I'll call the hospital from a pay phone so it can't be traced back to me."

"Tell Mama. I'll call her at Charlie's. That should be safe enough. I doubt they would wiretap a bar."

"I'll do that." He hung up.

*Michael?*

An innocent question? Or something else? Why would he be asking her friends about her whereabouts when it should have been obvious she didn't want anyone to know?

She shook off the question. She was becoming paranoid. Suspecting everyone. He was probably just worried about her. That was all. But if he started to ask questions, then others would as well. Maybe she should call him, tell him she was all right.

*No!* She'd broken contact with everyone but Jack, and now she had to break it with him as well.

She shook off the misgivings and drove by one more marina on the way to her motel. She stopped and went to the office. It was closed. She looked toward the docks. Lights blazed from a small cabin cruiser, and loud music blared into the night air. Several men stood on deck, beer cans in their hands. She decided to ask them if they'd seen the boat she was seeking. She worked to minimize her limp as she approached them.

"Hi," she said as she reached the boat.

They glanced at each other. One waved a beer can at her. "Hey there. Come aboard."

She stepped up onto the boat.

"I'm looking for some friends," she said, "but I guess they gave me the name of the wrong marina."

"Hell, lady, you can stay with us. We're more fun."

"I bet you are," she said, "but I promised." She handed them the photo of the boat.

"That's one beaut of a boat," said a towheaded man.

"Have you seen it?"

One of them looked at the boat thoughtfully.

"Isn't that the bloody boat that nearly ran us down earlier?"

The second man looked at the photo more carefully. "Hey, it *is* the one. I recognize the rigging. Arrogant bastard."

"What happened?" she said.

"Cut in front of us. Almost swamped us."

"Do you know where they were heading?"

"Out to sea."

"When?"

"Just a few hours ago. We were coming in from fishing, and that damned boat came tearing down the river. If that's where you were heading, I don't think you'll find it."

"Why do you think that? Maybe they just went out fishing."

He shrugged. "Don't usually use that kind of speed on a leisurely fishing trip."

"Did you see the name?"

"I did," said one of the guys in back. "Thought about reporting him to the Coast Guard. It was the *Phantom*."

"Did you?"

They looked blank.

"Report it to the Coast Guard?"

The guy shrugged. "Nah. Figured he would be long gone."

"And our booze was running low," said another with a chuckle.

"Any idea which marina it might have come from?"

"No."

"If you were going to a party there, why didn't you know the name?" asked the young man who'd invited her aboard.

"Just wondered if it was the same boat I was looking for. Must have gotten the wrong message about the date."

"Invitation's still open."

"Some other time. Are you going to be here a while?"

"Another week unless the spirit moves us. We started in New York and plan to sail to the Keys."

"A charter?"

"Nope," said the towhead. "My present for finishing Harvard."

"Nice present."

"Like I said, come back. We party every night."

Her mind in a turmoil, she left. Had someone discovered she was here? Or had the boat left on its own for some reason?

Or was it even the right boat? The manager of the first marina said there were several similar boats around.

She looked at her watch. Nearly nine, and she was tired and hungry. She would stop at a fast food place and resume her search in the morning. She felt a glow of triumph. She had the name. If only she could find the registration. That might lead to the owner, and the owner to someone else.

Ben landed in Brunswick. After breaking every traffic law to catch it, the flight had been more than an hour late leaving the gate.

How to find her quickly?

*If* she was here.

Big if, but gut instinct told him he was right. She was not the kind of person who would skip off on a vacation when people around her were being threatened. She had a purpose and destination in mind.

He rented a car at the airport, then on a hunch swung by several marinas he knew from his last trip. The office was closed at many of them, but at a few places he saw several boats with lights on, so he approached them all, asking if they'd noticed a young blond woman asking questions. No one had.

He came to a marina whose parking lot was nearly empty. There was one boat here—a cabin cruiser—with lights still on. He hurried up the dock, realizing he was running out of time. It was nearly eleven.

The deck of the cruiser was empty, but he heard loud voices

from inside. He stepped aboard and knocked at the door to the cabin.

A young man in swim trunks opened the door, paled when Ben showed his credentials. Probably had drugs of some kind inside.

"I'm looking for woman," he said. "She might have been asking questions about a boat. She's pretty, late twenties. Short, taffy-colored hair. Wears a leg brace."

He saw recognition flash in the man's face at first, then it faded when he mentioned the brace.

"What's she done?"

"She hasn't done anything. At least nothing wrong. But her life might be in danger.

Indecision flickered across the man's face, then he said, "There wasn't a brace."

Damn, he should have figured.

"Dark blue eyes? Good figure?"

"That's her. Looking for a large fishing yacht. We told her we saw one heading seaward this afternoon. Asked her to stay and party but—"

"When?"

He shrugged. "A few beers ago."

He nodded. "Did the boat have a name?"

"She asked that, too. It was the *Phantom*."

"Thanks."

Relief flooded the young man's face.

Probably his own as well.

*Robin Stuart was still alive.*

Now he had to keep her that way.

# chapter twenty-six

*Robin grabbed a salad at* a take-out restaurant, then called Charlie's on her disposable cell phone and asked for Mama. She heard pub noise in the background.

"It's Robin," she said.

"Hello," Mama replied simply. "The lady's fine."

Mama was being very cautious. Robin sent a silent thank-you to Jack Ross.

"Thanks," she said.

"Ah, your new gentleman friend's been asking for you." Like Mrs. Jeffers, Mama was an incurable romantic.

"What did you tell him?"

"The truth: How should I know?"

Robin smiled to herself. "Good."

Mama hung up.

If she ever decided to get out of newspapering, Robin decided she would create the Little Old Ladies' Fine Detective Agency. Between Mrs. Jeffers and Mama, they could be highly successful.

Then the smile disappeared. Michael Caldwell again. She rather wished she felt confident enough in herself to accept the fact that Michael found her irresistible. But she found that hard to believe. She had never been irresistible to anyone.

She headed back to the motel. She was strung too tight, though, to go to sleep. After making sure she'd fastened all three locks, she ate her salad while watching the news on television. Nothing from the Atlanta area about the murders.

She took a hot shower, then settled in bed with her map and list of marinas. She should be able to cover all the remaining ones tomorrow. Then what? What if she came to a dead end? What if she never discovered the boat's registration? The name alone didn't help. There were probably a thousand *Phantoms* along the Georgia and Florida coast. And even if she did find the registration, would it lead only to an endless trail of shell corporations?

ATLANTA

"An FBI agent is in Brunswick." The words were laced with anger.

"Not officially. I would know. I just asked for an update on the investigation."

"And?"

"Ron Holland said everything was on hold until the grand jury session next week. Meredith County and the state are resisting federal participation. Unless we can get some evidence from the Stuart woman, we're not going in."

The two men sat together on a bench on MARTA, Atlanta's rapid rail system. It was eleven p.m. and the car was nearly empty. Meeting this way was safer than telephones now.

"Then why did Ben Taylor take a plane to Brunswick?"

His companion's eyes changed, flared.

"News to you?"

"Yes. I was told he took a few days' leave. He's overdue some downtime."

"He's been circling around Robin Stuart for the past week. I think he's gone to meet her," said the man dressed in an expensive silk suit.

"You think she told him where she was going?"

"No. I planted enough doubts in her mind about him. But I think he discovered where she's gone. If he's going to Brunswick, then I suspect she's there, too."

"Why wouldn't he tell Holland?"

"Maybe he has suspicions of his own. Maybe he doesn't trust his superiors."

Alarm leapt into the younger man's eyes. "What do you want me to do?"

"Find out what his partner knows."

"I'll talk to him tomorrow morning."

"What do they have so far?"

"Nothing. Dead ends. Can't seek search warrants without cause, and there is no cause. They don't even have enough evidence to enter the investigation, which is why they pushed for the grand jury."

"The tracks are well covered except for that damned source. Until we know who it is, we can't plug holes he might open."

"Robin Stuart probably doesn't know much more than she already printed in the newspaper. If so, there's nothing to worry about."

"There's a lot to worry about if she's in Brunswick. This morning I told the captain of the *Phantom* to move the boat to the Keys."

"So . . . what's the problem?"

"If she can find the slip, she can get credit card numbers, descriptions. Pieces of the puzzle."

"I thought you had a bargain with the woman. Her family for silence."

"Her sisters have disappeared. We can't find them. We can't find her. You've been damned little help."

"We checked with the paper's attorney when we heard she was missing. He said she left for a few days to consider what she's going to do next week," the younger man said.

"Like the agent?" A raised eyebrow showed disbelief. "Both of them? At the same time?"

"Don't panic."

The older man fixed him with a stare. "I don't panic. I fix things before they get out of control. She may not name her source, but her disappearance worries us. So does Taylor's trip."

"Maybe she hasn't gone there."

"I'm not willing to take that chance."

"How would Taylor know where she's gone? No one else seems to know."

"He went by her house. He must have found something in

Stuart's house because then he and his partner paid a visit to Amy Boatright's house, the widow of Mark Boatright. You remember him. Then Taylor rushed off for a plane. Bought a ticket just an hour before the flight left. Not normal vacation planning."

The younger man swore softly under his breath.

"If Taylor's gone to Brunswick after visiting her house, you can bet she's there," his companion said. "He hasn't wanted to let her out of his sight. I planted some suspicion in her head, but if they get together . . ." He stopped, then continued, "Make yourself useful. I want to know what happened at the Boatright house."

"I can't be too obvious."

"Why the hell do you think we're paying you so much?"

"How do you know he went to the Boatright home? Are you following him?"

"We had someone watching Stuart's house."

"Isn't that risky?"

The older man shrugged. "Different people. Different cars. Besides, cops are used to following, not being followed."

"What if the agents noticed them?"

"They didn't."

"This is getting out of hand. Fire inspectors investigating the fire. The bureau trying to find ways to weasel in. DEA will be next. How could you be so stupid as to kill those officers?"

His companion stiffened, then glared at him with cold eyes. "My people had no choice. They saw me with Paul Joyner—a rumored drug lord with the chief deputy sheriff?"

"So you escalate. And escalate."

"I've contacted our people in Brunswick. They know what to do if she starts asking questions down there. In the meantime I want to know what Taylor's partner knows."

"I thought you wanted her alive."

"I did, but if she's getting close . . . she's better off dead. I doubt her source will go to anyone else after that. Not if he wants to live."

"What about the information she says she's given to other people?"

"I don't think she has that much. Not yet, anyway. Otherwise it would be in the paper. It's a chance we'll have to take."

The train slowed and the older man stood, rocked as it came to a stop. Then he slipped out the door and was gone.

Robin's stomach churned when she rose the next morning. She yearned for hot coffee but there wasn't a machine in her room. She took a quick shower, then ran a comb through the wet, short curls. No dryer. It would just have to dry on its own. Then she slipped on a pair of slacks and a shirt.

Forty minutes later, she arrived at the first marina on her list. This time she started at one of the larger ones. She parked in the lot and strolled down the docks toward the larger boats. None looked like the one she was seeking.

She went to the desk. "Hi," she said with a brightness she didn't feel.

An appreciative look came over the man's face as he looked up from a magazine. "Can I help you?"

She handed him one of her recently printed business cards and gave him the speech. Like the man yesterday, he was instantly interested. Yet when she mentioned the *Phantom*, she noticed something shift in his eyes, even as he shook his head.

She asked the same questions she'd asked the day before, then said she would like to look around.

He hesitated, then said, "Don't go bothering anyone."

As she left, she turned and saw him pick up a phone.

She tried to keep her gait even. It was more difficult today. She'd walked too much yesterday, and now the ankle ached more with every step. Should she hurry toward the car? Something in his demeanor told her he knew something about the boat. That meant others in the marina would as well.

She would give herself a few moments. She walked to the dock and down it, hoping to find people aboard the boats there. She struck gold halfway down with a couple who were walking toward her. They held tennis racquets.

She stopped them. "Hi," she said brightly. "I'm trying to find a boat called the *Phantom*. I want to interview the captain for a story I'm writing about deep-sea fishing. A friend took a trip with him and told me he was really knowledgeable."

One of them made a face. "The *Phantom* left yesterday, and we weren't sorry to see them go," said the woman. "The crew kept to themselves. Arrogant as the devil. Complained about everything."

"Really? The clerk didn't remember a boat like that."

"Jimmy. He's as bad as they were."

"Do you know the name of the captain?"

"Stefan something." They looked at each other. "Something like Fisher. I thought it funny that a fisherman was named Fisher. That's how I remembered it. I do know he was foreign. Had a pronounced accent."

"How long had they been here?"

"I don't know," the man said. "Since we've been here. Three weeks. I hear they're here often."

"Come on," said the woman, tugging at her companion's hand. "It'll be too hot for tennis."

Robin thanked them and started back to the office. The clerk had lied to her and she wanted to know why. She watched as the young couple got into a small convertible, then she went to the door of the office. It was locked.

She knocked at it, but no one came. Frustrated, she looked around. No one.

Where had he gone?

Then with terrible suddenness, she was aware of someone next to her, pressing a gun into her side.

"Be quiet, Ms. Stuart, and walk toward the parking lot."

She knew if she did, she probably wouldn't survive.

She glanced around. No one in sight.

"Move, bitch," the man said with sudden viciousness.

Maybe there would be someone in the parking lot. Maybe . . . she could pretend she was terrified.

*Pretend?*

Her bad foot hit a stone, and she stumbled slightly. She turned around and looked at her captor. "I . . . have a bad leg."

"Yeah, that threw us off," he said, his hand righting her. "We were told to look for someone in a brace. Get going."

She limped more than necessary, slowing their progress on the short walk to the parking lot. She passed her car.

"That way," her captor said. She followed the line of his gaze and saw a dark sedan with tinted windows. She knew once she reached it, she was probably as good as dead.

Her gun was in her purse, but with one in her back she wasn't foolish enough to try to use it.

"Who are you?" she said.

"You didn't hear what I said. Walk. Naturally. Toward that car."

"If I don't?"

"Then you can die right here."

"I have information with other people . . ."

"Move," he ordered again, the gun pressing even deeper into her side.

A car horn blew. Her captor looked to the dark sedan.

*A warning?*

The blast of the horn sounded again. She was aware of a car roaring toward them, then screeching to a halt between where she and her assailant stood and the dark sedan. Her captor spun around as the door opened and Ben Taylor burst from inside, a gun in his hand.

But her captor had a second's advantage . . .

Robin threw herself at him and the shot went wild.

He knocked her to the ground. She rolled over and saw Ben jump her attacker, both of them landing on the cement. Ben hit the man's head against the pavement and the assailant went limp.

She looked up. Two men from the parked car were racing toward them. A van squealed into the parking lot.

"Ben!"

He looked up and saw the van coming, then grabbed her hand. She resisted, leaned down and picked up her purse, then let him push her through the open door into his car. She scooted over to the passenger side as the two men neared the car. The motor was idling, and Ben stepped on the gas. The car seemed to jump, then accelerated.

The two men scattered as Ben steered toward them, then took a sharp right, barely avoiding crashing into the oncoming vehicle. Then they were over a curb. The car sped onto the highway, the van accelerating behind them.

She turned back. The van was only yards behind them. She doubted it would take much time for the dark sedan to follow. Ben swerved just as a shot rang out. She landed against the door. She managed to fasten the seat belt and he swerved again, driving from one side of the road to the other as she heard another shot.

Every nerve leaped and shuddered as the car swayed. Ben made one more turn and the car headed straight toward a truck coming in the opposite direction.

# chapter twenty-seven

*Ben jerked the steering wheel* and whipped the car around the corner, barely missing the truck.

He glanced through the rearview mirror. The van was just behind him. He watched the driver frantically swerve to avoid hitting the truck and ram into a parked car, effectively blocking the street. The horn blared. Whoever drove the dark sedan, the one that had been waiting in the parking lot, was completely blocked.

Ben turned another corner at full speed, then drove south.

"Do you have a phone with you?" he asked Robin as he made yet another turn and slowed.

She didn't answer for a moment and he glanced at her. Her fingers clutched the handle of her purse with a death grip. Her face was frozen. So it wasn't only the purse. He remembered her telling him about the automobile accident. The terror, a kind of acceptance. The crash. Was she reliving that during his wild dash to safety?

He wanted to hold her, but neither of them could afford that at the moment. Instead, he had to snap her out of it. "Call 911 and report the accident," he said. "Say you heard gunfire, that people in the car and the van might have been shooting at each other. Then hang up. Sound hysterical."

"That won't be hard." The voice was weak but a spunky humor was in it.

He threw her another glance. Hardly. He'd discovered she was not the hysterical type.

Her hands shook slightly as she said exactly what he told her, then turned the phone off.

"Quick thinking, deflecting his shot. But foolish. He could have turned the gun on you."

"Better you than me?" she asked dryly.

"True," he said, trying to contain a smile. "I can take care of myself." Her face relaxed slightly. Her grip on the purse didn't seem quite as tight.

He drove two more blocks, then turned again on a side street and traveled another three blocks before he heard wailing sirens. He had to get rid of the rental car. No question that the perps had taken the license plate number.

He turned into the parking lot of an abandoned convenience store and drove to the back, where they were completely hidden. He put the car in park, but didn't turn off the ignition.

He turned to her. Her face was pale.

"Why did you run away without an explanation?" He tried to temper his words, but he realized his voice was cold. Hard.

"I didn't know I had to give you one," she shot back.

"You step from one disaster to another. That's your business," he continued caustically. "Problem is, you leave chaos for everyone else in your wake."

She looked stricken, and he wanted to take her in his arms. God, he'd wanted to do that since he watched her throwing herself into her assailant to deflect his shot. She came too damn close to being killed.

"I'm grateful for your help today," she said stiffly. "Very grateful, in fact. But I had my reasons."

"You always have your reasons. They're not always good ones." He had to give that to her.

Her eyes met his. "Maybe you're right," she admitted.

God, but she got to him. The vulnerability in her eyes just then drained his anger.

He itched to touch her face. He started to reach out to her, then hesitated. Bad idea. She hadn't wanted him around. She didn't trust him.

Still, something in him responded to the fear that still lingered in her eyes. Even now he wanted to ease it.

He touched her face, pushed back some errant curls. Attraction rippled between them again. Fueled, he knew, by the adrenaline they both felt.

The air was thick with emotion. His fingers stroked her cheek, then curled around her neck, easing the tension. Her arms went around him, her breath whispering against his lips.

Then his lips met hers, lightly at first, then hungrily with all the anger and frustration he'd experienced in the last two days. Her lips moved against his, responding with an intensity that shook him. She opened her mouth, and he plundered it, ravishing and taking and giving.

Somewhere in his consciousness, he heard another siren. And another.

He moved away.

Robin looked stunned, as stunned as he felt. All the feelings between them, all that distrust and anger had exploded into something that went beyond reason.

Somehow he forced himself to put the car in gear. This was not a good place to be.

His hands shook slightly as he turned the car out of the parking lot and toward the interstate.

Robin felt as though lightning had flashed through her body. Yearning and wanting filled her.

She moved closer to him as he carefully drove just under the speed limit, his gaze keeping to the road. She looked at his face.

His jaw was set, a muscle knotted in his cheek.

He was silent, and so was she, until he asked directions to where she was staying.

She was stunned by the impact of that kiss, the feelings it had aroused in her.

Only hours earlier she hadn't trusted him.

Now he'd saved her life.

But she'd also heard the anger in his voice and it went beyond the words.

He knew she hadn't trusted him. And she feared she had damaged something fine that had been building between them. They were almost to the motel when he spoke again.

"You didn't answer me when I asked why you felt you had to run away without telling anyone."

"I met my source Sunday night. He told me Hydra had someone in the FBI. Then I received a call at the hospital after Mrs. Jeffers was admitted. Someone who knew you were with me. He told me if I spoke to the grand jury my family would die. He also said he would know, that someone close to me was working for them. Someone who also had access to grand jury deliberations."

"And you believed it? Did you think that someone was trying to get you to doubt me?"

"Yes," she said in a small voice. "I also thought that maybe one of your superiors could be involved. You have to report to them and . . ."

"And you couldn't tell me that?"

She reached for his hand and she laid hers on it. "I should have told you. Everything was happening so fast. I didn't know who or what to believe."

"You trust me now?"

"Yes."

"I could have staged that whole thing, you know. Just to get you to confide in me."

Robin heard the deep irony in his voice and felt the bitterness behind it. Saying she was sorry wasn't going to help anything, and she knew it. She just wished his tone wasn't so cool, so controlled, when she still tingled all over from the kiss.

"And you thought . . . exactly what, when you came down here?" he continued.

"I thought if . . . I could get some more information, then the name of the source wouldn't be so important."

"That damn source is going to get you killed as well as God knows how many others. God save me from amateurs."

"I'm not an amateur. I'm a reporter," she protested. "How did you know where to find me?"

"I found a photo of a boat jammed in your printer."

"You searched my home?" There was some indignation in her voice but it didn't sound that convincing, rather as if she thought she should protest.

"We didn't know whether you'd been kidnapped," he said.

"You disappeared from an agent." He paused, then added caustically, "You might well have ruined his career in the doing."

"Why? I wasn't under arrest. It was voluntary."

"I suspect it was voluntary because you thought we would watch you if it wasn't."

"Wouldn't you?" she challenged.

"Most likely," he admitted wryly.

"How did that photo lead you here? Why Brunswick?"

"Trust goes two ways, Robin," he said in a flat voice. "So far I've gotten damn little. From now on, you want information, you give information. Where did you get the photo?"

"My source," she finally said.

"A deputy with the sheriff's department." It was a question as much as a statement.

"Yes," she admitted. "Now how did you know it was taken in Brunswick?"

"The widow of a Meredith County deputy. Her husband was killed in the line of duty several months ago. A lot of deaths around that department. I asked about fishing trips. She remembered her husband had been on several in south Georgia.

Her gaze riveted on him. "Something to do with the murders?"

"I'm thinking there's a lot of coincidences."

"So you were sent here?"

He hesitated, then replied, "No. I took personal leave."

"Why?"

"I knew you were afraid of something. From your actions, you had to think there was a leak inside the bureau."

"My source said he'd been told . . ."

"That could have been an excuse to keep you from coming to us."

"No. He was scared. Not just scared. Terrified. For his family as well as himself. He said there was someone else who talked too much, and his family was killed. That's why he came to me. He thought I could make enough noise that no one could cover it up."

"Who in the bureau? Did he have any clue?"

She shook her head.

He thought about his office. He would bet his life that it wasn't Mahoney. Hell, he'd already done that more times than he wanted to remember. Holland? He doubted it. Just as he couldn't see any other agent he knew being involved. He didn't mix much. He couldn't return invitations. But he'd worked with them all for years. None lived beyond their means.

"What now?" Robin asked.

"Getting a new car is a priority."

"What about the one I was driving?"

"I don't think you want to go back and get it." He turned and studied her. "Did you leave anything in it?"

"No. Just a map."

"Did it have a hotel name on it?"

She shook her head. "I bought it at a minimart."

"Nothing else?"

"Everything is in my purse."

"The photos?"

She nodded.

"That's why you grabbed it," he said. "You know you could have gotten us both killed."

"Instinct," she whispered. "The original photo . . . my notes were in there."

"What about clothes? Other personal items?"

"At the motel," she said.

"I notice you're aren't wearing the brace."

"Too easy to identify me."

"Is that wise?"

"It was supposed to come off next week, anyway," she said.

He digested that. He knew how careful she had been about it. "Anything else in the car that would give them a clue? A receipt? A parking ticket?"

"No."

"Sure?"

"I've been careful."

"You've been talking to marina operators. Did you use your name?"

"No."

"The motel?"

"A different one there, too."

He was grudgingly impressed. She was good, better than he would have thought.

"Where did you learn all this?"

"Books. Movies." She thought for a moment, then added, "Logic." She paused, then added quickly, "I hope."

He had to smile at that. "Sometimes illogic helps. The unexpected."

"What about my car?" she asked. "I know I can't get it now, but I can't leave it there, either. It belongs to a friend of mine."

"Where are the keys?"

"My purse."

"I have a few friends down here. I'll ask one of them to pick it up."

She stared at him for a long time. "Is this going to get you in trouble?"

He shrugged. "Probably."

"Why are you doing this?" she asked.

"Damned if I know," he said and turned all his attention to the road ahead. Ben pulled in at her motel, drove slowly around the parking lot, then backed into a parking place, concealing the license plate from the rest of the lot.

"Move over to the driver's side," he told her. "Stay here until I signal you to come inside." He paused while she handed him her room key.

"I have a gun with me," she said, her fingers tightening around her purse.

"Where did you get that?"

"Yesterday. In Savannah."

"You said you know how to use it?"

"On targets."

"It's different with a breathing target."

"Have you ever killed anyone?"

He didn't answer. Instead, he stepped outside the car, mashed down the lock on the door, and waited until she slid over to the driver's side. Then he went inside her motel room. Almost instantly he appeared back at the door and gestured for her to come inside.

The room looked even smaller to Robin than it had before. And dingier.

Ben locked the door and turned to her. His granite eyes pinioned her with a long, silent scrutiny. Sparks of longing shot through her as she remembered the way his lips felt against hers.

She needed it now. The adrenaline rush had faded, and she realized how close she'd come today to being killed.

But he was grim-faced. Probably regretting that kiss.

Her heart thumped against her rib cage. She'd made so many mistakes. Suspecting him. Being careless enough to leave the jammed paper in her printer. And yet if she hadn't, then . . .

He would not have found her. She would not be here. Maybe she would have simply disappeared.

What she hadn't counted on was how glad she was to be with him, to see him. She was too aware of his presence, close enough to feel the heat from his body.

The connection was still there. Even when she'd had her doubts, it had been there in her, an intense physical awareness, but something even stronger. Something she'd fought. Was that why she hadn't let herself believe, even for the smallest second, that he could be part of a conspiracy?

She resisted the tangible impulse to reach out and touch him. His body's stiffness, the chill in his eyes warned her away.

He broke off the eye contact. "Have you been using your cell phone?" he asked.

"I have a throwaway phone," she admitted.

He shook his head. "Let me have it."

She was committed now. She handed it to him.

He punched in several numbers. "Carl," she heard him say. "I need a favor. A car drop and a credit card."

He listened for a moment, then said, "Where?"

Another pause, then, "Okay. Two hours."

He turned the phone off and handed it to her. "Let's get the hell out of here."

"You think they can find us?"

"They're resourceful," he said. "If it's true they have a mole in the bureau, they know I could be with you. I'll be getting some cell phone messages. Who calls and with what urgency may tell us something. Pack what you have. They've probably checked your credit cards. Now they'll be checking motels for a woman who paid cash."

"I have a prepaid credit card I've used since arriving."

"Should have known," he muttered more to himself than to her.

"Where are we going?"

"To long-term airport parking. Exchange a license plate."

"Isn't that illegal?" she said, stunned by the pronouncement.

"They'll get it back. We're merely borrowing."

But he would be doing far more than that, and she knew it. He was jeopardizing his career. Who *he* was.

*For her.*

For someone who hadn't trusted him. Lead settled in her stomach. She glanced at him. His jaw was set and his lips thinned. The silence was deafening.

Robin settled back into the passenger's seat. Now, she sensed, was not the time to ask more. It was enough he was with her.

Two hours later they drove to a well-known restaurant.

The car sported the new license plate, taken from a car at the back of the airport lot. It had taken Ben about one minute to change the two. She acted as lookout. He wondered whether it was the first time she had purposely committed a crime.

Before going into the restaurant, he checked his cell phone. Five calls. Two from Mahoney—one from the office and one from his private cell phone. Two from Holland. The fifth was not a number he recognized.

He couldn't call Mahoney. This was a career breaker, and Ben knew it. He could find work in private security. He wasn't worried about that. He *was* worried about keeping up payments for Dani's treatment.

By God, he wanted Hydra. And he damn well didn't want anything to happen to Robin Stuart.

They went inside, Ben holding the door open for her. He

requested a table for three with as much privacy as possible and they were escorted to a table in back. He took a seat where he could see the entrance, glanced quickly at the menu, and put it on the table.

She made her selection just as quickly and placed the menu on his.

"Did you discover anything in Brunswick?" he said.

She didn't hesitate this time. "The name of the boat. The marina where it was moored. The fact that the marina was covering for whoever leased the slip."

He waited.

"I'm pretty sure the name of the boat is the *Phantom*."

"Registered where?"

"I don't know. I just discovered where it had been moored when those thugs showed up. I don't know where it is registered or who owns it. It apparently left yesterday."

He didn't like that. Obviously someone was right behind her. Or ahead.

"What do you know about the boat?" he asked.

"That members of the sheriff's department were treated to fishing trips several times a year. Part of a grand plan, I think."

"What grand plan?"

"Systematic conditioning to corrupt them. Small stuff at first. An extra twenty dollars for tipping off a gambler or bootlegger about a raid, the protection of certain people in the county against DUI and gaming charges. Then the corruption grows until they're so deeply involved they can't go to the authorities. The fishing trips add to the peer pressure."

"And who's the main person involved? The sheriff?"

"I don't know," she said. "He must know about the petty stuff. I'm not sure he knows about the murders."

"Why give him a pass?" he asked harshly.

"Because of the way . . . some deputies talk about him. There's not the anger toward him as there is about—" She stopped suddenly.

"You're not going to tell me who your source is," he said wearily.

"I can't," she said.

"Do you know how quickly we might be able to wrap this up if I know?" he snapped.

"What would you do with the information?" she argued. "What if there *is* an inside person at the FBI? My source . . . his family could die."

"I have people I can go to."

"I can't depend on that."

The door of the restaurant opened, and Carl Andrews walked in. Carl had been at Quantico with him and Dani, had even competed with Ben for Dani. They hadn't been friends, but two years ago when Ben had been sent to Brunswick on a joint task force with the DEA, Ben had saved Carl's life, although the latter's arm had been shattered. He'd left the FBI on a disability and started a private high-tech protection firm.

He'd told Ben then that if he ever needed a favor . . .

Ben had never intended on taking him up on it. He didn't owe anyone and didn't want anyone to owe him. But then, he'd been breaking a lot of rules lately.

Carl slid into the booth next to Robin. He nodded to her as Ben introduced her as Mary Murphy, then turned his attention to Ben.

"How's Dani?" Carl asked.

"In rehab again."

"Sorry to hear that."

"So am I," Ben said.

"What's going down?"

"I need a car picked up, buried for a few days. Some people might be watching."

"Is it hot?"

Ben glanced at Robin.

She shook her head. "No. The owner is a friend of mine. He loaned it to me."

"You said you needed a credit card," Carl said. "You can have one of mine."

"I'll repay all the charges," Ben said.

"You in trouble with the bureau?" Carl asked.

"If I'm not now, I will be. Does that change anything?"

"Not with me. The bastards pushed me out."

Carl took the keys to the car and written directions to the marina.

"I'll be in touch," Ben said.

"Please do," Carl said dryly, then he rose and left without ordering.

"Who was that?" Robin asked. "He didn't sound like a friend."

"He's not. But he thought he owed me."

"You didn't like collecting," she observed.

"No."

"Who's Dani?"

For a moment, he almost told her it was none of her business. But seeing Carl had brought back memories. And not good ones.

"My wife," he said curtly.

# chapter twenty-eight

*"Your wife?"*

"My ex-wife." He emphasized the *ex*. "And the subject isn't open to discussion."

She wanted to open it.

Had he made a Freudian slip when he said wife instead of ex-wife?

Why should she care? He'd shown disdain for her occupation, her decisions. He was here now because he wanted to know what she knew.

"Sorry," she said coolly. "I didn't mean to go somewhere sacred."

"It's not sacred. It's just no one's business but mine."

Robin wasn't hungry after the conversation, but Ben, as always, was. He ordered a steak sandwich and shoveled it down while she picked at a salad. Twenty minutes later, they went to the car and got inside. It was hot, having sat in the coastal sun, but Robin needed it to heat the chill in her bones.

Ben had completely shut her out with his comment about his ex-wife. He had become unreachable in that moment.

*Rehab?*

He'd said nothing about his wife in the short time she'd known him. But though it had been short, it had been a lifetime in some ways. He'd been there every time she'd needed him.

And then she'd turned that against him.

No wonder he was so angry. And he was that. There had

been no recriminations. No second-guessing, but he was freezing her out.

She wanted the warmth back, that feeling of belonging they'd shared the night he'd brought her home from the Meredith County hospital and he'd massaged her leg.

"I'm sorry," she said. "I should have trusted you."

He started the car. "No particular reason you should."

He was wrong. There were lots of reasons she should have trusted him. "Why are you helping me?"

"I want these guys as much as you do," he said. "And if you're right about a mole in the FBI, I want to know who it is."

She watched him as he drove. "We should return to the marina."

"Why?"

"I think the attendant knows something. The registration would be there. So is whoever paid the rent in the slip. It's all we have."

"I don't think that's a good idea right now," he said.

"Then what?"

"I'm going to find out who owns the marina. Start at the top."

She stared at him. "How did you happen to be at that particular marina?"

"I figured that's where you would go. I'd already checked out several."

She suspected that wasn't the complete truth. "No other reason?"

He ignored her question. "You said the attendant at the marina knew something. Why?"

"He denied knowing anything about the *Phantom* but some people on a boat said it had been there for a while, and that the attendant really paid a lot of attention to the captain."

A muscle throbbed in his cheek. "I might have led them to you."

"How?"

"I left the deputy's widow's house and went directly to the airport. We were careful. But someone could have found out. I bought the ticket in my name. I didn't have time to do anything else."

"Could they still be following you?"

"I don't think so, but I'm not underestimating them. Not again."

A chill ran through her, and it had nothing to do with the air-conditioning. "Will your friend be okay?"

"Carl? He's really quite competent. He'll be all right."

"I don't want any one else hurt."

"It's a little late for second-guessing."

"I'm not second-guessing. You have some leads now you wouldn't have had before."

"I would have gotten to them."

"You're infallible, and I'm an idiot. Is that it?"

"No, that's not it. You're definitely not an idiot. That's the damn problem. But you are an amateur. And you're alone. You have no resources."

"I have you," she defended herself.

"Not something to brag about," he said.

"Where do we go now?"

"A library," he said. "We can use their computers. No way to trace us."

"You don't have to do this," she said. "I'm safe now. You can go back. No one saw you. No one would be the wiser."

"And what would you do?"

"I want to protect my sisters and Mrs. Jeffers and the man who trusted me."

"That means you would continue."

She knew her silence answered him.

She also knew that he was driving toward Savannah. She loved Savannah, almost as much as she loved the Golden Isles. But he was taking her away from where she hoped answers would be.

Still, one look at his face, and she decided not to protest.

"Tell me everything that happened at the marina," he said. "Your impressions. Trust your instincts."

"The attendant gave me the creeps. I told him I was a travel writer and at first he seemed very receptive. Then I asked him about a boat named the *Phantom*, said a friend of mine told me what a great time he had fishing on it, and that gave me the idea for a story on marinas on the Southeast coast.

"He shook his head as if he didn't know anything about it,

but some people said the boat had been moored just a few slips down, and had been for a long time. Said the crew seemed to keep to themselves.

"I started back to the office. This time it was locked. That's when someone approached me with a gun. The attendant must have called."

"What else did those people tell you?"

"That the captain's name was Stefan, last name maybe Fisher, that he was foreign, and that the crew was arrogant. Seemed to think they got special privileges from the marina management. That's all they knew."

"Interesting," he said.

She suddenly realized he knew something about that marina. It was simply too convenient that he "just happened by" at the right time.

"You know something about that marina? You weren't there entirely by accident."

His lips crooked into a tight smile. "I'm beginning to understand why you're a good reporter."

She waited for him to go on.

"I was here three years ago on a task force with the DEA. A cartel was running drugs into Brunswick. Used both steamers and smaller craft. Brunswick was perfect for their purposes. Access to the Intracoastal Waterway but away from the larger shipping channels. Not a big port, it wasn't monitored that closely."

"What happened?"

"We caught a shipment coming in on a small freighter delivering cars. We confiscated the ship, arrested some bit players, plus the connection in Brunswick, but we never got the money guys. The perps wouldn't talk, not even to get a lighter sentence. It was obvious they were more afraid of the cartel than a long prison term."

"And the marina?" she asked.

"We heard some smaller shipments of coke were coming into that marina but we could never prove it. Some thought it was just a decoy to keep our attention off the small freighters that used the port. The DEA continued to monitor it for a while but their agents never came up with anything, and the investigation was dropped. Prematurely, I thought."

"Three years ago," she mused aloud. "That's when my source said the boat trips started. Could they have shifted operations up to the Atlanta area?"

"Makes sense. Their market was the Southeast. The DEA and the Coast Guard heightened their surveillance of ports on the southeast coast. The local police are really working at intercepting shipments traveling on the interstates. Private planes flying within the country are a natural."

"And Meredith has private airstrips."

"Several of them."

A surge of excitement flowed through her. "You think all this is connected?"

"I don't think anything at this point. I just remembered the suspicions about that marina and decided to wait there for you this morning. I figured you would show up, if you hadn't already. It was my best chance."

"Do you think the same people own the marina today that owned it three years ago?"

"Not on paper," he said. "We made several visits, went through their books."

"Won't they be looking for whoever picks up my car, then? Isn't Carl in danger?"

"He's a pro. Plus he knows the picture as well as I do. He was almost killed in that drug bust. He'll have someone else pick it up, make sure the car is clean and that he's not followed. It's what he does, Robin. He trains executives here and abroad to take precautions against kidnapping. He knows every trick in the book and then some."

"Did you suspect your case three years ago might be connected with Meredith County?" she asked.

"Maybe I should have, but I didn't. My boss suspected that Hydra and a money-laundering operation might be connected but it wasn't until I saw a picture of that boat jammed in your printer that the pieces started coming together. When the widow I saw yesterday, Amy Boatright, confirmed it was Brunswick, I thought it was a heck of a coincidence. After your reception at the marina, I'm sure they're related."

The story danced in her head. She could see the headlines in 48-point boldface letters. INTERNATIONAL DRUG RING

BUSTED. Even more important, her family would be safe. And Sandy.

"You don't need my source any longer," she said. "You know where to look now. You can go—" She stopped suddenly.

"Go where?" he said. "If you're right, and there is someone in the FBI involved, then you and I are dead. You and that photo are the only link. I assume that whoever gave you that photo can in some way be traced back from it." He steered the car off the interstate and stopped at a traffic light.

"There has to be someone you trust."

"You weren't listening just now," he said.

She went back over the conversation, then remembered one important word. *Prematurely.* The investigation ended prematurely. Only someone very high up could cut short an investigation.

She saw a sign for Savannah, and he took the exit. So now she knew for sure where they were going. She wasn't sure why yet.

She leaned back against the door and watched him. For the moment, they were no longer adversaries. But neither were they entirely united in common cause. Tension stretched between them like strung wire. She hadn't trusted him, and now he didn't trust her. He might never again.

She openly studied him. He obviously hadn't shaved this morning. He had the dark hair and complexion that made five o'clock shadow more obvious than on men with a lighter complexion. She could well see him as a bandido in a film. He had a moody intensity and dark sensuality that radiated bad boy. Yet she'd discovered he was no bad boy at all, but a reluctant hero who was quietly present when needed.

*Dani.* His wife. Robin longed to know more about her, how he still felt about her. There had been something earlier between Carl and Ben that was subtly antagonistic. Something about Dani. Dani Taylor. Something that had left a deep scar on him.

She had thrown away what small part of himself that he had given her, and she sensed that he was not a man to offer it again. Her loss. God, what a fool she'd been.

He parked at a meter in front of a row of buildings on Bay

Street and guided her into a small storefront library. It was little more than a hole in the wall, but it had computers and a welcoming woman at the desk. He'd known exactly where to come. He'd obviously been here before.

Computers were available thanks to the fact it was summer, and few students were working. They each took a station side by side.

"I'll go after ownership records of the marina," he said. "Someone else checked them three years ago, and it might have been sold since then. In any event, I want to know the history of ownership. You check newspapers for advertisements of any charters of the *Phantom*. Or any mention of the boat."

She used the library password to sign on to the Net and started searching for Phantom/boat. Over twenty-seven thousand entries. She immediately gave up on that and went to the Brunswick newspaper. She searched for Phantom there. Nothing.

She looked at sport fishing. Again nothing.

She glanced over at Ben, wondered whether he was using his FBI access. Property sales were public records, but were they available to the general public on the computer?

Loneliness filled her as she watched that intensity that had caught her the first day she'd seen him. He was hunched over, his eyes intent on the screen in front of him. She should have that same intensity. Instead, she was far too aware of him, angry at her vulnerability with him. She hungered for his touch, for that rare half smile that so attracted her.

He was obviously unaware.

She turned back to her computer. The people she'd talked to at the last marina had said the captain of the boat was named Stefan and he had an accent. The last name was something like Fisher.

Nothing under Stefan Fisher. She tried Fischer.

A hit. Thousands of hits. Stefan Fischer was evidently a very popular name. She started to narrow it. Brunswick. Captain. Nothing.

Ben had stopped. He glanced over at her screen. His eyes asked the question.

"The captain of the *Phantom*, according to the boaters I talked to. But the last name might be spelled wrong."

"Time to go. We've already been here too long since I signed in, but I can access information you can't." He hesitated, then entered "Stefan Fischer."

Ten minutes later, he exclaimed, "Bingo."

"What is it?"

"If it's your Fischer, he has an arrest record. Drug possession. Charges were dropped. No conviction."

"When? Where?"

He cracked a slow smile. "Atlanta. Eight years ago."

"Can you find out why?"

A librarian interrupted them then. "We're closing."

She turned off her computer, and Ben did as well. Then they left the library.

The street was nearly empty, and the sun was dipping in the west. Both of them studied the cars around them. Several other people were exiting a nearby parking lot and getting into cars, but nothing looked suspicious.

"Hungry?" he asked.

"No. Where do we go now?" She realized with those words that she had given up the last resistance to him. He was a partner now, a cool, objective partner.

"I want to make some phone calls," he said. "Then we'll find someplace to stay. You need some sleep."

She needed much more than that. Much, much more, but he'd turned unapproachable.

She had to settle now for his help.

Ben thought about using Robin's temporary phone but they'd used it too much now. Someone might have been able to track the number down. Choice now was another temporary phone, or a pay phone.

He decided on a pay phone. They wouldn't be in Savannah much longer.

He called Mahoney's cell phone. Hung up. Then rang again. No one answered.

Ben went back to the car. Mahoney would know what to do. Go down to the coffee shop they frequented. It was a code they'd worked out as they drove to the airport yesterday. Was it just yesterday?

He stood outside the car, waiting as the minutes ticked away. Robin was inside. He didn't want to get back inside with her.

Hell he didn't.

It had been all he could do to keep his hands off her these past few hours. No, all day. Ever since he saw the perp holding a gun on her, and the way she'd dived into the bad guy to deflect his shot. Otherwise, Ben might well be in a body bag.

He'd purposely kept her at a distance, though he'd wanted to pull her into his arms after they'd sped away. He knew she was receptive. It had been in her eyes. Gratitude. Regret. Confusion.

He didn't want gratitude, or regret. He was damned tired of regret and gratitude. He wasn't going down that street again. Dani hadn't trusted him, either, until it was too late. Without trust, love was worthless.

Not that he loved Robin Stuart. He lusted over her. She intrigued him. She challenged him. And God knew it had been a long time since he'd held a woman in his arms. She'd responded to him with all the passion she brought to everything she did. All the fire he'd once had and lost.

But he'd learned in the past few days that law and press didn't mix. Would never mix. And he was damned if he was going to go through the same agony he did years ago.

So far, just getting away from killers had kept him occupied. So had the need to find answers. The fact that he hadn't finished the job three years ago grated on him. The fact that three police officers, and maybe more, had died because of that failure was lead in his gut.

He glanced at his watch. Twelve minutes. He only hoped that Mahoney had been at the office, that he could get to the coffee shop. The door of the car opened and Robin stood, stretched. Her eyes were red-rimmed, probably from exhaustion. but the light was in them. Light of battle? Or something else?

He went back to the pay phone and called the pay phone at the coffee shop. Mahoney answered immediately. "Where are you? The U.S. attorney is going nuts."

"What about Holland?"

"He wants to be able to give Ames some answers."

"Anything happening with the case?"

"Nada. Zero. Zip."

"Did Ames ever say why he wanted to see me?"

"He thinks you might know something about Robin Stuart's disappearance. He swears that if you helped her he will have your badge."

"He doesn't have any authority to do that."

"Well, he has Holland antsy." He paused. "Find anything?"

"Maybe. Can you check back on a case involving a Stefan Fischer? He was arrested for drug possession eight years ago in Atlanta. No conviction. I want to know what happened. Why it was dropped. Who the attorneys were."

"Will do."

"As quietly as possible."

"What does he have to do with anything?"

"He's captain of the boat that took out the sheriff's deputies off the coast of Georgia."

Silence. "You're not suggesting there might be some connection with the drug case down there?"

"I think there's a chance that Hydra might have moved to Atlanta, though some drugs may still come in through Brunswick. What better cover than a boat frequented by law enforcement?"

Mahoney swore. "I remember how we protested that the investigation was being concluded too rapidly."

"Yeah. See if you can get that information."

"What do I tell Holland?"

"That I'm on vacation and must have lost my cell phone."

"And if someone finds out I've been looking into this Fischer?"

"You're going back over old drug cases."

"You're going to get me fired."

"I hope to hell I get *someone* fired. And indicted."

"Who?"

"I'm narrowing the possibilities."

"How's Ms. Stuart?"

"The less you know, the better."

"Yeah, I know. How do I reach you if I find anything?"

"I'll find you."

"That's what I'm afraid of," Mahoney grumped.

Ben hung up. He hated to involve Mahoney, but his partner was in a better position than he to check on an old case. If he could find the case, he could go to the cops who handled it.

He went back to the car.

Robin was still outside, leaning against the car. He wondered how her leg was doing. She had the brace in the car but wasn't wearing it.

They both got into the car.

"Are you going to tell me what that was about?"

"The U.S. attorney is after my scalp. He believes I helped you escape."

"I'm not under arrest."

"No. You have every right to be here. Which makes me wonder . . ."

"Joseph Ames?" Her eyes widened. "You don't think he can be involved."

"I don't think anything at the moment."

"He has a great reputation as a prosecutor."

"Yeah," Ben said unenthusiastically.

He started the car, then glanced at her. He saw the wheels turning inside. *The U.S. attorney.* The one person who would have the authority to gather information, to continue investigations. To stop them.

The one person no one would suspect.

He dismissed the notion. All he had was the fact that he was angry about Ben's disappearance during an important case.

He turned on the ignition. He really wanted a different car, and now with Carl's credit card he could get one. If anyone was on their trail, he meant to shake them off.

He wasn't ready to take Robin back to Atlanta. Not until he knew one way or another whether Ames was involved. The likelihood of being believed was dim, and most certainly he would be taken off the case at best, killed at worse, with suspension and a career loss very real possibilities.

And Robin . . . even worse.

He knew one thing. They had to leave Savannah.

He found a map in the glove compartment. He wanted to revisit the marina. He wanted to break in and find what records they had. A few moments on their computer. The pure idiocy of that thought showed his desperation.

Robin looked at him intently, then said, "I didn't tell you everything. There's a beach house."

# chapter twenty-nine

*Ben turned off the ignition* and stared at her. "What beach house?"

"My source said that in addition to the boat there was a beach house that was used by the deputies."

"What else didn't you tell me?" he said, a hard edge in his voice.

He probably thought she was withholding information again. For once she was innocent. All her attention had been focused on the boat and who owned it after the attack on her.

"That's all," she said. "A beach house. But not a family retreat. More for a men's night out. I truly forgot about it."

"Where?"

"Fernandina Beach in Florida. Not far from Brunswick."

He swore under his breath. "You know we lost time. They're probably cleaning that up as well."

"It was stupid. I was concentrating on the boat. And San—my source didn't have an address. A private van always took them to both locations."

She saw something flicker in his eyes at her slip, but he didn't say anything.

"I wondered at the time why not Jekyll," she said. "Could be because the island is state owned, and homeowners lease property from the state. I suspect they have rather stringent requirements. A foreign corporation wouldn't qualify. The other nearby islands are pretty much year-round residences. Fernandina is the next closest beach. Still on the Intracoastal Waterway."

"Some separation probably isn't a bad thing for them," Ben said, picking up the thread. "Different states. Different records. If someone picked up on the boat, they might not automatically pick up on the property."

"A building on land will be harder to hide," she said. "There will be bills. Someone to contact in case of an emergency. Taxes."

He took his gaze from the road and glanced at her for the briefest second. "I understand why you're a good reporter."

"I don't think you consider that much of a compliment."

"If you're asking whether my opinion of your profession has changed, it hasn't," he said. "Mostly vultures who don't care who they hurt as long as they get a headline."

"And you lump me in that cauldron of unprincipled opportunists?" She tried to ignore the contempt in his voice, the wound it carved deeply inside her.

"I think *you* are principled," he conceded. "If . . . impulsive."

"But still an opportunist?"

He didn't answer.

She wasn't sure which adjective she most objected to. Opportunist or impulsive. The latter, she thought, was his euphemism for foolish.

"Why do you dislike the press so much?" It was a question she'd wanted to ask before. She knew a lot of cops didn't trust the press, but she'd never felt such outright hostility before meeting Ben.

"You don't want to go there," he warned.

"I do."

"A reporter destroyed someone I cared about," he said in a flat expressionless voice. "Not for the public good. Just a headline. Another got one of my witnesses killed because the agent in charge trusted him."

Both the words and the tone chilled her. After their wild escape this morning, he'd touched her briefly, and they'd worked together this afternoon in quiet companionship. She thought they'd reached a truce of sorts, even if he kept her at arm's length.

Or so she'd thought.

The connection she'd felt earlier was still there. She saw it in his eyes, and the way he'd reached out to her earlier. Reluctantly, perhaps, but the sparks were still there. The electricity. Even tenderness when he lowered his guard.

But she was back to the place when they'd first met, when she'd felt his blatant distrust of the press. Now she knew part of the reason—but not the whole of it—and she had no answer unless she knew more details.

Judging by the shuttered look of his face, she wasn't going to learn more.

He started the car again, headed south and stopped at a Mexican restaurant.

It was nearly ten, and day had turned into night.

Robin wasn't really hungry. She'd had a late lunch, and her stomach churned. She wasn't usually subject to nerves, and she seldom lost her appetite.

But she was a bundle of the first, and the latter was definitely gone.

After they were seated, she played with some chips after ordering. "Something's worrying you."

"I've been thinking more about Joseph Ames."

"Why?"

"He wanted to see me the day I left. I left before having a chance to meet with him. And, too, because he changed his mind about asking for an immediate contempt of court order against you. Because they were afraid you *would* talk? Your caller said someone would know exactly what went on in that room. That would include only the judge, Ames, and the grand jurors. I was just in there for twenty minutes."

She still had a difficult time believing Joseph Ames could be involved.

She studied his expression. She was learning to read him. "You don't really believe it?"

"There's so much scrutiny before you get that kind of appointment. That's a mark against it, but after the past week, I don't know what I believe. I do know that it's unusual for Ames to become so intimately involved in an investigation at this stage. And he stuck out his neck a mile on the subpoena. He wants to run for higher office. Jailing reporters is not a popular thing to do . . ."

She thought about the implications of what he was saying. *A U.S. attorney.* What a story—*if* it were true. A lot of ifs were involved. Then a knot settled in the center of her stomach. If true, how much further did it go? "That investigation you told me about in Brunswick," she asked. "Who closed it down?"

"Joseph Ames," Ben said flatly. "He said the trail had gone cold. No sense wasting more resources. I argued, but was then reassigned to a white-collar case."

A chill ran through her. "So maybe the protection my source referred to wasn't the FBI after all. It was someone in a better position to control events," she said.

"Maybe."

*Tell him about the source.*

She couldn't. Her training had been so strong, and Jack Ross's experience so searing, that reneging on her promise would be like tearing part of her soul out.

How could she make him understand that?

"Tell me more about the beach house," he said.

"I don't know much about it. My source mentioned it. He was there two years ago. Once. He was far more impressed by the boat."

"Do you have the address? Mahoney can check it out."

"He didn't have the address. A van took them down, just as it did for the boat trips. Just once, though. But he described it and gave me directions."

He looked skeptical.

"There have to be records of ownership," she said hopefully.

"Unless like the murder site in Meredith County, it goes back to a corporation in the Seychelles Islands."

She started. She hadn't known that. Bob Greene hadn't been able to trace the Somerville Group back that far. He'd only found a corporation and an attorney he couldn't reach.

"It's one of the most protective offshore banking venues there is," Ben continued. "Someone can incorporate there with all local Seychelles stand-ins. All you need is a registered office and a Seychelles' resident to sign as subscriber for incorporation. Only one shareholder and one director are required for incorporation but nominee service is offered to maintain the owners' privacy. Every path in this maze leads to the Seychelles Islands. I think your boat and beach house probably do as well. The difference on a house is that someone has to pay taxes, utility bills, and more importantly have someone available in case of an emergency. There might be some clues there."

"We're going to Fernandina Beach?"

"Yep. Unless you want to go home."

She shook her head.

"It'll be dangerous," he warned her. "They know now you are aware of the boat. They may or may not think you know about the house. If they do, it's probably been cleaned. If not, there might be people staying there. Dangerous people." He let that soak in.

"I want to go. It's my story."

"It's our lives," he corrected. "And some justice for those cops. You have to promise to do what I tell you."

She started to bristle, then relaxed. She *was* an amateur. He was the professional here. But she hated the professional tone, the lack of warmth, the implication that she was a burden.

He finished his meal. She started to reach into her purse to pay the bill but he was a second faster.

Then they were back in the car and heading south. Nearly eleven now and they had a long drive. She leaned back into the seat. She felt safe with him. More than safe. Warm. Tingly warm.

It wasn't enough. She wanted so much more.

She'd never ached inside like this before, or regretted more something that had been lost. She wanted to reach her hand out and put it over his. She had to be satisfied with closing her eyes and willing herself into falling into a shallow doze.

Ben stopped at a small town just north of Brunswick. They were both tired, and her directions to the beach house would require daylight. Better to get some sleep tonight and start out at dawn.

He had Carl's credit card, and he'd had damned little sleep the past four days. And Robin was curled up in the passenger's seat sleeping.

He stopped first at a convenience store, filled up with gas

and bought a razor and shaving cream. He bought two T-shirts emblazoned with dolphins. One medium. One large.

When he returned to the car, Robin was still asleep. He drove to a motel and registered under Carl's name, then drove the car to the assigned unit.

She looked peaceful. And appealing. Too damned appealing.

One reason he'd hesitated to stop was the agony of sharing a room with her. But he damned well wasn't going to leave her alone. She'd probably steal his rental car and try to save the world on her own. Again.

He shook her, and she merely sighed. "Come on, sleepy-head," he said. She protested without opening her eyes. He wondered when she'd last slept a night through. He reached down and picked her up, then carried her through the door. Her eyes fluttered open, then opened wide as he dumped her on the giant king-size bed.

He'd asked for two double beds. He should probably return to the office, but no, that would draw attention to them. He would take a chair. Wouldn't be the first time.

He took off her sandals. He debated doing more, then decided not to. Instead, he pulled the sheet and cover over her, his hand touching her cheek and lingering there for a few seconds. He eyed the chair. Then the very big bed of which Robin Stuart took up a very small part.

Exhaustion was crushing him.

He checked the locks, then took off his socks and shoes and lay down on top of the covers. Just for a few hours.

Robin woke up, her body curled against another.

She looked toward the window. It was still dark outside.

Drowsily she inventoried herself. No sandals, but she still wore the clothes she'd had on all day. Still, the warmth of Ben's body warmed hers in the air-conditioned room.

She didn't want to move. His warm breathing against her neck was an aphrodisiac that was irresistible. So was his body against hers.

Her eyes adjusted to the dark. She had apparently thrown off covers and gravitated toward him. That they both still wore clothes told her that he had carefully tried to preserve a wall between them.

But one of his arms had fallen across her back and she snuggled into him, her body aching for his.

She stayed that way, reveling in his nearness, when he pulled her to him. She wriggled her body around until she faced him and her cheek rubbed his.

"Hmmmmm," he moaned softly, drowsily, as if not entirely awake.

She leaned over and kissed him, lazily at first, then his lips began to respond with increasing passion.

Robin regretted her clothes, and his. She wanted the friction of his skin against hers, the heat exchanged and absorbed. Most of all she wanted to feel him inside her, feel his strength and power and her own tumultuous reaction to him.

His mouth pressed down on hers. Sensations ignited in the core of her as his tongue seduced its way into her mouth. Her lips moved against his, responding with an intensity that seemed to spur his. His body tensed, and she felt him grow hard next to her. She touched his jeans, which were straining, and she unzipped them.

His eyes opened halfway, dark eyelashes partially covering them. A sexual electricity sparked between them as his hands made heated paths up and down her body, then they slid down her back to her buttocks and unzipped her slacks and pulled them down.

She unbuttoned her shirt and slipped off her bra, feeling wanton and sexy in a way she never had before. There was something so sensuous—even primeval—about him, about the way her body responded to his slightest touch.

She wasn't sure he was fully awake or even that he fully realized what was happening, the sudden explosive coming together. His eyes closed all the way, then with a heavy sigh his kiss deepened. She wasn't prepared, though, for the sudden, raw violence as his lips hardened against hers, and his arm pulled her so tight against him she felt every muscle of his body.

She wanted him. She wanted him with every fiber of her being. She wasn't sure what had happened in the past few days. She only knew that she wanted to satisfy the fiery craving throughout her body, one so fierce and needy that nothing else mattered but satisfying it.

A moan ripped from his throat as her body played with his, inviting him, seducing him in a way that astounded her. She'd never been the aggressor before, but she was very much that now.

Then he became an equal in lovemaking. His hand touched her hair with unexpected tenderness. It was only a moment but then she knew it wasn't only lust on his part but something gentler, sweeter. Still he hesitated just a moment. She arched her body. He moved over her, hesitating just a fraction of a second before entering her.

Her legs went around him, drawing him even closer to her, until he was so deep in her she felt he was touching her soul. She felt his tenseness, the struggle within him, then heard the curse, low and mumbled, as he started to move inside her, a rhythmic movement that brought whimpering sounds from deep in her throat.

The exquisite electricity ignited every nerve end and coursed through her body. She responded, moving her body in concert with his in a primitive, sensuous dance that sent ripples of heat racing through her bloodstream. He was so strong inside her, so full, so compellingly complete. His every movement aroused such incredible sensations, she felt like an eagle racing toward the stars. As his body moved with more and more urgency, she thought she could stand no more, that the ecstasy was too great to bear. Then one last thrust exploded in thousands of radiant streaks. Waves and waves of pleasure washed through her.

He slumped next to her, his hand fondling the triangle of hair just above her legs. Awash in rippling aftershocks of pleasure, she made a half turn, lying halfway across him, her head against his heart. She heard its beat, rush, hurried, as was his breathing.

She had never felt this way before, never experienced the splendor she did tonight, or the sense of belonging she felt with him. She reached out to touch his face, still rough with beard.

A groan started in the back of his throat and his eyes opened wide. His hands explored her as they had minutes ago, but this time with more tentativeness as if something had changed. She had changed.

Sex. Lust. Certainly that had been there, but she'd never felt anything so powerful, so wondrous. There had been a confluence of souls. Nothing else could account for the splendor, for the tenderness in his hands, in his almost wondering touch.

She'd never believed in love like this. She'd known him a week. Two? Real love was built from companionship. Similar likes. Similar values. Now for the first time she could understand how her mother, the gentle birdwatcher, and her father, the consummate warrior, got together. But their marriage had been unhappy.

Ben wrapped his arms around her, pulled her tight against him, and nothing mattered, only the beating of their hearts in concert. Not even the warning in the back of her mind that the heady sense of belonging—the contentment mixed with something close to rapture—waged war with the profound differences between them, that both of them might be stumbling down the path to disaster.

His hold on her loosened and he gently guided her over to her side. The first indication of dawn was filtering through the curtains, and she saw his eyes. Not curtained now. Not wary. Instead there was a tenderness she'd not seen before.

"It wasn't a mistake," she said, anticipating him.

He ran a finger down her cheek and sighed. "Of course it was," he said. "The time, the place . . ."

She put her finger to his mouth.

"Not now," she said. "We'll think about it later."

For now, for this instant, she was going to relish what she had.

To her surprise, his lips twisted into a wry grin. "That's a Scarlett O'Hara tactic."

That startled her.

"I do read," he said.

"*Gone with the Wind*?"

"Everything as a kid, even *Gone with the Wind*. One of my foster homes had a copy. I devoured anything around. Even *Alice in Wonderland*," he added with a mischievous humor she'd not seen before. "Escape, I guess."

"Foster homes?" He'd said he had no family. He'd not mentioned foster homes.

His face changed, as if he felt he'd said too much. Then he shrugged and touched her face. "You don't know anything about me, Robin. Nothing."

"Because you don't want me to know, even about *Alice in Wonderland*."

"Just not very interesting," he said. "I was a throwaway baby. Never knew who my father was. My mother gave me up when I was two. Grew up in foster homes. I learned early not to want anything badly. I learned not to form attachments. I learned not to depend on anyone but myself." He paused, then added, "Those are habits I can't break, Robin."

The words weren't self-pitying. They were matter-of-fact and that made them even more painful to hear. No wonder he'd never discussed anything personal. Her parents' marriage had been anything but perfect, but she'd always been loved by both of them.

His words, though, had been more than a painful admission. They had been a warning.

A warning she chose to ignore. "How did you happen to join the FBI?"

"I joined the army after high school. The state turned me loose, and the army was the means to an end. I went into military police and took college courses whenever I could. I finished college after being discharged and was recruited by the FBI. The bureau likes a military police background."

"And you like it?"

He shrugged. "As well as anything. I've always been good at puzzles. That's what most crimes are. Little puzzles. Big ones."

"And Dani?"

His hand stopped moving across her back. He sat up and looked at the window, at the first rays of sun pouring in. "It's late," he said abruptly. "We should be on the road."

He'd closed the door to his life again.

# chapter thirty

*Michael put down the phone* and stared out the full picture window of his condo at the Atlanta skyline. The sun was rising over the city.

He glanced at the clock. Seven a.m.

His life had become a nightmare, and not even the apartment he loved had its usual soothing effect.

He'd worked damned hard for it. He'd been the first in his family to go to college, and he'd had to work two jobs to manage it. All his life, he'd wanted enough money to never have to worry about bills again.

After college he had college loans to repay. He'd been happy to get a job with a large financial firm that did auditing for some of the largest corporations in the Southeast, but the beginning pay had been barely enough to live on, much less help his younger brother with college expenses.

Then he'd been assigned to work on an audit of a large Atlanta development company. He'd been young and eager, went deeper than the other auditors and found a number of irregularities, including payments to what appeared to be shell companies.

He also discovered some overlapping management funds with a company called Exotic Imports. He started to ask questions. The president of the company, James Kelley, called him to his office and answered them, not entirely to Michael's satisfaction. But Kelley told Michael what a great job he'd been doing and how impressed he was. He was going to tell the accounting firm he should have a bonus and a promotion.

When Michael went into his office the next day, he was told by his immediate supervisor that he was being moved upstairs, and that he was in line for a partnership. His salary would be increased by half.

Nonetheless, he told his supervisor about what he had found.

"James Kelley and his friends are among our largest clients," he was told. "It's because of him we have substantial government business. I know Kelley. He used to be a practicing attorney and he knows every mover and shaker in town. No one is hiding anything. Believe me, he's on the up-and-up. Now, I have this other job for you . . ."

Michael took the raise and more money over the next few years. Bonuses. Some from the company. Some from Kelley. He was given a sweetheart deal on his condominium. Then he was up to his neck in sludge, too deep to get out without losing everything, including his livelihood. He was Kelley's man, and he became the auditor for Kelley's various developments and partnerships. He knew Kelley was laundering money, but when the original partner, the one who asked for an audit, died in a fiery crash, Michael stopped asking questions. He knew by then that he had become entangled in Hydra, and he didn't know how to get out. *Alive.* Now others had died. Including three cops. He suspected Kelley, through foreign corporations, owned the land where the three cops were murdered. Then he was ordered to romance the reporter. She was asking too many of the wrong questions.

After all, Kelley told him, Robin Stuart was a cripple and would be grateful for attention from a good-looking guy like Michael. To Michael's chagrin, Kelley knew of every woman Michael had romanced and bedded. He realized then he'd been followed, photographed.

He'd liked Robin Stuart. More than liked her. She intrigued him. For someone who usually liked flashy blonds and great figures, he was taken off guard. Her smile was infectious, not fake. Her blue eyes lit when she talked. There was a guilelessness about her that appealed to him.

He'd enjoyed every moment with her, as few as they were.

She was everything that he'd wanted to be, and wasn't. He saw himself through her eyes and was sickened.

He was also aware that he knew too much, and too many people who knew too much died. Not only did he know too much, he had failed with Robin Stuart, and failure wasn't tolerated.

The voice on the phone had demanded as much. Find out where Robin Stuart had gone.

He thought he could deliver. He had been at Charlie's when Mama answered the phone. Though she didn't mention the name, he sensed Robin was on the other end. One phone call, and he could get the telephone records. He decided not to make that phone call.

Time for him to go to the authorities and try to get into witness protection. He knew he couldn't live the way he was living now, never knowing whether he was going to be the next accident victim. Nor could he live with himself if he had anything to do with any more deaths.

The problem was he didn't know whom to go to; whom he could trust.

He knew Kelley had cops on the payroll, including most of the Meredith County sheriff's department. He'd heard him brag about others. The FBI? The U.S. attorney's office?

Someone in Washington?

He poured himself a drink. The only person he thought he could trust was Robin. She'd withheld the name of a source despite heavy pressure. She might know someone who could be trusted.

He left his condominium and went to his favorite restaurant around the corner. He stopped and dialed her newspaper office, asked for the editor.

"It's about the stories she's writing," he said. "I have information for her."

"Who is this?"

"That's not important. But it's urgent I reach her."

"Bob Greene has taken over the story."

"I'll only talk to Ms. Stuart. I'll call you back in a few hours to see if there's a way I can reach her."

He closed the cell phone. His hands were shaking so badly he almost dropped it.

• • •

Robin took a quick shower and washed her hair while Ben shaved. Then he took a shower while she used the motel blow dryer to partially dry her hair and applied just a touch of lipstick.

She'd wrapped a towel around her after emerging from the shower, and she looked incredible. Her cheeks were flushed and her hair curled around like honey-colored silk as she dried it. Her blue eyes glowed from their lovemaking.

He glowed inside, too, but he was loath to admit it.

He touched her still damp skin, then leaned down and kissed her lightly. His heart slammed against his rib cage as the kiss deepened.

He forced himself to step back. He would stay here all day if she didn't get dressed. If *they* didn't get dressed.

"No one should look as good as you do in the morning," he murmured. "It should be against the law."

She gave him a delighted smile that touched him with its guilelessness, even a sweetness. "Thank you."

Damn but he wanted to put her back in that bed and stay there all day. So did a very important part of him. The towel *he* was wearing had a decided bulge.

He went into the room and pulled on his jeans, wincing at the tightness around his crotch. Robin came out of the bathroom and reached for a shirt.

He shook his head and dumped the contents of the bag holding his purchases from last night. The two T-shirts came tumbling out. "We might have to be Mr. and Mrs. today," he said.

Robin picked up one. "I like it."

She fastened her bra and pulled the T-shirt over it.

"It looks a lot better on you than mine will on me," he said. He wanted to touch her again. But then he would have to admit he felt far more than he should for her, that she had become far too important to him.

Couldn't happen. He hadn't been enough for Dani, and he wouldn't be enough for Robin. He didn't know how to give someone else a part of himself. He'd lost that ability when he was a kid. Now the bureau was his life, a good one.

*Which I might be throwing down a well.*

"Time to go," he said.

He looked outside, then took out their belongings while she finished dressing. Then he searched under the car for any tracking device. Natural precaution only. He felt fairly sure they'd evaded any pursuit.

They headed south. She curled up on her side of the front seat. Inches away yet really miles.

They reached Fernandina two hours later.

She had only very sketchy directions. "On the beach. Not far south of a restaurant with a net in the window. There was a blue pelican mailbox in front of a three-story cottage with blue trim."

That was all she had. "He said they came down in a van loaded with booze. I think they stayed drunk the whole time."

Hell, there must be dozens of restaurants. He hoped pelicans weren't popular on mailboxes. He drove as Robin searched the road. Several times she asked him to slow down, then to continue.

"It's been how long?" he asked.

"He said two years."

The pelican could well be gone.

Then he saw a seafood restaurant. They went past several blocks of beach houses.

"I see a pelican," Robin said excitedly.

He saw it then as well. A rakish pelican holding a street number. The house was a sprawling three stories that faced the beach.

No cars in the driveway. Curtains drawn.

The road was busy now with residents and tourists.

He drove past the house and kept driving until they reached a store. "Got a bathing suit?"

"No," she said.

"It's time to get one. Both of us." He stopped the car at the store.

She hesitated. "My leg . . ."

He turned. "What about it, other than it's beautiful? Just like the other."

And it was. There were scars but they were fading into the skin, and it was just as shapely as the other one. In fact, she did have lovely legs. Long, and strong.

"I can't," she protested.

"Where's the intrepid reporter I know?" he said. "Everyone will be looking at your body, anyway." He whistled then. An appreciative girl whistle. Or at least he tried. It wasn't very good.

She didn't look convinced.

He tried a different tack. "I want to see the house from the beach. I think we'd stand out in jeans and slacks, even with the T-shirts. You can stay in the car, though," he taunted.

She gave him a dark look and opened the car door.

They went inside. As with most beach stores there were bathing suits and beach gear. She picked out a simple one-piece suit and a cover-up. He chose some trunks and two beach towels, a small radio, and suntan lotion. He started to take Carl's credit card out. She shook her head and took out cash.

She was right and he knew it. He hadn't been asked for identification at the motel. He might well be asked in a tourist area.

She was in the wrong profession. The FBI should recruit her.

They stopped for coffee in a restaurant and changed clothes in the restrooms before leaving. She looked even better in the bathing suit than he'd envisioned.

He drove down to an area where cars parked for access to the beach. He put the two towels across his shoulder and carried the radio. She put the car keys in the pocket of her cover-up.

They took off their shoes and walked down to the beach.

He watched as she wriggled her toes in the sand. A look of utter joy crossed her face. "I haven't done that in nearly three years. There were times I didn't think I ever would."

He raised an eyebrow.

"At one point there was talk of amputating my leg," she said. "More than one point. Several doctors said I would never use it again."

He grabbed her hand and his fingers tightened around hers. He'd found himself forgetting about her damaged leg, mainly because she hadn't allowed it to interfere in her life or job.

"For our roles," he said, looking down at their linked hands.

She only nodded.

She walked slowly, carefully on the sand, and he matched his pace to hers. They went down to the water's edge and he treasured her look of pure bliss when the water washed over her feet.

Then they walked down the beach toward the house. The house was easy to spot with its Victorian architecture and blue trim. The beach was becoming crowded. Colored beach towels were spread out over the sand, and music blared from radios. Kids ran in and out of the water and built sand castles.

The house looked benign from their vantage point.

They reached the beach in front of the house. It had huge glass windows, a wraparound porch on the first floor, and a wraparound deck on the second. Smaller decks jutted out from doors on the third floor. A white painted picket walkway led down to the beach.

They stopped, spread out the towels, and sat down. Ben turned the towels parallel to the ocean to catch the sun. Others had already staked out nearby spots. "Take off the cover-up," he told Robin. "I'll douse you with lotion."

She took it off, and he rubbed lotion onto her back and neck. It gave him a good opportunity to eye the house, even as his hands ran over her smooth skin.

*Concentrate.*

No signs of life or activity.

Her skin was so damned soft.

*Hell, Taylor, do your job.*

He finished and turned his back while Robin applied the lotion to him, her hands kneading it into his shoulders, re-igniting all those fires that had raged last night.

"That's enough," he said curtly. Hopefully, they'd established themselves as another sun-loving couple. He looked for any glimpse of a light inside, movement. None.

Probably used only for entertaining. If so, it meant that some real estate firm provided management services. There had to be a contact person in the event of an emergency.

They stayed two more hours, at one point going into the ocean. She held out her hand to him and tempted him into the water. "We're tourists, remember," she said. "Beach lovers."

She was right. They did need to act like vacationers. He swam out beyond the breakers and she followed. She was a strong swimmer and he'd learned to swim in the army. They treaded water, moving with the swells, as they kept an eye on the cottage. Still no movement. If anyone was inside, they were hunkered down.

He touched her, relishing the feel of her wet and salty skin. Then a wave hit them and swept them under. She came up laughing, looking like a beautiful sea sprite. Tenderness hit him like a sledgehammer. It had been a long time since he'd felt that emotion that strongly. He'd forgotten how painful it was.

"Time to go," he said.

Her grin disappeared, and she followed him out of the water. He used one of the towels to dry himself off. He didn't offer to wipe her off. Proximity had a disastrous effect on him. He needed all his attention on the case at hand.

When they were through, he took her hand again and instead of returning along the beach, he ignored a Private Property sign and led her straight through the property. To the road. They passed trash cans hidden from the road by a decorative fence.

He stopped at one, put on his shoes. She followed suit. Then he lifted the top off the can and peered inside as she glanced around. One small bag. How often did they pick up the garbage? Once a week? Twice? This was Friday.

Probably just trash from a routine cleaning.

Nonetheless, he reached inside and took it.

They walked out on the road. Civic-minded citizens carrying their own garbage from the beach.

They looked through the contents in the car. Rags. Shredded papers, probably from a wastebasket. A crumpled paper bag from a fast-food restaurant. Then an empty envelope from a property management firm.

"Bingo," he said.

But Robin was disappointed. She had hoped for more.

Her skin was hot from the sun, despite the lotion, and her body still hummed from last night and his touches today. She might have a taste of sunburn but she didn't care. Despite the pressure to find something, she'd never enjoyed herself as much as she had today.

Watching him relax for the first time, really relax, had

made her heart thud harder. She wanted him to grin far more often, to laugh, to enjoy watching a flower grow.

But she'd been caught up in the chase again when he found the garbage, and she hoped for some dramatic television moment. Something far more substantial than the name of a management company.

Still . . . it was a beginning.

She flipped on her cell phone. She'd had it off for the last day, not wanting anyone to be able to trace it. But she had been gone three days now, and she needed to know whether there were any emergencies.

She checked the voice mail system. There were several messages. A list of them, in fact, since yesterday. Two were from the U.S. attorney, one from her paper's attorney, and two from her editor. She wasn't going to answer any of them. She didn't want to explain anything. Not yet. Then there was a text message from her editor. "Urgent. Someone says they have information about the murders. Will talk only to you. Needs answer this afternoon."

It was after noon. Just shortly, but after.

She relayed the message to Ben.

His lips thinned. "Could be a trap."

"I know. But I can't pass on it, either."

"I don't want you calling from here. Not yet. We can't be sure Ames can't get telephone records for the newspaper. It's not that difficult now to get warrants these days under the RICO statutes. I don't want anyone to know we've been here until we're gone."

"There are hundreds of calls going in and out of the office," she said.

"And your editor has one extension."

"I have to call," she said stubbornly.

He offered a compromise. "We'll stop at the management company first. Then I'll drive up into Georgia. A few miles away but hopefully if anyone's tracing the call, they'll think we're still lingering around Brunswick."

They changed clothes in the restroom of a fast-food restaurant. She changed back into slacks and a shirt, he to jeans and flowered shirt he bought at the beach shop.

Then they found the management company. The firm was

located in a real estate office. They were met at the door by an associate. "Can I help you?"

"Yeah, I hope so. Looking to buy a beach house. Ruthie and I just came into an inheritance. We always wanted a beach house and, well, now we can afford it."

The woman stuck her hand out. "We can certainly help you. I'm Carolyn Sawyer."

Ben introduced them as Bob and Ruthie Diddley from Atlanta, formerly from Texas. "Just call me Bo," he said. "Everyone does. Hell of a name, but what can you do."

Robin tried to look like someone named Ruthie Diddley.

"What exactly are you looking for?"

"Ruthie here found just the house she wanted."

A gleam came into the associate's eyes. "Come into my office."

It was more a cubicle than office. The woman sat down at her terminal. "What's the address?"

Ben gave it to her, and she sat down at a terminal and entered it. "I'm sorry," she said. "We manage the property, but it's not for sale. We have other great houses right on the beach."

"Everything is for sale," Ben said. "For Ruthie here, I'll pay just about anything. Maybe you can get in touch with the owner and make an offer."

He saw her write down a name on a pad. "Let me ask the property manager who handles it. If you'll just wait . . ."

"Maybe Ruthie can look at other properties while you do that."

"Sure," the woman said. She pressed a couple of buttons, then slid from the seat. "I'll be right back."

Robin quickly took the associate's seat, waited until she left the office, then pressed the back arrow. Nothing. The woman had closed that window. She typed in the address of the house, as Ben went to the door.

It came up on the screen, along with a corporation name and contact name. She pressed a key for billing information. *Access denied.* Apparently the woman's password would get her to the address but wouldn't go further.

"Darlin', you just might have to decide on something else,"

Ben said in a loud voice. She pressed the escape button, then pressed Listings on the menu.

The woman returned. "The person handling the property is out right now, but I'll pass on your offer. Or have you found something else you like? There's some outstanding values."

"Ruthie has set her heart on *that* house."

"I would be happy to show you others."

Robin managed to bring a tear to her eye. "I dreamt of a house just like that. Maybe you can convince whoever owns it. Like it doesn't seem anyone *really* lives there. Maybe," she added hopefully, "you know him."

"I don't," she said. "I asked several other people. They don't, either."

"Well, thank you, ma'am," Ben said. "We'll keep in touch."

"If I can have your number and address . . ."

"We'll be moving right fast," Ben said. "And I don't believe in cell phones. Takes away your peace of mind, always screaming at you. Don't you think?" He paused, then added, "We'll check back with you, though. My Ruthie is as stubborn as they come. If she wants that house, no other will do."

Then he was ushering her out of the office before the woman could stop them.

Once in the hot car, she turned to him. "Bo Diddley?"

"Better than John Smith," he said. "No one would make up a name like that. Shouldn't alert anyone."

"And Ruthie?"

He grinned. "I always liked that name."

The grin went straight to her heart. In the two weeks she'd known him, he'd never grinned. A slight, pained smile, maybe. But a sense of humor?

Never would have guessed it.

The smile left his face. "Did you get a name?"

"I did." She told him.

And watched his face change.

# chapter thirty-one

*"Say that again?" Ben asked.*

"James Edward Kelley. You know it?"

Yes, he knew it. Everything was beginning to fit.

"James Edward Kelley," he said, repeating her words. "He's president of a company called Exotic Imports. He's also one of the developers of a 'fly-in' community in Meredith County." He paused, then added, "He's involved in other developments throughout Atlanta. A mover-and-shaker type. Active in politics."

"I've heard of him," she said, "but I've never met him."

"We're beginning an investigation of his companies in a money-laundering case. There were hints he might have connections with Hydra. I was just assigned to that case when the murders happened. You sidetracked me."

"Why would he use his own house for something that could be traced back to him?"

Ben shook his head. "That doesn't make sense unless it's his private home and for some reason let it be used one or two times."

"Would it help to find a connection between him and our fishing boat captain?"

"It would be a trail, but only that. All we know is that someone has been providing free trips for county deputies. On the face of it, nothing too sinister."

"Except one of those deputies thinks it is," Robin said. She looked at him curiously. "Why didn't you tell the Realtor you were FBI?"

"And alert them? Give the bad guys time to clean up the books? There's a good chance that the realty company will take us at our word. Two new obnoxious millionaires with more money than sense." He paused, then said, "Robin, it's time to tell me who your source is."

She wanted to. She wanted to yell out the name. She wanted to tell him every word Sandy had said. But Jack Ross's experience had burned a hole in him, a hole that destroyed his career. It wasn't her secret to give. "I can't. You'd have to tell a judge if asked. Your boss. I just can't do it."

"You've been nearly killed twice—and Mrs. Jeffers almost died, too. I think you've respected your promise long enough. And I won't reveal it unless you agree. Now I feel like I'm fighting with one hand tied behind me."

She was silent.

His face turned grim as he started the car. "Time to get out of here," he said.

The companionship between them was broken. She sat in stiff silence as he drove off the island. He'd trusted her with what he knew. She hadn't done the same.

Why couldn't he understand that it wasn't her secret to share?

They stopped on the other side of the Georgia line, and Robin used the pay phone to call Wade Carlton, her boss.

As soon as she said "Wade," he demanded, "Where are you? Everyone's going crazy looking for you, including me."

"I needed to get away. You said I could."

"I didn't tell you to stay out of contact," he said. "The U.S. attorney has called Mason a dozen times, and myself a few more, demanding to know where you are and threatening to throw all of us in jail for obstruction of justice."

"That's interesting."

"It's more than interesting. It's weird. Even Mason thinks so." He slowed down long enough to ask, "Now where are you?"

"On my way back. Any progress on the story?"

"No. Bob still hasn't been able to break through the maze of corporations. The sheriff's department says they have leads but none they can make public."

"I got your text message. Someone's trying to find me?"

"I don't know whether it's genuine or not. Maybe a trap. I do know I don't want you to go anywhere on your own."

"Someone's with me now," she said, "The FBI agent you met. Ben Taylor."

Silence on the other end. Then, "How did *that* happen?"

"He found me. I thought I might have discovered a lead in Brunswick. Ben Taylor tracked me down and saved me from some thugs."

"You told me you were going on vacation."

"I lied."

He chuckled over the phone. "I should fire you."

"It's a big story, Wade. Bigger than any of us thought."

"And more dangerous. I don't want you to do anything else on your—"

"What did the caller say?" she interrupted.

"Just that he had information, would only talk to you and wanted to know how to reach you. I knew he couldn't do it via your cell phone because you've turned the damn thing off." He paused again. "I think you should send him to Joseph Ames. He's certainly going after the case."

"No!"

"Why not? It's time for you and this paper to stop being the story and report it. I'm sure Ames will give us an exclusive."

"Whatever you do, don't go to him. Don't talk to him." She felt her voice rising.

A pause on the other end. "Are you implying what I think you are?"

"Yes." She had to get him off the idea.

"My God. Is that the big story?"

"I don't know yet. But we can't take the chance."

"Get back here, Robin." Wade's voice was flat.

"I'm on my way. Should be back late today. If that guy calls again, give him this number. It's a disposable cell phone. I've not been using it much because I didn't want it to be picked up by the bad guys." She read off the number of her throwaway phone.

"Can I reach you there, too?" he said ironically. "You worried the hell out of me."

"I'm sorry," she said. "I really am. I just didn't want to leave a trail."

Wade sputtered for a moment, then said, "I'll do it. But I swear if you try to meet with this guy alone, I'll fire you. I don't care how good the story is."

"It's nice to know you care."

Another sputter, and she hung up the phone.

When she got back in the car, she started recharging the disposable phone, and told Ben what Wade had said, including the fact that Ames was threatening her with obstruction of justice.

"He has no cause. You showed up in court. He's the one who wanted to put it off for a week. He's panicking."

"We still don't know if he's involved," she warned.

"I can't think of any other reason he would be calling you, and me. Wanting to know where we are."

"We just wait, then, for my caller. Maybe it's just a crank."

"Possible. But it's time to head back to Atlanta."

She nodded. "I want to visit Mrs. Jeffers."

They fell into silence then, her refusal to name her source hanging like a shroud between them.

Halfway to Atlanta, her disposable phone rang.

Only Wade had the number. And whoever he might have given it to. She took a deep breath, glanced at Ben, and pushed the talk button. "Robin Stuart," she said.

"Robin?" The voice was uncertain, shaky. And familiar. Her entire body tightened.

"Yes," she said.

"Are you alone?"

"No."

"I have to meet with you."

"I'm not sure I can do that."

"Do you trust who you are with?"

"Yes. Completely."

"FBI?"

"Yes. How did you . . ."

"Someone was worried you might be together. I was told to find out where you are."

"Why did they think you could do that?"

"I was asked to get close to you," he said in a toneless voice.

Stricken, she couldn't reply for a moment. She hadn't fallen in love with him, but she had liked him tremendously. She'd trusted him.

"Then everything was a lie."

A painful silence stretched over the miles. "Not everything," he finally said.

"What do you want?" she said.

"I want to get out. I don't want anyone else killed."

"Aren't you a little late?"

"I didn't have anything to do with the deaths."

Her breath caught in her throat. Michael had seemed too good to be true. Obviously he was. Now she wondered how she could have been such a poor judge of character.

For a moment she didn't trust herself to speak. She hated betrayal. How deep did Hydra go? How many other people had been corrupted by it? Could good people be corrupted? First Sandy. Other deputies. Now Michael. One thing she knew. Hydra preyed on weaknesses.

And how corrupted were they? Enough to lead her into a trap?

"Why should I trust you?"

A bitter laugh. "You probably shouldn't."

"Tell me now."

He paused. "I want to meet with someone who will give me protection. But I don't know who to go to. I know Hydra has penetrated different law enforcement agencies. I don't know the names."

"What can you give them?"

"I know two people directly involved. My . . . auditing firm has also been involved for years."

"I'm not sure what you want me to do."

"I'm tired of being scared witless," he said. "I would like protection, but . . ."

"I'm giving you to Ben Taylor," she said. "You *can* trust him." She didn't trust herself now.

Ben took the phone, holding it with one hand while he steered with the other.

He was asking the same questions she had.

Then, "What do you propose?"

His face tightened as he listened. Then, "Call back on the same number in two hours."

He clicked the phone off and handed it to her.

"What *did* he propose?" she asked.

"Nothing workable. He would admit everything. Problem is, he only knows two people directly involved and even then he probably doesn't have enough proof to convict them. He's a self-admitted liar and felon himself. I can't assure him protection at this point. We think Ames is involved, but we don't know it for certain. And we don't know how many others are involved. Apparently the whole Meredith County Sheriff's Office was on the take; others could be as well."

"Then what?"

He was silent for a long time, then, "They want you."

"You're thinking of a trap?"

"Something like that." He looked over at her. "But not with you. We'll do it with a decoy."

"What about the information we have now?"

"Leads, Robin. They're only leads. Suppositions. It could take us months to follow them. If we can draw them out and catch some little fish, they can lead us to the bigger ones."

"Did he mention names?"

"No."

"Why did you ask him to wait two hours?"

"I wanted him to sweat," Ben said coldly. "He's as guilty as the men who shot those officers and killed how many more deputies because they asked questions or balked at doing something illegal."

She was surprised at the depth of his anger. Ben usually didn't display emotions.

Except, she allowed, when he'd been angry with her.

"What if he changes his mind?"

"I heard the fear in his voice. He won't change his mind."

There was a hardness in his voice she'd never heard before. He'd been caustic before in some of his comments to her, but this was deeper, a condemnation that sent shivers through her.

"Isn't using a decoy risky? They might realize it's a trap."

"You're a civilian, Robin. We don't risk civilians."

"I can't be more at risk than I am now," she pointed out logically.

His body tensed.

She moved toward him and put a hand on his leg. She wanted the contact. She wanted the warmth she'd felt the night before. The tenderness, the belonging she felt with him. Michael's call had chilled her. The corruption of people chilled her.

"My wife put herself at risk," he said suddenly. "She always thought she was invincible, that she could put herself in deadly situations and survive intact. It doesn't work that way."

He'd finally opened a door.

"You have," she protested.

"I don't get personally involved."

"And your wife did?"

He didn't answer.

"What happened to her?"

He gave her a quick glance before turning back to the road. His fingers were tight around the steering wheel.

She didn't think he was going to answer.

"She was an agent, too," he finally said. "We met at Quantico when we were in training. I thought she was the most beautiful woman I ever met. Small. Dark. Brimming with confidence and fire and ambition. A lot like you that way."

"What happened?"

"We went in different directions after leaving Quantico, then met again several years later in Cincinnati. We married, although the bureau wasn't happy about it. Disapproval was clear in the assignments we were given. Mostly doing security checks. She decided to volunteer for undercover work. She was good at it, more than good. She was great. DEA started asking for her in our joint task forces. She was a good actress, a natural mimic, and had big soulful eyes that could convince anyone that the world was flat.

"Problem was she convinced herself that she could travel with addicts and lowlifes without some of it rubbing off. She took some drugs to 'be one of them' and became hooked herself.

"She's still hooked. We divorced five years ago. She didn't

want me telling her she needed treatment, and I couldn't stand by and watch what she was doing to herself."

Robin heard the pain in his voice and she started to understand him much better. His reluctance to get involved. His reticence about anything personal.

"What happened to her?"

"She was getting better," he said. "She was finishing a rehab program when a friend of hers, a reporter, sold a story to a national tabloid about the FBI agent who became a drug addict. It included some photos of her in less than . . . good moments."

A reporter. A friend. A so-called friend. No wonder he had such an aversion to reporters.

"She'd hoped to return to the FBI. After that story, it was made clear she wouldn't be coming back. A week later she took an overdose. I found her in time, and she survived, but she keeps returning to drugs. She's in her third program now."

"You keep in touch?" Her heart hurt for him. Deep pain shadowed his words.

*Beautiful. Small. Dark. Soulful eyes. Brimming with confidence and fire and ambition.* Sounded like a man still in love. She suddenly felt shut out. Clumsy. Unworthy. It was clear he still cared about Dani.

"Is Dani short for Danielle?"

He nodded.

"And Ben for Benjamin."

"No. It's just for Ben," he corrected.

"Do you see her often?" She couldn't stop herself from asking the question.

"No," he said curtly, and she knew the subject was closed. She looked at him and knew he wasn't really there with her. He was somewhere else, falling in love with a beautiful girl with soulful eyes.

She sat back in the seat. In those few moments, he'd told her more about his life than he had in all the hours they'd spent together. Grief had obviously carved a hole in his heart. He still loved Dani, or at the very least cared deeply about her.

How could she compete with a ghost? No, not a ghost. A living person who lingered in his memories.

*She couldn't.*

But she could do her job. Do it the right way. Prove him wrong about reporters. Some—most—had honor. They cared. She respected her job as much as he did his.

She was not going to be pushed aside. It was partly due to her efforts that the FBI had leads. She wasn't going to be left out now.

# chapter thirty-two

*They stopped at a rest stop,* and Ben called Mahoney, using the same method as before.

"I think you're right about Ames," he said immediately.

"What did you find?"

"Fifteen years ago Ames and James Kelley were attorneys in the same law firm in Washington. Kelley left under some kind of ethical cloud and moved to Atlanta. Ames moved here twelve years ago when the law firm opened an office here. Became active in politics and charities. Served as county chairman of his party. Gave large donations to the state and national party, and served on the board of several highly visible community charities. Hobnobbed with senators. No one was surprised when he was named U.S. attorney."

Ben remembered the disappointment in the Atlanta FBI office when Ames was named four years ago because he'd so little experience as a prosecutor. Still, the position was mostly administrative, and they'd rarely had problems getting the cooperation they needed from the office.

Except for shutting down the coastal investigation early, Ben had few complaints. Most of the attorneys in Ames's office were competent and had a good conviction rate. Agents usually had little difficulty in getting the warrants they needed. Ames was considered an aggressive prosecutor, an up-and-comer whose name was bandied about as a gubernatorial candidate.

"What about Fischer?"

"Strangely enough, or maybe it isn't so strange after all, the file is missing."

"No one remembers it?"

"I'm trying to chase down the arresting officer, but he left the department two years ago. No one knows where he went."

"You haven't told Holland yet?"

"He'll shit in his pants," Mahoney said. "The last thing he needs now is a politically popular U.S. attorney in his sights. But he's one of the good guys. He'll do what's right."

"I need to meet with him. Outside the office. Before anyone knows we're back."

"And I should tell him . . . what?"

"That I have some sensitive information. The bureau walls have ears. We don't need rumors flying around, and we can't dismiss the possibility someone else is involved, either in our office or in Ames's."

"We *could* be wrong, you know. Coming up with all the wrong conclusions."

"Maybe. But I might have a way of flushing the bad guys out."

"Okay, where do you want to meet?" Mahoney said.

"I doubt anyone will be watching Holland. They might be watching you, though. I think you should stay away right now." Ben paused. "Is he in the office now?"

"Yeah."

Ben named a hotel at the airport. "Ask him to meet me there. I'll be registered under Carl Andrews's name. I should be there in two hours."

"I don't believe it," Holland said grimly.

Robin watched him carefully. She wasn't as convinced as Ben that he was one of the good guys. She would never take anyone on face value again.

They sat around a coffee table. It was past seven p.m., nearly eight.

Ron Holland had been bemused when he first met her in the room. "The famous and elusive Ms. Stuart," he said as he shook her hand. Then he turned to Ben. "What in the hell is going on? I've been trying to reach you."

"You'd better sit down," Ben said.

Robin watched Holland's face during the long explanation of their trip, what they'd discovered. It changed from watchful to skeptical. "You have no real proof," he said when Ben finished. "Just coincidences, suppositions."

"I have a witness. A participant in the conspiracy who wants to come forward. He doesn't know who to trust."

Holland looked at Robin. "Your source?"

"No," Ben said. "But there've been too many dead bodies lately. He doesn't want his to be added to the count," he said cynically.

Robin wasn't quite so sure that was Michael's only reason but she let it slide.

"What does he have to offer?"

"A name. Problem is, it's mostly his word, and he's been in the middle of it."

"What's the name?"

"We won't get that until we promise protection," Ben said.

"And a deal which will further erode his credibility," Holland said. "What do you propose?"

"A trap. Our informant was asked to get close to Robin, try to find out what she knew. He failed at that, but now he's been ordered to find out where she is."

Holland was silent for several moments. "You think they'll come after her."

"I think right now she scares the hell out of them. They don't know exactly how much she knows, or who is giving information to her. They have to cut off that source."

Holland looked at her. "Who is the source?"

"I can't tell you that," she said. "I can tell you he doesn't know enough to be much of a help. He's been involved in some minor corruption at the sheriff's department and he overheard a conversation the night of the murders. Deputies had been warned away from that site. That's it. That's all he knows. You need more than that."

"You're willing to put your life at risk?"

"It's already at risk. So are my sisters', and their families', and my friends'."

"We can use a decoy," Ben said.

"You may not fool them then," she said. "My photo's been

in the paper. You need an overt criminal act. Then you'll have your building blocks."

Holland gave her a long, hard stare.

"She has a vividly inventive mind," Ben said wryly.

Holland looked from one to the other, then shook his head. "If you ever want another job . . . ," Holland said.

She watched Ben's face harden. *Dani.* He was thinking of Dani, she knew with a heart-twisting certainty.

"That still doesn't prove Joseph Ames is part of a conspiracy," Holland argued.

"I realize that. But if we start catching the little fish, they can lead us to the big one. If nothing comes of it, no one needs to know he was one of the targets."

"If someone learns about it, I could be headed to Outer Siberia. Or worse."

"I know I'm asking a lot," Ben said.

"Oh, hell. If he's guilty, he needs to be in jail."

"Do you have someone higher in the bureau you can go to?"

Holland thought for a moment, then nodded. Then he turned back to Robin. "I want you to be sure you want to do this. I can get you the protection, but there's always slipups, and now there's a wild card. They might have penetrated the FBI."

She looked at Ben. His eyes were shuttered, but she knew he was opposed to it. But she *wasn't* another Dani. She wasn't reckless. But she had to do this to get her life back. And she would be protected. Ben would keep her safe, whether he liked it or not.

"I'm sure," she said.

"I'll set it up," Holland said. "We'll get a safe house. And electronic wiretap warrants."

"That might lure Kelley, or his thugs, out of hiding," Robin said. "What about Ames?"

Holland and Ben exchanged looks.

Ben spoke first. "If Ames learns of the sting minutes before it goes down, what does he do? Would he risk a phone call?"

"And if he doesn't, and we do get Kelley, we can let Mr.

Kelley know that the U.S attorney knew about the raid in advance. I really enjoy it when rats go after each other."

"We'll have to get RICO warrants on both of them to tap their home and office phones as well as catch their cell phone conversations," Ben said. "Can we get one for Ames?"

"I'll damn well try."

"A U.S. attorney?" Robin asked doubtfully. "We don't have much."

"We have three dead cops and possibly a renegade prosecutor. We have a lot of latitude when it comes to organized crime. I'll get them," Holland said.

"You could destroy your career."

"Yeah? Maybe. Maybe not. A U.S. attorney would be a big catch. Do wonders for my career. If it goes south, well, I hate pencil pushing, anyway," Holland said with a quick grin. Then he turned to Robin. "You're one gutsy lady."

With that, Holland left.

Ben went over to her and put his hands on her shoulders. "Are you sure about this?"

"I trust you," she said simply.

He folded his arms around her. "I'm not so sure that's a good idea."

She looked up at him. "Because of Dani?"

"I never could protect Dani. She wanted more than I could give her. There were parts of me I couldn't share, and she grew to resent that." His gaze met hers. "She knew something was missing. She told me I was emotionally bankrupt, and she became more and more reckless."

She was indignant on his behalf. She'd felt his tenderness, seen his sweetness toward Mrs. Jeffers, his concern for others. She knew his anger and his sadness. She felt it now.

She touched his cheek with her hand. "You care far more than you're willing to admit."

"There are many who would disagree."

She took his hand and turned toward the bed. "I aim to convince you."

• • •

Robin prowled the safe house. The shades were partially closed, the curtains pulled. She glanced out of a corner and saw nothing but shadows that moved with the swaying trees.

The house was in southern metropolitan Atlanta, in one of the few remaining undeveloped areas. The sprawling house and barn had seen far better days. The paint was peeling, the carpets inside worn, and the grass overgrown.

It had been foreclosed on by the bank and was yet to be put on the market. The FBI had taken temporary custody for use as a safe house.

Mahoney explained that it was perfect for their purposes. The woods surrounding the house made good protection for the handpicked agents outside. Yet it would give any invaders a sense of privacy as well.

It was Monday evening, and they'd been here since morning. Mahoney came first, then other agents filtered in and took position. Michael called Kelley this afternoon, saying that he had visited Mrs. Jeffers, that she had told him that the FBI agent and her neighbor were staying at an old house she had told them about. She'd made him promise not to tell anyone.

She both hoped and feared that Kelley would react. He basically had an entire sheriff's department to call upon.

The moment anything happened, Holland was to call Ames and tell him about the sting. He only hoped Ames would use his cell phone or home phone to call Kelley and warn him.

Ben was outside taking a walk but really checking on the agents.

She smiled as she watched his brisk pace. He didn't do anything leisurely. And he always looked alone, even when he was with other people. There had always been a detachment, a deliberate separation between him and others.

Not so much last night as they spent the hours in each other's arms. She had purchased protection. Learned he'd done the same. They'd produced the small packages at the same time, then chuckled together at the evidence of joint desire.

She felt a warm rush inside at the memory.

She didn't know how long it would last. He'd said nothing about a future.

*It has only been a few weeks.*

Yet she knew. She knew with all her heart that he was the one she wanted. Needed. Loved.

He would say it was adrenaline.

Last night, lying in his arms, she knew the difference. She belonged there.

"How long have you known him?" she asked Mahoney, who was sitting in a chair in a corner. It couldn't be seen from the outside.

"Five years. Since he was transferred here."

"After Dani?" she asked.

"There is no 'after Dani,' " he said wryly.

"What do you mean?"

"Only that he still feels responsible. He still pays for rehab. It never works. He's hoping it will this time, but I don't think his heart believes it."

"But they're divorced."

"Doesn't matter to Ben. She doesn't have any family. Her mother died when she was at Quantico. He feels responsible for her." He looked at her shrewdly. "Her rehab bills take nearly all his salary. That won't change," he said, obviously warning her. "Ben doesn't change."

Pain surged through her. It seemed bottomless, as if it would swallow her whole. Ben obviously still loved Dani. Always would. No wonder he'd never voiced words she wanted to hear.

She turned away from the window and looked at her watch. Another hour and it would be pitch black. Lights were on in the bedroom, in this room. In the kitchen. For want of anything else to do, she went into the kitchen and made sandwiches and coffee.

*Would they come tonight?*

Or would they sense a trap?

She took Mahoney a cup of coffee and sandwich. She couldn't eat but sipped on the coffee, mulling over what Mahoney had said. Her thoughts must have been on her face because after a moment, Mahoney spoke up again.

"I didn't mean he's still in love with her. I meant that he loved her, and he doesn't give up on people when they don't do what he likes. He's unusual that way. He takes care of them."

"He said she called him emotionally bankrupt."

His eyebrows went straight up. "He told you *that*? Well, she's wrong."

Ben came back inside. "Everything's good outside. There's not much moon tonight, but our people have night-vision glasses."

She fought to keep from gazing at him, afraid all her feelings would be only too evident.

"What about a game of poker?" Mahoney asked.

"Why not?" she said. "But I don't have much money."

"We play for imaginary pennies," Mahoney said, obviously choosing to ignore the intensity in the room.

"I owe him about ten thousand dollars in pennies," Ben said. "He's a card sharp."

"Ah, you wound me," Mahoney said and took a deck of cards from his pocket.

"I don't understand why I have to go," Michael protested, as the driver of the van turned a corner. "I told Kelley what you needed to know."

"Time for you to get more involved," the man named Luis, said. "Mr. Kelley wants to be sure of your loyalty."

Luis had shown up at his condo an hour earlier, five hours after Michael had called and told him that he believed that Robin Stuart and an FBI agent were staying at a farmhouse. The agent, he said, apparently had gone off the reservation, ignoring summonses by his boss and the U.S. attorney.

Michael was cold, despite the heat of the Atlanta night. He'd agreed to help the FBI by setting this trap. He had not bargained on being a part of it.

Did James Kelley suspect something?

A number of automatic weapons lay on the floor of the van, along with several packages of ammunition. In addition to Luis and himself, there were two dangerous-looking men accompanying them. Four more were in a car behind them.

So this was what he had worked for?

"Your hands are shaking, friend," Luis said in what could

only be termed a sneer. Michael looked at his face, and knew he probably wouldn't live out the night.

"Don't worry," Luis said. "We took those three cops like they were in nursery school."

"The FBI is a little different."

Luis laughed his disagreement.

The car turned again and then parked. "You sure this is the house?"

Michael peered out the window. "I haven't been here but it's the right address."

"Now why don't you wander on up there and ask if your friend Robin is there?"

"Won't that be suspicious?"

"An old friend paying respects?" Luis said.

"What about you?"

"Don't worry about us."

Michael got out, hoping he didn't wobble. His legs felt like rubber. He walked slowly up to the door. He glanced around, noticed a few shadows moving away from the car. So he was the diversion.

The curtain moved slightly. Then he heard a lock being turned. The door opened.

A tall man stood in the doorway, a gun in his hand. Must be Ben Taylor. He hadn't met with him in person. Too dangerous. But they had talked.

"What the hell?" the agent said.

"Michael. I'm Michael Caldwell." Just then a shot ripped by him, and a number of shots sounded toward the back of the house.

Michael stood there, feeling like a truck had struck him. Then he saw blood starting to splotch his shirt.

The agent opened the door, sprayed the area beyond him. Then an arm went around his shoulder. Not a masculine one. Softer yet strong. Robin. Exposing herself to help drag him inside. Two shots hit the door, then he heard a soft sigh, and he fell as his support fell.

The cacophony of shots blasted through the building like the hell of war. He tried to crawl to Robin. Then everything went black.

• • •

"Damn it, don't you ever do what you're told?"

The words fought into Robin's consciousness, keeping the gray fog at bay.

"Don't you dare die," the voice intruded again.

The noise outside was gone, but the silence had its own thunder.

"Michael?"

"He'll live. Shouldn't, but he will."

She was tired. Really tired.

"Any . . . agent hurt?"

"Just you and Caldwell and some bad guys."

"Good," she said. He was pressing down on something, but everything was numb. She tried to move, but nothing seemed to work. Others crowded around her. She drifted off again. Ben was safe. Michael would live.

Good enough.

Robin woke in the hospital. Ben was sleeping in a chair next to her.

She moved and an involuntary groan woke him.

He was immediately at her side. His face was covered with dark bristle again, and his eyes were bloodshot.

"What . . . ?"

"A bullet hit an artery," he said. "You almost died from loss of blood. Nearly every FBI agent gave blood."

"You can't dislike reporters now. At least this reporter. I'm . . . a blood sister."

"You're a damn fool." But there wasn't any derision in the words. Rather something like worry. Affection. Maybe even . . . more than that.

"What . . . how long has it been?"

"It's Wednesday morning. You should rest now."

"What happened?"

"Their whole wall of cards collapsed. Lou Belize—a big drug lord—was killed but not before he implicated James Kelley. Four of their shooters were killed. Two survived and they're talking. Ron Holland called Ames to warn him about the raid, and in his arrogance Ames called Kelley. Apparently thought he was immune from electronic surveillance. He's been arrested. They're all fighting to make deals."

"The story?"

"All over the country."

She closed her eyes for a moment. Her big story.

"I think there's still a lot of story untold," he said softly, taking her hand.

"Have you been here long?"

"One day. Two nights," he said. He looked out the window. "There's been a stream of visitors to see you."

"I only want one," she said, her fingers tightening around his. "And only one story I want to tell."

He leaned down and kissed her, a touching of lips so light it was more like a soft breeze. "I'm kinda getting used to you," he said. "I didn't realize how much until I thought I would lose you."

"A reporter?"

"I suppose," he said with that half smile that had always fascinated her. "If *you'll* have a cynical worn-out agent with hardly a penny to his name."

She knew why now. Emotionally bankrupt? He was the richest man she knew. He had the biggest heart, even if he had tried to fence it with steel.

"Just try me," she said. "As long as he kisses better than he did a second ago."

And he did.

# epilogue

A YEAR LATER

The guest list kept growing, though all the intentions had been for a small wedding.

Small. Informal. Simple. That's what both Robin and Ben wanted.

Even then, Robin had three attendants, including Mrs. Jeffers, who served as her matron of honor. Being a matron of honor had been on her list. Another goal crossed off.

Considering what her neighbor had lost with good humor, Robin figured it was the least she could do. Her sisters, after hearing the story, had readily agreed.

Ben had only Mahoney as his best man. Carl Andrews, the former agent from Savannah, was among the invitees, though, and he sat with Dani Taylor, soon to be Mrs. Andrews. She had finished rehab nine months earlier and had remained free of drugs since.

Robin and Dani had become friends. After finishing rehab, Dani had moved to Atlanta, and Robin had helped her find a job with a recovery non-profit organization she'd featured in an article. Then Carl had started making frequent trips to Atlanta, and occasionally the four would go out to dinner together or have dinner at Robin's cottage.

"Ben doesn't give up on people," Mahoney had said the night she was shot. Robin had realized in the past months that her quiet, intense, introverted FBI agent had a heart far bigger than he admitted.

It had taken nearly a year for him to propose, partly because he'd been so busy with the case. But he also insisted that she be sure of her feelings, that she wasn't feeling gratitude or simply the remnants of the intense adrenaline they'd shared. He still felt that the failure of his first marriage was his fault. "You have to know me," he said. "I . . . I have a hard time sharing feelings. It destroyed my first marriage. I want you to be sure."

But he was wrong. He didn't have a hard time sharing, not once the barriers were broken. He protected. He gave. Not in superficial ways, but in the gut-deep meaningful ways. She'd known that in the beginning, and the next months only made her more sure. He was a caring man who'd created a hard shell to protect himself, and she saw more and more cracks as he helped Dani get a life back and helped Mrs. Jeffers build a new house and Michael Caldwell start again.

As for the Hydra case, they had been allies and opponents, she always wanting to know more than he could give her. She'd watched as one arrest had led to others. Lou Belize had been killed in the shoot-out at the safe house, but one of his companions—to avoid a death sentence—had confessed, and the walls started crumbling.

Hydra had been moving a shipment of cocaine from a private plane owned by James Kelley to a van for distribution among smaller dealers in Altanta when the Meredith County officers accidently stumbled on them.

Unfortunately, one recognized Belize, who was a suspected, but never convicted, drug dealer, along with Meredith Chief Deputy Sheriff Paul Joyner. The sheriff, apparently, had not been involved with Hydra but was convicted of taking bribes over the past twenty years. He had initiated—or continued—the systematic corruption that Hydra had exploited.

Those arrests led to others. James Kelley, largely due to Michael Caldwell's testimony, was recently convicted of numerous accounts of criminal conspiracy, tax evasion, and money laundering, and sentenced to forty years in prison. He turned on Joseph Ames to keep from spending his entire life in prison. Ames killed himself minutes before police arrived to arrest him.

Several Meredith County deputies were arrested as accomplices to a criminal conspiracy, and Sandy testified as to what he heard. He wouldn't be a coward again, he'd told her. He would always live with the regret he hadn't done more.

Because of his assistance in the case, Michael Caldwell received only a one-year sentence in a minimum security camp. He would leave this weekend. Carl had been in need of an accountant and, at Ben's suggestion, offered Michael a job in Savannah. A former crook to catch crooks.

As for herself, she'd won a year's worth of stories. A new headline every day. She'd won several regional awards for investigative reporting, and the paper had nominated her for a Pulitzer Prize.

Once that had been her dream. It still was a goal. But her dream now was a partner. A husband. A good and brave man to whom honor wasn't a word but a way of life.

"Time to go," Star said.

She stepped out. Mrs. Jeffers started down the aisle, her legs a bit creaky but her head high and a huge smile on her lips. Robin's sisters followed, then she took slow steps to the strains of "Beloved."

Ben looked grave. His eyes smiled, though, then his lips as she approached. Her heart swelled with love as he held his hand out to her and drew her close, to hell with the rehearsal instructions.

He leaned down. "I love you," he whispered.

Her hand tightened around his. Those whispered words—the smile in his eyes was the greatest award she could ever receive.

"Always," she whispered back before turning to the minister.

In 1988, **Patricia Potter** won the Maggie Award and a Reviewer's Choice Award from *Romantic Times* for her first novel. She has been named Storyteller of the Year by *Romantic Times* and has received the magazine's Career Achievement Award for Western Historical Romance along with numerous Reviewer's Choice nominations and awards.

She has won three Maggie awards, is a five-time RITA finalist, and has been on the *USA Today* bestseller list. Her books have been alternate choices for the Doubleday Book Club.

Prior to writing fiction, she was a newspaper reporter with the *Atlanta Journal* and president of a public relations firm in Atlanta. She has served as president of Georgia Romance Writers and board member of River City Romance Writers, and is past president of Romance Writers of America.